"I'M WHITE," CASSIE INSISTED BLINDLY.

"I lived ... onger than I lived ... think like a white...

Hunter l... face. If by sheer ... place for herself, Hunter would have bet money on Cass. But succeeding wasn't up to her.

This was a world where authority ruled and rank had its privileges, where being different was held in the gravest contempt. It was a world where men used Indian women for their pleasure and expected their wives to be inviolate.

It was a world where Cassandra didn't stand a chance.

"Beautifully written, it captures a time and place that seemed very real to me . . .
Characters are both noble and believable.
Highly satisfying."
Barbara Bickmore, author of *Deep in the Heart*

Other Avon Books by
Elizabeth Grayson

A PLACE CALLED HOME

SO WIDE THE SKY

ELIZABETH GRAYSON

Elizabeth Grayson

AVON BOOKS NEW YORK

SO WIDE THE SKY is an original publication of Avon Books. This work has never before appeared in book form. This work is a novel. Any similarity to actual persons or events is purely coincidental.

AVON BOOKS
A division of
The Hearst Corporation
1350 Avenue of the Americas
New York, New York 10019

Cover art by Glenn Harrington
Inside cover author photo by McLean-Wright Photography—St. Louis
Published by arrangement with the author
Library of Congress Catalog Card Number: 96-96910
ISBN: 0-380-77846-7

First Avon Books Printing: March 1997

Printed in the U.S.A.

RA 10 9 8 7 6 5 4 3 2 1

To
Renée Witmer and Carolyn Villeneuve,
the women who became the sisters I never had

Acknowledgments

Acknowledgments are wonderful things. They give authors a chance to say thank you to the people who enable us to do what we do.

As always the research people must come first. I could never have written *So Wide the Sky* without the material and expertise provided me by Eleanor Alexander. Her skill in gathering information on the Kiowa, Arikara, and Cheyenne, and her willingness to play "what if" helped me turn a photograph and an idea into a full-blown novel.

As always Charles Brown of the Mercantile Library Association of St. Louis came through with just the research I needed—this time on life in the Western forts.

Joyce Schiller of the St. Louis Art Museum once again gave me several lovely tidbits about objects from the period that enhanced my characters' world.

I would also like to thank my former colleague Sheila DeGraffe for being willing to turn her considerable expertise to defining a fictional character's speech pathology.

In preparing to write this book I have relied on my husband Tom, not only as fellow adventurer on the Wyoming prairie, but also as consultant on military uniforms and accoutrements. I would also like to express my appreciation for his sticking by me when the road was bumpy and full of unexpected twists and turns.

As usual, Eileen Dreyer deserves a big thank you, for service above and beyond. As do Kim Bush, Linda Madl, Libby Beach, and Tami Hoag. Without you guys, doing this wouldn't be half the fun.

And last but not least, a special thank you to Debbie Pickel-Smith for her friendship, her wonderful warm heart, her words of encouragement, and for holding my head.

Chapter One

Early March 1867
Department of the Platte

Trouble comes out of the west. Or so Hunter Jalbert's old Arikara Indian grandfather had taught him in the years when Hunter was struggling to prove himself as a warrior. Enemies loomed out of the lingering daylight for a final attack. Wild animals stalked down from the mountains in the dark. Whirlwinds tore out of the western sky.

Today trouble took the form of a white woman.

Hunter scanned the hills around the little draw where they'd agreed to exchange their wagonload of goods for a Cheyenne captive and felt the itch of premonition down his back. As sure as hellfire burned, they'd been set up for annihilation here.

A hundred Cheyenne warriors could be massing on the far side of the ridge. A score more might have their rifles trained on them from the outcropping of dun-colored rocks just off to the north. And here they sat—twelve troopers, two mule skinners, a captain and a scout—visible as gravel in an open palm.

When the messenger came to the fort offering to trade for an Indian captive, Hunter had urged Major McGarrity to negotiate a safer place to make the exchange. But McGarrity hadn't listened.

Drew Reynolds, the new spit-and-shine captain who was leading the patrol, hadn't heeded his warning, either. Hunter sliced a glance in Reynolds's direction. Word was that he had attended West Point and proved himself a hero in the war back East. But things were different here. Nothing the captain had seen fighting Rebs would prepare him for the way these tribes made war. Nothing he might have experienced in the battles between the North and South could teach him about the trickery and barbarity he'd face fighting Indians. And Reynolds was proving himself too arrogant to consult someone as lowly as his half-breed scout.

Well, the captain would learn, Hunter found himself thinking. If an arrow didn't get him first. If the Indians didn't scalp the lot of them.

It is a very good day to die.

The warriors' creed flashed through Hunter's mind, as much a part of him as his breathing or his heartbeat. It calmed him, enervated him. It made the waiting more difficult.

Just when they were ready to give up their vigil to the blowing and the cold, a party of Cheyenne emerged from a crease in the hillside to the right of the rocks.

Hunter stiffened in his saddle and shifted his gaze to where Reynolds sat his big bay gelding. "Hostiles, sir."

"I have eyes," the captain snapped. Reynolds turned to his men and shouted the order. "Stand ready."

Hunter saw the troopers free the flaps on their holsters and limber up their carbines. As the Indians approached, he did the same.

There were about a dozen Cheyenne in the party that cantered toward them. Because they were riding two abreast, it took a moment for Hunter to spot the woman in their midst. She rode as tall as some of the men, discernible from them only in the way her buckskin skirt flapped against her legs and by her ornate, high-pommeled saddle. As the party rode closer, Hunter could see that the woman's complexion was baked nearly as dark as the men around her, that her hair, slicked into braids with bear grease and dusted with vermilion along the part, was nearly black.

Hunter's breathing thickened with renewed suspicion. If this wasn't a white woman the Cheyenne had come to trade, then they were dead men. They might be dead men even if she was.

"What do you make of this?" Reynolds asked almost begrudgingly. He must be having doubts about the woman, too.

"I think we play it out," Hunter answered.

As the Indians made their way along the draw, Hunter shivered, wanting to spur his horse forward, to ride in shooting and howling like the warrior he'd trained to be. But years of fighting both Yankees and Indians had taught him patience.

The party of Cheyenne stopped less than a dozen yards away. The leader, a strongly built man wearing a war shirt trailing scalps and thick with beads, dismounted and motioned for the woman to do the same. Leaving their horses, they made their way to a midpoint between the two factions.

"Goddamned savages want us on foot," Hunter heard the captain mutter as he swung out of his saddle. "Come along then, mixed-blood," he added. "I'll be needing you to translate."

Biting back his reply, Hunter dismounted and followed Reynolds across the snow-dusted grass. The captain paused a few feet from where the Cheyenne stood with the woman at his side.

"I am a representative of the U.S. Army sent from Fort Carr, as you requested. Is this the captive you've come to exchange?"

The warrior acknowledged Reynolds first, then inclined his head in Hunter's direction. The captain's eyebrows lifted in surprise when Hunter accepted the greeting as a matter of course. But then, Hunter had been working with the army since '64 and had earned a certain reputation among the tribes.

Though the brave seemed capable of understanding Reynolds's words, when he spoke it was in his own tongue, accompanied by the appropriate sign language.

"I am Standing Pine, warrior of the Cheyenne," Hunter

translated as the Indian talked. ''This is the captive we have come to trade. Have you brought sugar and flour and meal as we asked? Have you brought ammunition?''

''There is no ammunition in the wagon,'' Reynolds answered brusquely. ''As you well know, the army has refused to trade for powder and shot you redskins can use to attack the stage stations and wagon trains.''

Reynolds's tone was belligerent, his words inflammatory. Hunter leveled a brief, quelling glance at the officer. Hadn't anyone told this man there was nothing to be gained by antagonizing the Cheyenne? Didn't the captain want the woman freed?

''We need ammunition to kill buffalo,'' Standing Pine insisted. ''It has been a hard winter. The hunting has been poor. We only seek to feed our families.''

''Well, I have no ammunition to give you,'' Reynolds said, and turned away.

''There is *food* for your families in the wagon,'' Hunter put in, addressing the Indian, halting Reynolds where he stood. ''There's flour and meal and bacon, potatoes and onions and canned fruit. There's cloth in colors that will please your women, knives and axes and cooking pots. Would you turn all that away for the sake of powder and shot?''

The brave paused a moment to drink in Jalbert's logic.

''Surely such goods would be welcome,'' Hunter added.

After a moment, Standing Pine inclined his head. ''It is true that the Cheyenne would welcome such gifts. I must see for myself what you have brought.''

With a nod, Reynolds granted permission for the Indian to approach the wagon.

The brave crossed the swath of grass to where it stood. He pushed back the flapping tarpaulin and looked at the boxes and barrels and sacks inside. Apparently what he saw among them pleased him, for when Standing Pine returned, there was satisfaction in his face.

''We will accept what you have given us in return for Sweet Grass Woman.''

Hunter had begun to nod in agreement when Reynolds spoke up. ''How do we know that this is indeed a white woman? She could be some squaw you're passing off on us for the promise of gain."

Hunter stared at Reynolds in astonishment. What he lacked in diplomacy, he made up for in pure arrogance.

Yet the Cheyenne met his demand with surprising equanimity. The woman had been standing with her face averted and her shoulders bowed, as if she were attending the words her betters spoke but never once acknowledging them. At a mumbled command from Standing Pine, the woman raised her head.

The woman's features were strong but more finely drawn than most Indian women's were. She had a firm chin and a mouth that didn't seem meant for smiling; a short, straight nose with a spattering of freckles; and brows that flared at the corners like a bird on the wing. The eyes that locked with Hunter's were pale, clear green, ringed by a corona of some mysterious darker color that was neither green nor gray. As he stared, Hunter did his best to plumb the depths of her. He found no warmth nor joy, no fear nor enmity. Her passivity assaulted him, decimating some fundamental belief about the light that should live in a woman's eyes.

And then he realized what they had done to her. High on her left cheekbone someone had marked her. A tattoo the size of a silver dollar spread like a star burst against her skin, deep blue lines radiating outward from a small hollow circle.

Beside him, Reynolds sucked in his breath. The captain wouldn't have seen an Indian tattoo before. He wouldn't know that they were worn as adornment as often as punishment. He would only see the disfigurement, the humiliation of being marked.

Even Hunter, for all his background and experience, tingled with shock.

Yet not so much as a ripple of acknowledgment disturbed the stillness in the woman's eyes. Either her captivity had turned her impervious as the surrounding hills, or she had retreated deep inside herself.

After a moment Reynolds seemed to recover. "Very well," he said. "I can see that the woman is white. We will take her back to the fort. You may have the wagonload of goods."

Standing Pine nodded, accepting the trade, and motioned two of his men toward the wagon. The muleteers who had been driving jumped down from the seat and untied their mounts from where they had been tethered to the back. The Indians took the soldiers' places, slipped the brake, and turned the wagon back toward the rocks. The other Cheyenne fell in behind.

Standing Pine watched them go. When the wagon had disappeared, he caught up the white woman's wrist and thrust it in Reynolds's direction. "She is yours now," he said.

Hunter saw the captain flinch, sensed his reluctance to take the woman's arm, to contaminate himself by touching her. Reynolds's reticence fired something bitter and hot in Hunter's chest.

Goddamn the man for considering himself superior! Goddamn him for refusing to touch her! How could Reynolds revile a woman who had done nothing to warrant it, a woman who must have suffered barbarities no white man could even contemplate? Hunter had lived with the white's scorn for so many years, he thought he was immune to it. Reynolds's treatment of the captive made him realize he was not.

Then, just as Hunter moved to claim her, Reynolds reached out and closed his fingers around the woman's arm. He dragged her forward and a little way behind him in a gesture of both possession and instinctive protection.

"Since our transaction is completed, go in peace," Reynolds said, dismissing Standing Pine.

"I will go," the man answered, and spun away. He gathered up the reins to the woman's horse, jumped onto his own, and prodded it to a run.

Hunter recognized Standing Pine's retreat for what it was. The brave wasn't trying to catch up with the wagon; he was getting out of the line of fire.

With certainty humming in his veins, Hunter swung his gaze to the west. Three score of Cheyenne warriors bristled along the top of the ridge.

"Indians!" he shouted, and ran for his horse.

* * *

"Treacherous bastards!" Drew Reynolds pulled and fired his pistol as the war party swept toward them. He jerked the woman in the direction of his horse. "Might have known we couldn't trust these goddamned redskins!"

In the few seconds it took to cover the yards of snow-speckled grass, Drew Reynolds weighed their options. He could order the men to hightail it for the fort, nearly six miles away. They could dig in where they were and make a stand, or take cover and hold the Indians off while someone rode for reinforcements.

"Into the rocks!" he ordered, and waved his men toward the seam of broken hillside off to the north.

The woman at his side hung back as the troopers spurred their mounts away. Her resistance dragged Drew's attention from the enemy galloping toward them.

"Stupid squaw!" he shouted at her. "Don't you appreciate being rescued?"

Giving no sign she understood, the woman continued to twist against his grip. Drew cursed, shifted his hold to her middle, and flung her up on his horse's back. To prevent her from scrambling down the opposite side, he clamped his hand around her lean, muscled calf and hauled her back into the saddle. Before she could squirm away, he caught up the gelding's reins and swung up behind her.

As Drew prodded his horse toward the rocks, the air around them trembled with the thunder of hoofbeats. Whoops of bloodlust swelled at their backs. Arrows hissed past. Drew bowed his body around the woman and rode for both their lives.

A barrage of covering fire erupted from the rocks as they scrambled up the slope. The blast and smoke of a dozen carbines rolled over them. Drew looked back just in time to see several Indians pitch off their horses.

Tightening the reins, Drew breached the perimeter of broken stones and guided his mount into the relative safety of several towering boulders. He pulled the woman to the ground as he dismounted.

"What do you know about this, woman?" he demanded, rage whining in his head. He tightened his grip on his captive's arm and forced her to her knees. "Were you part of their plan to lure us here?"

Wide green eyes stared up from that dark, disfigured face.

"If my men die because of you . . ."

"Captain?"

Drew shuddered and turned.

Jalbert came striding toward them. "The hostiles are pulling back."

Drew nodded in acknowledgment. He loosened his hold on the woman's arm. "Do you mean the raiders are gone?"

"I'd say they're forming up for another go at us," the man replied.

Drew nodded, took a breath, and scanned the field before him. In the long, grassy dip between the hills the Cheyenne were riding in circles, building momentum for the next attack.

Serendipity had given him and his men a far better field position than he had any right to expect. Before them lay a swath of level plain and the cover of the rocky hillside. Behind them the ground rose steeply, the earth crumbling away at the crest like a breaking wave. Drew had always liked fighting with a hill at his back, but today they'd have to keep careful watch. If the Indians who had gone off with the wagon circled back, they could pin his men down in a cross fire.

"You two troopers, get up to the lip of the hill," Reynolds ordered, then motioned Jalbert to follow them. "Make sure they keep their eyes open. We don't want those red bastards getting the drop on us."

As Jalbert went to do as he'd been bidden, Drew continued to assess their position. Behind the impromptu breastworks, his men could hold the Indians off for a while, at least. He'd made certain they were issued extra ammunition before they left the fort this morning. Yet against such numbers, the rounds and their position could do only so much. They needed reinforcements.

Still clinging to the woman's wrist, Drew crept forward to where his sergeant crouched in the lee of a waist-high pillar of crumbled stones. "Prepare to send a rider to the fort," Reynolds instructed in an undertone. "Pick your best man, Sergeant O'Hearn, and give him the fastest horse we've got."

"That'd be yours, Captain."

"Then let him take it. Have him head for the top of the hill and circle east. Let Major McGarrity know we need reinforcements. Tell him we'll hold on here as long as we can."

As the wiry sergeant scuttled away to do the captain's bidding, Jalbert took his place behind the rocks.

"The sentries are posted at the rear, sir. I took a good look around up there myself. There isn't anything to see for miles. My guess is that Standing Pine headed straight for the village with those supplies."

"Very good," Reynolds answered, his attention shifting again as the riders who had been circling at the far end of the draw began to form up for another charge.

"Captain," Jalbert asked, reclaiming Drew's attention, "what about the woman?"

Reynolds turned to where the Indian captive crouched in the shadow of the jumbled stones. What was going on behind those empty eyes? he found himself wondering. Where did this woman's loyalties lie?

Without answering Jalbert, Drew shifted the pressure on the woman's arm, forcing her down beside him, onto her back. He jammed his knee between her legs, pinning the drape of her buckskin skirt to the ground.

"I think it's best, Mr. Jalbert," he answered, "if I keep her here with me."

Reynolds saw the distaste in the scout's dark face as he turned to go, but it didn't matter what such a man thought. Drew had learned early how treacherous Indians could be—and he wasn't sure he could trust this one any more than the rest.

As the beat of the Indian charge grew louder, Drew glanced down, addressing the woman. "I don't know what you think or what you want, but until this is over, you just lie quiet. If you give me so much as a lick of trouble, you'll wish you'd stayed with the savages."

He wasn't sure she understood his words, but his meaning seemed clear. The woman closed her eyes and turned her face away.

Then the horsemen charging up the valley claimed all of

Drew's attention. It was as if the Cheyenne rode in some primitive ballet: the horses and riders a blur of grace and speed, of fury and daring, sweeping toward them over the windswept ground.

His appreciation didn't stop Drew from snatching up the sergeant's rifle, notching it into his shoulder, and sighting on one of the lead horsemen. The brave and his mount went down hard. More riders swarmed in his place, circling and firing. One of the men to Drew's left fell back, an arrow in his shoulder. He heard Sergeant O'Hearn cursing farther down the line. His hat was gone and blood was streaming from a gash at his hairline.

Still, the troopers held their own. Five or six Indians rushed their left flank and were driven back. A few breached the rocks and the line of soldiers. From the corner of his eye Drew saw Jalbert shoot one of the braves from his horse. He wrestled a second to the ground and dispatched the man with the war club Drew had seen tied to his saddle. Reynolds gave an almost imperceptible nod. The mixed-blood could be trusted, at least this far.

Then, as if by some prearranged signal, the Indians withdrew.

"Hold your fire!" Drew shouted, and quickly reassessed the situation. He knew his men could never bear up under continued attack. They were hopelessly outnumbered, and wounds had begun to take their toll. One of the muleteers lay dead, and two more men were moaning in agony. They couldn't hold the Indians off for more than another charge or two.

"Jalbert," Drew called out and waited for the scout to arrive. "Is there another way out of here?"

The scout spared a glance for the woman, then shook his head. "Even if we were able to retreat a few at a time, it would end up a race back to the fort. And carrying our wounded, we couldn't win."

Reynolds acknowledged the half-breed's assessment. They were safer here than they would be if they left the cover of the rocks. Still, this was damn grim business.

Already the band of riders at the far end of the draw were winding up for another attack.

Then from the south came the sound of a bugle. Both Drew and Jalbert perked up like hounds on point. The familiar notes of the call to arms drifted to them, clearer than before.

The Indians seemed to hear it, too. The whirlwind of riders slowed just as a column of bluecoats emerged from the dip of land to the south.

"It's Captain Parker," Jalbert reported, climbing to his feet to watch the fresh troops fan out to the right and left. From behind their makeshift breastworks, a cheer arose. "Parker must have been out on patrol when our man reached him."

"The Cheyenne see Parker, too," Drew observed, rising to stand beside the scout. Relieved of his weight, the woman who had been sprawled beneath him curled and drew her knees up to her chest.

As the line of soldiers advanced, the clot of warriors at the far end of the draw dispersed. They scattered in all directions like a good break on a billiard table.

Parker's troops pursued them, but from where Reynolds stood he could see that they'd never catch the Indians. He was beginning to appreciate the army's frustration at the way Indians could disappear into this country like barn mice into a hayloft.

At the midpoint of the draw, Captain Parker left the main body of his men. These seasoned troops would ride down the hostiles as best they could.

Reynolds bent and caught the Indian captive's wrist. He pulled her to her feet as Parker approached. "Well, whoever you used to be, madam," Reynolds told her, "whoever you are now, I'm taking you home. And God help you when we get there."

Chapter Two

The solid wood-and-stone structure of the North Platte Bridge spanned the wide churn of coffee brown water. It breached the gap between the mat of yellow grassland that rolled off to the north and east and the windswept foothills that rose in humps toward the snowy, pine-capped summit of the mountains to the south. At the far end of the bridge, on a bend in the wagon road that had carried thousands of settlers to Oregon, sat the United States Army outpost Fort Carr.

An unprepossessing cluster of log and rough-sawed buildings, of half-finished barracks and tents, the fort was still impressive enough to make Sweet Grass Woman stiffen in the saddle. She sat even straighter than before, though for the length of their ride she had refused any warmth or comfort that might be afforded by her proximity to the cavalry officer whose horse she shared.

She refused to accept anything from such a man. He believed that she had helped Standing Pine lure him and his men into an ambush. He had shamed her by forcing her to lie beneath him in the dirt, shamed her by thrusting his knee between her legs as if she were a common woman to be taken at his will. Even now he rode with one hand twisted in the belt at her waist as if she were his prisoner.

But Sweet Grass Woman knew very well what she was and took no joy in it.

The sentries who guarded the gate at the north end of the bridge snapped to attention as they approached, but not even the strictest military discipline could prevent one of the troopers from breaking rank and gesturing to his cheek as they passed by. His reaction to the tattoo the Kiowa had etched into her cheek made the breath catch in her throat. Sweet Grass Woman knew these men were only the first of many who would stare, speculate, and scorn her in the days to come.

The column rumbled onto the bridge's cottonwood decking, the sound of the horses' hooves on the planks reverberating inside her chest. An icy wind tore at her hair and clothes, chilling her to the marrow of her bones. Crossing the river seemed to take forever.

When they finally reached the southern bank of the river, the captain shouted orders, and the troopers melted away, some to stables, some to dismount before tents and barracks, a few to seek the small separate building where there must be someone who cared for the wounded and prepared the dead for burial.

It was only her captor and his scout who continued around the end of a row of buildings and onto a half-built parade ground. A flag she'd once thought of as her own snapped in the wintry breeze.

They were just drawing up before the large log building at the northern end of the field when an officer came out onto the narrow, covered boardwalk that ran across the front. At the sight of them, a scowl gathered his mouth so tight it all but disappeared into the bristle of his beard and mustache.

The captain dismounted from his horse and dragged her down. His grip was painful, almost insulting. It took every bit of her determination to keep from twisting away. With a hand on her elbow, he maneuvered her to stand at the foot of the wooden steps.

The older man loomed over her, his gaze sliding up from her moccasined feet to her buckskin dress, from her vermilioned hair to the crest of her cheek. The star-burst tattoo stung as if it had been cut and colored only the night before.

"... this ... captive ... goods for?" he demanded.

Sweet Grass Woman strained to make sense of the big man's words. She had spent three years as a slave to the Kiowa and six with the Cheyenne. It had been nearly seven years since she'd heard English spoken aloud. She trembled in frustration at the sound of it, angry with herself for needing so desperately to understand, appalled by how little of her native tongue she had managed to remember.

"We ... gave ... wagon ... goods ... get ... captive ..."

The big man nodded. " ... said ... you ... trouble ... Cheyenne?"

The men's words came in a torrent after that, too thick and fast for Sweet Grass Woman to grasp. She knew they were discussing the meeting with Standing Pine, the ambush, and her. Her return. Her fate.

She strained closer, aching to make some sense of what they were saying.

As the two men talked, a crowd began to gather. There were troopers in sweat-stained shirts and dusty canvas pants. A cluster of traders and buffalo hunters wandered up and stood off to one side, their eyes alight with speculation. Three women in bonnets and swaying skirts came rushing from one of the cabins at this end of the compound. They stopped dead in their tracks once they got a look at her. Settlers who'd been shopping at the trading post up by the bridge ambled over to find out what was happening.

The shame of being forced to stand there on display sent humiliation seeping hot beneath her skin. She linked her fingers and held on tight, fighting to keep her hands from her burning cheeks, to keep from acknowledging the many ways the Kiowa had marked her.

The murmurs came as she knew they would, tainted with sympathy, disdain, and horror. They came in a language that shouldn't have seemed so foreign in her ears. With the hiss of incomprehensible words, the crowd and the buildings and the dread closed in. The smells of sweat and onions and the white man's privies. The musky taste of fear and the burn of bile in the back of her throat. Her muscles twitched with a need to run.

Then she caught sight of the mixed-blood scout with his close-cropped hair and his white man's clothes, standing a little way apart. His face was broad and bony and impassive. In spite of his expression, she recognized the pity in his eyes. And it shamed her.

From somewhere deep in the bedrock of her soul, she dredged up pride enough to glare at him. To square her shoulders, to lift her chin.

She had relied on pride to see her through worse times than this. Pride had kept her from screaming and cowering as Julia had when they were taken by the Kiowa. It helped her endure the years of beatings and servitude, helped her bear the shame of being marked and gambled away to the Cheyenne.

But pride could not ease the turmoil in her blood or slow the wild, fierce thunder of her heart. She was afraid, afraid in a way she had never been before. Afraid of what she'd been and what she'd become. Afraid of what might happen after this.

In the years of her captivity, she had learned to fear for things not nearly so intransigent as her death.

The crowd fell still when the older officer turned his attention from the captain to her.

"You . . . English, girl?" he demanded, raising his voice. Sweet Grass Woman shook her head. She didn't understand English well enough to grasp more than bits of what he was saying. She couldn't remember nearly enough to make herself understood.

". . . you tell . . . name? . . . you tell . . . you come from?"

She shook her head again. She didn't know the words for *Vīh́' ō ŏts Hé?e* in this other tongue.

The people gathered at the edge of the parade ground watched and waited. The air grew thick with questions, curiosity.

The officer frowned, as if he were trying to decide if her silence was one of genuine confusion—or simple defiance. She could sense his mounting frustration, his annoyance with her.

At the periphery of her vision she could see the mixed-blood scout. She could tell by the way he pursed his lips that he could make her understand, help her answer, but he could not do that unless the bearded man asked.

Then he inclined his head and lowered his eyes.

Sweet Grass Woman instantly understood what he meant and did the same.

In that moment of submission, the tension between her and the man at the top of the steps seeped away.

"Me"—he thumped himself soundly on the chest, trying to communicate another way—"Major Ben McGarrity."

She nodded.

"You?" He pointed at her.

She stared back, realizing that before she'd misunderstood. He wanted her English name, not the name the Cheyenne had given her. He wanted to know who she'd been when she was fifteen and traveling down the Santa Fe Trail with her family—not who she was now.

To Major Ben McGarrity Sweet Grass Woman didn't exist. To him Pale Eyes, as the Kiowa had called her, had never existed. To him, to the captain, to these white men and women, she had not existed for nine long years. A shudder ran the length of her back. Only if she could give her English name would she exist for them again.

She wet her lips and groped for the unfamiliar syllables. She shaped her mouth around them for the first time in so very, very long.

"Cas-san-dra." She spoke the word so softly Ben McGarrity had to lean closer to catch it. "Cas-san-dra M-M-Mor-gan."

He smiled at her as if delighted by her accomplishment. It was like the moon coming out from behind a cloud. She was a person again in this white man's eyes.

She wondered if by reclaiming her white name, she had ceased to exist for the Cheyenne. In spite of an inexplicable sense of loss, she felt her face warm at McGarrity's pleasure.

"Cassandra Morgan," McGarrity announced to everyone who had been straining to hear. "Her name is Cassandra Morgan."

She heard her name echoed in a score of voices as the people in the crowd repeated it among themselves, shaking their heads.

Amidst the buzz came a single, strangled word. A voice strained with incredulity.

"Cassie?"

She turned to seek the source of her name, the diminutive her family and friends had used when she was a child. She turned to where the cavalry captain stood. His face was slack, the bleached-out color of the winter sky.

"Cassie," he breathed again. She could hear the hope and dread mingled in his tone. His gaze moved over her as if he were seeking the truth in her features and not her words. "Cassie?"

She studied him, too, wondering who he was, looking for some hint to his identity. What she saw before her was a tall, broad-shouldered man, a few years older than she was herself; a somber man with a long jaw and resolute mouth, draped in a bristly brown mustache. She saw side whiskers creeping down to accent his hollow cheeks, a fringe of wavy, chestnut-colored hair flaring at the edge of his collar. Deep creases crimped the corners of his eyes, whose color was the cold, clear gray of Navajo silver.

Something about his eyes stirred recognition way down deep, miles below the level of conscious thought. It made her mouth go dry, made the breath hover in her throat.

He nodded once, as if he had reconciled some question inside himself. Or inside her.

Touching the center of his chest, he spoke, his voice prodding, testing her. "It's Drew. Drew Reynolds."

Disbelief spiraled up inside her ribs, evaporating every dram of air. Her hands tingled. Her head went light.

Drew?

The memory of another time came flooding back. Drew Reynolds had grown up on the farm adjoining theirs in the hills of Kentucky. He was the boy Cassie Morgan had followed around and idolized for as long as she could remember. Drew Reynolds had been her first playmate, her first nemesis. Her first love.

But Drew was dead. She had seen him fall with an arrow in his back during the attack on their families' wagons. She'd seen him die. Even in the fear and brutality and turmoil of the first months of her captivity, she had grieved for him.

This couldn't be Drew alive before her now. This couldn't be Drew, the army captain who had handled her so callously—and with such contempt.

McGarrity's voice boomed above them, demanding explanations. "Captain Reynolds . . . this woman . . . you know?"

She stared at the man who claimed to be her childhood friend, still not sure that he was who he claimed to be. Yet somehow she could make more sense of what he was saying than she had been able to make of any of the English she'd heard spoken until now. Perhaps she understood because she knew he was explaining to Major Ben McGarrity about how their parents decided to leave Kentucky for a better life, about the trip down the Santa Fe Trail, and the Kiowa attack. Perhaps she understood because the echoes of her own lost language were beginning to stir inside her.

Once Drew Reynolds had finished explaining about the past, McGarrity motioned the three women forward. In the thick babble that followed Reynolds's revelations, she managed to catch a few of the major's instructions. She heard him tell the women to "take . . . scrub . . . good," to "make . . . presentable."

The women shifted their gazes from McGarrity to her, their expressions marked with dismay. The woman in the flower-trimmed hat, the sweet-faced one a few years younger than the major, addressed him at some length. From the way he listened to what she said, Sweet Grass Woman surmised she was McGarrity's woman, McGarrity's wife.

The major's mouth narrowed at the corners before he waved a young sentry in their direction.

As the women moved away, the sentry took Sweet Grass Woman's arm. Instinctively she jerked her elbow free.

The crowd buzzed like a swarm of bees, as if someone like her had no right to resist.

The major glared at the sentry, across at his wife, and then at her.

"Jalbert!" the major finally bellowed. "Explain . . . all my wife . . . want to . . . eat . . . clean!"

The half-breed came toward her. He was so tall she had to look up, so broad she felt somehow diminished by his nearness. She raised her chin, determined not to let him see how overwhelmed she was.

He must have seen it anyway. When his gaze sought hers, there was calm and understanding in his eyes. "Do not be afraid, Cassandra Morgan," he told her in Cheyenne, his voice soft and coaxing as if he were taming a balky colt.

"I have not been Cassandra Morgan for a very long time," she answered him.

His full mouth narrowed almost imperceptibly. "You are Cassandra Morgan here."

"My name is *Vīȟ' ō ŏts Héˀe.*"

"Sweet Grass Woman," he translated, the words sounding unaccountably precious on his tongue. "I am Lone Hunter, but these whites call me by my Christian name. They call me Alain Jalbert."

Sweet Grass Woman nodded, acknowledging the point he'd made. She would answer to Cassandra Morgan when these whites spoke to her.

"What is it these people want of me?" she asked him.

"The women want you to go with them. They have food prepared . . ."

She was not so easily bought off as to trade her cooperation for a bite of bread. "And what else?"

"They want to bathe and dress you in clothes like theirs."

"I bathed this morning in the creek," she offered. "I greased my hair and my body to prepare myself for the exchange. I am wearing my marriage dress."

Lone Hunter inclined his head. "The ways of The People and the ways of whites are different, as you well know. Can you not remember how it was before you were captured?"

She had schooled herself not to think about that time, not to remember. As the years passed and she had given up hope of either rescue or escape, it had been easier to deny herself the memories. She had become a girl without parents, a home, or a childhood. She had become somebody else.

Now she was suddenly afraid to relinquish who she had become with the Cheyenne. How could she give up being Sweet Grass Woman—who had cured skins that were prized beyond all others, who could quill and bead the finest shirts and moccasins—to become an unformed girl she barely remembered?

She drew a long, slow breath. "Perhaps I remember some of it."

"You must let them do what they will with you," Jalbert advised, "if you want them to accept you."

Terrible bleakness dragged at her. It had been huddled deep inside since the day she had been taken by the Kiowa, a fear so cold it burned, a yearning so deep it pierced the chambers of her heart. But it was only when the Cheyenne chiefs had decided to send her back to the whites that she realized what that terrible needing was.

"Do you believe that these whites will accept me?" she challenged Jalbert, her voice breathless and small. "Do you think they will claim me as one of their own now that I have returned to them—especially as I am?"

She could see this was a man who would not lie. "Go with them," he urged her instead of answering. "I will come if that will make it easier."

She inclined her head, needing his company, agreeing to do as he asked. She turned to follow the women, shamed by the sweep of relief she felt when she heard him fall into step behind her.

Chapter Three

❋

"Cassie Morgan," Drew Reynolds muttered under his breath. "Well, I'll be damned!"

Even as he watched Sally McGarrity and her compatriots lead the woman captive in the direction of the major's quarters, Drew couldn't quite believe that this squaw was who she claimed to be. How could this woman with her stiff, greased braids and tattooed cheek be the girl he'd grown up with back in Kentucky?

That Cassie's hair had shone in the sun, the golden brown color of hazelnuts. Her skin had been satiny, all pink and cream. And not even as a child had she been so thin. By the time she turned fifteen she'd rounded out. With sudden and unnerving clarity, Drew remembered just how soft Cassie had been when she curled against him, how well her breasts had filled his hands.

In spite of not wanting to believe this Indian woman was who she claimed, in spite of being appalled by what had befallen the girl he'd known, Reynolds could not find it in him to refute her words. When he'd first looked into those pale, desolate eyes, something had stirred up cold, unwelcome memories. He should have recognized the shiver of recognition for the portent it was.

For if this was indeed Cassie Morgan, there would be far

more questions than the few Major McGarrity had asked so far. Questions about what happened that day nine years before when both Cassie's family and his own were massacred. Questions about the attack, about who had been taken captive, about how he'd managed to survive. About why he hadn't carried on a search for the captives once his wounds had healed.

The questions would disturb the memories he'd finally managed to suppress. In a way, coming west had helped him do that. He had finally been given a posting that would enable him to seek vengeance against the savages who had destroyed his family and shattered his life. But coming west had also put Cassie Morgan in his path—Cassie who would stir up memories of that day like the layer of fine, dark silt at the bottom of a pond.

What was worse, her arrival raised questions Drew wasn't sure he wanted answered. If Cassie had survived those nine long years of captivity, could his sister be alive, too? Was Julia living among the Indians? And if she was, had she become as soiled and debased as Cassie Morgan?

Cas-san-dra Mor-gan.

Sweet Grass Woman whispered the name to herself as she followed the women through the parlor and into the kitchen of what she surmised were Major Ben McGarrity's quarters. They were clearly prepared for her arrival. A sawed-off barrel intended for use as a bathtub stood before the hearth. An assortment of bodices, skirts, and underclothes had been draped over the chairs. The table was an inch deep in fripperies.

As the three white women went about flapping toweling and heating water, Sweet Grass Woman eased toward the jumble of brushes and combs, hairpins and ribbons, bottles of scent and tins of pomade. Half-hidden in their midst was a beautiful ivory-backed looking glass. For a sharp, breathless moment, Sweet Grass Woman simply stared at it.

Not once in all the years since the Kiowa had scarred her had Sweet Grass Woman allowed herself to peek into one of the traders' mirrors. Not once had she sought her reflection in a stream. She had been determined not to acknowledge the stamp of shame Little Otter and her sisters had cut into her face, the scar that declared her a Kiowa slave. When Gray Falcon had claimed her and taken her to live with the Cheyenne, she discovered that women of the tribe adorned themselves with all sorts of tattoos. After that, the mark she bore no longer mattered.

But she knew it mattered here at the fort. It mattered now, among the whites. She'd been shamed by the sentry's reaction when they had crossed the bridge, and she'd seen the women's expressions of shock and dismay. She needed to know what they saw when they looked at her.

For a long moment she stared down at the mirror's ornate back and gathered her courage. Slowly she flipped the mirror to the opposite side and leaned above it.

The image in the looking glass was not that of the clear-eyed Kentucky girl with a ready smile. It was not that of the Kiowa's half-starved captive. An Indian woman peered out at her, a woman with wind-burned skin and vermilioned hair, with pale green eyes and a vulnerable mouth. *A woman with a blue star-burst design scored deep in the skin of her left cheek.*

Sweet Grass woman closed her eyes and remembered how the Kiowa women had held her down, remembered the heat of her blood welling up as Little Otter pierced her skin, remembered the way the finely ground pigment burned when they rubbed it into the cuts. And this was how they'd left her, scarred, disfigured. An abomination in the eyes of the whites.

The flush of rage and futility scorched her face and throat, belly and chest. Marked as she was, she could never deny what she had been. She could never escape into another life. And because they had no use for her, the Cheyenne would never take her back.

The realization left her shuddering.

"Cassandra?"

She swung around at the sound of her name. She refused to let these women guess what she'd been doing, or sense her shame. Sweet Grass Woman was too proud to allow anyone to gain such an advantage. Wasn't Cassandra Morgan at least as brave?

"Cassandra." The woman spoke again. It was the one she had come to think of as Major Ben McGarrity's woman.

"Me"—the white woman thumped herself on the chest just as the major had done—"Sally McGarrity."

Sweet Grass Woman inclined her head. She'd been right about the pretty one belonging to the major.

"And . . . ladies . . . friends." Sally McGarrity pointed to the large woman whose deep red hair was scraped into a fuzzy knot on the top of her head. "Alma Parker," Sally said, making the introductions.

"And Sylvie Noonan." The small, sleek mink of a woman stepped forward.

Again Sweet Grass Woman inclined her head.

Sally McGarrity seemed a little breathless after that, or perhaps it was the thought of what lay ahead that taxed her.

"We . . . you . . . bath," she said with the appropriate hand motions.

All three women had donned voluminous canvas bib-aprons in anticipation, as if they expected to have to fight tooth and nail to get her into the wooden tub.

Nothing could have been farther from the truth. Mere feet from the warmth of the kitchen fire, the tub steamed invitingly. From somewhere in the murk of Cassandra's memories came the feel of warm, soapy water lapping against her skin, of how the heat and joy of it crept all the way into your bones.

Obviously thinking she hadn't understood, Sally McGarrity made her way to the tub, extended one arm, and pantomimed washing it. "Bath," she offered hopefully.

"Bath?" The woman named Sylvie chimed in helpfully, bending over the tub and going through identical motions.

Sweet Grass Woman waited.

"You"—the red-haired woman pointed from her to the tub—"take bath!"

The woman joined her friends. The three of them stood bent over and pantomiming. Sweet Grass Woman easily read their expectant expressions.

Slowly she smiled. It was a smile that had little to do with acquiescence and understanding, and everything to do with satisfaction and amusement.

The women beamed—and converged on her.

They swept the beaded trade blanket from around her shoulders and took her herb and medicine bags out of her hands. They removed the clattering bone bracelets, the rings from her fingers, and the tiny copper bells from her ears. They untied her woven belt and deposited it—her awl holder and her knife—well out of reach. They pulled off her moccasins and unlaced the soft rabbit-fur leggings.

When she made no move to do it herself, the women stripped her buckskin dress away. It had been her wedding dress, and while it was a good deal less ornate than the one most maidens wore, Sweet Grass Woman was proud of it. She liked its deeply fringed yoke, the rows of elk teeth sewn across the front, and the wide, intricate bands of beads she had added to the sleeves. She had worn it today to impress the whites, and because if she had not worn it, Gray Falcon's new wife would have claimed it for her own.

With the removal of the dress, Sweet Grass Woman stood before the white women, straight and strong and naked. She stood as she had so often among the Cheyenne women when they'd all gone to the creek to bathe. But instead of nodding in acknowledgment of her slender waist and well-muscled flanks, these white women blustered and flushed and turned their heads.

"...help us!...not one bit...modest!" Alma Parker gasped and went to take the steaming kettle from over the fire.

Keeping their eyes carefully averted, the other two wrapped Sweet Grass Woman in a sheet and led her toward her bath. Water lapped even deeper in the tub as Alma Parker poured from her kettle. Steam rose in welcoming billows.

Discarding the sheet, Sweet Grass Woman stepped over the rim of the sawed half barrel. For a split second the water in the tub seemed cold against her skin, icy cold, burning cold. Then the cold turned blazing hot. She yowled and recoiled, jumping back.

Sally McGarrity and Sylvie Noonan grabbed her by the arms and forced her toward the tub.

Sweet Grass Woman twisted in their grasp. Did they want to burn off all her flesh?

Pulled off-balance and with one foot still stinging from being scalded, Sweet Grass Woman lost her balance and crashed backward, taking the two women with her. They landed in a jumble on skirts and petticoats and long, bare limbs.

Alma Parker screamed.

A split second later the front door banged back on its hinges and the mixed-blood Jalbert loomed over them.

". . . hell going on . . . ?" he demanded.

"She . . . get . . . tub!" the redheaded woman shouted, waving her now-empty kettle.

Sweet Grass Woman could see that Jalbert was perfectly capable of plucking her off the floor and depositing her in the scalding water.

"*E-hao-hoˀta!*" she protested. "*E-hao-hoˀta!*"

Jalbert's eyebrows shot upward in surprise. " . . . says . . . water . . . hot."

The room went still. The white women exchanged stunned glances.

". . . never thought . . . test it," Sally McGarrity admitted, simultaneously pushing up onto her elbows and dragging the discarded sheet over Sweet Grass Woman's nakedness.

Jalbert let out his breath. ". . . seems . . . someone . . . tell . . . Cassandra . . . what you mean."

"Well . . . certainly . . . sit . . . watch . . . bathe!" Alma Parker huffed in disapproval.

Shooting the woman a glare that would have withered someone less formidable, Jalbert cleared one of the chairs, thumped it in the doorway, and sat down facing into the parlor.

"I won't look," he promised.

Sweet Grass Woman froze in the midst of climbing to her feet and gaped at Jalbert's broad back. *She had understood every word.*

Excitement filled her. She wanted to share the joy of that

discovery with the major's woman, who was steadying her, but she had no way to tell her.

While the three women scurried around adding cold water to the tub, Sweet Grass Woman searched her mind for any English words she could remember. There were Cheyenne words, Kiowa words, Sioux words, words in German and French. There was a whole vocabulary of hand talk for communicating with tribes whose language she did not know. And there were English words, a few locked away—house and food, face and hands, tree and sky. She needed time to remember, time to roll the words round on her tongue. But she could not do that here. She would practice the words when she was alone.

"Cassandra," Sally McGarrity said, gesturing. ". . . bath ready . . . water no . . . hot."

The women stood back solicitously and allowed Cassandra to climb into the tub without their help. Once she had eased down into the delicious, fluid warmth of the bath, Sylvie Noonan and Sally McGarrity loosened and brushed out her braids. Alma Parker picked up a cake of strong-smelling yellow soap and started scrubbing her face with it.

When Cassandra reached for one of the bars of soap to wash herself, the women pushed her hands away. Employing energetic, businesslike strokes, they bathed her from the soles of her feet to the top of her head. They used a scrub brush on her knuckles, her elbows, and her knees. They soaped and shampooed her hair until the bear grease and vermilion floated in a scum on the surface of the water.

When the women had dumped and filled the tub again, when they had washed her clean by the white world's standards, Sweet Grass Woman lay back in the water. Her muscles were lax with the rubbing and the warmth. Her mind was exhausted by the emotions of the day. Behind her she could hear the women talking, preparing towels to dry her, and clothes for her to wear.

Then from beneath the fringe of her lashes, she saw Alma Parker gather up her things. Before she realized what the white woman meant to do, she had crossed to the open fire and dumped Cassie's beautiful buckskin dress into the roaring blaze.

"No-o-o-o!" Sweet Grass Woman howled, coiling toward the front of the tub, reaching out in an attempt to snatch the butter-soft deer hide from the flames. "No-o-o-o!"

Jalbert was across the room before she could blink. He shoved Alma Parker aside and reached into the fire. But even as he lifted one corner of her wedding dress, the flames chewed upward and inward, consuming the hide so quickly that he had no choice about letting go of it.

He turned from the blaze to where Sweet Grass Woman huddled against the side of the barrel. She sensed his awareness of her, the leap in his pulse. In the instant before he turned away his eyes, already bright with anger, flared hotter.

"You . . . not burn . . . anything . . . her," he ordered, turning on the three women.

". . . nothing here . . . few dirty—" Alma Parker began.

"You . . . not . . . burn . . . things!" Hunter told them fiercely. ". . . all she has!"

Sweet Grass Woman was grateful for his defense, embarrassed that he should reveal to these white women what the destruction of this meager pile of belongings would mean to her. Still, Jalbert had stepped in in time to save her beautiful beaded blanket and her moccasins, her belt and leggings, her medicine bag and precious store of herbs. She would need all the magic she could muster in this strange new place.

". . . think . . . Jalbert . . . right," Sally McGarrity intervened. ". . . think . . . let . . . keep . . . things."

With the disposition of her belongings settled, Jalbert stomped to his chair in the doorway. Once he was settled, once the women had caught their breath, they converged on her. They helped her out of the tub, rubbed her dry, and slid her into a loose, flowing gown embroidered in blue. They fluffed her hair with a towel and brushed it dry. They smoothed some strange, flowery-smelling cream into her face and hands. Once they were satisfied with their efforts, they gestured for her to remove the gown that she was wearing and gave her another, done all in white.

Knee-length pantaloons came next, followed by stout

woolen stockings that knotted above her knees. The women fastened a stiff, boned cloth around her middle, then proceeded to tighten it with laces at the back until Sweet Grass Woman could barely breathe. They lowered two thick flannel skirts over her head and tied them with bands around her waist.

Sweet Grass Woman did not remember that white women wore so many clothes when she was a girl.

Sylvie Noonan wrestled a dark blue skirt down over the mound of underskirts and Alma Parker buttoned the matching bodice all the way up the back. It took the three of them working together to force her feet into the stiff black boots that laced halfway up her shins.

How did white women accomplish anything trussed up in all of this? Sweet Grass Woman wondered, hoping they were finished.

But while Alma and Sylvie emptied the second tub of water out the kitchen door, Sally McGarrity took up a brush and began on Cassandra's hair. She dragged the thick mane this way and that, combing and coiling. Finally she twisted it into a knot on top of her head and stabbed it in place with hairpins. They put earrings in one of the holes in her ears, and fastened a small gold-colored flower to the rise of her breast.

They fussed and tweaked until she was done to their mutual satisfaction, then stepped back to admire their handiwork.

Sweet Grass Woman sat very still. In truth she could barely breath for the constriction around her ribs and the high, stiff collar. Her feet were going numb in the high-topped shoes and each and every one of the hairpins was poking her scalp. She felt like a wildflower that had been plucked and pruned and painted until no resemblance to what she had been remained.

After a flurry of whispers that seemed to indicate that the women were satisfied, Sylvie Noonan lifted the ivory-backed looking glass.

Sweet Grass Woman was gone from the mirror's silvery surface, dissolved in a barrel of bathwater. Nor had the girl who had inhabited this body years before appeared in her place. The woman reflected within the ivory frame appeared to be white, with heavy, gold-streaked hair, a sprinkling of freckles across her nose, and calm, pale eyes. She wore a high-necked gown that was trimmed with lace and seemed to affect an air of cool disdain.

Only one thing spoiled the image in the glass. This lady bore a dark tattoo.

Cassandra Morgan.

Cassie Morgan.

Cass Morgan.

Hunter Jalbert sat with his back to the proceedings and considered the woman being bathed and dressed and civilized in the room behind him. He couldn't help liking what he'd seen of her so far—and he'd seen a good deal more than any of them intended.

He fought down a grin of pure masculine appreciation as he recollected bursting into Major McGarrity's kitchen expecting blood and mayhem, and finding two of the officer's wives rolling around on the floor with their naked charge. Just one quick glimpse of that long slim torso and those shapely legs had convinced him that whatever else she was, this Cass Morgan was a fine-looking woman.

And one with grit.

She couldn't have survived nine years with the Indians if that weren't so. He liked the way she'd held her peace while Standing Pine was negotiating her release. She'd handled herself with dignity once they returned to the fort and hadn't let either Ben McGarrity or Drew Reynolds intimidate her. And when Alma Parker had incinerated her wedding dress, she'd behaved far more reasonably than any of them had a right to expect.

Hunter rubbed at the back of his neck with one broad hand. He could never reveal that Cassandra Morgan had been married to a Cheyenne, that she might even have borne him children. He could never let on that her Cheyenne husband probably hadn't been the first man to take her. Whites never seemed to grasp that a woman captive had no choice about submitting. It was that or die, either by Indian torture or her own hand.

Explaining it wouldn't keep these well-meaning wives from judging her, or labeling her a whore for doing what she'd had to do.

As if the tattoo on her cheek wasn't label enough.

Hunter shifted in his chair, suddenly impatient. He'd spent the whole damn afternoon dancing attendance on these four women. He did have other concerns, concerns that—

"Mr. Jalbert?" It was Sally McGarrity's voice, sounding uncertain and hopeful. "Mr. Jalbert, what do you think of our Cassandra?"

Hunter turned from his long, fruitless perusal of the McGarritys' parlor. And caught his breath.

Before him stood a woman whose thick coiled hair shone the rich, golden brown of buckwheat honey; whose sun-kissed cheeks glowed pink with recent scrubbing; whose eyes were the clear, pale green of a forest pool. She wore a gown of violet-blue, that defined her narrow waist and embraced the curve of her breasts in a way any man alive would like to.

In the bathing and dressing and primping, Sweet Grass Woman had disappeared. Somehow Hunter hadn't expected to resent the transformation. He hadn't expected this sense of loss.

He hadn't expected the woman who took her place would be so beautiful.

"Mr. Jalbert?" Sally McGarrity's voice came again, more uncertain, less hopeful. She wanted reassurance—for both Cassandra and the three of them.

Hunter grappled with his feelings, trying to dredge up the kind of compliment women longed to hear.

"Mistress Morgan," he said, once he'd unglued his tongue from the roof of his mouth, "I can't think when I have seen a lady more lovely than you."

The words were trite. Abashed, tongue-tied men must have mumbled them a million times, yet the three wives beamed.

Cassandra stared, a line of concentration between her brows. He repeated the words in Cheyenne, just for her.

A small, slow smile appeared on her face, a smile that held so little hope and so many grave misgivings.

Before any of the women could respond, Ben McGarrity

came banging into the house. ''That girl decent yet, Sally?'' he demanded as he barreled through the parlor and into the kitchen.

Hunter stepped back to give him room.

''We've scrubbed her clean and given her something respectable to wear,'' Mrs. McGarrity assured her husband.

The major pulled up short and made a perusal of the women's handiwork. ''You've done a damn fine job, by the looks of her. Turned her into a regular buckskin Cinderella.''

''Cinderella?'' Cass whispered as if from somewhere long ago she remembered the name. Judging from the tentative curl of her lips, she must have guessed that the major was issuing compliments.

A wave of damp, suffocating heat rose in Hunter's chest. He wasn't sure if this woman was someone he should pity or vow to protect. What he did know was that he had to get away, out to where the wide, windy sky was growing dark.

Before he could make good his escape, the major turned to him. ''Jalbert, if you don't mind, I'd like you to stay on to supper. We'll be keeping Miss Morgan here with us, at least until we determine whether she has family somewhere. We need your help to make her understand that.''

''Well, sir, it's not that I don't appreciate why you want me here, but I do have other duties . . .'' Hunter was never included in fort society, and the unexpected invitation to dinner made him uneasy.

''Damn your other duties!'' The major's scowl brought his eyebrows together. ''You hired on as a translator, didn't you? Then consider this an order: stay to supper.''

''Yes, sir,'' Hunter answered begrudgingly.

While the two men were concluding their negotiations, Alma Parker and Sylvie Noonan had been putting on their shawls and gathering up their things.

Sylvie paused on her way to the door to pat Cassandra's shoulder. ''I know all this seems strange to you, dear, but you'll feel at home here soon enough.''

Alma Parker frowned and followed Sylvie out the back door.

It had barely closed behind them when Private Montgomery, the major's striker, came in carrying a covered pot and a basket of sundries to complete their evening meal. While the enlisted man, who worked as the McGarritys' servant, set supper on the hearth and began laying the table, Sally ushered everyone into the parlor.

It was furnished in army-outpost style, with a battered settee, two mismatched chairs, and several much-mended tables. But Mrs. McGarrity had added special touches of her own. The embroidered homily, "Home Is Where the Heart Is," hung over the fireplace. A fine brass lantern clock, several daguerreotypes of men in uniforms, and a troop of ceramic dancers were arrayed across the mantel. A snarling bearskin rug took up most of the floor.

Hunter motioned Cassandra to one of the chairs while Mrs. McGarrity lit the oil lamps.

"Have you found out any more about where Cassandra comes from?" Sally asked her husband. "Does she have family back East?"

The major settled himself on the creaky settee. "Captain Reynolds told me he didn't think there was anyone left. I figured I'd send an inquiry telegram to Kentucky anyway, in case there's a branch of the family Reynolds doesn't know about."

"Ken-tuck-ee?" Cassandra asked softly.

The three of them turned to stare at her.

"Ken-tuck-ee?"

"What about Kentucky?" Hunter prompted in Cheyenne.

"It is where we came from. Where Drew and I grew up," she answered in the same language.

"Do you have kin left back there?"

Cassandra shrugged. "Did my parents survive the attack on our wagons?" she asked, her face intent.

"Didn't you see what happened?"

"I thought I did," she answered. "But I thought I saw Drew die, and now I know he did not."

Hunter could sense the glimmer of hope in her and couldn't bear to extinguish it. "Maybe Captain Reynolds can tell you what happened," he reassured her. "We'll ask him tomorrow."

Hunter translated the conversation for the McGarritys.

"But surely Captain Reynolds would have told us if there was anyone left," Sally McGarrity said, concern in her voice. "If Cassandra doesn't have family to take her in, whatever will become of her?"

That question weighed on each of them as they sat down to a supper of spicy venison stew, baking powder biscuits, and apple tart. It was the best food Hunter had ever encountered in the military, but Cass Morgan and her fate prevented him from giving it the attention it deserved.

Sally McGarrity was right. Without a family to offer her protection, where could Cassandra go? Marked with that tattoo, she would never fit in, either here on the frontier or back in the States. How would she make her way in a society that would never accept what she'd become, in a world that had changed in the last nine years even more than she had?

Hunter found his gaze drawn to Cassandra often during the meal. He watched as she ate, the way she adapted to what the McGarritys seemed to expect. She bowed her head for grace. She took note of Sally McGarrity's table manners, picking up her spoon only when Sally did, wiping her mouth with the napkin when she was done.

Was Cassandra remembering or mimicking? Hunter wondered. Was she a white woman who had become an Indian, or an Indian who must now become a white woman?

That she was still alive proved that she was able to adapt to whatever came.

When the meal was finished and the dishes had been cleared away, Sally McGarrity rose and gestured for Cassandra and Hunter to follow her. She showed them to an alcove at the back of the kitchen that had been partitioned with a drape of army blankets. Beyond it stood a packing crate washstand, a straight-backed chair, a narrow iron bedstead, and a battered trunk. Judging from the fatigue pants and the empty gun belt left hanging on a peg, the major's striker was being displaced, sent back to the barracks for the duration.

"Tell Cassandra this is where she will be sleeping," Sally McGarrity instructed, pointing to the bed made up with linen sheets, a faded quilt, and a buffalo robe. "Tell her her things have already been put in the trunk, and that there is a night-dress in there for her to wear.''

Hunter did as he'd been bidden.

''Tell her that if there is anything she needs, she should just call out and either the major or I will come to her.''

Cassandra nodded in acknowledgment when Hunter was done.

''And then tell her good night,'' the major's lady instructed. ''We turn in early.''

Hunter sought Cassandra's gaze, struggling with a need to touch her, to reassure her. To tell her somehow things would be fine, though he had no right to promise that.

''Good night, Cass Morgan,'' he said instead.

She curled her lips in a slow, sweet smile. ''Good—night—to you, A-lain Jal-bert,'' she whispered in halting, but perfectly adequate, English.

Chapter Four

Drew Reynolds tossed his hat on a hook to the left of the door and followed the rocking chair's rumbling rhythm through the parlor to the kitchen. He found its occupants as he knew he would. Lila Wilcox was ensconced in the creaking chair. His daughter Meggie was wrapped in the quilt her mother had made her, snuggled up in Lila's arms.

Lila raised her chin from where it had been resting on Meggie's white-gold curls. "She stayed awake waiting for you as long as she could."

Drew heard the disapproval in Lila's voice and let out his breath in a sigh. "Meggie's just going to have to understand that some things keep me from being home with her."

Tonight that had been writing a report for the War Department on the skirmish that had taken place with the Cheyenne this afternoon, and the repercussions it was bound to have. Disastrous repercussions—at least for him.

"Begging your pardon, sir, but how would a child just barely four years old come to understand your working every day from reveille till well past taps?"

Of course Meggie wouldn't understand, Drew acknowledged. But what was he to do? The army didn't make provisions for widowed fathers. God knows it didn't make provisions for any officer's family beyond their designation as camp followers.

Drew deliberately turned from Lila Wilcox's uncompromising frown, dipped water from the bucket near the kitchen door, and took a drink. If Laura hadn't died on the long trek west, Drew found himself thinking, if Fort Carr wasn't set down in such a godforsaken place, if either he or Laura had kin back in the States, he'd have already made arrangements for someone more suitable than the company laundress to look after his daughter.

When it became clear Drew wasn't going to answer her, Lila Wilcox went on. "And what about my own duties? With you keeping me here so late, how am I to get my washing done? Meggie or no, the men still want clean clothes."

If there were anyone else to care for Meggie, Drew would have sent Lila back to her wash. At first the officers' wives had taken pity on them and had looked after Meggie during the day, but none of them had offered to make the arrangement permanent. The other laundresses at the fort had more than enough to do looking after their own ragtag bands of children. Only Lila and her infantry sergeant husband, Will, had already raised their four sons to manhood.

"Well, then," Drew answered, turning to her with a sigh, "don't you think you'd better go and spend some time bent over your washtubs?"

"In the dead of night and weather as cold as this?"

Drew took Meggie in his arms, relieving the laundress of any reason to stay.

Lila accepted the dismissal and heaved her ample self to her feet. But before Drew could usher her out the door, she turned to him. "I hear tell you brought an Indian captive back with you this afternoon."

Drew nodded, determined not to let Lila suspect the way his belly clenched in response to her inquiry. In a community as insular as this, there were no secrets. Still, Lila Wilcox seemed to know more about everybody's private relationships than anyone should.

The entire garrison had seen him bring Cassie Morgan into the fort and heard him claim to have known her long ago.

Even those who had not gathered before McGarrity's office knew by now that the Cheyenne had used the promise of her exchange to lure the small detachment of cavalry into a trap.

Drew had said all he intended to say about that and about Cassie, but Lila would want to know more. And Drew refused to provide gossip for Lila to share over the laundry tubs in the morning. He positively refused to give any hint that Cassie's return had stirred up the caldron of dark emotions inside him.

"What did you hear?" he asked the tall, rawboned woman before him.

Lila's eyes narrowed. "That the woman was a Cheyenne captive. That they tattooed her with some heathen design. That no matter how she scrubbed, Alma Parker couldn't get it off."

Drew bit his lips to hide a smile. Alma Parker would consider it a personal affront that a white woman had been marked in such a way and would take it upon herself to eradicate the tattoo however she could.

For Cassie's sake, Drew wished she had succeeded.

"I heard," Lila went on when Drew remained silent, "that the woman returned from the Indians is someone you know."

"Our families came west together years ago," was all Drew said. He wasn't about to reveal more about the attack than he already had. From the day he'd left Fort Union for West Point nine years before, he hadn't spoken about it to anyone.

"Well, Lila," he said, shifting his daughter in his arms, shifting the woman's attention to safer concerns. "I suppose it's time I put Meggie to bed. Take the morning at your tubs, if you need it. I'll keep Meggie with me or have one of the enlisted men look after her."

"Very well, Captain Reynolds." Lila tightened her shawl around her shoulders and opened the back door. "Good night."

Drew hugged his daughter close as a swirl of winter cold swept through the room.

Once Lila was gone, he made his way through the parlor to the alcove off his bedroom where Meggie slept. He pulled back the sheets and woolen blankets and settled her in the narrow iron bed. He stood for a moment looking down at her. Asleep his daughter looked the perfect angel. Awake, she was a child, a responsibility, a problem Drew didn't know how to solve.

If only Laura had lived . . .

Drew cursed the useless regret and bent to stroke his daughter's hair. It was gossamer, like threads of spun silver and gold. "We'll find a way through this, Meggie-girl," he whispered. "I promise you."

His daughter stirred as if she'd heard, shifted beneath the covers, and settled again.

Bless the simplicity and innocence of children that they should sleep so soundly, Drew thought standing over her. He certainly wouldn't sleep this night. He wouldn't dare close his eyes. He never slept when something happened to remind him of the massacre. And tonight, after Cassie Morgan's return, it would be worse than it had ever been.

He made his way back to the kitchen and reached for the tall pewter pitcher he kept on the uppermost shelf in the pantry. Taking both a tin mug and the pitcher to the table, he sat down heavily and fished out the bottle of whiskey hidden inside.

For the most part, Drew didn't hold with drinking spirits. He'd seen what liquor had done to some damn fine officers. He'd seen the shame of it and the mistakes they'd made with their men's lives. But whiskey had its uses. Sometimes a man needed something to calm his nerves. Sometimes a man needed something to help him forget. But certainly Captain Andrew Scott Reynolds, grand-nephew to famed General Winfield Scott, had no intention of letting the devil's brew get hold of him. He was a better man than that.

Pulling the cork, Drew poured a judicious amount of whiskey into the cup. He recorked the bottle and put it back. There was no sense inviting a second drink.

Once the bottle was stowed safely away, Drew downed the liquor in a single draft. It burned along his tongue and down his gullet. It kindled a fire in his chest and seared a hole in his belly. But somehow whiskey had never been able to thaw that frigid place where the nightmare lived.

Nothing ever thawed it.

Sighing, he pushed to his feet and paused in the parlor to take a cheroot from the humidor and light it with a splint from the fire. He snatched his overcoat from the peg by the door and stepped out onto the covered porch. There was a puncheon bench against the wall, and he settled himself there to enjoy his cigar.

It was cold tonight and would be colder still by morning. He didn't envy the men on sentry duty. He was glad he'd served his stint as officer of the day last week, when the weather had been at least marginally warmer. Still, it wasn't the weather or even the bite of the sharp west wind that chilled Drew Reynolds to the marrow of his bones. It was memories of the summer he was seventeen—and tonight there was no escaping them.

June 1858
On the Santa Fe Trail

It hadn't begun like a day that would change a man's life. The same sun that had followed them from Kentucky chased the morning stars away and painted the high, thin sky primrose pink and peacock blue. The same hot wind that had battered them on the Kansas prairie set the gray-green sage to rustling and hummed in the branches of the piñon trees. The animals that had brought them as far as this lowed and stirred, wanting to be watered and fed just as they did every morning.

Drew had risen with the sun, going about the duties he'd performed each day since they'd left Kentucky. He'd stirred the embers of the fire and added wood. He fetched water from the creek so his mother could start breakfast. He helped his father and his older brothers with the animals.

On the far side of the clearing Drew could see that Cassie Morgan was helping her father with their animals, too. She was the oldest in a family of girls and had learned things most females never did: how to plow a field and keep the furrows straight, how to sharpen an ax and turn spindles on a lathe, how to yoke oxen to a wagon and drive a four-horse team. When they were younger, her accomplishments had been considerable enough to convince Drew to let her tag along when he went tramping through the woods or fishing in the creek that divided his father's property from hers.

When she was a child, acting as her father's surrogate son had pleased Cassie, but since she'd turned fifteen last winter, she'd become more interested in genteel pursuits. She was perfecting her sewing and her cooking. She had taken more interest in spinning and weaving and looking after her younger sisters. Cassie had also developed a sudden and most flattering interest in him. Drew grinned at the memory of how flustered he'd been when instead of greeting him with a cuff on the arm as she had for years, she'd slipped her hand through his and smiled up into his eyes.

Almost as if she knew Drew was thinking of her, Cassie slid him a sidelong glance from across the clearing. He answered it with their secret smile, feeling the sweetness of the plans they'd made well up in him. She would make him a perfect wife—just as soon as she was old enough, just as soon as he could secure a parcel of land and build a cabin. His brothers, Matt and Peter, had promised to help him do that when the day came for him to claim Cassie Morgan as his bride.

"Oh, Drew, do stop mooning after Cassandra," his sister Julia teased as she brushed past him with an armload of folded bedding. "The look you get on your face whenever you see her is quite revolting. Besides, she'll probably meet some dashing frontier scout when we reach Santa Fe and forget your name."

Drew caught up with his sister and gave her long, reddish braid a tug. "You just wait and see what happens in Santa Fe, feather-wit," he told her. "Neither a scout nor one of those fancy Spanish *caballeros* will come between Cassie and me."

Julia laughed as if she knew better, and spun away.

The small train of five wagons passed the morning grinding its way up one of the rocky ridges that made up the Sangre de Cristo Mountains and faced a steamy afternoon of rumbling down the narrow, twisting canyon on its opposite side. Since Cassie had spent most of the morning walking to lighten the load, Drew took her up behind him on his horse when they stopped for nooning.

He liked riding double with her, liked having her arms entwined around his waist and the feel of her breasts against his back. But being as close as this made the sweet, sultry longing rise between them. Tempted though they were to lag behind or seek the privacy of a side canyon where they could kiss and touch and be together, they were mindful of the constant threat of Indians. Cassie's father, Jess, had spotted three painted-up braves watching their progress this morning, and he had warned everyone to stay together.

As the afternoon advanced, the sun burned hot out of a silver-bright sky. The air in the narrow canyon shimmered, and dust devils danced ahead of the wagons, as if leading the way. The travelers lapsed into a weary silence that was broken only by the rattle and jolt of the iron wheels over broken stones, the rhythmic clatter of hooves, and the lowing of thirsty animals.

Then from somewhere just ahead came the hollow boom of rifle fire.

Drew pulled his horse up short. For an instant no one in the wagon train moved. No one breathed. Then all at once his oldest brother, Matthew, toppled from the seat of the lead wagon. A second shot dropped one of his oxen in its tracks.

The men reached for their rifles. The women gathered the children and scrambled for cover.

All except Matt's wife. Maude surged to her feet in the box of the first wagon and started screaming. Visible as a lightning rod and howling like a banshee, she seemed to lack the presence of mind to take up the reins and get their wagon moving again.

Until she did that, they were corked up like bugs in a bottle.

From their vantage point slightly higher in the canyon, Drew could see Peter leave his wife and his wagon and sprint toward the head of the line. Peter would take care of Matt.

He would get them moving again. Peter was good and solid and capable.

Drew had hardly completed the thought when he saw the flare of fire high up on the cliff. The impact knocked Peter sideways. He staggered, stumbled, and lay still.

"Peter!" Drew bellowed, though he figured it was probably too late for his brother to hear him. "Peter!"

Peter never moved. Blood pooled beneath him and glistened in the sun.

Behind Drew, Cassie moaned in fear.

Bile and fury choked him. Drew jerked his rifle from the sheath at the side of his saddle and dismounted. He dragged Cassie down with him. They found cover in the boulders to the right of the trail. From there, nearly twenty yards behind the wagons, they could see the battle unfolding.

More than a score of Indians had dug in on the cliff side off to the left. Bullets and arrows came thick and fast, ricocheting off the canyon walls and slamming into the sides of the stranded wagons. Safely hidden up in the rocks, the Indians could fire down on the wagons forever.

From where he and Cassie had taken cover, Drew couldn't get a clear shot at the raiders. Yet he couldn't see how to cross the open ground and reach the wagons either.

Below them, they could see two of Cassie's sisters cowering behind a wagon wheel with their fingers in their ears. The men were shouting back and forth, planning strategy as they paused to reload.

If only Matt's wife would stop screaming and pick up the goddamned reins, Drew thought. If only she would drive the wagon out of there, they could run the gauntlet and escape. None of them would survive unless she did that.

Drew's muscles burned with the need for action, but without jeopardizing his position, there was nothing he could do.

The fire from the hillside came constant as a drumroll. The defenders could hardly show themselves to shoot back, and the firing was taking its toll.

The horse that had been tied at the back of one of the wagons lay dead, pincushioned with arrows. A firebrand flared, blackening one of the tailgates. A water bucket spewed its precious contents onto the earth.

Behind the rear wagon, Claire Morgan was reloading for her husband. Farther down the line, Drew's mother was crouched beside his father firing relentlessly at the savages who'd killed her sons.

"We're all going to die," Cassie whimpered.

"It's going to be all right," Drew soothed her, though he knew very well it wasn't.

Two more oxen dropped in their traces. The canvas on the second wagon began to flame. In the midst of a deafening fusillade, Jess Morgan staggered backward and fell.

"Papa!" Cassie moaned, and buried her face against Drew's chest. He hugged her hard and cursed.

The gunfire from the wagons was dwindling when Drew spotted a small band of braves snaking along the southeastern rim of the canyon. They were circling around, preparing to attack the wagons from the front.

"I have to go down there," he murmured, half to himself. "I have to warn them."

Cassie's head came up. Fear and grief had drained the color from her skin, until those pale, clear eyes fairly blazed. "No, Drew!" she whispered. "Please don't leave me."

He checked the prime on his rifle, charted his course across the open ground. Once he'd done that, he turned to Cassie.

"Promise me you'll stay here. That no matter what happens, you won't show yourself. That once the Indians leave, you'll get on that horse and ride back the way we came."

He could see Cassie understood why Drew wanted her promise. He waited just long enough to see her nod.

"I love you, girl," he told her, and kissed her hard.

"And I love you!"

Drew launched himself down through the tumble of rocks toward the open ground.

Once he reached it, he realized that the Indians had done more damage than he and Cassie had been able to see. His mother was sprawled beside the rear wheel of their wagon, an arrow in her chest. Their hired man lay near her, his head half–blown away. A child lay curled up and still, one of Cassie's stairstep sisters. And still Maude kept screaming.

Drew sprinted down the slope in a hail of gunfire. He had to make it to the wagons, had to warn whoever was left of the newest danger.

But before he could reach the wagon at the back, he felt a jolt of impact in his thigh and his left leg crumpled beneath him. He fell headlong, grinding his face in the dirt. He lay there panting and confused, sucking in the thick, grainy dust of the canyon floor. It wasn't until the pain swarmed over him that he realized he'd been shot.

He lay there, dazed, wounded, trying to think. Exposed. Vulnerable and defenseless. He worked the pistol from his holster and started to crawl.

"Pa! Pa, they're coming around the front!" he yelled above the roaring in his ears, above the constant blast of gunfire.

But no one answered.

Shots kicked up dirt on his right and left. An arrow sliced past. Drew crawled faster, dragging his useless leg, leaving a smear of blood on the yellow earth.

His ears rang. His lungs burned. He ran with sweat. The wagons seemed only marginally closer when he raised his head.

He saw dust rising at the foot of the canyon. Matt's wife's screaming went suddenly still. The raiders had reached the lead wagon. That meant he'd failed.

They were lost. Every one of his family and Cassie's would die here, brutally, uselessly. Drew squirmed toward the wagons anyway.

The firing went on around him. The report of the rifles rang hollow in his ears. Sweat rolled down his temples and stung his eyes, mingling freely with his tears. Still, he clawed at the powdery earth. He pulled himself along, closer to the nearest wagon, toward the edge of the shade.

New pain exploded through the muscles of his back. It flared white hot, blaring, biting deep. Drew shuddered and fought for breath. The canyon blurred and shimmered around him, tinted orange and yellow by the sinking sun, red and brown with drying blood. Then the colors faded away and blackness swooped in like carrion birds.

Drew sat on the puncheon bench with his head in his hands, sweating as if it were summer, not ten degrees. His heart was rattling around inside his chest and his half-smoked cheroot lay ground to powder between his feet.

God Almighty! he thought, letting out a shaky breath. After all this time, why were the memories still so close, so vivid and invasive? He still saw his mother's broken body when he closed his eyes. He could still taste the dust and the blood and the fear, still feel a sharp, fresh ache in those old wounds.

He should be able to control this, to make it go away. Instead he felt raw inside, as if he'd been split open and exposed to the world. The best of him and the worst. The moments of which he was proudest—and most ashamed. Things he longed to put away and didn't know how.

He wished he could blame the freshness of these memories on Cassie's return. But if he was honest with himself, he had to admit that the memories were always there. Lurking just below the surface of conscious thought. Waiting for some provocation so they could rise from that cold, viscous place inside him. And when they did—

"You all right, Captain?" It was the sentry walking his rounds who spoke as he came down along the neat row of log cabins that served as the officers' quarters.

"I just stepped out for a breath of air," Drew answered, his voice sounding rusty and thin.

"Then you must be breathing mighty deep, sir," came the young soldier's reply.

Drew's shoulders stiffened. "And why do you say that, corporal?"

"Because you were sitting in that very same place, in that very same position, when I made my rounds an hour ago."

Drew supposed that was true. His knuckles ached with the cold. In spite of the sweat still crawling down his ribs, the tips of his ears had begun to burn.

"Thank you for reminding me how long it's been," he

answered with a grimace that he hoped would pass for a smile. "I have a lot on my mind."

The corporal bobbed his head as if he understood. "You go on into the house, sir. Get some rest."

Drew came to his feet and went inside as if he meant to take the corporal's advice. But instead of making his way to his bedchamber, he returned his overcoat to the peg, lit both of the oil lamps in the parlor, and set them atop his campaign desk. Before seating himself, he took the bowl from his wooden paint box and filled it from the water bucket.

With meticulous care, he laid out the things he would need. The metal tubes of pigment, the ivory palette, the three small badger-hair brushes, and a rectangle of fine rag paper. Using a slightly larger piece of blotting paper behind it, Drew tacked both papers to the lid of the box.

There was something soothing about preparing the paint, about the slow, smooth circles it took to mix the pigment and the medium, about the way it kept a man's mind from wandering. When he had moistened and then thinned the colors to his satisfaction, he began to paint.

Though he had easily mastered the tight, meticulous drawing style taught to cadets at West Point, Drew painted without sketching first. He let his brush flow across the paper, let the colors and movement take him. Painting was one of the few spontaneous acts Drew Reynolds ever allowed himself.

Tonight he used a sweep of yellow-green to conjure up the prairie they'd ridden through this afternoon and one of brown for the gash of dun-colored rocks where they'd made their stand. He painted quickly, the way the grass was winnowed by the wind, the way the winter light grayed and flattened the mass of stones. He painted with a fierce and focused concentration that didn't allow for thought or memories.

He flinched at the sound of Meggie's voice.

"Papa? What are you painting, Papa?"

Drew had to take a long, slow breath before he could turn to where his daughter stood in the bedroom doorway.

"I'm painting something I saw this afternoon."

She came toward him, barefoot across the rough, chill

floorboards. She'd catch her death of cold. He ought to get up and search for her slippers.

Meggie stopped beside him and regarded the painting with a critical eye. "There isn't any red," she said after a moment. "You never paint with red."

Instead of answering her, Drew washed out his brushes and put them away. He reached to scoop his daughter up in his arms.

"So, Meggie, what brings you out here in the middle of the night?"

"I had a nightmare," she told him. "I was afraid."

Drew looked down at his child and nodded. "I know how scary nightmares can be," he answered. When he continued, his voice had gone rough and low. "Sometimes I have nightmares, too."

Chapter Five

The sobbing woke her, the dry, persistent fight for breath; the soft, pitiful gasps of a frightened child. Cassie came awake clutching the edge of the buffalo robe, her fingers tangled in the thick, rough hair. She swiped at her cheeks with her hands, feeling guilty and ashamed. Only the dream ever made her cry.

She might have known she'd dream tonight, after being driven from her home by her Indian husband, after being used by Standing Pine to bait the soldiers, after coming to a place that seemed so strange.

"Cassandra?" Sally McGarrity pushed back the blanket curtain and stood in her nightdress and cap, a candle in her hand. "Cassandra . . . all right? . . . have . . . dream?"

"A dream," Cassandra nodded. "When Kiowa—" She bit her lip, searching for the words. "—took me."

Sally set the candle aside and came to kneel on the pallet Cassandra had made for herself on the floor.

". . . you doing down here?" she asked, drawing Cassandra into her arms. "Oh . . . doesn't . . . matter, does it?"

Cassie resisted Sally's embrace at first, uncomfortable with her closeness, the sense of being confined. But there was warmth in Sally McGarrity, warmth and comfort, compassion and tenderness.

My mother held me like this, Cassie found herself thinking. She stiffened in Sally's arms. It wasn't good for her to remember things like that; it wasn't safe. If she thought about what her life used to be like, she'd want to go back, and there was no going back. No family, no friends, no home in Kentucky.

"There, there," she heard Sally McGarrity whisper.

Cassie knew there was no family left. It would do no good to ask Drew about the massacre. Drew's survival was miraculous enough. She dared not hope that Ma and Pa had lived to start the trading post they'd dreamed about in Santa Fe. She knew in her heart that Susannah, Lucy, Faith, and Janey were dead, not flirting with beaus or happily married and having children of their own.

She fought down the wave of grief she'd held inside for nine long years. There was no time for grieving now, just as there had been no time for it when she and Julia had been fighting to stay alive.

Julia.

Cassandra closed her eyes. Julia weighed heavily on her conscience, a burden of truth she had to share with Drew. But how could she explain what had befallen Drew's treasured younger sister? She could not tell him through Alain Jalbert, not in Hunter's words, not with Hunter there to hear her. They must speak of it alone. She must somehow find the words to tell Drew about Julia herself.

Sally McGarrity gradually loosened her hold on Cassandra and smoothed back her hair. "Better now?" she asked.

Cassie nodded.

"You want . . . bed . . . there?" she inquired, indicating the narrow iron bedstead.

"Pokes me," Cassandra answered, jabbing with her finger.

Sally McGarrity laughed and came to her feet. "Straw ticks do that. You want"—she gestured as if she were pouring from a pot—"coffee? It's getting light."

Without waiting for an answer, Sally went into the kitchen. Cass heard the rumble of the coffee grinder and smelled the thick, dark essence of the beans. Taking a moment to search out her blanket and moccasins, Cassandra joined her.

She was surprisingly comfortable sitting across the table from this woman she had known less than a day. But then, Sally McGarrity seemed content with Cassie's silence, content to wait for the coffee to boil.

Taking care not to stare, Cass studied the older woman, seeing kindness and warmth in her deep blue eyes; the soft, sweet line to her mouth, waving strands of silver in her auburn hair. She seemed possessed of an abiding serenity, an infinite calm. It must have made her the perfect foil for the major's energy.

He rumbled into the room a short time later as the two women sat over steaming cups of coffee. "... three ... after six," he grumbled, glaring at his pocket watch, "... that bugler ... blown ... yet!"

His words were cut short by the sound of the trumpet.

"There!" he said, closing his watch with a snap. "Finally."

"Coffee, Ben?" Sally asked, already reaching for the pot.

He sat forcefully, gruffly, the way he did everything, and reached for one of last night's biscuits.

Sally passed him a cup of coffee and the jam. The smile he gave her was only one step short of adoration.

"I want you ... Cassandra ... office," he said around bites of his breakfast. "There ... questions ... answered. Want ... about ... Cheyenne ... I'll see Jalbert ... there, too ..."

"Can ... you ... time ... Cassandra ... talk ... Captain Reynolds?" Sally inquired, and Cass looked up. "They ... things say so many years."

Ben McGarrity nodded, downed the rest of his coffee in a single draft, and surged to his feet. "Bring Cassandra ... after guard ..." he instructed, and dutifully bussed his wife's cheek.

Sally smiled and watched him go.

Cassie saw the softness in the older woman's eyes, the abiding tenderness in the curve of her lips. Sally loved her big, bluff husband. She had found her special place in the world. And what Cassandra wanted more than anything was to find a place of her own.

Chapter Six

Drew sat braced in the corner of Major McGarrity's office, awaiting Cassie Morgan's arrival. He thought he had prepared himself for this morning's meeting. He thought he could look at Cassie, hear her voice, and not feel the terrible clutch of shock, revulsion, and pity he had the day before.

In a way he had succeeded. What Drew felt as the major ushered Cassie and Mrs. McGarrity to chairs in the cramped office at the rear of the headquarters building was none of those things. It was stunned surprise.

There was nothing in this young woman to revile or pity. She was dressed in a rich, blue bodice and matching skirt, with a furl of ecru lace cresting at the base of her throat. Her taffy-colored hair draped low on her cheeks and fell in glossy ringlets from beneath the back of her deep-brimmed bonnet. With a soft half smile and discreetly lowered lashes, Cassie was alluring, coquettish, astonishingly beautiful.

The promise of that beauty must have been evident in the girl Drew had known: in the sculpted bones of her face, in the ivory glow of her complexion, in the clear, arresting eyes. As a young man he had seen all that, but he had never understood that one day Cassie would possess a loveliness that could turn a man inside out.

Yet he knew the Indian tattoo was lurking like the serpent

in the Garden of Eden, hidden in the shadow of the bonnet, disguised by the drape of her hair. It would always be there, evidence of the years Cassie had spent with the savages, marking her in a way she could never erase.

Certainly Drew could never forget it. He couldn't allow himself that luxury.

The ladies were just getting settled when Alain Jalbert shouldered his way into the room.

McGarrity waited only long enough for Jalbert to assume the empty chair.

"Well then, let's get started," McGarrity began. "I want to know about the Indians, I want to know how many Cheyenne were in the band where she was living. I want to know what alliances they've made with the Sioux. I want to know how many warriors Red Cloud and his lieutenants can muster against us come spring."

Jalbert sent the major a long, assessing glance. "And what makes you think she'll tell you any of that?"

"Of course she'll tell us," Drew spoke up. "Why wouldn't Cassie tell us?"

Jalbert's eyebrows rose, and Drew felt the sting of the half-breed's contempt. "Because she's been living with the Indians all this time. Because she probably considers herself as much Cheyenne as white."

Drew's outrage was caustic and hot. "But the savages killed her family!"

"You said it was the Kiowa," Jalbert put in softly, "who attacked your families' wagons."

"Yes," Drew acknowledged. "The Kiowa."

"And she's been living with the Cheyenne."

Drew scowled with distaste. Redskins were redskins. He didn't care to make such fine distinctions. He didn't like the friendly camp of Sioux clustered at the western perimeter of the fort. He didn't trust the mixed-blood Jalbert, and his spontaneous translations. He wasn't pleased that Cassie's return from the dead was forcing him to change his thinking about who and what she was.

Still, how could there be any question of where her loyalty lay?

"Why don't we let Cass tell her story in her own way?" Jalbert suggested, shifting his gaze to McGarrity. "If you've got questions when she's finished, you can ask them then."

McGarrity glanced across at his wife before he nodded. Jalbert relayed the request to Cassandra, then translated as she began to speak. "I will start with the day the Kiowa came. The day they attacked our wagons. The day they made me their captive."

McGarrity nodded again. "Go on."

"Drew"—she glanced hesitantly in his direction—"and I were riding together a short distance behind the wagons when the Indians began to fire down from the walls of the canyon. They trapped our families in a narrow place where there was no way to escape. They fought bravely, but there were many more Kiowa than there were of us."

The fear Drew had felt nine years ago clawed at his throat as she spoke. He remembered the blind, raw panic of being pinned down, of being outgunned. Of being helpless.

"Only when they were sure that everyone in the wagon train was wounded or dead," Jalbert translated as Cassie went on, "did the Kiowa show themselves. Some climbed down the cliff. Some rode into the canyon from the ends. That is how they found me—hidden among the rocks where Drew had left me when he went down to the wagons to fight."

Cassie sliced another glance in his direction, acknowledging that the worst of the telling still lay ahead.

Drew swallowed hard, fighting for breath.

"Only Drew's sister Julia and I were not hurt in the attack. One warrior bound our hands and guarded us while the other Indians killed and scalped our families."

That day came back to Drew in horrific detail. He smelled the coppery corruption of blood and violence and sudden death. He tasted the rime of dust on the back of his tongue. He heard the wracking of Julia's ceaseless sobs. He'd lain in the rough, sparse grass a few yards away from Cassie and his sister. But he was broken, immobile. Too badly hurt to lift a hand, too weak to hold a pistol and grant them release.

Sweat crawled down Drew's ribs and beaded in the fringe

of his mustache. His hands were shaking when he wiped it away.

"Tell us the rest," McGarrity prompted her.

Cassandra nodded, a shudder moving through her. "The Indians looted all the wagons, and set them on fire. They tied ropes around our necks and marched us west. They pulled Julia and me along behind their horses and beat us if we stumbled or couldn't keep up.

"We had been marching for three days when we reached the Kiowa village. There were other prisoners there, and they herded all of us together. The women and children poked us with sticks and tore at our hair and clothes. They tortured some of the men."

Cassie's voice wavered, and Jalbert paused in his translation, concern showing in his eyes. "Once—once all that was over," she continued, "they began to divide us up. Some of the children were given to Kiowa mothers who'd lost a child. Most of us were taken as slaves. One of the warriors from the canyon claimed Julia, and another claimed me."

"Then you don't know what happened to my sister?" Drew burst out, unable to bite the question back. "Did Julia kill herself rather than submit?"

Cassie looked deep into his eyes. She seemed reluctant to speak of Julia's fate, yet he sensed that when she did, he would finally learn the truth.

"I think we should let Cass explain what happened in her own way," Jalbert said, and rose to secure a dipper of water from the bucket that stood outside the major's door. Cassie drank gratefully and handed it back.

"For the first months we stayed at the same encampment," she went on once Jalbert had resumed his place, "and I saw Julia every day. We would meet when we went to the creek for water or were sent to gather roots or wood. Though it was forbidden, we would whisper to each other in English so we wouldn't forget the sound of it.

"Then late in the fall, the warrior who owned Julia went to winter farther south. I did not see her again until the bands came together for the summer hunt," Jalbert continued translating.

"Julia had changed while we were apart. She had grown pale and thin. I tried to spend as much time with her as I could, but the brave who owned her caught us speaking English, and both of us were beaten. After the gathering, Julia's Kiowa family returned to the south."

"Dear God," Sally McGarrity said. "Was there no chance to escape? Didn't you try to run away?"

Cassie bit her lip as if she were not sure how to answer. "Where would I run to if I had?"

Cassie's resignation made Drew angry. She should have at least tried to escape. She should have died trying.

McGarrity leaned forward from his perch on the corner of the desk. "But how did you come to be with the Cheyenne?"

Cassie drew a shaky breath and raised her head. "I was wagered in a horse race. Gray Falcon won me for his wife."

Sally McGarrity gasped.

The major cursed low in his throat.

Drew shuddered with the chill that ran the length of his back. Visions of what being wife to a warrior meant swam through his mind: some red bastard tearing at her clothes, dark hands mauling her, a savage grunting and panting between her thighs.

Gooseflesh rippled along Drew's arms. How had Cassie stood the degradation? How had she survived the shame? Good women killed themselves before submitting to an Indian. Why hadn't she?

He lifted his hand to rub the gooseflesh away and saw the half-breed watching him. Jalbert had known all along what had happened to Cassie. He had known how repulsed Drew would be, and he was arrogant enough to sit in judgment.

Drew was quivering inside when he reached across to take Cassandra's hand. "It doesn't matter," he told her, responding to the challenge in Jalbert's hooded eyes. "What matters is that you survived, that you have been returned to us."

Drew hadn't noticed how pale Cassie had become until her color came flooding back. "Do you mean that, Drew?" she whispered, her face suddenly shining with hope.

"Of—of course he means it," Sally McGarrity answered. "We're all glad you're here at the fort, aren't we, Ben?"

The major scowled. "Of course we're glad. Now, missy, just how long were you with the Cheyenne?"

"I lived with the Cheyenne for six years," Cassie answered.

"Did you always live with the same band?"

"Most of the time," Jalbert translated for her.

"And where was that?"

"We lived with Black Kettle's band until the attack on the Sand Creek encampment. We were fortunate to escape with our lives from Colonel Chivington's troops."

Cassandra's quiet revelation sent shock ricocheting around the room.

"Oh, my Lord!" Sally gasped.

The major scowled.

Even Jalbert's calm seemed ruffled by Cassie's answer.

Only Drew maintained his composure. He had read early accounts of Colonel Chivington's victory over the Indians in the newspapers back East and it seemed an infinitely well-planned and well-considered action. Chivington had come upon the encampment in the early morning while the Cheyenne were still abed and had his men ride down any hostiles who tried to escape. Only later did it come out that Colonel Chivington had attacked a company of Cheyenne that was under the army's protection, and that his men had slaughtered Indians who hadn't even tried to resist.

Still, considering that the redskins had been raiding in the Colorado territory for months, considering what Drew himself knew of savages, he'd had no trouble defending Chivington's actions to his fellow officers. That had given him a reputation as an Indian hater, but it had also gotten him assigned to Fort Carr when many of his classmates from West Point were fighting bureaucracy back in Washington.

Cassie ducked her head before continuing. "It was after Sand Creek that we took what we could salvage and made our way north toward the Republican River."

That single fact defined the stance Cassandra's Indian husband had taken. He had allied himself with the raiders. Under Red Cloud the Cheyenne and the Sioux had wreaked havoc most of the previous year. They had attacked travelers on the

Bozeman Trail, harassed Forts Phil Kearney and C.F. Smith, and massacred poor Captain Fetterman and his men just before Christmas. Now they were holed up in their winter camps, but come spring . . .

"But why did the Cheyenne agree to trade you back?" McGarrity asked after a moment, and waited for Jalbert to repeat the words.

Cassie's chin came up. Her eyes were hard, her mouth drawn tight at the corners, as if his question had touched her on the raw.

"My husband no longer wanted me," she answered. "And no other warrior would take me to wife. I am childless, barren. Of no use to a husband. Of no use to the tribe. That is why they gave me back."

Drew could barely believe what he was hearing. White women never spoke of such private things. While they might whisper among themselves, no lady would make such a declaration. What shook him even more was that Cassie almost seemed willing to bear some warrior's child. But how could she consider that after what the savages had done to both their families?

McGarrity pressed on, still determined to get his answers. "Ask her if she knew Standing Pine meant to use her to lure Captain Reynolds's patrol into that ambush?"

Jalbert did not even bother to translate. "She didn't know," he said.

"You're sure of that?" McGarrity asked with a frown.

"Absolutely, sir."

"You aren't even going to ask her?"

The half-breed shook his head. "I saw her face when the hostiles came over the rise."

McGarrity shook his head in disbelief. "How can you be certain that after a few days here at the fort, she won't steal a horse and hightail it back to report our strength?"

"The Indians don't want her," Jalbert answered steadily.

"So she says." The major studied the half-breed seated before him. "Can you guarantee she hasn't been sent to spy on us?"

Drew wanted Jalbert to be right in this. Though Cassandra

might be marked, violated, soiled by her years with the savages, there was still enough of the girl he'd known in her to make Drew long to believe in her.

Jalbert looked across at Cassie and back at the major. "I'd stake my life on her loyalty. Now, Major, if there isn't anything more you want me to ask her, it seems to me . . ."

The way Jalbert had appointed himself Cassandra's guardian offended Drew. The half-breed had no rights where Cassie was concerned.

"I've nothing more now," the major conceded. "I still want more specifics about the Indians she's been living with, though that can wait."

"Then if we're done, perhaps Mrs. McGarrity could take Cass home?" Jalbert suggested. "Talking about this can't have been easy for her."

Sally McGarrity came to her feet. "It's been a rather taxing morning for all of us."

"Please," Drew spoke up, appalled at the way his voice broke on that single word. "I still don't know what happened to my sister."

Cassie turned her eyes to his, her face marked with compassion and regret. "We must—speak—of Julia—when—we are—alone."

The words, carefully enunciated in clear but halting English, stunned them all.

McGarrity was the first to recover. "By all means," he offered, "use my office."

Jalbert turned to Cassie, obviously reluctant to leave her. "Do you want me to stay? Do you want me here to explain to Captain Reynolds—"

"We will—manage," she told him.

Drew saw the flush rise in Jalbert's face. The mixed-blood didn't like being shut out. Still, Drew was glad Cassandra had chosen not to share their secrets.

Jalbert followed the major and his lady out the door.

With a knot in his chest Drew watched them go, wondering if he really was ready to learn what had befallen his Julia.

* * *

Cassie's throat tightened as Alain Jalbert and the McGarritys left the confines of the major's office. Talking about her captivity had forced her to remember days when terror clawed her raw, weeks when she'd been forced to submit to a life she had not chosen. She was exhausted by the memories, by the explanations, by a sense of failure. She wanted the telling to be over, but she knew the worst still lay ahead.

She dreaded exposing the parts of her captivity that dealt with Julia. Those days were too painful, too filled with her own powerlessness and guilt. Yet she could not refuse to tell Drew Reynolds Julia's fate.

She felt his gaze on her and looked up into the pewter gray eyes she remembered so well. He sat before her so much harder and grimmer than the boy she'd known. Lines were scored deep around his eyes and mouth. A few silver threads streaked his chestnut hair. Had she changed as much as he had since that day in the canyon?

"I—I thought—you were—dead," she told him, fumbling for the English words. She needed to hear how he had survived. She needed to buy herself a little time before they talked about Julia.

"The Kiowa came damned close to killing me," Drew admitted, glancing away. "I crawled under one of the wagons and very nearly burned to death."

"I could not—watch—" she whispered, "—once they began the—" She made the motion with her hands. "—scalping and—the killing. I saw you fall. I saw you—take an arrow in the back. I thought you . . ."

Drew nodded and silence swelled between them. She began to think that talking about that day was as hard for him as it was for her.

"It was the smoke from the burning wagons," he finally went on, "that brought a patrol from Fort Union. They were the ones who rescued me. They were the ones who buried our families."

Her throat closed up and her eyelids burned. She had learned not to cry during those early days with the Kiowa. Indians thought tears were a sign of weakness, and she could not afford for her captors to think she was weak. *Weak like Julia.*

"I am—pleased that someone—buried them."

She did not tell him that she had imagined vultures circling above the canyon, gliding down to tear at the mangled remains of the people she'd loved. No one must ever know that was part of the nightmare haunting her.

"The men from—Fort Union—did they—care for you?"

Drew gave an uncomfortable shrug. "I was more dead than alive when they found me. I had taken a ball in the leg. It was broken. The arrow cracked a couple of ribs and one of them had put a hole in my lung. And there were burns . . ."

She could see the sweat bead up on his brow. He knotted his hands to still their trembling.

She understood how painful the memories could be. Yet to see Drew respond to that day the way he was shocked her. She had thought a man would be stronger than a woman, that Drew would be stronger than she.

But then, Drew had suffered as much as she had. They had been so young and fragile and unformed that dusty afternoon when they had lost everyone they cared about—including each other.

Drew's unexpected vulnerability gave them common ground where the truth Cassandra had to tell might come a little easier.

"I did recover from my wounds," he continued suddenly, "and all I could think about was riding out and killing Indians."

"Did you?"

Drew shook his head. "The commander at Fort Union wouldn't let me. He said he wouldn't waste his men and horses chasing Indians they'd never catch. He wouldn't let me go alone. He kept me confined to the fort so I wouldn't run off. He convinced me that if I wanted to kill Indians, the way to do it was to join the army."

Cassie nodded.

"I gave him permission to submit my name to the military academy at West Point, but I didn't want to wait through four years of schooling to go to war. When the appointment came through, the colonel all but threw me on the stage and sent me East. It didn't take me long to realize that fighting Indians as an officer was going to be a whole lot different than fighting them as an enlisted man.''

''Is that why—you came back. To fight Indians?''

Drew nodded. ''I'd have come back sooner, but the war—'' He must have seen the confusion in her face. ''Do you know what has been happening back East while you've been here?''

''Gray Falcon said—the army was—ordering soldiers away from the forts—to do battle—with each other. That was why—it was a good time—for the Cheyenne to fight . . .''

. . . the invasion of the whites.

It was only here and now that she realized how much her view of the world had changed during her years with the Indians. Turmoil rose in her chest like smoke from a smoldering fire. She felt raw inside, ashamed and confused.

Cassie had known there were enemies who threatened the hunting ground and the welfare of the Cheyenne nation. The warriors talked of little else. She knew those enemies were white like her. Yet when Gray Falcon had ridden out, she had helped him prepare for battle. Being who and what she was, how could she have done that?

Drew was so caught up in explaining the war to her that he didn't seem to notice how ragged her breathing had suddenly become. He didn't seem to see the shame burning in her face.

As he talked, Cassandra fought to gain control of her emotions. She couldn't think about this now. Not while she was with Drew, not when there were other things they must discuss.

''. . . after I got my commission from West Point,'' Drew was saying, ''I married Laura. Her father had been my cartography instructor. She and I—''

''Laura?'' Cassandra started as if awaked from a daze. ''Are—are you—married?''

''I'm widowed,'' he answered. ''My wife died on our way out west.''

''Widowed,'' she echoed.

It seemed so strange that Drew's life had gone on without her, that he had been wounded and resurrected, that he'd gone to school back East, fought in a war, and gotten married. Once he had been at the center of her world. How could all of this have happened and her not know?

She felt as if there were a hole in her life, years ripped from the fabric of who she was. She had the past and she had now. The only thread that spanned the gulf between them was Drew, and now even he had become somebody else.

''Do you have children?'' Cassie asked, dreading the answer.

''I have a daughter.''

Cassandra nodded, her throat too tight to speak. Once, she had dreamed of being the mother to Drew's children, of holding his gray-eyed babies to her breast. She knew now that she would never mother any child, much less one of Drew Reynolds's children.

''Oh, Drew,'' she breathed. ''How old—''

''Meggie's four.''

He didn't say any more about the girl. Perhaps that was because he didn't want her to know about his Meggie, that by knowing she might somehow taint his daughter. It was a realization that twisted inside her like the blade of a knife.

''But then,'' Drew went on, ''there is time enough for us to talk about this later. Now I want you to tell me about Julia.''

The moment was upon her, and Cassie felt less prepared to tell him about Julia now than she had been when the others left.

He sat beside her, tense and grave, hunched as if he were husbanding his strength against the pain. But it was Cassie who would determine how much pain Drew Reynolds would bear, and how much she would take upon herself.

She began to speak because she had no choice. ''I—told you—that when I saw Julia at the summer—gathering she was''—Cassandra motioned to the shape of her own face—''pale and thin. The next year—she was very sick. She—'' Pantomiming, Cassie breathed fast and low.

''Panted?'' Drew asked and Cassandra nodded.

''—when she went for water or wood. Fevers came on her in the night. She—coughed, and there was—blood. It was the wasting disease.''

''Consumption.''

''Yes.''

Drew stared past her as if he were trying to conjure Julia up before his eyes. Cassie hoped he was seeing his little sister as she was that last morning at the campsite with her reddish hair shining in the sun and her voice filled with laughter. She didn't want Drew to imagine Julia the way Cass had seen her last, with empty eyes and skin so translucent you could almost see her life's blood seeping away.

''Did you care for her?'' She could hear the ragged edge to Drew's deep voice. ''Did anyone care for her?''

She looked deep into his eyes. ''The woman Julia—belonged to was very—kind. She took plants and made—medicines for Julia—to drink. She—bathed Julia with water—when the fever was high. She let us talk in English when I came to—visit in her lodge.''

Drew's mouth thinned before he asked the question. ''Did Julia die?''

She reached across and took his hand. It was a gesture completely foreign to the way she'd been living. The Cheyenne were warm and giving people, but they did not touch to offer encouragement or comfort. The impulse harkened back to her childhood, to the closeness she and Drew had shared before the Kiowa raid had destroyed their world.

She curled her fingers around his palm. It was callused and warm. With the contact, Drew seemed to become more real to her, more vivid and intense. He became more the boy she'd admired, more the man she'd once loved.

''Yes,'' she whispered.

He brought his opposite hand to cover hers. ''Were you with her?''

''No.'' She waited, tense and trembling, wondering if he would ask more about his sister's death. Wondering if she would lie to him or tell him the truth.

Drew let out his breath, and when she looked up he'd

closed his eyes. "Then may God grant peace to our Julia's soul."

At his words, the fear went out of her.

They sat silent for a few moments more, and Cassandra could sense that Drew's grief for Julia was already seasoned by time and tears. He had given up on his sister long ago.

Cassandra was weary, too. Worn by the day and the memories and the terrible confusion. The weariness made her want to lie down with her back to the earth and stare at the sky. Made her want to feel the wind blow over her as if she were dust.

Then Drew's hands tightened on hers and she felt the tide of strength and fortitude rise up between them—renewing him, renewing her.

"Thank you for telling me the truth," he whispered. "I know talking about this is difficult. But I had to hear about Julia from you."

Cassie inclined her head in answer and curled her fingers more tightly around his hand.

Hunter watched Cassandra and Drew through the half-open door. He hadn't meant to watch them. He hadn't planned it. He'd looked up from the map spread out on the table in the front room of the headquarters building and seen them framed in the narrow opening.

They had asked to be alone so they could speak of the captain's sister, and in spite of understanding the reason for the request, Hunter resented being shut out. He'd liked Cassandra's dependence on him, enjoyed the intimacy of giving voice to her words, the responsibility of filtering this strange and confusing world for her. He'd liked knowing she trusted him to do that. It had made him feel connected to her in a way he'd rarely felt connected to anyone.

Now she'd made it clear that there were some things too personal for him to know. Yet he knew. By watching the dip of her head and the way Reynolds looked at her, Hunter could surmise at least a few of Cassandra Morgan's secrets.

Cass sat with her shoulders bowed toward the captain, her profile framed by the brim of the deep blue bonnet. She talked quietly, the gravity of the words and the difficulty of expressing herself in English drawing her brows together. As she spoke, the harsh, proud lines of Drew Reynolds's face crumpled, going vulnerable, revealing a depth of love and pain Hunter had never imagined the man could feel.

Reynolds's sister must have died while she and Cassandra were captives. Hunter saw the captain's hands knot in futility and frustration as Cassie spoke. His lips compressed, and he looked away.

At length the captain bent closer, his words soft, intense, demanding.

When he was done Cass lowered her lashes, drew a long, unsteady breath, and raised her gaze to his. Hunter could see how she was struggling with the words, read the frustration in her gestures as she explained. What she was telling him was either a difficult truth or a desperate lie.

Then, as if to make what she was saying easier to bear, Cassandra reached across and touched the captain's hand. It was a simple gesture, one of comfort and compassion, one appropriate to a conversation as deep and serious as this. But at that contact, something inside Hunter shattered.

With that clasp of hands, with the brush of Reynolds's flesh and hers, Hunter knew he'd lost his chance for something he was only beginning to realize he wanted: a lasting bond with this strange and beautiful woman.

When they had completed negotiations with Standing Pine the day before, Cassandra Morgan had stepped into the no-man's-land between whites and Indians, the world Hunter had inhabited all his life. Over the years he'd come to appreciate its subtle dichotomy, the advantages and the compromises, the freedoms and the injustices. But until Cass stepped inside, Hunter had never realized how isolated he had become. Until she came, he never dreamed his life could be more than what it was.

He had never thought to find a woman whose life had taken on that same frustrating duality. He had never considered seeking a woman like her to be his companion, but now he felt as if Cassandra Morgan had been sent to him to care for and protect.

He was the only one who would ever understand the bigotry and suspicion she would face by being marked, the insults she would bear, the inequities she would live with every day. Only he would know how to ease her way and comfort her. By rights, Cassandra Morgan should have turned to him.

Yet Hunter could see that already she was reaching out to Drew Reynolds, to the life and society that once had been hers by right of birth. Hunter had seen enough of the captain's motives and prejudices to doubt that Reynolds would give much of himself to a woman like her. But perhaps with his help, with his sponsorship, Cass could make a place for herself in Reynolds's world. It would be a perilous place, a tenuous place. A place where survival would have to pass for happiness.

And if Cass failed . . .

Hunter didn't want to think about what it would be like for Cassandra then. He didn't want to think about what it would be like if she turned to him as second-best. And no matter what happened, Cass Morgan could never want or need to be with him as much as Hunter suddenly wanted and needed her.

Weary all the way down to his bones, Hunter turned from the crinkled map, from the scene taking place behind that half-open door, and made his way outside.

He stood on the wooden porch while the world went on around him. Mule skinners cursed their teams. Soldiers on fatigue duty hammered new shingles onto the roof of the barracks across the way. A few friendly Indians wandered up toward the sutler's trading post. Hunter stood in the midst of the activity and the people and the noise and had never felt more alone.

Chapter Seven

Drew couldn't help thinking how good it was to be with Cassie even after all this time. How natural it seemed to help her with her shawl and offer his arm. How right it felt to ask if she wanted to meet his daughter.

"What—happened to your—wife, Drew?" Cassie asked as they made their way out of the headquarters building and onto the path that skirted the parade ground.

"She died of a fever on the way out west."

"How long—" she wanted to know. "How long ago was that?"

Drew had to think back. The last months seemed jumbled, compacted somehow. They had left Fort Leavenworth the first of October—too late, as it turned out, to miss the first of the season's howling blizzards. They'd been caught on the flats west of Scott's Bluff and hadn't known whether to batten themselves down to withstand the storm or forge ahead to Fort Laramie. They'd decided to press on, and with Laura and Meggie lying bundled in layers of blankets and buffalo skins in one of the army ambulances, they'd fought their way through the freezing wind and pelting snow. Meggie had done fine in spite of the hardship, but by the time they reached the fort, Laura was coughing and feverish. The following morning the doctor diagnosed her ailment as pneumonia, and by midnight she was dead. It had happened too fast for either Drew or Meggie to comprehend.

"Laura passed on in November," Drew finally answered.

"I am—sorry—for your loss," Cassie said, fumbling with the English words. "How is your—little girl getting on—without her mother?"

Drew felt a nudge of conscience that he hadn't been more attentive to his daughter's needs. "Well enough, I suppose."

Their walk had taken them across the compound to the bake house, one of the two sandstone buildings in the fort. After Lila Wilcox's tiny cabin, it was Meggie's favorite place.

Though a chill, damp wind that promised snow had pursued them all the way, the bakery breathed summer in their faces when they opened the door. The air inside was heavy, ripe and yeasty with the smell of baking bread.

Meggie was wrapped in an apron from her neck to her toes and up to her elbows in bread dough. As soon as she caught sight of him, she abandoned her work.

"Papa, Papa!" she cried. "Sergeant Goodwin's letting me help him mix the bread!"

The announcement was hardly necessary, and before Drew could stop her, Meggie had thrown herself against him. In one big hug, she had covered his crisp uniform blouse and dark blue trousers with a loaf's worth of flour.

"Oh, Meggie!" Drew admonished her, scowling at the mess she'd made of him. Still, he bent and caught her up in his arms.

"We already baked—" She skewed her face trying to remember. "How many loaves did we bake, Sergeant Goodwin?"

"Eight dozen," the round-faced sergeant answered. "Ninety-six."

"Did you know that there are twelve loaves in a dozen?" Meggie asked him.

"As a matter of fact I did," Drew answered, swiping at a smudge of flour on Meggie's cheek.

"And you know what else?"

"I'm afraid I don't have time for guessing games, Meggie." Drew was already wondering how long it would take to get back to his cabin and brush the flour out of his uniform. With Sergeant O'Hearn laid up with his head wound, and his company one lieutenant shy of full strength, Drew was trying to keep a closer eye than usual on afternoon drill.

"I brought someone by," he continued, "I want you to meet."

Meggie reluctantly opened the scope of her regard to include the woman at his side, and he felt his daughter stiffen. Drew proceeded with the introductions anyway.

"Meggie, this is Cassie Morgan. We have known each other since we were barely bigger than you. Cassie, this is my daughter Meggie."

"Hello, Meggie," Cassie greeted her.

Meggie simply stared.

"What do you say, Meggie?" Drew prodded her, torn between the concern that Meggie was going to ignore Cassie's greeting completely or mention the Indian tattoo,

"Hullo," the little girl finally murmured, and buried her face against his shoulder.

"Since Laura died, Meggie hasn't taken much to strangers," he hastened to explain.

"I think she's wonderful, Drew," Cassie answered, shifting around behind him to get a better look at his child. "She has your eyes."

He supposed he'd hoped that Meggie would show some affinity for his old friend. Perhaps she would have if he'd been able to give Meggie and Cassie time to get acquainted, but time was a luxury he didn't have today.

"Thank Sergeant Goodwin for letting you help," he instructed his daughter. "And let me get that apron off."

"We still got baking to do," Meggie protested.

"It's time to go find Lila."

The little girl stood with her hands propped on her hips and a mutinous expression on her face.

"Lila will have finished her washing by now," Drew said as reasonably as he could. "Lila will take you home, give you something to eat, and read to you."

"I don't want to take a nap," Meggie answered, not the least bit fooled by the euphemism.

"Go along now, lass," Sergeant Goodwin offered, trying to help. "Somehow I'll manage to get this baking done without you."

Meggie waited a moment longer before relenting. "I won't take a nap," she muttered, and turned her back so Drew could work the strings on her apron. He fumbled with the knots and then had the devil's own time fastening the row of velvet-covered buttons down the front of her coat.

Meggie spent the time looking Cassandra up and down. He'd seen court-martial panels who looked less formidable.

"Thank Sergeant Goodwin for letting you help," Drew prodded his daughter a second time.

"Thank you, Sergeant Goodwin," Meggie offered obediently. "I'll come back and help tomorrow."

Drew cast the sergeant an appreciative glance as he ushered the two females toward the door.

The weather had worsened outside, and they were all but blown toward the small hardscrabble encampment where the company laundresses lived. Every fort had a soapsuds row made up of tents or tiny makeshift cabins with cauldrons of wash water steaming out front and lines full of laundry radiating like spiders' webs across the back.

The sound of hoofbeats, war whoops, and gunfire erupted behind them just as they reached the head of the row. Drew gave Cassie and Meggie a shove toward the nearest cabin and grabbed for his pistol.

Three riders swooped past headed for the clutch of ragtag tepees perpetually clustered to the west of the fort.

Young bucks, Drew managed to reason through the blood drumming in his head. Friendlies liquored-up and looking for trouble.

The concept of friendly Indians was not one Drew had managed to assimilate. Still, he knew that they were part of life here at the fort. This was how the bureaucrats back in Washington wanted their Indians—tamed, living near supply depots, dependent on the whites for clothes and food. It wouldn't further anyone's aims to shoot a friendly Indian by mistake.

Though his heart continued to thump erratically, Drew

eased the hammer down and holstered his pistol. He looked around for Meggie and Cassandra. They were scrambling to their feet a few yards away.

"She knocked me down!" Meggie sputtered, outraged. "She made me get mud on my coat!"

"It's all right, Meggie," Drew assured her.

"Lila won't give me a star for inspection if I have mud on me!" she wailed, and burst into tears.

Cassie came to her knees beside the child and began scrubbing at the spots with the tail of her shawl.

Meggie yelled louder.

The racket brought Lila Wilcox from her cabin near the middle of the row. She seemed to take in the situation at a glance. "Now, Miss Meggie, what's all this crying about?"

There was no question that his daughter had a flare for the dramatic. Meggie related her tale of woe, complete with pitiful sniffles and reproachful looks in Cassie's direction.

"Well, seeing as how it's not your fault, child," Lila said, coming to take the girl's hand, "I'll overlook the mud and brush it out myself once the spots are dry."

Meggie drew a shuddery breath, as if she were only partially satisfied.

Once the child had been quieted, Lila looked Cassandra up and down. Drew could see it wasn't a cursory inspection, either. Certainly Lila saw how the mud had soaked into the front of Cassie's skirt and the way the jostling had set her hat askew. Between that and the lock of hair that had worked loose of its pins, the tattoo on her cheek was clearly visible.

"So you're the one," Lila murmured at last, and turned her head, dismissing Cassie as if she were invisible.

Drew couldn't allow an army laundress to snub a woman he was escorting, and cleared his throat. "Cassie, may I present Mrs. Lila Wilcox," he began in a voice that rang with command. "Lila has taken care of Meggie since we came to the fort."

Cassie inclined her head.

"And Lila, this is Miss Cassandra Morgan, lately of Kentucky."

"And even more lately of the Cheyenne, the way I hear tell," Lila said under her breath.

Drew glared, angry at Lila's outspokenness and then proud of how calmly Cassie met the older woman's gaze.

"How do you do?"

"'Bout as well as a body can expect," Lila answered, though a faint, dull flush had begun to creep into her cheeks.

Confused by undercurrents he couldn't quite fathom, Drew went on. "I was just bringing Meggie over from the bake house."

"You needn't have done that, Captain Reynolds. Old Goodwin and I had things worked out."

"I thought I might just as well. I know you've been falling behind on your other duties."

"And I do appreciate your help," Lila said almost begrudgingly. "But then, Meggie always enjoys spending time with her pa, even if it's only a few minutes he can spare in the middle of the day."

Drew felt the sharp edge of Lila's tongue, but chose to ignore the sting.

"Well, then," he answered. "If you and Meggie are set for the afternoon, why don't I see Miss Morgan back to the major's quarters?"

"Why don't you do that?" Lila agreed. "Miss Meggie and I have a couple of special things we've been planning, don't we, pumpkin?"

Meggie nodded and tugged Lila toward the tiny cabin on soapsuds row.

"Good-bye, Meggie," Cassandra called after them. "Good-bye, Mrs. Wilcox."

Both of them chose to ignore her.

"Poor little tyke!" Sally McGarrity sniffed as she and Cassandra made their way up toward the river and the bridge where the sutler kept his store. "I wish you could have seen Meggie when they arrived! Captain Reynolds kept her fed and clean enough, but he'd bundled her up—"

"Bundled?" Cassie's understanding of English was growing quickly, but there were still words and phrases that puzzled her.

"Wrapped her up," Sally explained, gesturing. "He made her wear every speck of clothing she owned. And Meggie wasn't talking—not a word. Not even to him."

Cassie found it hard to believe that Meggie Reynolds had ever been silent.

"She'd lost her mother, after all," Sally went on. "Barely four years old and left alone with only her father to tend her. Not that he didn't try. God knows, Drew Reynolds is a man who tries. But he didn't have any idea what that baby needed."

Cass fumbled through the unfamiliar words in Sally's story and seemed to catch the drift of it.

"Alma, Sylvie, and I took turns keeping Meggie while he got settled. We held her, petted her, and made her dresses. She was growing out of all her things, and Drew had no idea what to do about it. We played with her and fed her gingerbread."

"Gingerbread," Cassie said, remembering.

"We talked and talked to Meggie, and finally Meggie started answering back." Sally's mouth tilted in a smile. "And she hasn't stopped talking since."

Cassie nodded, struggling to take everything in. "Drew said her mother—only died in—November."

Sally scowled and huffed. "I daresay the captain barely knows that poor woman is gone except that she's left him with that child. Lila Wilcox has been a godsend. She's a rough-and-ready sort, but she's been good for Meggie.

"Still," Sally went on, "that child needs more than Lila can give her. She needs love, and I just don't know if Captain Reynolds is the kind of man who can show affection."

Cassie thought of how Drew had been when they were growing up in Kentucky. He'd loved to tease and joke. There had always been warmth in his eyes, and he treated people with an easy kindness that made them like him. She had seen the change in him this morning. He had pressed her to tell him about Julia, spoken sharply to the bakery sergeant and Lila Wilcox. He had been impatient to hand Meggie over to

Mrs. Wilcox and to leave Cassie herself at the McGarritys' door. It was as if Drew were always somewhere else, focused on something far more important.

She and Sally were just passing the cavalry stables when Alain Jalbert came by on his horse. Both women turned to watch him. Today Cass saw the warrior in him, the pride in the way he carried himself, the war club tied to the back of his saddle, the medicine bag on a thong around his neck. The man seemed to have taken it upon himself to protect her in this strange new place, and she was glad of it.

"Another singular fellow, our Mr. Jalbert," Sally observed, and opened the door to the sutler's store before Cassie could ask what she meant.

Cassie had been in trading posts before, though Gray Falcon had been careful about which ones. White captives were at a premium when it came to bartering with the army, and her Cheyenne husband had been too practical to let some enterprising trader make a profit selling his wife back to the whites. Still, the smell of curing furs, gun oil, sizing, and spices was familiar. So was the dimness, relieved only by two lanterns hanging from the cabin's crossbeam and the glow from the alcove around back where three men sat gambling.

Sally had invited Drew to come for supper, and she had insisted on going to the store to get some "delicacies." As Mrs. McGarrity went about her shopping, Cassie wandered around the room. Though she could see that the stock was low, probably because of the difficulty of winter travel, there were still all manner of goods Cassie had rarely seen in the posts that catered to the Indians. There were gleaming steel needles, spools of thread in rainbow colors, bolts of strong, high-quality cloth.

A box of small, bright scissors caught her eye. Cunningly designed to resemble the cranes she'd seen fishing in the lakes up north, the scissors lay in a box at the edge of the counter beside trays of thimbles and tiny copper bells. She took a pair of scissors out of the box and slid her thumb and forefinger into the holes to test their weight. She worked the blades and saw that the bird's bill opened and closed as if he were singing. Cassie wanted the scissors almost more than she wanted to draw another breath.

The traders who came to the villages and most of the trading posts she'd visited put out small goods for the Indians to steal. It was a sign of goodwill on the traders' part, a sign that they were willing to indulge the Indians' enjoyment of a little harmless pilfering in preparation for the hours of earnest trading that would follow. Usually the objects weren't as fine as this, or as expensive. But the scissors were out where anyone could finger them, not back on the shelves.

Glancing up to see if the sutler was occupied, Cassie slipped her fingers from the holes in the handles of the tiny scissors and made as if to put them back. She palmed the scissors instead, and just as she was pocketing her prize, a big man in a sweat-stained shirt and battered hat loomed out of the shadows and grabbed her wrist. He dragged Cassie across the room to where the sutler and Sally McGarrity stood bargaining.

''Hey, Jessup,'' he jeered, ''you need to keep a closer eye on your inventory when there's In'juns about.'' The man's grip tightened, forcing Cass to open her fingers. ''These scissors belong to you?''

Sally McGarrity stared, taking in the scissors still tucked in Cassie's palm and the guilt she knew shone in her face.

Sally's eyes widened. ''Cassandra!'' she murmured in horror.

Cassie's flush sizzled all the way to her hairline.

The sutler, Jessup, let his hard, black gaze slide over her, coming to rest on the tattoo that peeked from beneath her bonnet brim. His eyes lit at the sight of it.

''Don't you make no mistake, girl,'' he told her. ''This here's a respectable sutler's store, not some redskin trading post. We don't put things out for squaws to steal.''

New humiliation burned in Cassie's cheeks. She couldn't think how to defend herself.

Instead Sally McGarrity spoke up for her. ''It's a natural mistake for her to make if that's how things are done at the Indians' trading posts. Put the scissors—and all the rest of this—on my husband's account.''

Cassie stood nailed to the spot while Jessup bundled up the scissors and Sally McGarrity's purchases. She knew she should apologize, though the thought of speaking one word to the man behind the counter made her skin crawl. She would address herself to Sally once they got outside. But even when they reached the street, Cassandra's tongue seemed glued to the roof of her mouth.

They had walked a fair distance in the direction of the major's quarters before Sally spoke. "There are bound to be things that are different here from what you've grown used to," she began, "but we whites do not lie and we do not steal."

Cass hadn't seen that that was true when it came to the white men's treaties and Indian land, but she held her peace.

"If you're going to live among us," Sally went on, "you're going to have to learn to abide by certain rules."

Were they rules she had learned as a child and now forgotten? Cassie wondered. Or rules that had only come to apply because she'd been living as an Indian?

"I'm sorry, Mrs. McGarrity," Cassie said, finally finding her voice. "Nothing like—this—will ever—happen again."

"See that it doesn't, Cassandra," the older woman answered, and forged ahead.

"In the end that sly old horse threw the general," Drew said, grinning as he came to the end of his story. "And if horses could laugh, that one would have."

Cassie chuckled and stole another glance at the man who occupied the opposite end of the settee. This was the Drew Reynolds she remembered. He was charming and wry and affable. Tonight he had been an ideal dinner companion, arriving at the stroke of six o'clock with a tin of toffee for Sally McGarrity and a coil of ribbons for her.

The meal had gone well. With the help of the major's striker, Sally had put together a dinner of quail with peach and brandy sauce; roasted potatoes; some sort of desiccated green vegetable; and muffins served with the raspberry jam Sally had bought at the sutler's store.

If Drew had heard about the incident this afternoon, he

gave no sign of it. Cassie's cheeks burned just thinking what he would say about her thievery. From this day on, she vowed, she wouldn't take so much as berries from a bramble bush.

When she turned her attention back to Drew and Major McGarrity, they were still telling soldier stories. Cassandra had heard Cheyenne warriors do the same, sitting around the campfire until the moon had set. In those tales the Cheyenne seemed to venerate daring, to honor bravery in battle; these white soldiers spoke with humor and derision about their leaders and their own experiences. Or perhaps these white soldiers didn't tell tales of their bold and bloody deeds to impress the women, as the Cheyenne did.

As they sat in the quiet parlor finishing up the dishes of dried-apple cobbler with condensed milk, Cassandra unabashedly studied Drew. She recognized the confidence of the boy she'd known in the surety of the man Drew had become. She saw how the softness and vulnerability in his features had hardened with time and experience. Yet as the two men talked of what Cassandra was beginning to understand had been a long and brutal war, there were no shadows in Drew's eyes.

This morning when they spoke about the attack on their families' wagons, Cassie had watched those pewter gray eyes go dark with anguish and bitterness and grief. She knew without him telling her that surviving the massacre had affected Drew far more profoundly than anything that had happened since. He might be able to spin out tales of the Civil War, but she knew he would never voluntarily speak of what had befallen their families.

"I heard the old man was a tyrant," the major was saying about one of the officers when Cassandra picked up the thread of their conversation, "I'm just glad I never served under him."

In the brief silence that followed the major's words, McGarrity spooned up the last of his cobbler and milk and set his dish aside. "Well," he said, "as much as I hate to bring such a pleasant evening to a close, I need to head over to the telegraph office and see if the message I'm expecting has come through."

"If you don't mind, Ben," Sally McGarrity spoke up, setting her dish aside, "I think I'll go with you."

The major looked around at his wife as if she'd lost her mind. "For God's sake, Sally, it's twenty degrees!"

"Then I suppose I should wear my heavy cloak."

Sally McGarrity rose and took a soft brown garment from one of the hooks beside the door.

"But—but what about Cassandra and Captain Reynolds?" Ben McGarrity sputtered.

"Oh, they're old friends," she answered, handing him his overcoat. "I'm sure they can keep each other company."

Drew and Cassie laughed at how Sally bustled the major outside.

"I think Mrs. McGarrity meant to give us some time alone," Drew observed.

"Oh?" Cassie murmured. "Do we—need that?"

"I don't know," Drew answered. "Do we?"

Cassie wasn't sure what he expected her to say. They had already talked about the past, about the circumstances that had brought each of them here. They had spoken about Julia. Did he suspect—did Sally suspect—that there was more she could tell him about his sister's death? Was there more she wanted Drew to know?

"Sally has been—very kind," Cassie said instead. "Everyone here at the—fort has been—very kind." It wasn't exactly the truth, but she didn't want to mention either the incident with the sutler or the way everyone stared at her.

Drew seemed to know about the staring. "The longer you're here, the less of an oddity you'll seem."

She nodded, though she wasn't sure he was right.

"What do you intend to do with yourself, now that you are back with your own kind?"

Back with her own kind? Just what kind was that?

Cassie stared at Drew. He had been "her own kind" once, but he wasn't the man he'd been nine years ago. His experiences and his fears and his hatreds had changed him, just as the things she had done and seen changed her. But if Drew wasn't "her own kind" anymore, who was?

Only Alain Jalbert seemed as caught between two worlds

as she. Only Hunter seemed able to understand how it felt to be both the same and different from everyone else.

Still, Drew was right. She needed to think about what lay ahead. To do that she had to put the past to rest.

Cassandra knew the answer before she spoke, and yet she needed to hear the words of confirmation. "No one but you—survived—the attack on the—wagons, did they?"

"No one survived but me."

Drew's response boxed her in the way she knew it would.

"I'm sorry if I didn't make that clear this morning," he went on, "but I thought you knew."

"I expect I did," she admitted.

Drew turned toward her and laid his arm along the back of the settee. "Major McGarrity has sent inquiries to Kentucky," he said. "If he can't find relatives to send you to, we'll make sure you have what you need to make a life for yourself."

She tried to think what kind of a life that might be. It would not be the life she had envisioned when she was fifteen, a life with Drew and his children. No white man would take an Indian's leavings. She had long ago accepted that she would never nurse a baby or mother a child. Nor were the skills that had distinguished her in the Cheyenne camp of use to her here.

Her future stretched before her, barren and bleak. What was she going to do now that her life was beginning again? She'd started over twice before, once as a slave and once as Gray Falcon's woman. Who was she going to be this time?

As if he had recognized the depth of her confusion, Drew tightened his arm around her shoulders. "We'll do everything we can to help you find your place."

Her place. That was all she'd ever wanted, somewhere to belong. The thing that had always eluded her.

She looked up into his face, seeking confirmation. "Can you promise me a place, Drew?"

"I promise I'll do everything I can to help you find where you belong," he told her solemnly.

Cassie smiled up into his eyes, and though she had only meant to acknowledge his kindness, the moment their gazes met, awareness flared in both of them. Her skin tingled where his fingers brushed her shoulder. His eyes seemed to brighten. Her body suffused with heat. His breathing came ragged in the silence. The air went thick and sultry between them.

It could have been the rugged cast to his features, the wildflower scent of her hair, or the hollow ache of loneliness in each of them. It might have been his strength or hers, her need or his that made them suddenly so aware of the bond that linked them still. In the end it didn't matter what it was. The essence of what they'd shared years before drifted around them like lingering smoke.

"Oh Drew," Cassie whispered, "should it still be like this between us?"

"No," he answered her.

But it was.

The attraction was all scent and heat and promise. She recognized years-old desire in his eyes, saw a fresh tide of yearning erode the hard line of his mouth. Perilous expectation rose in her.

They came together as if the kiss were preordained, his mouth seeking hers, her lips opening in welcome. His arms tightened around her, drawing her against him.

Cassandra closed her eyes and savored him, responding and remembering all the intimacies they'd shared. The texture of his lips; the languorous perusal of her mouth; the taste of Drew were all wondrously familiar. The strength in that long, hard-muscled body and the tickle of his mustache were surprising and new.

She curled deeper into his embrace. He took full advantage of her willingness; circling her lips with his tongue; seeking the warm, sweet cavern that beckoned him.

Sharing so much of herself with Drew awakened a slow, deep need in Cassandra, a sharp, delicious quickening. She craved his touch and his taste and his tenderness in ways she never had when she was young. Cassie craved them as a woman did—a woman who had known pain, brutality, and loneliness; a woman who needed comfort, security, and peace. She ached for everything to be as it had been years ago when life was filled with joy and Drew Reynolds loved her, body and soul.

How clearly she remembered the spring they'd discovered each other. They had been sitting barefoot and ankle-deep in the icy stream that carved a meandering channel between his father's land and hers when Drew had leaned across and kissed her. He'd done it shyly, hesitantly that first time. Yet even then he'd kissed with a natural affinity for the act that was partly honest affection and partly burgeoning curiosity.

Cassie had loved him for as long as she could remember, and now that she had a chance to let him know, she kissed him back.

Her headlong willingness had turned the simple, experimental brush of lips to something else, something delicious and intoxicating, something forbidden. They had sprawled back on the new spring grass, touching and stroking and holding. In those first few moments they had learned how a spark could ignite between a man and a woman, learned the power of a single kiss to delight and tantalize and excite. They had withdrawn shaken by what they'd discovered. In some deep, essential way, they were children no more.

Tonight, as their lips parted and their tongues merged, there was an echo of that first discovery: the surprise and the elation, the awakening and the promise. What passed between them now was intense, adult. Their feelings had names, passion, yearning, and desire.

That those emotions should leap to life between them after all this time was poignant and bittersweet. But both of them knew this was the wrong time and place for them to feel such fierce attraction. They were the wrong people to touch and ache and need.

Slowly, shaken by what had passed between them, they withdrew from the embrace. Cassie sucked in a shuddery breath and shoved back her hair. Drew scrubbed his face with his hands and refused to look at her.

Still, the need was thrumming in them both, a subtle symphony played out in the beat of their pulses, in the hum of their sighs, and the chatter of Sally McGarrity's lantern clock. It was as if those few simple kisses had awakened something that had lain dormant in each of them—a ghost of who they'd been, a dream of what their lives might have been like if they hadn't lost each other.

But they had.

Drew shoved to his feet and stood over her. "This can't be happening. We can't let it happen."

Though she was quaking inside, Cassie looked up at him. "I don't know—that we can—help it."

He stared as if he were seeing her for the very first time.—her tattoo, her sun-browned face, the years she'd spent with the savages. She read the revulsion in his eyes.

"Damnit, Cassie! Can't you see how much we've changed? Don't you know we can't go back?"

"Oh, Drew," Cassie sighed. There was such wistfulness in her, a deep, fruitless longing for all that might have been. "Perhaps if we tried—"

Drew recoiled, breathing hard. "I don't want to try. There isn't room in my life anymore for trying."

He was possessed by that single-minded fury, a need for revenge that had swallowed him whole. She could not help but feel sorry that he had forfeited the softer parts of himself to something so cold and useless.

He crossed the room and snatched his hat and overcoat from the hooks beside the door. "Thank Mrs. McGarrity for inviting me to dinner. Tell her everything was delicious."

Cassie came to her feet. "Drew, please—"

He jammed one arm into the sleeve of his overcoat. "Tell the major I'm sorry I couldn't wait, that I'll see him in the morning."

"We can't—pretend that—nothing happened between us," she insisted. "We can't see each other—every day and—"

He stopped as he reached for the door latch and looked at her. His jaw was hard as granite, but there was turmoil in his eyes. "Nothing happened, Cassie. It might have, but we didn't let it. And we won't."

"But Drew—"

"It's too late for either of us to feel like this, Cassie. We aren't young and innocent any more. We've both lost too much." There was a hint of anguish in his voice that tore at

Cassie's heart. "We're who the Kiowa made us, and we can't go back."

"No, Drew, wait," she cried out, but he had already flung open the cabin door and fled out into the cold.

What in the name of God had he been thinking? What fiend from the bloody depths of hell had induced him to take Cassie Morgan in his arms? How could he have made such a monumental blunder?

Drew stomped along the path toward his quarters at the opposite end of officers' row. Beyond learning his sister's fate, he hadn't meant to renew his connection to Cassie Morgan. Officers didn't associate with women like her, women who'd been captives, women who had chosen to submit to the Indians rather than muster the courage to kill themselves. The lines of military society were carefully drawn, especially here, and women like Cassie had no place in it. But because they'd known each other long ago, Drew wanted to see Cassie settled either with relations back in the States or someplace out here where she could earn her keep.

Though the web of old ties and old guilts made him feel accountable, he'd done his best to make Cassandra understand that he couldn't be a part of her new life. He'd nearly had her convinced when she'd looked up at him, all lost and forlorn, and he'd instinctively reached out to comfort her.

Once he felt her heat and vitality beneath his hands, something old and compelling had taken hold of him. He'd been utterly beguiled, caught in a force so elemental that he was helpless against it. One moment he'd been patting her shoulder, and the next he'd been kissing her.

The sweetness of her mouth had drawn him in, sent the blood singing in his veins. A bolt of longing had melted his bones. He'd tingled and burned as if he had connected with some wild blaze of energy.

He'd gone years without experiencing anything so intense, so reckless and headlong and out of control. Never once with Laura had it been like that—not even when they made love. And in a secret, dark place in his heart he'd been glad of it.

Life and the Indians and the war with the South had taught

him a lifetime of hard lessons. In these last nine years he'd stopped believing in everything but hatred and revenge. The emotions Cassie had stirred up in him tonight were as terrifying as they were miraculous. But they demanded more faith in the world than Drew had left.

When he reached his own small cabin, the light in the kitchen was burning bright. Lila Wilcox was in there, probably sitting with Meggie asleep in her arms; humming some sad, sweet melody; and keeping time by the creak of the rocking chair.

He shuddered at the thought of facing Lila after what had passed between Cassie and him. Lila had a way of reading people, of sensing what went on behind their eyes that was downright unnerving. If he went in there now, she'd take one look at him and surmise a good deal more than he wanted anyone knowing.

Extracting one of the fine cigars he'd tucked into his pocket before leaving the house, Drew settled himself on the bench in front of the cabin. He went through a gentleman's ritual of clipping and lighting his smoke, blew several agitated puffs, and scowled out toward where a few tattered snowflakes were drifting in the wind.

He didn't like Sally McGarrity's treating Cassie's return from the Cheyenne as if it were some grand reunion between him and her. In spite of what had fired up between them tonight, that wasn't what it was. He had come west to kill Indians, and he couldn't afford to get distracted.

The government might well be paying annuities so the tribes would keep their treaties, but as long as the whites kept moving west, the Indians would keep resisting. No peace would come to these western lands until the Indians were annihilated, and if Drew had reasons of his own for wanting to see that, so be it.

The skirmish after Cassie's exchange had whetted Drew's appetite. Once the snow was gone and the grass was green, the Indians would ride out. War was coming; all he had to do was wait until spring to exorcise his demons.

"Reynolds? Is that you?"

The sound of Major McGarrity's voice shook Drew from

his musing. When he made as if to rise, the major waved the gesture away.

"I was surprised when Sally and I got back and found you gone," the major began.

Drew shrugged, taking care not to meet McGarrity's eyes. "Cassie seemed—tired."

McGarrity appeared to accept his explanation and extended a crumpled paper for Drew to read. "It's the telegram I was expecting from Kentucky. I wanted you to see it before I showed it to Cassandra."

"Have you found some Morgan relatives?" Drew asked hopefully, and tilted the foolscap toward the light.

Ben McGarrity shook his head. "Not a soul. It's as if they all either lit out or died shortly after your families left."

"The men probably fought in the war," Drew offered, "and that part of Kentucky was pretty much overrun. I doubt there's much left standing. Cassie's family and mine saw the trouble coming. That's why our parents sold out and headed west."

Not that the trail to Santa Fe had proved any safer.

"You can't think of anyone else back in the States who would take her, can you?"

Drew thought Cassie's mother had had family somewhere along the eastern seaboard, in Philadelphia maybe. But he couldn't for the life of him remember. "Doesn't Cassie have any ideas?"

"I haven't asked her, but I don't think she wants to be shunted off to relations she barely knows. After what she's been through, I hardly blame her. I doubt she'll find a very warm reception back in the States, anyway."

McGarrity didn't mention the tattoo; he didn't need to. A mark like that would be even more damning back East than it was here.

Forcing that unsettling thought from his mind, Drew shoved over on the bench and took out a second cigar. The major accepted it gratefully and sat down beside him.

Once he had it lit, McGarrity went on. "This pretty much leaves Cassandra's future up to me. She's too old to send off to school somewhere. From what I hear, there are missionaries coming to minister to the Sioux in Minnesota. I suppose I could send her to them once they get settled. Certainly her knowledge of Indian languages and customs would make her useful."

They smoked for a time in silence.

"She'll end up a whore if I turn her out," McGarrity offered.

Drew nodded. "Perhaps that's what she's been, living all this time with the Indians."

Ben McGarrity's face twisted with disapproval. "Even with the Cheyenne, being some brave's wife is worth a little respect."

Drew scowled but acknowledged the point.

"And there's nothing between the two of you?"

Though the taste of Cassie's kisses lingered on his mouth, Drew shook his head.

"Sally thought there might have been something years ago."

Drew exhaled a plume of smoke. "Mrs. McGarrity's right; there was something between us once," he admitted. "But Cassie's not fifteen anymore, and a lot has happened to both of us."

"Since you once had feelings for the girl, we thought you might—"

Drew was suddenly afraid of what the major was going to suggest. "Of course I'd like to help Cassie," he broke in, "but there doesn't seem to be much I can do."

"We thought you might take her on to cook and clean and look after Meggie, since Lila Wilcox has duties elsewhere."

Drew let out his breath. "I don't know that Cassie would be a suitable choice."

McGarrity shrugged. "You wouldn't be the first officer to hire an Indian woman to look after his children. But perhaps you're right. Perhaps she isn't suitable," he said. "There may be an enlisted man who's looking for a wife and wouldn't be so discerning. Or maybe we can find a place for Cassandra as a laundress. At any rate, she's welcome to stay with us for a while longer. Sally seems to enjoy having a protégé."

Drew looked long and hard at his superior officer and wondered if he was being manipulated. Were he and Mrs. McGarrity keeping Cassie around in the hopes that something would develop between them?

Before Drew could say more, the major snubbed out his cigar and shoved to his feet. ‘‘Don’t stay out here all night, Reynolds. I can’t have one of my captains getting frostbite.’’

Drew gave McGarrity a quick half smile. ‘‘No danger of that, sir. I’ll finish this cigar and go inside.’’

‘‘Good night, then,’’ the major said, and headed toward home.

Drew finished the cigar, but didn’t move. McGarrity had given him something to chew on, and Drew would just as soon do that out here.

He did need someone to look after Meggie. Lila Wilcox had been a temporary solution at best, and he had to have someone to depend on when he was out campaigning. Meggie needed stability after all these months of turmoil. He’d only need to hire Cassie for a year or two, just until Meggie was old enough to go to school back East.

The biggest problem with hiring her was the expense. A cavalry captain made seventy dollars a month, and that money came to frontier outposts at wildly irregular intervals. Lila’s services had been a bargain because as company laundress she received regular army benefits and could charge men for cleaning their clothes.

He would have to give Cassie money enough for housing and food and whatever else she’d need to keep body and soul together. Still, McGarrity’s idea had merit.

Before he committed himself, Drew meant to think this through. Nine years ago he’d dedicated himself to avenging his family’s death, and he couldn’t let anything—or anyone—prevent him from fulfilling his destiny.

Sally McGarrity seemed stunned to find Hunter standing on her porch just after seven o’clock the following morning. She peered at him around the edge of the door, blinking like an owl caught in a beam of lantern light.

‘‘Good morning, ma’am,’’ he prompted her, hoping she’d invite him in out of the cold. ‘‘I hope you won’t mind that

I've stopped by so early. I want to say good-bye to Cassandra, if I can."

"Good-bye?" Sally asked, glancing past him to where his horse stood saddled up for travel. "Are you going somewhere, Mr. Jalbert?"

"I've had orders to Fort Laramie. Colonel Palmer needs a translator and sent for me."

He'd specifically asked for "that half-breed Jalbert," and though Hunter didn't usually respond to the names white men called him, something in the tone of the colonel's telegram rankled him. It was almost as if Palmer were reminding Hunter how separate he was from the rest of the world and how singular his existence had become. It reminded Hunter of how much all that had begun to chafe him, and Sally McGarrity's reluctance was making him itch again.

"Well, then step inside," Sally invited, clutching at the neck of her dressing gown as she opened the door.

That's why she hasn't let me in, Hunter thought, more than a little relieved. It had to do with modesty, not who he was.

"I didn't mean to disturb your breakfast," he apologized removing his hat, "but I need to be on my way if I want to reach the old stage station at Box Elder Creek by nightfall."

"Well, we can't very well have you going off without telling Cassandra good-bye, now can we? Do sit down here in the parlor while I go see if she's finished dressing."

Hunter did as he'd been bidden and heard the murmur of feminine voices from the back of the cabin.

He wished he *had* been able to leave without saying good-bye. But he was concerned for Cass, worried she wouldn't be able to get on here at the fort without his help. Or at least that's what he'd told himself.

He refused to admit he wanted to see her before he left. No woman could have gotten under his skin as quickly as this. Certainly none of the women he'd smiled at and courted and slept with over the years had touched him the way Cass Morgan had.

But then, none of them understood who he was or his place in the world—at least not the way Cass was coming to understand it. She was as caught between the whites and the Indians as he was. That bound them in a way that went deeper than friendship, deeper than physical attraction. Cass touched something at the core of him, and he responded with both fascination and fear.

Sally bustled back into the room. "Cassandra is nearly ready," she informed him. "Won't you have a cup of coffee while you're waiting?"

"I'd like that very much," he said.

She brought him some from the kitchen. The flowery, gold-rimmed cup and matching saucer seemed out of place between his big rough fingers, though her offer of it made Hunter feel unaccountably welcome in her home.

Sally turned from him with a nod. "Then if you'll excuse me, I'll see to my own toilette."

For all the daintiness of the cup she'd served it in, Sally McGarrity made army coffee, strong and hot. Hunter had drunk most of it when Cass appeared in the doorway from the kitchen.

She was wearing the clothes she'd had on the day before, a dark blue dress that highlighted the gold in her upswept hair and clung like a lover's caress to her every curve.

The cup and saucer rattled a little in Hunter's hands as he came to his feet.

"Sally says you're going away," she said in Cheyenne.

Hunter ducked his head in acknowledgment, needing a moment to set the cup aside and pull his suddenly disordered thoughts together.

"I got orders to Fort Laramie this morning," he told her, and wished like hell he was staying. "I'm sorry I have to go. I know it would be easier for you to get settled if I were here to help. But when the army buys your services, you don't have much more choice about following orders than anyone else."

Cass lowered herself to the settee, and Hunter resumed his seat on the opposite end.

"I know about following orders. It would be better for me if you were here," she said, "but I will manage. I always have."

He heard a soft, almost-reluctant confidence in her voice. It was the kind of confidence that came with having faced the worst and fought her way through. It made him want to help her this time, to do what he could to make her adjustment to this strange, new place easier.

"I'm not sure how long I'll be gone," he went on. "A week, maybe more. By the time I get back you'll probably be all settled and speaking English like you never forgot a word."

Cass nodded.

"Is there anything you need before I go? Did your talk with Captain Reynolds go as you had hoped?" He'd seen enough of her conversation with the captain through the half-open door to know how it went.

An expression passed across her features like a cloud across the moon. "My talk with Drew went well enough. What I would like to know," she said, her mouth bowing a little with confusion, "is why everyone behaved so strangely when I told them I had been at Sand Creek?"

Hunter wondered how he could explain that having been at Sand Creek was like admitting you'd been to hell and back. Right-thinking officers everywhere considered the Indian loss of life a blot on the army's honor.

"The attack on the encampment at Sand Creek represents a very dark day for the army," Hunter began. "Chivington's volunteers should never have ridden into that camp. Lives were needlessly lost in Black Kettle's village, and many hold the army responsible. Ben and Sally McGarrity believe that there is no excuse for that kind of carnage, and so do I."

He didn't say a word about Drew Reynolds. For all Hunter knew, Reynold's sympathies might well lie with Chivington.

"So many women and children were lost," Cass agreed, as if she were conjuring up images of that day two years before. "The soldiers at Fort Lyon had told the chiefs that we would be safe if we camped at Sand Creek, so most of our men were away at hunting camps. There was no one to fight when the soldiers rode in, though Black Kettle did his best to protect us.

"He raised the United States flag the president had given

him when he went to Washington. He raised a white flag of surrender, but the soldiers kept killing and killing. His wife was terribly wounded, and my friend's little girl was shot down before our eyes.''

''How did you get away?'' Hunter asked, not able to help himself.

''Some of us ran into the narrows at the head of the creek. A few of the men who had been left to guard the camp held the soldiers off until nightfall. We stole away in the dark—but had to leave so many behind.''

Hunter stared at the woman before him, seeing both the pain in her eyes and the resolution that hardened her mouth. This woman had survived more hardship than most people saw in a lifetime. She would adapt to life at the fort with or without his help.

Assured of that, Hunter had no reason to stay—except that he wanted to stare into that remarkable face and savor the unexpected connection he felt with her.

That realization was enough to bring him to his feet. ''I—I'm sorry for what you went through at Sand Creek,'' he stammered, not knowing what to say. ''There are plenty of whites who hate what happened there and want to make certain it won't happen again.''

''But it will,'' she said, an odd resignation in her tone. ''In the fight between the whites and the Indians, it is bound to happen.''

''Perhaps we will all find a way to live in peace,'' he suggested, wanting it to be true.

''Have the white and Indian parts inside you found a way to make their peace?''

The question startled him. Cass's perceptiveness was the very thing that attracted him, but it also brought her too close. She seemed able to see through him in a way that no one ever had, giving her the power to touch him or hurt him or turn him inside out

Hunter jammed his hat on his head and bundled his buffalo coat around him. ''Well, then,'' he told her gruffly, ''I need to be on my way. I just wanted you to understand it wasn't my choice to leave you to fend for yourself.''

She rose gracefully from the settee and walked him to the door. ''Thank you for all you have done to make my way easier here,'' she said.

He adjusted his hat and nodded. ''I've been glad to help.''

She smiled at him, a bright, intimate smile that turned him warm inside. It was the first real smile he'd seen her give to anyone. He felt privileged, and absurdly pleased with himself.

Hunter grinned back.

''Have care in your travels to Fort Laramie,'' she said, opening the door. ''Find a warm place to spend the night. There's the scent of snow in the wind.''

He sniffed once and realized she was right. ''Tell Mrs. McGarrity good-bye for me.''

Cass stepped out onto the porch and watched him mount up. She smiled and waved him out of sight. Hunter rode a full ten miles before he was even aware of the cold.

Chapter Eight

It took Drew a week to make up his mind about hiring Cassie—seven miserable days of riding patrol in raging blizzards, of relieving half-frozen sentries, of struggling with balky horses, cantankerous men, and surly officers. It was a full seven nights of smoking cigars in the howling wind, of painting until the lamps burned low, of standing and watching his daughter sleep.

McGarrity's idea made perfect sense: if Drew took Cassie on, Meggie would have someone to care for her, and Cassandra could make a living for herself. He couldn't for the life of him figure out why committing to that was proving to be so difficult.

He finally arrived at the major's quarters late in the afternoon of the seventh day. Sally McGarrity fluttered like a schoolgirl when she found him at her door.

"How lovely to see you, Captain Reynolds!" she exclaimed, and ushered him in.

Drew stepped gingerly onto the worn rag rug before the door, stomping the snow off his boots before he moved beyond it.

"Goodness me! Hasn't this weather been terrible?" Sally chattered as she went about hanging up his hat and overcoat. "Cassandra and I have been all but housebound. But then, there are piles of mending to do. I'm convinced that every soldier in the fort dropped off something that needs a button or a patch."

"The laundresses or the tailors should be taking care of that, ma'am," Drew offered earnestly.

"Oh, yes, Captain Reynolds, I know. This all belongs to Ben, but I swear he's the most careless man—" She glanced up at Drew and colored prettily. "But then, I don't suppose you came by to talk to me about needlework, now did you, sir?"

Drew smiled and inclined his head. "It's always a pleasure to pass the time with you, ma'am. But I admit I was hoping to have a word with Cassie Morgan."

Sally led the way to the kitchen at the back of the house. Cassie glanced up from her sewing as they came in. At the sight of him, a bloom of pink rose in her cheeks.

She was beautiful sitting there by the fire. She wore a princess-style gown of deep wine red, and the sleek knot of her honey brown hair shone in the lamplight. With the shadows hiding the tattoo, she might have been some proper young matron from back in the States who had never so much as seen an Indian.

"Good afternoon, Cassie," Drew greeted her.

"Good afternoon, Captain Reynolds."

"How have you been?"

"Mrs. McGarrity and I have been keeping busy."

Drew turned his most charming smile on his hostess. "I wonder, Mrs. McGarrity, if I might have a word with Cassandra in private."

Sally's face immediately brightened. "Why of course you may! I have some letters I've been meaning to write. If you need me, just sing out."

As the older woman disappeared in a flurry of rustling skirts, Drew settled himself in the chair Sally had vacated. Now that the moment to make the proposition was upon him, Drew felt a sharp, inexplicable kick of nervousness.

"I—I was wondering," he began, "if Major McGarrity showed you the answer to the telegram he sent to Kentucky inquiring after your relatives."

"He showed me," Cassie replied, never glancing up from her stitches. "He showed me the one from Philadelphia, too."

So the major had tried to track down Cassie's mother's kin. By the sound of it, he'd had as little luck locating them as he had her Morgan relations.

"I was wondering if you'd made any plans."

"For my future?"

The discussion was starting out the way their previous one had, only this time Drew didn't intend to get sidetracked. "I know that as accommodating as the McGarritys have been, you'll eventually want to move on from here. I thought if you were ready to make that decision—"

Cassie's fingers stilled over the cloth on her lap, and she slowly looked up. "You made it quite clear the other evening, Drew, that beyond a certain friendly concern, you didn't much care about my future."

He felt the color come up in his face. "I didn't mean to imply that what you do doesn't matter. We've known each other all our lives, and I can't help feeling responsible . . ."

She let out her breath in a hiss. "You don't need to feel responsible for anything where I'm concerned."

Having her absolve him didn't help. "What I mean to say, Cassie, is that I want you to come and work for me."

She blinked twice in what appeared to be genuine surprise. "Work for you?" she echoed warily. "Just what is it you want me to do for you?"

"I need someone to look after Meggie," he told her. "The officers' wives were wonderful to her when we first arrived, and Lila Wilcox has done her best since then. But I need someone permanent, someone I can count on to care for Meggie for a year or two, until she's old enough to go to school back East."

Cassie looked at him long and hard, then deliberately turned her head so he could see the star-burst tattoo. "And you're willing to entrust your daughter to me?"

Drew stared at her a moment, then averted his eyes. "Is there any reason why I shouldn't?"

Cassie hesitated and flushed. Her chin came up in a gesture

of challenge that any fool would recognize. "Well, I did once steal from the sutler's store."

Drew had been appalled when he heard what she had done. He'd been ashamed for her, outraged at how morally corrupt Cass had become after her years with the savages. He'd said as much, and Jalbert had taken him aside to explain how Indian traders put things out for their customers to steal, that what Cassie had done was make a natural mistake.

"You don't intend to steal from him again, do you?" Drew finally asked.

She shook her head with such vehemence that her earrings danced.

"I'm not making this offer lightly, Cassie," he went on. "What I want is someone kind and caring to look after Meggie. After all that's happened, she needs security, someone she can count on to be there to feed her, and wash her, and put her to bed. She needs to have someone to hold her when she cries, someone to play with her, and teach her things. I can't be a soldier and do that, too."

"Does soldiering mean so much to you?"

Drew didn't even hesitate. "It means everything."

"More than Meggie?"

"Yes."

"More than anything else in your life?"

"There isn't anything else in my life. There isn't room for it," he answered honestly. "And you know why I feel the way I do."

Her expression darkened.

Drew took a breath and began to lay out his requirements. "I'll be needing you to keep house: do the cleaning and the wash, see to securing our rations, and cooking the meals.

"I can't afford to pay you much, but I'll give you room and board. You'll have to stay in my quarters once I leave on maneuvers, anyway, so it seems silly for you to pay rent somewhere else. We can curtain off the kitchen the way the McGarritys have, so you'll have a little privacy."

Drew felt better now that he had it all laid out. "You've always liked children, Cassie. You'd be good at this. Will you accept the position I'm offering?"

Cassie hesitated so long Drew wasn't sure what to think.

"No," she finally answered.

Drew stared at her, heat creeping up his neck. "What do you mean, 'no'? I'm offering you a place to live and a way to earn your keep. It's a hard, cold world out there, Cassie, and jobs are scarce." He didn't say that jobs would be especially scarce for a woman like her.

"I don't want to be your housekeeper."

Drew scowled in exasperation. "Then what in hell *do* you want?"

She focused those cool, clear eyes on him. "I want to be your wife."

Drew couldn't have been more stunned if she had pulled out a pistol and shot him. "You want to marry me?"

She nodded. "You're willing to hire me to do the things wives do. Wives cook and clean. Wives take care of a man's children—"

"Wives share a man's bed," he countered, and pushed to his feet. "I'm not asking you to do that!"

He filled the silence with his pacing, his bootheels rumbling on the wooden floor.

"If I live in your house," Cassie told him softly, "I think it will end up like that."

"The hell it will!" he thundered. Yet even while the denial was on his lips, Drew found himself imagining what it would be like to have her warm and willing in his bed; to share deep, sultry kisses and caress her; to thrust himself inside her and feel those long, slim legs around him. *To know that every time they did that, he was taking some Indian's leavings.*

"I swear to you, Cassie, if you agree to live in my house, I won't so much as touch your hand."

She looked at him, looked into him, looked through him. "After last week, I don't believe that's something either of us can promise. And besides, it's not the only reason I want to marry you."

He eyed her uncertainly, trying to imagine what was going on inside her head. Was she going to tell him she loved him?

"What's the other reason?" he demanded.

"I need somewhere to belong." There was a starkness to

the declaration, an obdurate insistence that booked no doubt. "When I realized no one was going to rescue Julia and me from the Kiowa," she tried to explain, "I did my best to make a place for myself. I did the same when I was traded to the Cheyenne. It's how I survived.

"Now that I've been returned to the whites, I have to make a place for myself again. I know that won't be easy because of the way I'm marked." Cassie drew a shaky breath, as if what she intended to say were hard for her. "If I lived with you—even if we never touched, never so much as kissed—everyone would believe I was your whore. They would mark me in an entirely different way, in a way that would be even harder to overcome. I would never be able to make a place for myself when Meggie left, and you had no further need of me."

Drew opened his mouth to speak, but Cassie went on. "If you married me, I would be a part of something, part of your and Meggie's lives, part of a family."

What Cassie wanted was really amazingly simple: a home where she could feel safe and people to love her. Wasn't that what everyone wanted?

Everyone but army captains bent on revenge.

Drew dropped into the chair beside her and rubbed at his eyes. What would it be like coming home to her, sitting across the table from her as they ate their meals, watching her holding Meggie? What would it be like to have Cassie in his bed?

Once when they were young, Drew had been able to envision scenes like those, to imagine how sweet marriage between them could be. Now Cassie wanted him to pick up the shards of those broken dreams and make a new reality.

As if he could go back.

As if she could.

There was no question what marrying Cassie would cost him. He would forfeit the respect of other army officers, perhaps even their trust, and advancement through the ranks. But then, he'd never had the hankering for stars on his collar. All he'd ever wanted was blood and glory—and vengeance.

"Please, Drew," Cassie offered softly. "I know it can't be the way it was between us when we were young, but please don't ask me to settle for less than I deserve."

Dear God, what did she deserve?

More than she had. More than she was likely to have if he turned her away.

Sitting there in Sally McGarrity's cozy kitchen, Drew found himself wishing Cassie had never come back. He had convinced himself that she was dead. He had grieved for her. Why wasn't that enough?

She made him remember what it was like to lie helpless when she and Julia needed him, to see that their hands were bound and stained with blood, to know that two shots from his revolver could set them free. If he had been able to reach the pistol, if he had been able to aim the gun and pull the trigger, Cass wouldn't be here now, bringing back memories to torment him.

For a long, desperate moment Drew stared into Cassie's pale, marked face and wondered which was stronger, his guilt or his fear. But then, he had always known the answer.

Drew was trembling inside when he reached across and took her hand. "Would you, Cassandra Morgan, do me the honor of becoming my wife?"

Hunter stopped just outside the big double doors of the cavalry stable to watch Cass plow toward him through the snow. She was like some bright angel, some fancy he'd dreamed up while riding alone across the vast, wintry prairie. The hood of her faded cloak framed a mass of honey hair he wanted to rub between his fingertips and a face that was all the more arresting for its blatant imperfection.

He grinned in greeting and wondered if she'd missed him.

"Well," Cassandra Morgan said, huffing a little with the exertion of stomping through the drifts of snow, "you took your damned time getting back from Fort Laramie, Alain Jalbert!"

Hunter blinked at her in astonishment. "My God, Cass, you're speaking English! And cussing, too. How did you make so much progress while I was gone?"

"I didn't have much choice," she admonished him.

"No, I suppose you didn't," Hunter murmured, sorry all over again that he'd been ordered away.

"I did fine while you were gone," she said with a touch of pride. "If you'd been here to help, I might not have remembered so many English words so quickly."

That was probably true, and he was unduly pleased she had managed by herself. He was pleased with Cassandra Morgan for a good deal more than that, everything from the way she'd stood up to Ben McGarrity that first day to the deep, sweet curve of her lips. The fatigue of his long, cold ride melted away just seeing her smile.

"So why were you looking for me?" he asked, hitching his saddlebags and his war club over one shoulder and turning toward the friendly camp and the tepee that was his home.

Cass fell into step beside him. "I've come to ask for your help."

"My help?" he asked, teasing her. "It seems you've gotten on extremely well without my help. What do you need?"

"I want you to teach me how to be a soldier's wife."

Hunter stopped dead in his tracks and stared at her. "A soldier's wife?"

"I'm marrying Drew Reynolds at the end of the week."

Hunter's knees wobbled as if someone had landed a sucker punch. "You're marrying Captain Reynolds? Captain Drew Reynolds?" *The man who hates Indians? The man who could barely touch you the day you were exchanged?*

"Yes, I am," she answered, a hint of defiance in her tone.

He told himself he shouldn't be surprised. He'd watched Cassie and Drew that day at headquarters. He'd seen how they looked at each other, how they touched. He'd sensed the intensity of the bond between. Hearing this shouldn't leave him so hollow and shaky inside. It shouldn't make him want to grab her by the shoulders and shake her hard.

He curled his lips in what would have to pass for a smile. "Well then, I suppose congratulations are in order."

If Cass had heard the contradiction in his tone, she ignored it. "Thank you," she said.

"Isn't this marriage a little—sudden?" he asked in spite

of himself, not sure why he was so angry, why he wanted to rip off Reynolds's head.

"I suppose it is. But Drew and I were promised years ago."

Years ago. How old could either of them have been? Sixteen? Seventeen? Even if they'd loved each other with all their hearts, a world of things had happened since then. Monumental things. Life-changing things.

"Are you sure this is what you want?" *It's none of your goddamned business what she wants.*

"You aren't just marrying Captain Reynolds because—" Hunter hesitated, "well, because you don't know what else to do?"

He saw a dull red stain creep into Cassie's cheeks. "Drew needs someone to care for his daughter," she told him a little too carefully. "I need to secure my place if I'm to live among the whites."

Hunter stared at her, wondering if it was possible to "secure a place" anywhere. He never had. He'd been an outcast among his half brothers and half sisters in the big house in St. Louis, a stranger among the Arikara when he'd gone back to his tribe, and a misfit in the Confederate Army. Being a respected scout came as close as anything to belonging somewhere. Still, he understood how needing acceptance could push her into this.

"Have you thought—" he began and stopped himself, wondering what he was about to ask. Had she thought about how driven Reynolds was, how much he hated Indians? How difficult life with him was bound to be?

Had she thought about marrying him instead?

That idea shook Hunter even more than the announcement of Cassie's nuptials. He had never once considered taking a wife.

"Thought what?" She turned those wide, pale eyes on him.

In spite of standing out in the snow, Hunter went hot all over. Flushed and feverish and panicky.

"Have you thought," he fumbled, "that marrying Drew Reynolds might not be everything you expect it to be?"

"Few things are what we expect," she answered coolly.

"And a marriage between us serves both our purposes. Still, I want to be a good wife to him, the kind an officer needs."

The kind of wife Drew Reynolds needed and Cassandra would make were miles apart.

Hunter did his best to squirm out of the obligation. "Why haven't you asked Sally McGarrity to teach you what you need to know?"

Cass ducked her head. "Not everyone on the post approves of Drew marrying me, and because they think Sally brought us together, some of the women—"

"Alma Parker," Hunter guessed.

Cass flushed and nodded. "She's gone out of her way to make things . . ."

"Difficult?" So Alma Parker opposed the match. It was the first time he and Alma Parker had agreed about anything.

"Will you help me learn what I need to know?" Cass looked up at him, her eyes wide and soft with trust.

Trust he'd wanted so much to win. Trust that damned him as surely as stealing from the poor box.

The anger came again, so strong he couldn't see.

"Let me get this straight," he drawled around the hot, bitter knot twisting in his throat. "You want me to teach you things an officer's wife needs to know—things like how not to get caught stealing from the sutler's store?"

He saw the pain flare up in her eyes and had never felt more like a bastard.

In spite of his gibe, Cassie Morgan held her ground. "You understand the differences between my life with the Cheyenne and the one I'll be living with Drew," she insisted. "You know how these women behave and the mistakes I might make. You could teach me the things I've forgotten about living among the whites."

Hunter stood, his muscles taut, his fingers clamped tight around the saddlebags. "You can't just slip back into the life you left nine years ago."

"Because I'm marked."

"Damn the mark!" he thundered at her. "You can't go back because you've changed. You've changed not so much in the ways that show, but in the ways that don't: the way you are, the way you think, the things you believe.''

''What do you mean?''

Hunter tried to breathe more deeply, to still the tremors racking his insides. He didn't want to be part of this. He didn't want to help Cass Morgan be a better wife to someone else. Still, he didn't seem able to deny her.

He nudged the hem of her skirt with the toe of his boot. ''What are you wearing under there, Cass? Are you wearing those bright, shiny lace-up boots Sally gave you, or are you wearing moccasins?''

The color in her cheeks deepened. ''The shiny boots hurt.''

Hunter gave her a stiff-lipped smile. ''I imagine they do. I'll warrant Sally McGarrity's boots hurt, too. And Alma Parker's boots and Sylvie Noonan's boots, but they wear them anyway. It's what ladies do. They suffer to be fashionable, even out here, because they believe that maintaining certain standards of gentility is important. They wear corsets that constrict their breathing and skirts that drag in the fire . . .''

Cass nodded. ''I'll get used to the boots,'' she promised him.

Hunter shook his head. ''Will you? Well, perhaps you will. But you miss my point. Because you spent nine years with the Indians, you won't ever again see the world as a white woman does. You've learned to deal in practicalities. You'll always see what is, when your white friends will see what ought to be.''

''But I'm white,'' Cass insisted blindly. ''I lived among the whites a whole lot longer than I lived among the Indians! I'll learn to think like a white again.''

Hunter looked into her pale, determined face. If by sheer resolve a person could make a place for herself, Hunter would have bet money on Cass. But succeeding wasn't up to her.

This was a world where authority ruled and rank had its privileges, where being different was held in the gravest contempt, and sense and sensibility were held in low esteem. It was a world where men with Reynolds's prejudices used Indian women for their pleasure and expected their wives to be inviolate. It was a world where Cassandra didn't stand a chance.

"Oh, Cass," Hunter sighed, unbearably weary all at once. "If you're determined to marry the captain, I can't stop you—"

"But you will not help. You're not going to teach me what I need to know to succeed as an officer's lady."

Hunter knew that if he denied her help, he would be severing the bond between them. It was a connection he was loath to break; a fine, sweet, profoundly uncomfortable connection that meant more to him than almost anything else.

"It's been my observation," he said, measuring out his words, "that success in marriage depends a good deal more on who you are and what you believe than on what you know. But if you're determined to rush headlong into wedded bliss with Captain Reynolds, then I wish you every happiness."

She must have known he lied.

As he turned toward his tepee, his bed, and the solitude that seemed suddenly so appealing, she stood and shouted after him, "I will make Drew a proper wife. I will be an officer's lady. I will make a place for myself here at the fort!"

"Not in a hundred lifetimes, Cassandra," Hunter murmured, and hoped he was wrong.

Only a fool would be afraid of a four-year-old, Cassie chided herself as she made her way along officers' row through the falling snow. After what she'd seen and faced and survived these last nine years, the prospect of spending the afternoon with Meggie Reynolds shouldn't turn her all quivery inside.

Drew had made it clear that they would be married regardless of how his daughter responded to her, but Cassie knew things would be better for everyone if she could win Meggie's trust.

Cassie had come fully armed to do that. A drawstring bag full of surprises dangled from her wrist, and Sally had helped her make a plate of fried cakes dusted with sugar. Cassie figured no child could hold out long against a plate of sweets.

Cassandra knocked for a good long while before the door to Drew's cabin creaked open. Lila Wilcox peered out at her.

"What do *you* want?" The woman's hostility wafted toward Cassie on the smell of bleach, naphtha, and strong lye soap.

"Drew told you I was coming to pay a call on Meggie this afternoon, didn't he?"

Lila hesitated and scowled. "I suppose he might have mentioned that."

"Then do you think I can come in?"

Lila opened the door in grudging acquiescence, and Cassie stepped inside. Meggie stood peeking at her from behind the blind of Lila's ample hip.

Cassandra hunkered down to greet the little girl. "Hello there, Meggie. It's good to see you again. I hope you like surprises. I have several in my sack, and they're just for you."

Having set the bait, Cassie rose and shifted the plate of fried cakes from hand to hand as she removed her cloak. Lila huffed, hung it on a peg to the right of the door, and led the procession into the kitchen.

In spite of Lila's presence in the cabin, there were no woman's touches here. The table was bare except for a slate and piece of chalk. A pitiful collection of tin plates and mugs, a pitcher and a few chipped crockery bowls sat on open shelves. The rough wood floors were unadorned.

Cassie remembered the thick furs she had spread over the ground cloth in Gray Falcon's tepee. There had been bright blankets on the cots, paint and embroidery decorating the inner lining of the tent, parfleches and other colorful objects stacked here and there. How much cozier that had been than this.

Still, there was an ornate rocker pulled up before the fire, with a colorful quilt draped over one arm. Cassie walked to the trestle table and set down the towel-draped plate of fried cakes.

"Whad's in 'ere?" With one fist jammed in her mouth, Meggie's words were all but unintelligible.

"I made some good things for us to eat," Cassie said, hoping to coax Meggie closer. "I thought you and Lila and I could have a party."

The little girl eased out from behind the older woman's skirts and looked up at her for permission. Still radiating dis-

approval, Lila nodded that having a party would be all right.
"Ca' we hab tea?" Meggie asked around her hand.
"I'll put the kettle on," Lila said, and went to do it.
While Lila puttered at the fire, Drew's daughter looked Cassie up and down. Cass settled on one of the benches beside the table and let her. She'd always thought that making friends with a child was a lot like taming a wild animal; you had to wait for them to make the first move.
Eventually Meggie did, taking the fingers from her mouth and coming closer. "What's that on your face?"
Cassandra might have known it would be the first thing Meggie would ask about. "It's a tattoo."
"Can I touch it?"
Cassie nodded and sat stone still while small, spit-wet fingers traced first the circle and then the star burst that radiated from it.
"How'd you get it?" Meggie asked.
"The Indians put it there."
"Does it rub off?" the little girl asked, stroking experimentally. Meggie's fingers left dampness in their wake.
"No."
"Did it hurt when they put it there?"
"It hurt a lot."
"How did they do it?"
"Meggie!" Lila admonished from where she stood spooning tea into the pot.
As if Meggie suddenly realized how close she'd come, she took two steps back. "You must have been bad for them to do that," she said. "You must have been very bad for them to want to make you so ugly."
Though it was hardly the first time Cassie had heard that sentiment expressed, the words lodged like arrows in her heart. She told herself that they were the defensive words of a frightened child, that Meggie hadn't meant to hurt her, but excuses never helped.
"I tried to run away," Cassandra admitted after a moment. "That's why the Kiowa marked me."
She didn't tell the wide-eyed child that it had hurt far more to be considered Little Otter's property, to know that once

the women had tattooed her, she would carry the mark of her servitude for the rest of her days. With the tattoo marring her face, she could never truly belong to herself again. That realization sliced more deeply now than ever before because she wanted so much to make a new life with Meggie and Drew.

"It's not good to run away," Meggie pronounced solemnly.

"Sometimes it is," Lila corrected her, breaking into the conversation from across the room. "Sometimes a body needs to run—when there's danger or something's hurting too bad to do anything else."

Cass looked up, surprised by the woman's defense. But before Cassie could thank her, Lila had turned back to the fire.

"Looks to me like this here tea is ready. Does that mean we can find out what kind of treat Miss Cassandra brought you?"

With a smile and a flourish, Cassie flipped back the towel she'd put around the fried cakes to protect them from the snow.

"Oh, I do like fried cakes!" Meggie exclaimed, settling herself at the table and waiting for the women to do the same. "Don't I, Lila?"

Though there wasn't all that much conversation as they ate, a good deal of the constraint Cassie had sensed when she arrived had evaporated. Lila was gentle and firm with her young charge, correcting her when she tried to dunk a piece of fried cake into her milk and tea. She encouraged Meggie to talk about the snowman all the laundresses' children had built earlier in the week, about how she was learning to write her name, and about how her father sometimes let her ride up in front of him on his big bay horse.

While Lila was clearing the plates away, Cassie dug into her bag of tricks. She bypassed the top the major had whittled, the paraphernalia she'd brought to play the moccasin game, and pushed aside the ball of string and the big black buttons for making "hummers."

At the bottom of the bag was the doll she'd been working

on all this week. She had fashioned it from doeskin; stuffed the body with batting; embroidered eyes, a tiny nose, and a rosebud mouth. She had attached thick, pale skeins of horsehair clipped from the tail of the major's palomino and dressed the doll in a blouse, a jacket, and a skirt made from scraps she'd found in Sally's rag bag.

With a pleasant feeling of pride and anticipation, Cassie took out the doll. The little girl didn't seem to have many toys, so surely she would welcome—

"No-o-o-o!" Meggie howled when she saw the doll. "No! No! No-o-o-o!"

Cassie's bright hopes turned to ashes in her chest.

"Meggie, look," Cassandra said as calmly as she could. "She's a nice dolly."

The little girl slapped at her, nearly knocking the doll out of Cassie's hands.

"No-o-o!" she screamed.

"Meggie," Lila interceded. "Meggie, all Miss Cassandra wants is to give you the doll. Won't you take it?"

"No!" she howled again, tears spilling from those big gray eyes. "I don't want it!"

Lila hitched Meggie up onto her hip. The child clung to her like bindweed. "What's the matter, dumpling? Why don't you want the doll?"

"Mama," she sobbed.

"You want your mama, sweetheart?" Lila asked, trying to interpret the child's distress. "You know that your mother has gone away to live with God in heaven. Your papa has explained all that."

"Mama," Meggie wailed.

"What about Mama?" Cassie asked.

"Mama's not in heaven. You shrinked her!" she accused before burying her face in Lila's neck.

Lila and Cass exchanged startled glances.

"Of course I didn't shrink her!" Cassie began. But then, seeing the color of Meggie's hair, Cass could well imagine that Laura Reynolds's might have been this same pale, white-gold. It was because of Meggie's fairness that Cassie had asked to clip the strands from the tail of the major's horse.

''The doll wasn't meant to look like your mother,'' Cassie went on. ''It was supposed to look like you.''

''Then—'' Meggie snuffled, glaring at Cassie from one red-rimmed eye, ''then why is she—she wearing Mama's dress?''

Her mother's dress? Cassie thought back to the fabric she'd used. It had come from a pretty but well-worn gown. One, now that she stopped to consider it, that would have been far too small to fit Sally McGarrity's more generous curves. Was it possible that she had inadvertently used a length of cloth that had once belonged to Laura Reynolds?

''I'm sorry,'' Cassandra said, feeling her own throat tighten. ''I—I didn't dress the doll like your mother on purpose.''

''How do you suppose that happened, then?'' Lila challenged, speaking loudly to make herself heard above Meggie's wailing.

Cassandra told her.

''Good Lord! Do you really think that's it?'' Lila's big, rough-skinned hands were rubbing circles on Meggie's back.

''I can't imagine anything else. Drew must have given Sally his wife's old things.''

''And to think Captain Reynolds told this poor little tyke that once he married you, you'd be taking her mother's place.''

''Is that what he told her?'' Cassie gasped. ''Then what must Meggie be thinking?''

Going around behind Lila, Cassie tried to look into Meggie's face, tried to take her hand. Meggie mewed at her and curled up tighter in Lila's arms.

''Meggie,'' she began, trying to think what was most important to say, ''I want you to know I didn't do anything to make your mother go away. I haven't come to take your mother's place. I *will* be marrying your father. I *will* be coming to live in this house. But all I want is to be your friend.

''I'm going now, and I'm taking the dolly with me. I'll keep her safe for you. If you decide you want her, all you have to do is ask. All right?''

If she expected any sign that Meggie had understood, Cassie was destined to be disappointed. She tucked the doll into her bag and quickly gathered up her things.

Lila waited as Cassie flung on her cloak. "I'm sorry about this," she said, her voice gruff and deep.

"No sorrier than I am," Cassie answered.

"Meggie's a good child, really," the laundress continued. "Coming all this way, losing her mother, not having anyone to count on has been hard on her."

"I imagine it has."

"I think you marrying the captain will be good for her—for her and the captain both. They're two lost souls."

Cassie had sensed that somehow Drew had lost his way. She just wasn't sure she was the one to guide him back.

"You have a good heart," the laundress continued, surprising both of them with her candor. "Just keep in mind it takes time to make a difference in someone's life."

Cass looked into Lila Wilcox's eyes and saw unexpected acceptance there, understanding, and what might be the beginning of a friendship.

Cassie gave Lila one of her rare smiles. "That sounds like good advice," she said. "I'll do my best to take it. And, Lila, thank you."

"I just want to see them happy," Lila said, opening the cabin door for her to leave.

"So do I," Cassandra assured her. "So do I."

Chapter Nine

Every girl dreamed of the day she would marry her first love. Cassie had started dreaming about marrying Drew when he had carried a slingshot, instead of a cavalry pistol, and stolen ribbons from her hair. Now that Drew had asked her to marry him, every one of those girlish fancies came rushing back.

She had seen too much of life to imagine Drew still cared for her. Years had passed. He had been married to someone else. She had changed in ways that neither of them wanted to face. Though he might still feel the pull of that old attraction, Drew's decision to make her his wife was a practical one—based in reason not romance. Yet when she took her place before the minister in the McGarritys' tiny parlor, Cassie felt a reckless surge of hope.

She wanted this marriage to work. She needed to find a bit of peace by being part of this man's life, and she hoped by some stray miracle they could find a way to love each other.

''Dearly beloved,'' the parson began. ''We are gathered together in the sight of God and this company, to join this man and this woman in holy matrimony . . .''

The members of ''this company'' were decidedly sparse. Because Drew had been concerned that Meggie might not behave in an appropriate fashion, he had gone ahead and made arrangements for her to spend today and tonight with Lila Wilcox. Cassandra had asked Sally to send a note to Hunter Jalbert, thinking he might relent and come to befriend her. But word came back through one of the corporals that Jalbert had ridden out again on army business.

So it was that when Cassie and Drew stood up before the minister to pledge their lives, Major and Mrs. McGarrity were the only witnesses.

"Will you, Andrew Scott Reynolds," the parson intoned, "have this woman, Cassandra Claire Morgan, to be your lawfully wedded wife? Will you love her, comfort her, honor and keep her in sickness and in health, and keep thee only unto her, for as long as you both shall live?"

"I will," Drew responded.

The minister turned his gaze on Cassie.

As she repeated the words, she stared at the handsome man she was taking as her husband. In his full-dress uniform, Drew was all buffed and brushed and shiny, all serious and intent. All closed up tight within himself. She wished she could find some hint of emotion in his eyes. Instead they were as cool and impenetrable as silver mirrors, reflecting back her own fragile hopes and towering uncertainties.

As Drew repeated the rest of his vows, she wondered if he understood how much she wanted to please him. To that end she'd packed all of Sweet Grass Woman's belongings in a battered trunk. She had dressed for her wedding in a white woman's full regalia: a borrowed gown of watered silk, a laced-up corset and horsehair hoops, stockings and ribbon garters, and the excruciatingly pointed, shin-high boots. She was as proper—and as uncomfortable—as she had ever been in her life. She just hoped that the changes she was making in herself would mark today a new beginning.

Once Drew had spoken his vows, Cassie clasped his fingers tightly in her own and pledged to love and honor and obey him, to care for and comfort him for the rest of his days.

Then Drew produced a plain gold band from his pocket. He turned one of his rare, sun-bright smiles on her and eased the circlet of gold onto Cassie's finger. "With this ring I thee wed," he whispered.

Cassie went warm all over.

But the ring caught at Cassie's knuckle. Drew wiggled and turned the narrow band, trying to force it on.

"Oh merciful heavens!" the parson breathed.

She could sense Sally's dismay and Ben McGarrity's growing impatience. But most of all Cassie saw Drew scowling down at her as if he were only now seeing in those strong, capable hands who she was and what she had become.

Cassie pulled her finger out of his grasp and twisted the ring in place. "We can proceed now," she suggested pointedly.

The parson mumbled his way through the final blessing and declared Drew and Cassandra man and wife. Sally rushed over to envelope Cassandra in a hug. The major reached across and shook Drew's hand.

It wasn't until McGarrity and his wife had turned to sign the marriage certificate that Drew approached Cassandra. "I suppose it's time I kissed my bride."

The kiss he gave her was perfunctory, but his mouth clung to hers just long enough to remind her that she would be lying with him tonight, that they would be making love. The thought of that spawned a tight, fluttery anticipation in Cassie's throat.

Major McGarrity's striker and Sergeant Goodwin had contrived to provide the couple with a wedding cake and a few glasses of punch. Still, without the toasts and music and dancing, the celebration didn't last long.

Drew and Cassie took their leave and made the walk down officers' row just as the sun was melting away. If word of the captain's wedding had gotten out, there was no sign of it. Men returning from afternoon assembly brushed past them, but no one stopped to offer congratulations. Cassie knew that most of the people in the fort disapproved of her, but she had hoped that someone would wish Drew well.

Once they reached his quarters, Drew set about the business of lighting the lamps and replenishing the fires. While he was busy, Cassie took more careful note of her new home. The layout of the cabin was more or less the same as the McGarritys', with the front door opening into the parlor, a bedroom through a curtained doorway to the left, and the kitchen attached at the back of the house.

Though it hardly seemed possible, Drew's accommodations were even more spartan than the major's. There was nothing in the parlor but a chair, a china mantel clock, and a scarred campaign desk. Having no desire to inventory the furnishings in the bedchamber, Cassie wandered into the kitchen and set the remains of their wedding cake on the table.

She sensed Drew's entry into the room in the same way a compass knows which way is north. She turned and watched as he tended the fire, seeing how the orange glow of the flames threaded his hair with copper and gold. Cassie stood watching Drew and felt as if she had been waiting for this moment all her life.

Only when he turned away from the fireplace did Drew seem to realize she was there. "You haven't taken off your cloak," he said, coming toward her.

"I—I've hardly had a chance."

"Then why don't you let me help you?"

Cassie's fingers stumbled over the braided fastener at the throat. Drew waited in silence, then swept the heavy garment from around her shoulders. He dropped it onto the bench beside them, where it pooled and shifted, sliding to the floor with a whisper of silk.

It was the only sound in the quiet room, the only movement.

Cassie stood with her heart beating high in her throat, more aware of Drew than she had ever been of anyone. He stood over her, tall and broad and vital, smelling of bootblack and tobacco, of wool and cedar and cold winter air. Of strength and assurance and security.

She wanted to reach out to him, but she didn't have the courage. It had been years since she'd made love, years since she had truly given herself. She wasn't sure she remembered how to do that, no matter what she'd promised. Could she respond to Drew? Would she reveal too much about her past as they made love? Would she know how to please him?

As if sensing her doubts, Drew breached the distance between them. He curled his hands around her shoulders. He whispered her name, as if he were calling her back to a time when life was simple and their love was all that mattered.

He lowered his mouth and kissed her, brushing her lips as if she were a giddy girl, and he a shy, inexperienced boy. He kissed her as he had that day down by the creek, as if they had all the time in the world to explore what they'd discovered together.

He drew her closer with nothing more than the invitation of his mouth. Their kisses flowed one into the next with only a slow withdrawal and a gradual deepening to mark the completion of one and the beginning of another. He raised his hands to cup her face, his palms broad and warm against her.

But beneath the brush of his fingertips the tattoo throbbed, reminding her of who she was and what she'd been, reminding her that she was ugly when she wanted to be beautiful.

Drew must have sensed her uneasiness, for when he raised his head, his eyes were dark with confusion. "Cassie?" he murmured. "What is it, Cassie?"

A cold, deep sadness spread inside her. Things weren't the way they should have been. Yet for this one night she wanted to pretend they were.

She longed to imagine that they had been married with their families looking on, that they had come home to a house Drew and his brothers had built, that they were looking to a future blessed with love and joy and children.

For this one night she needed that.

Cassie reached for Drew and gave herself up to pretending. As if he understood, as if he needed the pretending as much as she, Drew swept her up in his arms and carried her off to the bedchamber.

The room was small and chill, with the colors of sunset spilling across the foot of the bed. By that faint roseate glow, Cassie could see that the pillows had been fluffed, that the sheets had been turned back and sprinkled with lavender. Two fat beeswax candles, a bottle of wine, and two stemmed glasses sat on the rickety nightstand. Someone—probably Sally—had done her best to turn this barren room and this rusty iron bed into Cassie's bridal bower.

Seeing that, Cass went still inside. Once, she might have

dreamed that her life with Drew would begin with soft, smooth sheets that smelled of lavender, with candles and wine, but she wasn't sure she could pretend she deserved all this.

When Drew lowered her to the edge of the bed and stepped away, she was afraid he meant to leave her there.

Instead he began to remove the intricate trappings of his uniform. The rasp of leather and the faint jingle of buckles as he unfastened his sword belt and scabbard set Cassie's nerves on edge. It seemed to take forever for him to unwind the red mesh sash that encircled his waist. It took longer still for him to tug off his cavalry boots.

When he was done, he paused to look at her with puzzlement in his eyes, almost as if she was a gift he'd asked for long ago and didn't know what to do with now.

Though she was quaking inside, Cassie lifted one hand in invitation.

Drew smiled and padded toward her.

"Oh Drew," Cassandra whispered. "I—I want to thank you for agreeing to this. For marrying me in spite of everything."

He laid his palm against her cheek, against the tattoo as if he were blocking out that part of her life.

"Oh, Cassie, no," he said on a sigh. "After all you've been through, you should have whatever you need. I only did what was right by taking you as my wife."

Cassie swallowed hard. She had wanted to be more than a responsibility, more than an obligation to the man she'd loved for as long as she could remember.

As she sat silent, wondering if she could tell him that, Drew's hands found their way into her hair. He plucked the pins from her chignon one by one and let the thick, buttery brown coils spill down her back. He tangled his fingers in those loosened strands and sought her mouth. He closed his eyes and nibbled at her. He sipped and tasted. He lingered and savored, and when he raised his head, Cassandra could hear the uneven cadence of his breathing.

Drew came to sit beside her on the bed and reached for the row of glass-domed buttons at the front of her bodice. His knuckles grazed her skin as he worked over them. Cassie shivered with a strange, anticipatory heat.

As her gown fell open, a swath of skin, her corset and chemise lay revealed in the widening vee.

"God, you're beautiful," he breathed, tracing his fingertips along a line from the hollow of her throat to the gathers at the top of her chemise. "More beautiful than I remembered."

In response to those whispered words, Cassie lifted one hand to his cheek and guided his mouth to hers again.

As their kisses deepened, Drew slipped his hand through the opening at the front of her gown and cupped her breast. The possessive way he held her, the slow, gentle kneading, the sweet, melting sensation as he circled her nipple with the pad of his thumb turned Cassie soft with longing. Something warm and fluid pooled down deep in her loins, something she dimly recognized as feelings of eagerness and pleasure.

It had been years since she had responded to any man, since she had done more than lie with her eyes closed and her fists knotted at her sides when a man thrust into her. She had wondered if she would ever feel the slow, sweet seep of need, the hard driving hunger of desire. Now that she knew Drew could make her feel what a woman felt, Cassandra gave herself to him, mind and body, soul and spirit.

Trembling a little with her own daring, Cassie sought the buttons down the front of his uniform tunic and the ones on the well-worn shirt beneath. When she had freed them all the way to his waist, Drew pulled her to her feet beside the bed.

They stood for one long moment staring into each other's eyes. There was still the gulf of time and pain and the past between them. But there was also the bridge of their mutual desire. Drew hesitated for a moment, then moved to span it.

He eased the sleeves of her opened bodice down her arms. Cass helped him shrug off his tunic and shirt. He loosened the tapes at her waist and pushed her skirts and petticoats to the floor. She splayed her fingers against his chest, aware of his breadth, his warmth. He ran his palms along the stiff-boned corset and spanned her waist with his hands.

He pulled her hard against him. The thrust of his arousal prodded her, and she lifted her hips against him.

Drew sucked in his breath as if he weren't sure he'd have another chance. "Oh Cassie," he moaned. "How could I have forgotten the way it was between us?"

He took her mouth again, ravenous and devouring. Together they fought the laces down the back of her stays and fumbled with the buttons on the front of his pants. Drew released his hold on her only long enough to slide the trousers down his hips and shuck his knitted underdrawers.

Cassie loosened the ties at the neck and dropped her chemise to the floor.

The last, lingering hues of daylight highlighted his broad shoulders and the long, hard-muscled contours of his flanks. They pinked the swell of her breasts and the gentle curve of her belly.

Drew ran one palm from her throat to her hips as if to reacquaint himself with every curve. Cassie let her hands stray over him, discovering a new manliness to him, a wondrous solidity and strength. She skimmed over the smooth, pale flesh where he'd been burned, sensed the echo of pain in his old wounds.

The touching was a ritual of renewal that neither of them questioned. Gradually the brush of hands became less a rediscovery and more a seduction. A strong, compelling eagerness drew them together. Their hips aligned, their bellies brushed. That contact was harsh and elemental, basic and irresistible.

Cass breathed his name.

Drew bound her to him as if he never meant to let her go. His mouth took hers with a swift, rough passion that blotted out everything but the scalding desire boiling up between them.

They fumbled toward the bed and sank down on it together. He rolled above her, his body hovering, sheltering hers. She trailed her hand along his side, closed her fingers on the jut of his hip, and pulled him nearer.

He lowered his head and took her nipple in his mouth.

Cassie arched against him, twisting and crying out as sweet, white heat melted through her. Tendrils of pleasure unfurled along her limbs. Deep at the core, her body throbbed.

Drew skimmed his big work-roughened hand down her body, across the smooth pale flesh of her belly to the nest of soft, damp curls between her thighs. The hot, wet suction of his mouth on her breast, the slow, rhythmic pressure of his fingers dipping inside her sent her senses spiraling. Her world dissolved around her. She was lost, adrift in sensation, moving restlessly beneath him.

She reached for him. "Please," she whispered, brushing her fingers along his shaft. "I want you. I want to be with you."

She felt the thrust of his manhood at the juncture of her legs and opened to accommodate him. He bound her to him, filling her body with his, claiming her passion, touching her soul.

She rose against him and called his name.

His mouth took hers with rough desire that denied memory and obligation and identity. It blotted out everything but the scalding need boiling up between them. Then there was only the wildness and the passion and this man. The heat, the frenzy, and the delight. And when their world came apart in a sweet-hot swirl of completion, they spun away into the bliss of the rosy dark.

It was late when Cassie finally stirred. There was cold, fresh moonlight spilling through the window. The air in the room tasted crisp and thin. She felt fragile, newly born, as if she might find the husk of who she'd been discarded on the floor among their crumpled clothes. The husk of Cassie Morgan. The husk of Sweet Grass Woman. The remnants of her past.

She was Cassandra Reynolds now. Cassandra Reynolds, the captain's lady. She was the woman she'd been born to be.

She looked across at Drew. His hair was tousled with sleep, his mouth bowed and soft, his face breathlessly compelling in repose. He had been the source of her rebirth. He was the one who had given her this new beginning. In the wonder of their joining, she had found the essence of a self she thought she'd lost. With his love and his passion, Drew had given her the means to reconcile the years of torment and move ahead.

She nestled against him, feeling grateful and contented.

But even the slight movement of her body against him jerked Drew awake. He grabbed her hard, rolling over her, pinning her to the bed. His eyes were bright and hostile.

"Drew?" she breathed. "Drew?"

"Cassie?"

He loosened his hold on her and lay staring into her face as if he couldn't quite believe that she was there with him.

"I'm sorry, Drew. I didn't mean to startle you."

"It's all right."

She felt the tension in his muscles ease, felt his weight shift against her.

"It's just that I've learned," he continued as if he felt compelled to explain, "never to sleep too soundly. Soldiers who do don't live long."

She nodded and reached up to stroke his cheek. "I won't hurt you, Drew," she promised. "You can sleep safe with me."

"Can I, Cassie?"

"Yes," she whispered and reached up to seek his mouth. She let her lips glide over his.

It was a slow, provocative seduction, hazy and languorous, blurred by the silent, sleepy hour and the moonlight. Her hands skimmed down his back, fingertips trailing, palms gathering in his texture and his heat. Her flesh slid beneath his, sleek satin against the hair-roughened skin of his chest and legs. Soft sinuous curves and hard, taut muscles.

With a whisper of invitation, she opened to him, welcoming his power and his vitality deep into herself. His weight bore her down into the feather tick as they moved together, prolonging each moment, sharing each sigh.

Drew closed his eyes and breathed her name as if he were invoking other times and other places. Cassie lying in the grass beside the stream. Offering herself in the darkened hayloft. Whispering that she loved him.

"Cassie. Cassie," he cried out.

And she came to him without reserve. Rising against him.

Sobbing with joy, shivering with elation. Humbled by the power of the bond between them.

He found his delight in her, and, locked in each other's arms, they drifted away.

The moon was down when they stirred again, shifting together as if the contact skin to skin were something precious. Cassie smiled with new contentment, new security. If tonight was any indication, she'd found a home at last. She sighed and nestled against Drew, resting her palm above his heart.

"Oh Drew," she whispered, pliant and elated, and secure within herself for the first time in years. "I'm so glad you were the man who made me a woman, the man who showed me what loving could be."

At her words, he went stiff and still beside her. So stiff and still, she wasn't even sure he was breathing.

Cassie raised her head. "Drew?" Her aura of well-being evaporated.

"Drew?"

He shrugged away and moved to the edge of the bed.

"Drew, please."

He rummaged through the clothing on the littered floor.

She trembled, realizing suddenly what she'd done. She had told him the truth, let reality intrude when both of them had been pretending.

"Oh, Drew, I didn't mean—"

But she had. She had wanted him to know how important it was for her to have experienced the wonder of making love before she'd learned about the humiliation and the pain. And Drew had taught her very well about the wonder.

Beside her, he pushed to his feet and jerked on his trousers. He threw on a shirt and left the room without a word.

Cassie wrapped a sheet around her and trailed her husband through the house.

She stopped in the doorway to the kitchen, watching as he snatched a tin cup and a pewter pitcher from the shelf of the makeshift pantry. Without once looking in her direction, he took them to the table and sat down on the bench.

Her discarded cloak lay pooled beneath his bare feet, crushed and forgotten.

He took a whiskey bottle from the pitcher, uncorked it, and poured a dram into the cup. He corked the bottle up again and downed the contents in a single draught.

"Drew," Cassie pleaded, fear crushing the air from her throat. She had wanted this to be their new beginning, and now she'd ruined everything.

"Go to bed, Cassie," he all but snarled at her. "I don't want you here."

There was such cold finality in his voice that Cassie went.

Chapter Ten

"This is the most ridiculous thing I've ever heard," Drew grumbled as he guided his horse toward Lila Wilcox's cabin the following morning. "No one with sense goes on picnics in the winter." Drew had had plenty of "winter picnics" with the army and spoke with some authority.

Cassie glanced across at him, silent and adamant. She'd come out of the bedroom this morning, announced that they were taking Meggie on a winter picnic, and he hadn't been able to change her mind. Drew supposed he should be glad that Cassie had come up with something to do. After the way their wedding night had ended, with her alone in bed and him painting until almost dawn, he wasn't sure what she would say or do this morning.

He scowled, thinking back on the night before. He hadn't realized how much he had hoped that once he and Cassie were married they could recapture some of what they'd felt for each other years before. Last night he had determinedly shut his eyes and drawn on his memories of Cassie, of the simple wonder of their love, of their first erotic discoveries.

Yet from the moment he touched her, Drew had known this Cassie was different from the Cassie he had known when they were young. She was stronger and bolder, more skilled at making love. Her passion and willingness to offer herself for his pleasure had shattered any illusions he might have had.

He should have been angry and repulsed by the change in her, but instead her practiced kisses had turned his blood to flame. He had taken her mindlessly, helplessly, losing himself in the sweetness of her mouth, in the damnation of her flesh. Drew wasn't sure he could ever forgive himself for doing that. He wasn't sure he could forgive her for reminding him that he had been the first of many men to have her.

And the last.

He hadn't known how to face her this morning, so that when Cassie emerged from the bedroom and began poking through their stores, Drew had been glad for the diversion. While she'd been tucking things into a burlap sack, he had gone off to saddle the horses. He figured that after her years with the Indians, she would ride astride and as if she had been born in a saddle. He hadn't been wrong on either count.

As they pulled up in front of Lila's cabin, Meggie burst out the door and headed straight for him.

"Where have you been, Papa?" she demanded, stretching her arms toward him, wanting to be taken up in his saddle. "Lila said you'd be here *hours* ago."

Lila appeared in the doorway. "I didn't tell her any such thing. I said you'd be coming along when you'd finished up your business." She cast a glance in Cassie's direction. "And truth to tell, I didn't expect you for some time yet."

Drew ignored the laundress's gibe. "And did our Miss Meggie behave herself?"

"She was a perfect little lady," Lila answered. "I even took her to Sunday services."

"And you know, Papa, I slept in a funny little bed that pulled out from under Lila's big one. We had popcorn last night, and played a guessing game with walnut shells and a pea."

"Teaching her to gamble, are you, Lila?" Drew asked, telegraphing his disapproval with a raised brow.

"It wasn't me that taught her," said Lila with a laugh. "It was my boy Josh. He learned some mighty sinful ways when he was off fighting in the war."

"I'll have to have a word with his sergeant," Drew threatened.

"And what did you do last night, Papa?"

Under Lila's speculative gaze, Drew blushed so hard he thought steam might be billowing out from around his collar.

"I married Cassie," he finally said.

Meggie didn't spare so much as a glance for her father's bride. "So is Cassie going to be my mother now?"

"She's my wife," Drew answered slowly, wondering why he hadn't worked this out ahead of time. "So I suppose . . ."

"Your mother will always be your mother, Meggie," Cassie intervened. "What I'd like to be is your friend."

Meggie looked at Cassie speculatively, not quite willing to believe her. "My friend?"

"I thought perhaps today we could do something to mark the start of our new friendship," Cassandra went on. "I thought the three of us could go on a winter picnic."

"There's no such thing as a winter picnic," Meggie proclaimed without hesitation, proving herself every inch her father's child.

"That's only because you've never been on one," Cassie answered.

Drew figured he'd better step in to curb his daughter's stubbornness. "Look at it this way, Meggie," he suggested. "Do you think it would be more fun to ride out and try one of these winter picnics, or head on back to the cabin?"

"Picnic," Meggie answered, as Drew knew she would. Anything that involved riding horses won Meggie's immediate approval.

"Do you want to ride on my lap or astride?"

"Astride, please." For once in her life, Meggie had decided to be biddable.

Drew swung his daughter up into the saddle before him and looked across at Lila. "We'll come by later to pick up her things."

By some stray miracle, the weather had decided to cooperate with Cassie's plans. After nearly two weeks of gray skies and intermittent snow, the sun was beaming down so hard that Drew could almost hear the hiss of melting snow.

They crossed the bridge to the north side of the river and followed the track along the bank to the south and west. Red Buttes was about four miles out and had been the site of an attack on a supply train a summer or two before. Still, going there was safe enough this time of year, when the Indians were holed up in their winter camps.

As the three of them left the rutted trace that had taken thousands of settlers to Oregon, the river stretched off to their left. Today, after weeks of cold, it was hardly more than a glistening ripple of dark water bordered by a wide, grayish skim of ice. Meggie sang as they rode along, and Drew thought he recognized the words of a hymn, one she must have heard at services this morning. Cassie gradually picked up the tune, though most of the words eluded her.

They reached Red Buttes just before noon. While Drew saw to the horses, Cassie set to work making a fire. Once he was done, Drew and Meggie scrambled up the ridge of sandstone bluffs.

From the top they could look back across the wide, low landscape of the Platte River valley. In the flat, the river meandered across the landscape from southwest to northeast, a wide swampy channel hemmed with groves of cottonwoods.

It wouldn't be long before those trees would be in leaf, Drew found himself thinking. Lush spring grass would carpet the valley below. And with the spring, the Indians would come. They'd conspire to cut the telegraph line, to steal stock from the way stations and the travelers passing through. They'd harass the railroad survey parties down to the south. Drew smiled to himself. All he had to do was bide his time, and the enemy he'd been yearning to fight for all these years would come to him.

Since the snow had receded from the rusty red outcroppings at the top of the buttes, Drew settled himself at the edge and nestled Meggie between his legs.

"Look, Meggie," he said, bending close to point. "The eagles are fishing in the river."

The big birds swooped along mere feet above the surface of the ribbon of open water. They banked and dived and flapped away with fish clutched in their talons. They were magnificent, soaring into the azure sky, graceful and dark against the sun.

They had been watching the eagles for some time when Meggie turned her head to Drew. "So, am I sus'pose to be nice to Cassie now?"

Meggie's sudden question caught Drew like an elbow in the belly. He fumbled for an answer. "It would make *her* happy if you were nice," he finally said. "And if *she* is happy, I guess I'll be happy, too.

"Besides," he went on, "Cassie's going to be taking care of you when I go fight. It would ease my mind considerably if I knew you two got on."

Meggie considered his reply at length. "She's got that mark."

"Oh, yes, the mark."

"I don't care if she got it because she tried to escape from the Indians. I still think it's ugly."

Drew's attention sharpened. "Who told you that's how she got it?"

"She did. She said that was how they punished her when she tried to run away."

So Cassie had tried to escape. But when had she done that? And had she taken Julia with her?

"She won't mark me like that if I'm bad, will she, Papa?" Meggie asked in a very small voice.

Meggie's tone banished Drew's concerns about the past. Taking an uneven breath, he wrapped his arms around Meggie and bound her back against him. "Of course she won't mark you!" he whispered, rocking her against him, pressing his cheek against her hair. "Cassie would never hurt you. She's one of the kindest, gentlest people I've ever known. She likes little girls, and in time she will come to love you every bit as much as your mother did."

The thought of Meggie being marked the way Cassie was, of her falling into the clutches of the Indians as Julia had, lay in his belly like a canister of grapeshot. Meggie was his child, his responsibility. He would do whatever he had to do to keep her safe.

"No, Meggie," he reassured her, rocking again. "Cassie's

a good, kind woman. She would never hurt you. She'll take excellent care of you when I'm away."

"But what if she doesn't?"

For a moment Drew was confused by Meggie's continued concern. What else could he say to reassure her?

"What if she doesn't, Papa?" Meggie persisted.

Drew heard how her tone had lightened and realized he was supposed to threaten something outrageous. "Well," Drew drawled. "I could wait until Cassie's asleep and paint her green."

Meggie giggled.

"Or I could—make her eat carrots every meal for a month." Meggie hated carrots.

"Or I could tickle her."

Meggie laughed outright. "I think you should make her eat carrots. Green's too pretty a color, and Cassie might not be ticklish."

"Maybe we should go ask her," Drew suggested, slinging Meggie over his shoulder and getting to his feet. "Besides, aren't picnics supposed to have food?"

This picnic did. Cassie served up a concoction of tinned beef, potatoes, beans, onions, and desiccated vegetables with dumplings on top. Drew couldn't imagine how she'd managed to make something so delicious out of the army's nearly inedible ingredients. When the stew was gone, there were apples from the bottom of the apple barrel. Though Drew cut out the bad spots, they were pretty sorry specimens.

While Cassie was cleaning up and Meggie was picking up deadfall along the riverbank to build up the fire, Drew took out his paint box and pinned a paper in place. The buttes intrigued him, the subtle shadings in the stone, the hulking shapes, the contrast of the rusty red against the fields of winter white. He was mixing colors with water from his canteen when Cassandra wandered over to see what he was doing.

"I didn't know you painted," she said with some surprise. "You never did anything like that when we were growing up."

"It's something I started at West Point. They taught classes in drawing and mapmaking, and since I seemed to have an aptitude for scribbling, I decided to try my hand at watercolor."

"Will you show me something you've painted?"

Drew shrugged. He never showed his paintings to anyone. "Maybe later," he said, deliberately putting her off.

"Do you mind if I watch?"

He did mind. His paintings were something he did for himself. They were private, an outlet for thoughts and feelings he didn't know how else to express. For all that he'd taken her as his wife, he didn't want her to be part of this.

Meggie's scream cut off any evasion he might have made.

Drew and Cassie wheeled toward the river. Nearly forty yards from shore, Meggie hung half in and half out of the water, clinging to a branch embedded in the ice.

"Oh Jesus!" Drew moaned. "I never thought to warn her—" He tossed his paints aside and bolted down the bank.

"Hang on, Meggie!" he yelled to her. "I'm coming!"

"Hurry, Papa!" the child yelled back.

"Be careful," Cassie called after him.

Drew ran through the rime of snow and the yards-deep margin of dried grass at the edge of the river, slowing only when the ice turned slick and treacherous beneath his boots.

"Hang on, Meggie!" he could hear Cassie shouting. "Just hang on!"

Meggie hung on, her eyes wide in her pale pinched face, her red-mittened hands bright against silvery wood.

Fear clawed deep in Drew's chest as he scuffled forward, desperate to save his little girl.

"Papa, hurry!" Meggie begged.

"I'm coming as fast as I can."

The ice turned from cloudy white to translucent gray. Bubbles swelled and slid beneath the surface.

"Papa's coming," he promised.

The ice beneath him creaked and shimmied. Then everything shifted. The branch Meggie had been holding dropped, rebounded, and snapped with the report of a pistol shot.

Drew dived flat out across the ice.

Meggie screamed, and her shrill went silent as the cold, dark water closed over her head.

He scrambled closer to the hole on his hands and knees.

"Oh, God! Oh, Jesus, please!" he pleaded, fear shrieking through him. Would the weight of Meggie's clothes pull her right to the bottom? Would the current take her? Would she be trapped beneath the ice?

"Meggie! Meggie!" Cassandra bellowed the little girl's name as if by sheer force of will she could order her back.

Then miraculously Meggie bobbed to the surface at the far side of the hole, coughing and sputtering.

Drew slithered nearer and felt the ice dip beneath him, all but dumping him in the river. He dug in with his knees, his fingers, and the toes of his boots. He hung there breathing hard, still too far away to reach his daughter.

From somewhere off to his right Cassie was screaming his name. He turned to look and saw that she was out on the ice.

"Go back," he ordered her, "Go back!"

Cassie shook her head. "I don't weigh as much as you. I have a better chance of reaching her."

Drew ignored her, needing to find a way to get to Meggie himself. He shifted toward the hole again. Icy water lapped over the lip of the ice and flooded beneath him.

"Papa, get me!" Meggie wailed. "Papa, please!"

"Damnit, Drew, get back!" Cassie shrieked.

She was sprawled on her belly and squirming toward the hole from the opposite side. Even he could see she had a better chance of reaching his daughter than he did.

Cursing under his breath, Drew inched back.

Somehow Meggie was managing to cling to the slippery ledge of ice at the edge of the hole, to stay afloat in spite of the drag of her skirts and coat.

"Papa?" she mewed. "Papa?"

She was pale as parchment. Her lips were blue.

Drew's heart seized up inside fo him. "Cassie's coming," he reassured her. "You hang on until she gets there."

Back where the ice was thicker, Drew scrambled to his feet. From there he could see Cassie wriggling closer and closer to his daughter. She was six feet away. Three feet. Less.

She stretched out her arms.

Meggie made a grab for one of Cassie's hands. She missed and sank beneath the water again.

"Meggie!" Drew yelled and bolted forward. His daughter was going to drown. He'd failed again.

Cassie lunged for the hole and thrust both arms shoulder-deep into the water.

"I've got hold of her sleeve," she shouted and began creeping backward.

Drew stood frozen, helpless. He prayed Cassie didn't lose her grip on Meggie's coat, that the current didn't drag both of them down.

It seemed like forever before Meggie surfaced. Cassie wrapped her hands around both the little girl's wrists and began to pull her through the ice.

Drew started forward to help and Carrie warned him back again.

He could hear Cass babbling reassurances as she crab-crawled backward. He could see Cassie's back arch, sense how the muscles of her shoulders and arms were straining against the drag of Meggie's weight and the river current.

Gradually Cassie reclaimed his daughter. Her shoulders came first, then her back as far as her waist. Meggie's legs and feet appeared. She was kicking a little as if trying to help.

The two of them sprawled flat out on the ice, as if they never meant to move. Then slowly Cassie climbed to her knees and pulled his daughter toward her. She bound the child up tight in her arms, soothing her with words Drew could not hear, swaying gently.

Drew sucked in a ragged draught of air. He wiped the sweat from his face with one shaking hand and went out to meet them.

He caught Meggie roughly in his arms, surprised by how much he needed to feel that small shuddering body against his chest.

"Why?" he whispered against her, light-headed with relief when he should have been angry. "Why did you go out on the ice?"

"To see the eagles."

"The eagles?" he breathed, and hugged her tighter. "Oh, Meggie." Drew carried her back to the fire.

"We've got to get her out of those wet clothes," Cass said, gathering up Drew's discarded overcoat. "We've got to get her wrapped in this."

Working together they stripped off the little girl's things and rubbed the circulation back into her hands and feet. Meggie accepted their ministrations, shuddering and blinking in white-faced confusion.

"She's going to be all right, isn't she?" Drew mumbled, opening his own wet tunic and shirt and binding his daughter against his chest. Cassie draped Drew's overcoat around them and buttoned it tight.

"We need to get her to the fort."

They made the ride in record time. Meggie was still trembling violently when they got back. While Cassie bathed his daughter in a steaming bath with pungent herbs, Drew got down his whiskey bottle and made a sweet, weak toddy. He fed it to Meggie with a spoon.

He was still shaking inside, berating himself for not seeing the danger, furious at Meggie for scaring him, angry with Cassie for being able to rescue Meggie when he could not. He hated the panic that flowed in him. He hated being so naked to the world. He'd vowed not to care this much about anyone ever again.

Once they had scrubbed and dosed a modicum of warmth back into the little girl, Cassie eased her out of the tub, rubbed her dry, and bundled her into a nightdress. Meggie was limp when Cass was done. She lifted the child in her arms and carried her to her own small bed.

Drew sat stiff and still at the edge of the larger one, his own mug of whiskey clasped between his hands. Cassie turned to him when Meggie was tucked up tight and sound asleep.

"She's going to be all right, isn't she?" He hated needing reassurance, but couldn't seem to help asking.

Cassie looked down at him with compassion in her eyes. "I think she'll be fine. I don't see any sign of permanent injury, but you can have one of the medical orderlies take a look at her if you like."

"She won't get pneumonia?" He heard the quaver in his voice and cursed himself. "Laura died of pneumonia."

Cassie stepped nearer and stroked his hair. It took everything he had not to grab her and just hang on.

"I can't tell for sure," Cassie answered him honestly, "but her lungs seem clear so far."

He leaned his head against her midriff, accepting her touch, welcoming her tenderness. He could never remember being so shaken, so down-to-the-bone weary.

"Thank you for what you did," he mumbled against her ribs. "I'm not sure I could have reached her. I'm not sure I would have known what to do once we got her out of the river."

"At least we won't have to worry about her walking out on the ice again," Cassie said with what sounded like a smile.

"No," Drew agreed. "But there's no telling what mischief she'll come up with tomorrow."

"Then, I guess we'll have to be ready for anything."

As Cassie spoke, Drew felt her reach for the buttons on his uniform blouse.

"What in hell are you doing?" he demanded, pulling back.

Cass looked down at him with tenderness in her eyes. "This tunic's nearly as wet as Meggie's things. And I suppose those trousers are, too. I want you to put on something dry, then stretch out on the bed for a little while."

"It's not even dark," he argued, as he came to his feet and stripped his shirttail out of his pants. The effort made his head reel and his knees feel rubbery.

"But you're exhausted, aren't you? Being scared to death does that even to big, strong men like you."

Sometimes this new Cassie was entirely too wise. He couldn't bring himself to admit either that or how frightened he'd been. Not while she was standing there, watching him. Not while the ripples were still settling. Yet somehow he was glad she understood.

She gathered up his clothes as he removed them and waited while he tugged on a fresh pair of underdrawers. He sat down on the bed to put on his socks, then glanced across to the alcove where Meggie was fast asleep.

"She's going to be all right," Cassie reassured him. "And so are you."

He looked up into that pale, marked face, drawing warmth and courage from her eyes. Perhaps it was his momentary weakness, his need for comfort and concern that prevented him from resisting when she laid one hand against his shoulder and pressed him back onto the bed. Perhaps it was why he agreed to close his eyes, at least for a little while.

He heard her take the extra blanket from the chest at the foot of the bed, felt her drape the woolly folds over him.

"I want to take care of you, too, Drew," she told him so softly he wasn't sure he was meant to hear her.

At another juncture in his life he might have welcomed her offer. He just wasn't sure he could let her close enough to do that now.

Even as she rose through the hazy veil of sleep, Cassandra sensed that Drew was watching her. She fancied she could feel his gaze slide across her skin, from the crest of her brow to the curve of her cheek, from the slope of her throat to the rise of her breast. She fancied that she heard him breathe her name.

She turned to where he lay beside her in the moonlit darkness of their bedchamber. She could tell he was awake. She could hear the faint, uneasy flutter of each breath, feel his motionless rigidity. He was staring out of hollow, shaded eyes, looking back from some cold, dark place inside himself. It was as if he had been watching her for hours, intent and pensive—yet detached.

"Drew?" she whispered. "Drew?"

As if he were willing a world of distance between them, he shifted on the feather tick and rolled onto his back.

Cassie refused to allow the withdrawal, not with her own man, not in her own bed. Not when the dark pressed close around them, and they both seemed suddenly so very far from sleep.

She let the shift of his weight spill her against him. As she braced a hand against his chest, her fingertips hummed with a faint, focused resonance of a man in pain.

She curled against him, instinctively seeking to soothe him with the strong, sure contact of her own flesh. She drew him closer and he came, big and broad, resisting and relenting. His skin was hot and damp. He smelled of desolation, old terrors, and bad dreams. Of a boy's haunting memories and a man's new fears.

She whispered his name, calling out the torment deep inside of him. A breath ripped raw up the back of his throat as he tried to resist, and then his hands were on her, clawing at her hair, gathering the fabric of her nightdress in his fists. He shuddered; he sighed. He gave his emotions up to her.

They flowed over her jumbled and incoherent, raging and hot. She fought down a need to protect herself. She had demanded that he show her where it hurt, and now she refused to look away.

He gave up the words in a whisper as frayed and fragile as the ribbon in a family Bible. "Oh, God, Cassie," he gasped. "I could have lost her. She could have drowned."

His shudder racked through them both.

"It's all right, Drew," Cassie murmured back, holding him as tightly as she could. "We got her. We saved her. Meggie's safe."

"Safe." He scoffed a jagged laugh. "No one's safe. No one's ever safe. Not Meggie or Laura. Not Julia or you. I've never been able to keep anyone safe."

With those whispered words, she recognized the parched, brittle agony of his soul.

After Julia died, she had eaten and slept and breathed this shame and futility. She had wanted to stop feeling and thinking and waking every day. Yet somehow she had groped her way beyond it. She could help Drew do that, too.

"Oh Drew," she whispered, holding him more tightly than before. "Let this go. Forgive yourself and stop remembering. Let me help you."

Deliberately, she stretched up along his body and sought his mouth—his sweet, soft mouth, draped in the fine dark silk of his reddish mustache. A score of memories returned with the taste of him, memories of slow, tart kisses stolen in an apple tree; of snuggling in the hayloft the night she turned fifteen; of a sun-warmed rock beneath her back as they made love. And with them came the need to make more memories. New memories. Memories potent enough to warm a night when the wind blew cold and the future lay shrouded in uncertainty.

Cassie set about that task, trailing her fingers over him, testing the texture of his flesh with her fingertips. She skimmed them down along his side, then up along the arc of his ribs. She sought the dark, flat disk of his nipples in a nest of downy hair. She entwined her legs with his and pressed close.

Drew gasped and shuddered as she touched him. She felt him strain beneath her hands, his muscles tightening. As she stroked him and held him and soothed him, she sensed the need for forgetfulness grow in him. It was as if he wanted to lose himself, to forfeit the guilt and responsibility for a little while.

They both needed that: to touch on a more than physical plane, to obliterate the past in a rush of new pleasure, to share the bliss they could find together. She wanted this joining, this loving both for Drew and for herself.

And he seemed to want it as fiercely as she. He grabbed her hard, his arms enfolding her, his hands splayed against her back. He rolled above her.

"I need you, Cassie," he whispered.

She felt as if she had been waiting half her life to hear the words. Drew needed her, to love and pleasure him, to understand and heal him. To be his wife in every way.

Her throat was too tight to speak. Instead Cassandra gave her answer with her eyes. With her hands. With her hips rising against him.

She slipped her trembling fingers beneath the waistband of his underdrawers and eased them down his hips. He lifted away her heavy bedgown and fit his body to her, length to length.

She sucked in her breath at the intimacy of the contact, at the way his chest crushed down on hers, at the brush of their bellies, at the weight of his manhood nestled between her legs.

She looked up into his eyes and knew that he was here with her in a way he hadn't been with her the night before. He was letting her see his turmoil and his pain. He was giving her this chance to touch the bare, cold places where the real Drew lived.

Cass opened her arms and her heart to him.

He came to her with a kiss that crested and swirled with both dark emotions and breathless need, with a touch that set her shivering, with a love that had not been diminished in spite of him denying it.

She offered him the redemption of her mouth, the salvation in her touch, the benediction of giving himself to her. She willed him to believe that sharing his deepest self, that loving like this could make a difference in his life. That it could help him find his way after nine long years of being lost.

She felt the fervor build in him. In her. In both of them.

She breathed his name, calling him to her.

He came, sinking deep into the succor of her woman's core. The joining of bodies was sweet beyond all bearing. She ached with the delight of being one with him, with having him give all of himself to her. She brushed her palms up his chest, contoured them to the strong, straining column of his throat, and curved them along the slope of his jaw. She drew him down into her kiss.

As their mouths merged it was as if they were completing a cycle of their lives: a sweet beginning, a time apart, and a fierce reunion. An act of welcome, of coming home.

They held tight to the moment, savoring the splendor and the sweetness, the magnitude and the magic. They sighed and shifted and settled as the fervor ebbed away.

They lay tangled together amidst a mound of tumbled bedclothes. Cassie turned her head and pressed her mouth against Drew's ear. "I love you," she breathed, the words harkening back to a time when they'd come easy, a time when neither of them had understood their magnitude, a time when they were young.

The answer seemed to rise in Drew, too swift and strong for him to deny. "I love you, Cassie. I love you, too."

Drew slept soundly, dreamlessly, as he had not slept in years. He awoke alone. The covers on the far side of the bed were tumbled, but cool to the touch. Cassie had been gone for quite some time.

Cassie.

Images of the previous night blurred in his head, of hands and hips and tumbled hair. Of kisses and caresses and promises.

Cassie. Oh, God, what had he done?

Drew rolled to the edge of the bed and sat for a moment with his head in his hands.

The nightmare had started it. In the dream he had been stretching, reaching—but not for the pistol to save Cass and Julia from the Indians. This time he had been grabbing for Meggie's small, red-mittened hands, trying to pull her from the river. He'd fought so hard to reach her, to rescue her, but in the end, he hadn't been able to save his daughter, either.

When he started awake, Cassie had been in bed beside him. She had come to him with her tenderness and her warmth. She had soothed him with her touch. And when she offered him the solace of her body, he had snatched her to him and held on hard.

Drew cursed the memory and shoved to his feet, stepping gingerly on the ice-cold floor. He scrambled for his socks and underwear. He broke the skim of ice in the water pitcher and prepared to shave.

It took everything he had to face himself in the mirror, knowing he had let Cassie see his frustration and his fear, knowing he had opened himself and let her touch the raw, secret places inside him. Knowing he had given up every part of himself as they made love.

He lathered his face and skimmed the straight razor along his jaw.

He could still taste her in his mouth, still feel the imprint of Cassie's hands against his skin. He remembered every word they'd said to each other, every sigh they'd shared. He had told Cassie that he loved her. How could he have done that?

Wiping away the last of the soap, Drew reached for his trousers and shirt.

What was he supposed to say to her this morning? Could he tell her that he'd lied? Would she understand if he told her he couldn't care for anyone now?

The thought of facing Cassie, of extinguishing the light in her eyes, made him damn whatever twisted bit of fate had brought them together. Yet he knew he must find a way to make her accept that last night had been a mistake, that he didn't love her after all.

By the time Drew buckled his sword belt around his waist, he thought he had prepared himself to face her. He meant to behave as if nothing untoward had happened between them. If he did not acknowledge the weaknesses he'd shown her, she might not acknowledge them either. If he didn't put actions to his words, she might understand how much he regretted telling her he loved her.

His resolve carried him as far as the kitchen door.

Drawn up before the hearth, his wife and child sat dozing in the rocking chair. They were bundled in a well-worn buffalo robe and the delicate appliqué quilt Laura had made for her daughter. Meggie lay lax against Cassie's chest, one arm curled around her neck. Cassie sat with her tattooed cheek pillowed on Meggie's hair.

The swell of unexpected tenderness caught him hard.

Everything that mattered was snuggled up in that rocking chair. It was all he could do to keep from kneeling beside it and gathering the two of them in his arms. He wanted to hold them and protect them and keep them safe.

As if he could.

As if anyone could.

As if he dared to take that chance.

Standing there, Drew was forced to admit how much he needed to hear the swell of Meggie's laughter. He wanted to be able to curl into Cassie's sustaining warmth. But no man could live on such thin fare as that. Nor could he endure if that warmth suddenly cooled or the laughter fell silent. Drew couldn't claim and hold this woman and child because he knew he could never protect them.

From out on the parade ground came the bugle call for reveille.

Drew straightened slowly, squaring his shoulders, raising his head. He owed his allegiance to his parents and his brothers on whose graves he'd sworn revenge. He must honor those vows or lose himself. He owed his energies to the army that was giving him his chance for revenge. And in the end, dedicating himself to those things was infinitely safer than loving a woman and a child.

Drew's heart beat thick inside his chest; he knew he had made his choice, that there was no going back. He took one last look at where Meggie and Cassandra sat curled together. Then without so much as a word of good-bye, Drew left the cabin.

Chapter Eleven

It's nothing, Cassie told herself, rubbing away the gooseflesh along her arms. No one is watching you.

Yet someone was. She had awakened this morning with the hum of anticipation in her belly. She felt the prickling down her back as she heated Drew's shaving water and fed him breakfast, as she kissed him good-bye and sent him off to headquarters. It was the third week of their marriage, and Cassie was doing everything she could think of to be a good wife to him.

But as she followed Drew out the cabin door, the sense of being watched became stronger. She sheltered Meggie with the wing of her cloak and looked around. On the parade ground a squad of new recruits were being put through their paces by a bawling infantry sergeant. A trio of muleteers stood smoking together. Three friendly Indians rode past, one with a mule deer across his saddle. No one so much as looked in her direction. Still, the queasy feeling persisted.

"It's nothing," Cassie muttered under her breath and led Meggie down the steps.

On the porch next door, Sylvie Noonan took one look at the two of them and went inside, slamming the door behind her.

Or maybe it's everything.

These last weeks had been difficult. Only the McGarritys and Lila Wilcox had accepted her marriage to Drew. She and Drew had not been invited to Amos Parker's birthday party, or to the Noonans' for an evening of charades. Several of the laundresses had pointedly turned their heads when Cassie passed, and Drew had confined one of his men to the guardhouse for referring to Cassie as "the captain's In'jun whore." Even Meggie had suffered; Sylvie Noonan's children had held her down and streaked her face with mud so she'd be "just like her Indian ma."

And once the Indians started raiding, Cassie knew the resentment against her would worsen.

Trying to ignore the foreboding, Cassie and Meggie set off toward the sutler's store. Cassandra tried to avoid the place, hating to be reminded of the day she's stolen the scissors. But it was necessary to buy from Jessup now that the quartermaster's stores were down to salt pork and hardtack, rice and beans, cornmeal and flour. There hadn't been any coffee or sugar in weeks, and the entire compound was suffering through the deprivation. Even Alain Jalbert's hunting parties hadn't been able to keep ahead of the fort's demand for game. The first supply train of the season couldn't come too soon.

As she and Meggie followed the mucky path along the side of the cavalry stables, a new ripple of uneasiness chased up Cassie's spine. This time when she looked, she caught sight of an Indian woman lurking behind one of the commissary wagons.

When the woman motioned Cassie toward her, Cass hastily looked away. She could not speak to an Indian and give the people here at the fort another reason to doubt her sympathies. But as they reached the corner, Cassie recognized the woman. Only something of grave importance would bring Runs Like a Doe all this way.

Cassie gave the woman a nod of acknowledgment and hustled Meggie along ahead of her. What could Runs Like a Doe want?

Nothing that should matter to you, came Drew's voice in her head.

But it did matter. This woman and her family had befriended Cassie when Gray Falcon brought her to the Cheyenne camp, and she owed them for teaching her how to make a life there. She owed them for taking her in when her husband divorced her and removed her belongings from his tepee.

Cassie saw the wide double doors to the cavalry stable gaping halfway down the barn and knew what she must do. She dragged Meggie inside and approached the young soldier on stable duty.

"Good morning, Private," she greeted him.

The wiry, dark-haired private turned from where he had been forking hay into the nearest stall. She could see right off he knew who she was.

"M-M-M-Morning, ma'am," he managed to gasp. He was looking at her as if he expected her to pull out a knife and take his hair.

Cassie smiled grimly and forged ahead. "Captain Reynolds was telling us last night at supper that you had a new litter of kittens here at the barn."

The private's expression softened.

"Meggie would very much like to see the kittens."

"The kittens," he mumbled.

"Perhaps you could show them to her while I see about something at the commissary?"

"Oh, yes, please!" Meggie begged.

The private nodded. "An' they're as fine a batch of feelines as I've ever seen. I'll be happy to show Miss Meggie the kittens."

"Thank you," Cassie murmured. "I shouldn't be long."

With Meggie safely out of harm's way, Cassie ducked out of the barn and hurried over to where Runs Like a Doe was waiting.

"I would hardly have known you, Sweet Grass Woman," the Indian woman greeted her, speaking in Cheyenne. "You are much changed in these last weeks."

Knowing there was danger in being seen together, Cassie caught the woman's arm and dragged her into the shadows.

"Why have you come?" she asked urgently.

"I come for Blue Flower," Runs Like a Doe answered. "I have ridden two sleeps to ask your help."

"What is it Blue Flower needs of me?" Cassie asked, already knowing she could not refuse.

Runs Like a Doe's face was lined with worry. "She has birthed a fine strong boy but has no milk to feed him. Every woman in our band has weaned her children, so there is no one who can nourish him. Though Blue Flower tries to give him what he needs, he grows weaker every day. Soon he will die if we cannot find a way to feed him."

Cassie's heart went out to Blue Flower. She had lost her only daughter at Sand Creek more than two years before, and her pregnancy had helped her recover from the loss. How deeply her friend would grieve if this child died.

"Why hasn't Sharp Knife killed a mother antelope for her milk or stolen a cow?" Cassie asked. "Why have you not given Blue Flower a brew of white baneberry leaves to increase the flow of her milk?"

"If we had not tried those things, would I have come all this way? They say," Runs Like a Doe went on, "that the sutlers at the forts where the whites can trade have milk that comes in tin cans."

Cassie nodded, remembering the can of milk Sally had bought the night Drew came to dinner.

"I need you to buy this white man's milk so Blue Flower's child will live."

What Runs Like a Doe wanted seemed simple enough. Cassie would buy the milk and Runs Like a Doe would take it back to the Cheyenne village. No one need know what she had done.

"Do you have money?" Cassandra asked. "These white sutlers take money for their goods."

The Indian woman took a handful of coins from a pouch at her waist. "Is this enough?" she asked.

"I do not know," Cassie answered. "I will buy as much milk as I can with it."

Cassie's mouth went dry as she approached the sutler's trading post. She could feel Jessup's eyes on her the moment she stepped inside. She made a circuit of the big, dim room, taking note of the large stock of milk that stood on the shelves behind the counter. The milk must be expensive if Jessup put it there.

"Is there something you want?" the sutler asked, sauntering toward her.

Cassandra swallowed down her dislike and spilled the handful of coins on the counter. "I want as many cans of milk as this will buy."

Jessup counted the money and set three cans of milk beside the coins.

"Is that all I get?" Cassie asked in dismay.

"Condensed milk is damned expensive."

"How much is it exactly?"

"It's not cheap back in the States," he began, "and after having someone cart it all this way, I don't think a dollar a can is too much to ask."

A dollar a can! Even Cassie realized how outrageous that was. She also knew that three cans of milk were not enough to keep Blue Flower's baby alive.

"How many more cans do you have?" she asked him.

"More than you can afford to buy," he taunted. "Unless you mean to steal them."

Heat burned in her cheeks, but Cassie ignored it. "How many more cans of milk do you have?"

He turned to look. "Fifteen."

If Blue Flower were careful, she could make eighteen cans of milk last long enough to give her son a start in life.

"I will take them all."

A sneer lifted one corner of Jessup's mouth. "And just what do you intend to do with all these cans of milk, Mrs. Reynolds?"

Cassie stood her ground. "I don't know that that's any of your concern, Mr. Jessup."

"I s'pose it's not," he answered. "What does concern me is how you mean to pay for them."

Cassie swallowed hard. She had $2.29 in the change purse Drew had given her. It was all she'd need, he'd told her, to see to their household expenses until the end of the month. She fumbled the money out of the purse.

"You're forty cents shy of six cans of milk." Jessup was enjoying the hint of desperation he sensed in her.

What was a child's life worth? Cassie found herself wondering.

Anything, came the answer. Anything.

She looked down at her wedding ring. It was all she could offer in payment—the ring or herself. She shuddered at the thought of what it would be like to lie beneath this horrible man.

Then a remarkable phrase flashed through her head. "Just put them on my husband's account," Cassie said. It was the phrase Sally McGarrity had used to pay for her goods that first day at the store, the day Cassie had stolen the scissors.

Jessup glared at her. "You sure about that?"

Cassie stood firm though she was quaking inside. "Do you want to sell the milk or don't you?"

Jessup nodded and made a notation in a big, clothbound book. "You want this in a box?"

"A burlap sack will do just as well."

The cans weighed a good deal more than Cassie expected. It took both hands to carry the bag, and the cans kept banging her shins as she hobbled toward where Runs Like a Doe was waiting.

"You got them!" she exclaimed.

Cassie nodded and handed the Indian woman the bag. "Add water to the milk to make it last," she cautioned.

Runs Like a Doe reached across and grasped Cassandra's hand. It was an uncharacteristic gesture, one that spoke of deep gratitude and abiding trust.

Cassie clasped the woman's fingers in her own, missing the friendship she'd shared with her and her younger sister.

"Take care as you ride out," Cassie admonished. "Now that the weather is better the soldiers are spoiling for a fight."

"It is the same in Standing Pine's camp. There will be blood on the earth when the summer comes," Runs Like a Doe whispered and turned toward the scattering of tepees to the west of the fort.

Cassie made her way back to the cavalry stables, where

she found Meggie knee-deep in kittens. She stood watching the child and wondering how she would explain buying all those cans of milk when the sutler's bill came due.

"Meggie!" Cassandra Reynolds called out as she hauled the buckets of water up the riverbank. Behind her the Platte glistened like quicksilver, a soft, dawn-pink mist rising off the water, but Cassie couldn't stop to watch it. She had to be back to the cabin in time to fix Drew breakfast before first drill. "Meggie, do come on!" she shouted again.

The little girl came running, a bouquet of buttercups clutched in her grubby, mud-stained hands. "Look, Cassie!" Meggie crowed. "I picked them myself."

After weeks of unsettled weather, spring had finally gained a toehold on the prairie. The wind still gusted out of the west, but now there was the scent of earth in it, of life and growing things. Rains boiled over the plains and blew away. Beneath the wide, wild sky the grass was greening.

Cassie knew what that meant; all the women did. The winter truce was over; the men were preparing for war.

When Cassie pushed through the door to the cabin a few minutes later, she found Drew standing in the middle of the kitchen. "There's no hot water for shaving," he complained.

"I just came back from the river. I'll put some on to boil."

The corners of Drew's mouth tightened beneath his mustache. "I'm not sure I can wait. And why would you go all the way to the river when there's bound to be water in the water wagon?"

"She says that water's dead," Meggie answered helpfully, plopping the mangled wildflowers on the table.

"Dead?" Drew echoed. "What nonsense is that?"

Cassie pretended she didn't hear him and hastily poured water into a small pot hanging over the fire.

"Water that stands all night is dead," Meggie continued, repeating the explanation Cassie had given her weeks before when they'd begun the dawn trips to the river.

"Cassie?"

"I'll have hot water for you shortly," she promised.

"Cassie?" Drew persisted. "Is 'dead water' some kind of redskin foolishness?"

Cassie stood without meeting his eyes. Over the years she had learned that a subservience sometimes deflected questions she did not want to answer.

"Cassie?"

She could hear the disapproval in his tone, the conviction that he was justified in questioning her.

"The Cheyenne start every day by dumping out the old water and getting fresh," she explained as simply as she could. "It's something I got used to doing."

"And you explained that to Meggie with some Indian fable?"

"I suppose I did," she conceded.

"Well then, let me make this clear to you," he blustered, standing over her. "I won't have my daughter exposed to heathen ways. Don't tell her any more stories. Don't expose her to any more Indian superstitions. And I won't have you practicing them either.

"You said you wanted a place to belong. I married you to give you that. The very least I can expect is for you to act like an officer's wife. Giving up your Indian ways is the start of that."

As if giving up my Indian ways will make a difference, Cassie thought begrudgingly. The tattoo on her cheek prevented anyone from seeing who she was or how she behaved. Even Drew.

"Do you understand me, Cassie?" he demanded, still towering over her. "I'll hear no more about water going dead overnight."

When she inclined her head in assent, he wheeled and went off to finish dressing.

"I didn't think he'd get so mad about it," Meggie whispered when he was gone.

"You had no way of knowing," Cassie consoled her. "And he's right. I should never have told you that story."

"But I like your stories. Knowing about the Indians keeps me from being afraid when I see them here at the fort," Meggie admitted after a moment.

Cassie sighed. "Be that as it may, I don't think I'll be telling you stories anymore."

Once the water over the fire began to steam, she filled Drew's china shaving basin and took it into the bedroom.

While Meggie finished breakfast, Cassie set about her tasks for the day. Someone—and she had a very good idea who—had been leaving her fresh game. There had been pigeons last week and a clutch of quail the week before. This morning two plump rabbits were on the step when she went outside. Taking time to skin them was what had made her late getting down to the river. Now she added salt to one of the buckets and put the rabbits in to soak.

"What happened to their hair?" Meggie asked.

"I skinned them."

"Skinned them how?"

Cassie didn't think Drew would like her regaling Meggie with the details. "Well," she said, "I imagine it's a little bit like the way a man squirms out of his knitted underclothes."

Meggie hooted with laughter, then clamped her hands over her mouth as Drew came back.

"I haven't time for breakfast," he told Cassandra just as reveille sounded. "And tonight I'm holding extra drill. This new group of recruits is as green as grass. Half of them have never sat a horse, and some barely know one end of a rifle from the other. We have to work them hard so they'll be ready when our orders come."

She heard the eagerness in Drew's voice. He wanted to fight. He needed the riding and the shooting and the death to avenge their families' massacre. She just couldn't help wondering if once he'd had his chance to kill a few Indians his need would ease, or if the hatred had already bitten too deep.

Cassie slid another slice of corn bread onto Meggie's plate. "Then you won't be home for dinner?" she asked him.

When he shook his head, she continued. "I want you to know that I'm sorry about the water."

"I shouldn't have to remind you that you're Cassandra Reynolds now, not some Indian squaw." He left with the ring of bootheels and the slam of the front door.

Cassandra stared after him and sighed. Somehow the Cheyenne way of thinking had become ingrained in her. The basic beliefs, the innate practicality, the reverence for nature were as much a part of her as her heartbeat or her breathing. Hunter Jalbert had tried to tell her how much she'd changed, but she'd refused to believe him. What she had to find was a way to put that life behind her and become the woman Drew needed her to be.

After she washed the breakfast dishes, Cassie went in to the bedroom and pulled her small, battered trunk from beneath the bed. Inside were her belongings, her beaded blanket, her leggings, and her moccasins; her jewelry and her tools; her precious herb and medicine bundles.

Drawn by the creak of the trunk lid, Meggie appeared at the foot of the bed.

''What are those?'' the girl asked, staring at the leather-wrapped bundle Cassie had taken from inside the trunk.

''This,'' Cassie said, picking out an angled buffalo bone, ''is a scraper. This one's a flesher.'' She held up an angled tool with a metal blade. ''And these are some pegs and an awl.''

''What are they for?''

''Well, I thought I would tan those two rabbit skins,'' Cassie told her, ''and make you a pair of slippers.''

''You're going to make me slippers from real rabbits? The hopping kind?''

Cassie laughed. ''I think all rabbits hop.''

Meggie threw her arms around Cassie's neck. Cassandra hugged her back, liking the weight and warmth of that solid young body in her arms.

It's almost as if she's mine, almost as if she belongs to me, Cassie found herself thinking. But the little girl wasn't hers. She was Drew's—Drew, who didn't want the responsibility of a daughter; Drew, who had long ago pledged himself to something else entirely.

Cassie frowned at the irony as Meggie squirmed away.

''It will be awhile before the slippers are finished. First I have to prepare the skins. Then I'll cut the pattern—''

''Can I help?''

''If you like,'' Cassie answered, ready to close the lid of

the trunk. But before she could, Meggie reached inside and fingered the object lying on top of Cassie's beaded blanket.

"Is this the doll you made for me?"

Cassie nodded, watching the little girl, wondering what she was thinking. "Would you like to hold her?"

Meggie hesitated, then took the doll. She ran her fingers over its face and hair. "I remember that Mama's hair was the same color as this," she said. "And I always liked when she wore this dress, because it had a lot of red in it."

Cassie waited, a strange, breathless heat collecting in her chest.

"Papa said Mama is an angel now, that she comes and watches me while I sleep," Meggie confided. "Do you think that's true?"

"If your papa says it is."

"Cassie?" Meggie's voice shook a little. "I can't remember my mama's face. How will I know when she comes to me?"

Cassie didn't know much about angels, but she was learning more about being a mother every day.

"Oh, Meggie," she breathed, drawing the little girl into her lap. "Mothers always know their babies, and their babies know them."

"How do they know?"

"They know it with their hearts," she said, pressing one hand against Meggie's chest. "There's a special kind of love between mothers and daughters that isn't like anything else."

Meggie stared up at her. "Papa said your mother died when you were little. Is that how you got to know about the special love?" she asked in a whisper.

Cassie closed her eyes against the sudden sting of tears, remembering her mother, feeling a bond with the woman who'd given her life that she hadn't felt in years. "That is exactly how I know," Cassie whispered back. "Do you think," she continued after a moment, "that it would help you remember your mama if you kept the doll?"

Meggie hesitated, then nodded her head. "I think it might."

"Very well, then," Cassie said, closing the lid and pushing

the trunk back under the bed. "Bring your dolly along. We need to start work on those rabbit skins."

Cassie was on her knees scraping the second rabbit skin when Lila Wilcox happened by carrying two huge baskets of clothes.

"Seems like I just get one load of clean clothes delivered, and there's an even bigger pile of dirty ones waiting to be washed," she complained, setting the baskets aside and lowering herself onto Drew's back step. "And can they pay me? No! There's not a soul in this whole damn fort with so much as a penny to bless him. If the paymaster don't come soon, there'll be a whole year of credit on everyone's books!"

"It's the quartermaster's wagons I'm waiting on," Cassie confessed. "Drew keeps promising that there will be more than salt pork and cornmeal to eat once they get here."

The older woman huffed. "Looks like you got some rabbits, anyway."

"Someone left them on the step this morning."

"Oh?" Lila angled. "Any idea who?"

Cassie lowered her eyes. It was not unusual for the officers' ladies to have admirers, but she'd heard favors generally ran to flowers and poetry. She guessed she just wasn't the kind of woman who inspired verse.

When she didn't answer, Lila turned her attention to what Cassie was doing. When she realized what it was, she gave a snort of derision and shook her head. "You just can't let a body forget how you got here, can you?"

"What do you mean?"

"Not one wife here at the fort would touch a dead rabbit, much less skin the critter," Lila admonished her.

With a huff of frustration, Cassie realized that Lila was right. And just this morning she'd been vowing to try harder to fit into her wifely role.

"As if anyone *could* forget where I came from," Cassie challenged, "once they got a look at my face."

"Some of us might be able to."

Cassandra glanced up at Lila in surprise.

"Stopping by every day or so like I've been doing," Lila continued, "I've got so what I see is how you are with that little girl. I see that you take time with her, that you play with her and teach her things. It makes me look at what you are down deep. And now that I can do that, the outside just don't matter so much.''

Cassie didn't know what to say to her. She hadn't dared to hope that what Lila said was possible.

Certainly Drew hadn't learned to look past the tattoo. He blew out the light when they made love. He closed his eyes when he kissed her so he could pretend she was the Cassie he'd loved nine years ago. Knowing that made her want to rage and weep and shake him.

Yet Lila had given her hope that Drew might learn to see her as she was. At least she had to believe that it was possible.

When Cassie didn't respond, Lila gestured to where Meggie was serving ''tea'' and ''cakes'' to her dolly.

''Where'd she get the doll?''

Cassie sat back on her heels and glanced across to where Meggie was playing. ''She saw it with my things and asked for her. Said she couldn't remember her mother's face, that she thought it would help.''

''Do you remember yours?'' Lila asked after a moment.

''My mother?'' Cassie asked, calling up the image of Claire Morgan, seeing her standing over the hearth of their house in Kentucky. ''Of course I remember my mother, but I was a whole lot older than Meggie was when I lost her.''

Lila heaved a gusty sigh. ''Sometimes it's a curse to remember the dead. When I look at Josh, all I can see is him roughhousing with his brothers.''

''I didn't know you'd had other children,'' Cassie said, thinking of the big, rawboned corporal who served in Noonan's infantry.

''I lost three of my boys in the war: James at the first Bull Run, Richard at Chancellorsville, and Emmett at Petersburg.''

Cassie sensed the depth of Lila's pain, as if the most vital reason for living had been ripped away. Cass understood in a way she might not have mere weeks before. She understood because of Meggie, and the realization frightened her.

Lila pushed to her feet as if she were irritated with herself for remembering. ''I guess I'm not likely to get these shirts and socks and drawers dried before nightfall if I don't get at it."

"Oh, wait," Cassie said, springing to her feet and rushing into the house. When she came back she was carrying what looked like a small, dark crock of grease.

"What *is* that?" Lila asked.

"It's an ointment for your hands. I noticed the last time you came how red they were."

Lila took the crock and sniffed it. "What's in here?"

"Well, there's bear grease and beebalm, beardstongue and blanket flower—"

"Will it work?"

"I use it myself sometimes."

Lila thought that over. "So you know about herbs?"

Cassie nodded. "Most Indian women do since they don't have patent medicines to rely on."

"Do you know anything that can help an aching back?" Lila asked. "Will was helping the blacksmith shoe horses yesterday, and by nightfall he could hardly move."

"I'll brew something up and send it over with Meggie."

"Thank you," Lila said, hefting the baskets again.

"I'm glad I could help."

Lila nodded. "And you think on what I said now, girl, about giving folks a chance to look beyond the mark on your face. A fool's as blind as those who can not see."

Cassie watched Lila disappear toward soapsuds row and knew that here at Fort Carr she'd found at least one true friend.

Cassandra heard the front door slam and looked up from the dandelion greens she was slicing just as Drew loomed in the kitchen doorway. His eyes were blazing, and his face was like fire. He crossed the room in two long strides and waved a paper in Cassie's face.

"What in the name of God were you thinking?" he thundered.

Meggie looked up from where she was rocking her dolly to sleep in her arms.

"Whatever are you talking about?" Cassie asked, moving

to where Meggie was sitting, lifting the little girl to her feet, and propelling her out the open door. No child should be privy to her parents' arguments; whatever had Drew so upset was between the two of them.

Once Meggie was safely outside, Drew shoved the paper into Cassie's hands. "Do you know what this is?" he demanded.

Cassie stared at the words and numbers on the page. Though her ability to read English was coming back, she couldn't make much sense of them.

"It's the sutler's bill—a list of the things that have been charged to my account since the first of the year."

Cassie's stomach lurched.

"The way this works is before the paymaster gives any of us our wages, the sutler collects his due. Do you have any idea how much Tyler Jessup took out of my pay?"

Cassie stared at the figure at the bottom of the column, her heart in her throat.

"One hundred and thirty seven dollars," Drew answered for her. "Nearly half of what I made in four months' time. I expected the bill to be high. I told you to buy what you needed to make some clothes; I didn't want you going around in someone's castoffs. And because the commissary wagons didn't come until last week, we bought more from the sutler than we might have ordinarily. But there's this"—he pointed to an item two thirds of the way down the page—"thirteen cans of condensed milk. When I first saw the notation I thought it was a mistake, so I went to check with Tyler Jessup. And do you know what he told me?"

Cassie knew.

"He said *you* bought the milk, *eighteen* cans in all, and carted it off in a burlap sack."

There was no denying what she'd done.

"Now, Cassie," Drew asked with exaggerated patience, "since I've already paid for all that milk, I'd like to know what you did with it."

Cassie had known all along she'd have to own up to this. She just figured she'd have some warning, some time to make up a story Drew would believe. She knew how he'd respond to the truth.

Deliberately she bowed her head. While she was with the Kiowa and Cheyenne, she'd learned to subjugate herself, to acknowledge her mistake by silence and servitude. It was one way she'd survived, and it only cost her pride.

But Drew wasn't Little Otter, who lived to see Cassandra humiliated. He wasn't Gray Falcon, who accepted her submissiveness as license for punishment. Drew stood over her waiting for an answer.

At length Cassie dared to raise her head. A child was alive because of her, and she refused to disavow what she'd done to save it.

"A woman I knew, a Cheyenne woman, came to me and asked for help," she began, explaining as simply as she could. "Her sister's child was dying for want of milk. I bought the cans so the baby would live."

She heard Drew suck in his breath.

"Let me understand this." His voice was so low and filled with fury that Cassie wished he were shouting. "You spent *my* money on milk so some *redskin* baby could live? You saved his life so that in a few years' time he can ride out in battle against me?"

Cassie knew he spoke the truth. There were years of fighting ahead, and the child she'd done her best to save would undoubtedly become a warrior.

Drew slammed his fist on the table beside her. "Damn it, Cassie, answer me!"

Heat built inside her, filling her chest, making her ears ring and fingers tingle. It had been nine long years since she had dared to feel either anger or pride. She'd spent those years bowing her head and biting her lip, suppressing her outrage, and fighting down her indignation. Suddenly those feelings raced through her blood like a dose of spirits.

"No baby will ever die if it is in my power to save it!" she vowed in a voice that shook with determination. "No white baby nor Indian baby, either."

"Well, you'd damn well better not let me catch you helping the Indians or their babies again. I came here to kill the redskins, not to coddle them."

Cassie stood her ground, her head high and her jaw clenched, holding tight to her convictions in the face of his anger.

"Do you understand me, Cassie?" Drew bellowed.

Before she could draw breath to answer, someone knocked on their front door.

Both of them clung to the moment, needing the question resolved between them. The silence thickened.

The knocking came again, louder and more insistent.

"Oh, Christ!" Drew spit, and spun away.

Weak at the knees, Cassie sank down on the bench beside the table. Over the drumming of her pulse, she could hear the conversation going on at the front door.

"Begging your pardon, sir," someone was saying. "Major McGarrity has asked me to inform you that the Sioux chief, Man-Afraid-of-His-Horse, has come into the fort. There's to be a dinner in his honor at seven o'clock."

"A dinner?" Drew echoed. "To honor some Sioux chief?"

"Yes, sir. At the headquarters building, sir. And the major says that the ladies are invited, too."

"Are they now?" Cassie could hear the sarcasm in Drew's tone. They'd been cut off from fort society all these weeks.

"Shall I tell the major that you and Mrs. Reynolds will attend?"

"Indeed we will," Drew answered, as if he had a choice.

Cassie heard the door bang closed, and a moment later Drew came bowling into the kitchen. "Who in hell is this Man-Afraid-of-His-Horse?"

"He's peace chief for the Sioux," Cassie answered. "He has an encampment up on the Powder River. There are many warriors at his command if he should choose to ride to war with Red Cloud, but so far he has steered a moderate course."

"And why would he come here?" Drew asked, giving voice to the very question Cassie herself was asking.

She glanced up at him and shrugged. "I don't know. He could have skins to trade, or prisoners."

"Where would they get prisoners?"

"Where did they get me?"

Drew nodded. "Well, it's safe to assume he wants something."

He hesitated a moment, staring into space, and then looked down at her. "It's too late to do anything about the milk, but this can never happen again. If we were at war, what you've done would be construed as giving aid to the enemy. You could be hanged for that, and I'd be court-martialed. Is that what you want?"

Cassie shook her head.

"Then you must promise not to help the Indians, no matter what." When she said nothing, Drew went on. "This is important, Cassie. Your actions could hurt everyone at the fort. They could compromise my position here."

Cassie inclined her head in acknowledgment; she understood the consequences of what she'd done. What's more, she loved this man. She loved his daughter, too. She didn't want to see either of them hurt.

It wasn't hard to speak the words when she had so much at stake. "I promise," she said, and wanted with all her heart for the vow to be true.

Chapter Twelve

Hunter translated Ben McGarrity's comments for Man-Afraid-of-His-Horse and watched the guests arrive. He introduced the chief's two companions to a flock of young lieutenants and eyed the entrance. He chatted with Mrs. McGarrity and stared at the door. Then Cassandra stepped into the room, and Hunter's mood settled like birds at sunset.

Marriage to the captain agreed with her, Hunter observed with a hitch of surprise. She looked lovely tonight dressed in a dimity gown of dusty blue. There was high color in her cheeks, and her hair shone gold in the lamplight. But it was the glow in those clear, pale eyes that convinced him she'd found what she needed. Hunter just wished she'd found it with him.

He should have been glad that the marriage between Cassie and the captain was working out. He should have been pleased that Cass had secured her share of happiness. Instead a hot, bright spark of longing sizzled in his gut. He wanted what Drew Reynolds had.

Hunter straightened as Captain and Mrs. Reynolds came up to be introduced and tried to ignore the shy, half smile that touched Cassie's lips when she looked at him.

"Sir," McGarrity began, addressing Man-Afraid-of-His-Horse, "may I present to you the commander of our second cavalry company, Captain Andrew Scott Reynolds. Captain Reynolds served gallantly in the recent war, and is the descendant of one of the United States' most decorated generals. He was also graduated from our military academy at West Point. The lovely lady with him is his wife Cassandra."

As Hunter translated, Man-Afraid-of-His-Horse looked the new arrivals up and down. He took in Drew's square-shouldered stance and his possessive grip on Cassie's elbow. He nodded with approval at the way Cass tipped her head differentially. But before he spoke, his gaze seemed to settle on the tattoo that marred Cassandra's cheek.

"I have heard much about the soldiers from this military academy," he said, addressing Drew. "Is not General Sherman, who came to Fort Laramie some months ago, a graduate of West Point?"

"Indeed he is," Drew answered. "There are many fine West Point officers serving on the frontier."

Man-Afraid-of-His-Horse took a moment to think that over. "And is it your counsel, Captain Reynolds, that we accept the treaty that was offered to us last spring rather than fight such men as these?"

"Of course you should sign the treaty," Drew replied. "The quality of our officers, our numbers, and our equipment are far superior to anything you redskins can muster. If you and your warriors choose to fight, your people will be annihilated."

Hunter broke off translation as soon as he realized the trend of Reynolds's remarks, but Man-Afraid-of-His-Horse seemed to understand them well enough.

The Indian's eyes narrowed. "And how is it that a man with views like yours is married to a woman who wears the Kiowa's mark?"

Hunter took it upon himself to answer. "Captain and Mrs. Reynolds were promised to each other before she was captured," he explained as simply as he could. "When she returned to the whites, they were reunited."

Man-Afraid-of-His-Horse nodded. "Because of nearly losing his bride, this man believes he has reason to hate all Indians."

Hunter inclined his head.

"Well, then," Man-Afraid-of-His-Horse said with a nod, "we must listen to such as he. Men with hatred in their hearts tell truths that others prefer to keep among themselves."

Before Hunter could respond to the chief's words or the colonel's inquiring gaze, Man-Afraid-of-His-Horse spoke directly to Drew. "I would not like to meet you in battle," he said. "But if I do, I will know to kill you first."

Hunter translated word for word, watching Reynold's eyes.

Cold amusement flickered and died away. "Then look to yourself, sir," Reynolds answered, and turned to go, making room for the next officer and his lady to be presented.

As the couples passed, Sylvie Noonan arched one brow in Cassie's direction and jerked her skirts aside.

At the deliberate slight, a fierce, slow-burning anger ignited in Hunter's belly. Sylvie Noonan had been willing enough to pity Cass when she was a poor Indian captive, but now that Cassie was her equal in military society, the woman refused to acknowledge her.

Yet if either Cassie or Drew saw what Sylvie had done, they gave no sign. They crossed the room toward where the crystal punch bowl stood amidst a muster of mismatched cups. Two garrulous young lieutenants strode toward them as if they were drawn both by curiosity and Cassie's exotic beauty.

When all of the line and staff officers had been presented and even Tyler Jessup had shambled in to join the party, Sally McGarrity ushered everyone to their places at the table. It was laid with immaculately ironed linen that suspiciously resembled bed sheets. An array of patterned china and silver gleamed in the light cast by the quartet of silver candelabra that graced the table. Stemmed wine and water glasses stood at every place. Hunter guessed that McGarrity had raided every household in the fort to set a table grand enough to impress the Sioux chief.

If Hunter was awed by the table service, he was even more surprised by the meal that was served by six efficient, white-gloved orderlies. It began with a savory onion soup, progressed to a course of poached white fish, a salad of field greens, and entrees of roast venison and quail. Parsleyed potatoes were offered around, along with the vile green mush the army passed off as peas. There were pickles and onions, rolls and biscuits, jelly and marmalade, water and wine.

Hunter ate sparingly and kept his eye on his companions, yet the meal went far more smoothly than any of them had a right to expect. Man-Afraid-of-His-Horse handled his cutlery well. He made polite conversation with Major and Mrs. McGarrity and listened attentively to Hunter's translations.

Yet in spite of their veneer of affability, Hunter knew every officer in the place was wondering when raiders would burst through the doors to take their scalps. After the Fetterman massacre the previous December and the skirmish when the Cheyenne traded Cass, everyone thought the Indians would swoop down out of the north as thick as mayflies.

That Man-Afraid-of-His-Horse should come to the fort when bands of Sioux were already warring off to the east didn't make sense. It didn't even make Indian sense, and that left a cold, hollow feeling in Hunter's middle. Still, he kept his misgivings to himself.

Doing that was easy when he could sit and watch Cassandra. She was luminous in the soft light of the candles. Her eyes shone bright and warm. Her smile came and went like sunbeams through a bank of clouds. She didn't say much, letting Drew, Captain Noonan, and several of the lieutenants monopolize the conversation. Still, she laughed at the jests and answered when someone spoke to her. She was handling with innate grace what must be an intimidating, new experience.

Hunter ached with regret just watching her. He longed for the brief time when she'd depended on and trusted him. For the few short days she'd lived in his world and shared a closeness Hunter had never had with anyone. But before he realized how much he wanted her, Cass had married someone else.

Hunter raised his glass of wine to his lips and grimaced at the bitter taste. He could see that Cassie's marriage wasn't perfect. The captain was a proprietary man, an exacting man, a man driven by demons of his own. But he was giving Cass security, a place in the world. He had given her a child to care for. They were things Cassie desperately needed, things Hunter himself could never provide. Though he wished he could make room for her in his life, Hunter knew Cass was safe. He knew Cass was provided for and, for the most part, content. He supposed what he wanted didn't matter much if that were so.

Still, when it came to Indians, the captain was unpredictable and dangerous. If Man-Afraid-of-His-Horse had responded differently, Reynolds might have set off his own little war.

"Sir?" Hunter looked up to find an orderly standing over him. "There's a man outside who says he needs to speak to you."

Hunter excused himself and slipped away. One of the Indians from the friendly camp was waiting in the shadows at the corner of the building.

"What did you find when you rode out?" Hunter asked.

"Nothing," the brave answered.

Hunter bent closer. "You must have found something. There has to be an encampment nearby. Man-Afraid-of-His-Horse wouldn't have ridden all this way with just two guards."

The tracker shook his head. "Up north are the winter camps. There is nothing else."

Hunter cursed under his breath. If he had been able to leave the fort, he'd have gotten to the bottom of this. He'd have found out why Man-Afraid-of-His-Horse was here. Still, he'd used this man before and knew he was reliable.

"No camp. No tepee. Nothing." The brave clarified and held out his hand for pay.

Hunter dug in his pocket for the agreed-upon amount. "And there's no sign?" he asked, withholding the coins for an answer.

The man shook his head and reached again. Hunter let the money go and watched as his informant headed off toward the friendly camp.

"What the hell is Man-Afraid-of-His-Horse doing here?"

he mumbled under his breath. "Just what the hell is going on?"

Arrogant bugger, Drew Reynolds thought as he glared down the dinner table to where Man-Afraid-of-His-Horse sat in the place of honor to Major McGarrity's right. What in hell was this savage doing here all gussied up in his war shirt and feathers? And why was McGarrity treating him like an honored guest?

Everyone at the fort knew that as soon as orders came from Omaha, they'd be riding out against the Indians. The army had the matter of the Fetterman massacre to settle with the hostiles. Once they started on the summer campaign, they might just as well clean out that rats' nest of Sioux and Cheyenne villages up along the Powder River and secure the Bozeman Trail all the way to Montana. With all of that ahead, Drew didn't see why McGarrity was bowing and scraping and giving parties for one of the redskins who'd be riding against them.

Drew settled back in his chair looking long and assessingly at the officers gathered around the table. Only Anderson, one of Noonan's young lieutenants, and Clark, who was too old and rum-soaked to have the stomach for a fight, spoke about their hopes for peace. The other men—the real men—were silent and every bit as itchy for battle as Drew was.

He shifted his regard to the others who had come tonight—the wives and the Indians—and caught one of the redskins palming a silver spoon. The man glared back, daring Drew to speak, knowing he could not. Drew swallowed a curse and looked to the women seated around him. Sylvie Noonan was too busy fanning herself to notice the thievery and Sally McGarrity was regaling Alma Parker with some story she'd read in *Harper's Monthly.* He did notice that Tyler Jessup and one of the chief's companions were using hand talk to converse and wondered just what they'd found to discuss.

Then Drew's gaze came to settle on his own wife. He smiled, thinking how well she was behaving herself. Dressed in a pretty new gown, with her hair curled and her hands folded demurely in her lap, she came close to being the woman he wanted her to be: not marked by her experiences, not cursed with strange and inexplicable loyalties.

Heat built up inside him just thinking about what Cassie had done. How could she have met with that Cheyenne squaw and given her food? How could she feel anything but hatred for the Indians? He'd tried to understand; he'd tried to be patient, but she kept giving in to her impulses and making mistakes. He wanted so much for Cassie to be the woman she'd been before, the woman she seemed to be tonight. Yet she kept failing, failing herself and failing him.

Only with Meggie were things as he had hoped. The child's laughter rang through the house for the first time since Laura had died. Meggie was growing, behaving herself, and learning things. Cassie was the reason, and for Meggie's sake Drew was willing to overlook most of Cassie's transgressions. But not all. Not the kind of mistake he'd discovered today.

Drew glanced up and found that one of the orderlies was offering him a selection of cigars and a glass of port. He took a cheroot from the box, trimmed the end, and lit it.

"This is every bit as elegant a meal as any I had back East," he commented to Lieutenant Braiden, who sat to his left.

He could see at the far end of the table that Man-Afraid-of-His-Horse had refused a cigar and was making some other request. With Jalbert inexplicably gone, McGarrity didn't seem to know how to respond to him.

The Indian raised his voice and asked again.

Everyone turned to see what Man-Afraid-of-His-Horse wanted. McGarrity gestured for one of the orderlies to find Jalbert, but Man-Afraid-of-His-Horse didn't seem willing to wait.

He repeated the words a third time and stared down the table to where Cassandra sat.

Drew looked to his wife. She was pale as whey and staring at the tablecloth.

A hush settled over the diners as Man-Afraid-of-His-Horse continued to glare at her.

Her chest rose and fell in agitation.

The room went still.

"Man-Afraid-of-His-Horse would like more water, if you please," Cassie finally said in a very small voice.

Drew's stomach tumbled, dropped like a stone off a cliff.

He heard the whispers begin, the buzz of speculation. Alma Parker and Sylvie Noonan exchanged knowing glances. Drew could well imagine what all of them were thinking.

At the head of the table, the chief held out his glass, and one of the orderlies leaped forward to fill it with water.

"You understand Sioux, Cassandra?" McGarrity asked quietly.

Cassie inclined her head. "I speak it, too."

"Then extend our apologies to our guest for not realizing what he needed."

Cassie did as she was bidden.

Drew would rather she'd shouted obscenities.

"Well then, Cassandra, have you any other talents we should know about?" McGarrity wanted to know.

Cassie raised her chin a little. "I speak Cheyenne and Kiowa and Sioux, a little German and a good deal of French. And I know some hand talk, too."

"You're a veritable dictionary, aren't you, my dear?" Drew muttered under his breath.

Cassie's color ripened, and she slid him a sidelong glance.

Drew scowled back, letting her feel his displeasure.

Jalbert returned from somewhere outside. "Excuse me, Major," he broke in. "One of the orderlies said you needed me?"

"Thank you, Jalbert," McGarrity acknowledged, "but it seems Mrs. Reynolds speaks the Sioux language and was kind enough to translate."

Drew intercepted the startled look Jalbert shot in Cassie's direction. Not even the half-breed had known about her facility for languages.

At the head of the table, Jalbert leaned across to McGarrity. "Major," he prodded, almost as if he and not McGarrity was the host tonight, "didn't you have some words of welcome for our guests?"

McGarrity nodded and came to his feet. "Let me say, gentlemen, how pleased we are that you have come to visit here at Fort Carr. It is pleasant to share a meal and have an opportunity to come to know you better. Perhaps gatherings such as this will help keep the peace between our two peoples. If there is anything we can do to encourage understanding between us, you have only to ask.''

Everyone applauded McGarrity's words, though not with as much enthusiasm as they would news of a campaign against the redskins.

Once Jalbert had completed the translation, Man-Afraid-of-His-Horse rose to give his answer. ''Indeed, we are pleased by this show of hospitality. I, too, believe that coming together helps us know each other's ways and each other's hearts,'' the Sioux chief began.

''The whites have shown us great generosity in the past. You have given us flour and utensils and cloth. You have given us tools and seeds. You have given us mirrors and bells and whiskey. But what you have not given us in a very long time is powder for our guns and lead for shot. Though we have great need of them, you have not allowed the licensed traders to sell them to us in their trading posts.''

Drew leaned forward in his chair. *So this was why the bastard had come.*

''During the long cold winter, it did not matter that we had so little ammunition with which to hunt for food. We tracked the deer and antelope through the snow and killed them with our arrows. But soon many of my tribe will gather to hunt buffalo. As you know, the buffalo are the center of our lives. They give us meat and skin, horn and bones, hooves and sinew—everything our families need to survive. And in order to kill enough buffalo, we need new supplies of lead and gunpowder.''

Drew had to admire the redskin's gall. He'd come to the fort to beg for bullets—perhaps the very bullets that would enable this chief and his braves to make war on the whites.

Once the Sioux had powder and ammunition, they would ride down on the stage stations and isolated ranches. They would harass the wood and hay parties sent out from the forts, and attack the gangs of men laying track for the Union Pacific. Just how witless did this Indian think they were to believe that all he wanted powder for was a buffalo hunt?

Drew saw that others were as affronted as he. Lieutenant Anderson's mouth hung open in surprise. Captain Parker braced forward in his chair. Even Sylvie Noonan's fan had halted in mid-swish.

"Surely you do not mean to deny us what we need to live," Man-Afraid-of-His-Horse went on, looking from person to person around the table as Jalbert translated. "Surely you see that no matter how generous you have been with other goods, by denying us what we need to kill the buffalo you deny us the life's blood of our tribe."

McGarrity shoved to his feet. "Man-Afraid-of-His-Horse must know I do not wish to see Sioux families go hungry. If it were in my power to allow you to trade for ammunition, I would ask Mr. Jessup to leave the table and open his store. But word has come down from General Crook in Omaha that in the Department of the Platte no ammunition can be sold to Indians. I cannot countermand the general's order. I cannot give you shot or gunpowder."

Man-Afraid-of-His-Horse faced his host, standing taller than McGarrity in his feathered headdress. "Is there no one to whom I can speak, no one who has the authority to change this general's order?"

McGarrity paused. "Perhaps Colonel Palmer at Fort Laramie would be willing to listen to your concerns," he suggested.

Man-Afraid-of-His-Horse took a moment to consider the major's words. "Very well, then. If you will grant me an escort to Fort Laramie so they know I come in peace, I will go and speak to this Colonel Palmer."

"Indeed, that's something I can do," McGarrity agreed. "Will dawn tomorrow be convenient for your departure?"

Man-Afraid-of-His-Horse inclined his head and rose to go. "I would thank you for your hospitality to me and my companions. This has been a most enlightening evening."

In a swirl of fringe and bobbing feathers, the Indians took their leave.

McGarrity motioned for silence the moment the door closed behind them. "Escort your women home," he ordered, "and get back here as soon as you can. This gives us an opportunity I never thought we'd have, and we need to prepare."

Amid the scrape of chairs and the stutter of footsteps, the officers and their wives rose to go. Orderlies swept away the remains of the meal. The bachelor officers took out maps and spread them across the tables.

Drew steered Cassie out the door, and they made the short walk to their cabin in silence. Only after Lila had left the house did Drew turn to Cassie.

"So, Cassandra, besides your facility for languages, what other things have you been keeping from me?"

Cassie turned to him, her mouth drawn tight. "You made it very clear you had no interest in what happened to me while I was a captive or what I learned while I was with the Indians. Out of respect for your wishes, I've held my peace." She drew the shawl from around her shoulders and stood with it bundled against her chest. "But since you've asked, I speak Kiowa and Cheyenne because I was forced to learn them by my captors. I learned Sioux and hand-talk so I could survive in the Powder River camps."

"And where did you learn German and French?"

"I learned a bit of each from the trading and hunting parties passing through. I thought that if I could talk to them, I might be able to convince one of those men to buy me back from either my Kiowa master or my Cheyenne husband."

"And just what did you offer them in exchange for that favor?" Drew knew perfectly well the only thing a woman captive had to barter.

"Does it matter what I offered? None of them were willing to pay my price. None of those men were willing to help me leave the Indian camps." She drew a long, ragged breath, her color high. "And now that I've returned, I can't imagine why I thought I belonged here."

Drew flinched as if she'd struck him. Of course this was where she belonged. His Cassie was white.

"What you said you wanted was a home, and I've done my best to give you that," he shouted in a voice that shook. "You said you wanted to be my wife, and I married you.

What you agreed to do in exchange was care for my child. But if that's proved so distasteful, perhaps I can arrange for you to go with Man-Afraid-of-His-Horse when he leaves tomorrow.''

Before either of them could say another word, Meggie appeared in the kitchen doorway.

''Papa?'' she mewed, sloe-eyed and rumpled with sleep. ''Papa, why are you yelling at Cassie?''

Drew tamped down his temper and went to scoop his daughter up in his arms. ''We were having words, Meggie. Words over something that has nothing at all to do with you.''

''You said you were going to send Cassie away. You won't do that, will you? I need her here with me.''

''Of course I won't send Cassie away,'' Drew assured his daughter, resenting the promise the moment it left his lips. ''But I need you to stay with Cassie now,'' he said, handing Meggie to his wife. ''I need to get back to headquarters.''

''How come you're always going to headquarters?'' he heard Meggie call after him as he shut the cabin door.

Drew stopped on the porch for a moment to collect himself. Though most of his anger was spent, it had left a bitter residue. Sharp, brittle pieces of disillusionment, shards of betrayal that settled way down deep. A simmering resentment.

The Cassie who'd faced him tonight wasn't the Cassie he wanted as his wife. He wanted the girl he'd loved nine years ago. He wanted the woman he made love to in the dark. He wanted someone quiet and compliant and grateful—especially after all he'd done to make a place for her.

He'd tried to understand what she'd been through. He knew it had been horrible, but he'd survived things, too. He'd survived them and gone on. Cassie had to do that. She needed to stop doing what was wrong for her and start doing what was right. She had to stop thinking like an Indian if she was going to make a life with him.

Drew blew a breath and scrubbed a hand across his face. He had more important things to think about than this, soldierly things, things he felt qualified to address. He'd deal with Cassie when he got home.

He entered the headquarters building not two minutes later

and found most of the officers already gathered around the table. The air was filmed with cigar smoke. An uncorked bottle of whiskey stood well within reach. Drew poured a tot into a glass and lit a cigar.

"Gentlemen," McGarrity began, calling the meeting to order. "Tonight Man-Afraid-of-His-Horse has given us a rare opportunity. In asking for ammunition and in being willing to ride as far as Fort Laramie in search of it, he is absenting himself from the villages up north. He has also provided us with a reason to send a wagonload of supplies and a cadre of men to those Powder River camps."

"But why should we give the hostiles more supplies?" Noonan asked. "Haven't we given them subsidies enough?"

McGarrity shook his head. "It's not what we give them, but the opportunity this gives us," the major illuminated. "It gives us a chance to see things up north for ourselves: to assess the mood of the tribes and the number of warriors they can field."

"You mean for our men to be spies," one of the young lieutenants observed.

"Not spies, precisely," McGarrity went on. "We won't make any bones about who we are, but the mission will be one of reconnaissance. We're going to observe as much in those villages as we can."

"It's bound to be dangerous work," someone said. "We won't want to provoke an incident."

"That's why I'm detailing Lieutenant Anderson and a dozen men to escort the wagon."

The men shifted, puffed at their cigars, and frowned down at the map. Anderson was not a popular choice.

McGarrity ignored the discontent. "Choose steady men, Lieutenant," he advised. "Men you trust to behave themselves. One misstep and some young buck will be sewing your scalps to his war shirt. Jalbert will accompany you. He'll keep you out of trouble, if he can.

"Now, Captain Reynolds." McGarrity's tone changed as he turned to Drew. "I want you to accompany Man-Afraid-of-His-Horse to Fort Laramie."

Drew stiffened, suddenly furious down to his boot soles.

Some damn lily-livered lieutenant was riding into the heart of the Powder River country, while Drew was supposed to nursemaid Man-Afraid-of-His-Horse.

"Colonel Palmer is no more likely to give the chief ammunition than we are," McGarrity went on, "but you must assure him that Colonel Palmer will telegraph General Crook and convince him to relent. Jalbert has recommended a translator to accompany you, and your Sergeant O'Hearn is familiar with hand talk, too."

Drew clamped down hard on his temper. He'd undertaken unpleasant duty before and knew what he must do. "Yes sir," he acknowledged without letting his feelings show.

"As for the rest of us," McGarrity went on, "we'll sit tight and wait this out."

"There haven't been orders, then?" Parker asked.

McGarrity scowled and shook his head. "Preliminary orders provided for a full-scale campaign again the Powder River encampments under Colonel Gibbon, but that action has been postponed."

The men's faces fell in disappointment.

"Have you had an explanation for the delay?" Lieutenant Braiden asked.

"Interference from Washington," the major admitted. "The faction in Congress sympathetic to the Indians has managed to get another peace commission appointed. Their specific objective is a treaty with the Sioux."

"Even after the Fetterman massacre, sir?"

"Blame the Bureau of Indian Affairs." In spite of his obvious effort to control his irritation, McGarrity shoved to his feet and started to pace. "If it were up to those damned bureaucrats, they'd give Man-Afraid-of-His-Horse and Red Cloud all the guns and ammunition they want.

"At least all the do-gooders have done so far is force us to postpone the campaign. Still, we have to be ready when orders finally come. That means placating Man-Afraid-of-His-Horse and getting the best information we can. Are there any further questions?"

No one spoke. The officers adjourned.

Drew left headquarters with all the rest. He wasn't happy

about his assignment, but had been a soldier long enough to take what duty he'd been given. Still, he cursed his abominable luck all the way home.

Cassie heard Drew slam into the house and rose from where she'd been sitting in the rocking chair. He bolted past her as if she were invisible, took down the pitcher, and poured himself a drink. He swallowed down the whiskey, then turned to her.

"I've been assigned to escort Man-Afraid-of-His-Horse to Fort Laramie," he announced. "We're leaving tomorrow."

She could hear in his voice that he wasn't pleased. "Do you know how long you'll be gone?"

Drew shrugged. "At least a week."

She nodded, a strange relief assailing her. "They aren't going to give Man-Afraid-of-His-Horse the ammunition he wants, are they?"

"No."

"Then why are they sending him off like this? Why are they making him think there's a chance he'll get it?"

Drew paced away from her, his shoulders hunched. "I don't know why this damn army does anything. I don't know why we went through that charade tonight. Or why the hell we aren't riding out to attack the Powder River encampments."

She could hear the ragged edge to his anger and was relieved that it wasn't directed at her.

"I have a long trip ahead of me. I'm going to bed." He crossed the room to put the bottle and the pitcher away. "Are you coming, Cassie?"

Though it sounded like a command, she shook her head. She didn't want to lie with Drew tonight, not after the way they'd argued and he'd threatened to send her away. She didn't want Drew's touch to stir her the way it did. She didn't want to hold him and touch him and pretend for him.

He stared at her for one long moment and spun away. She hoped he didn't wake Meggie, now that she'd finally gotten her back to sleep.

Cass sat down in the rocking chair near the hearth and

waited for the house to go dark and still. When it was she slipped outside. She only meant to go as far as the porch. As far as the road. As far as the river.

She was panting when she reached the fringe of trees along the bank. She was trembling with a need for silence, space, air.

She sucked in great lungfuls of it, deep, sweet mouthfuls of coolness and night. She shivered, grateful she had been able to escape for a little while.

When she could breathe again, when the thundering of her heart had died away, she paced through the saw grass that switched and rustled in the wind. She stalked along the edge of the river and watched the water flow past her, going fast and far away. She almost wished she was going with it.

She tried not to think about Drew, but there wasn't any help for it. He was in the center of this turmoil with her; this swirl of present and past, of who they were and who they'd been. He was as much a part of what bound her as he was a part of what made her want to run away.

She loved him. She had always loved him, and she wanted to find a way to be with him. She needed the security, the link to the past, the place in the world Drew gave her. She just wasn't sure how to have that without losing herself.

Meggie made staying with Drew necessary. Cass adored the child's endless questions, her sticky-faced kisses, and her baby laugh. She lived for Meggie's moments of unexpected wisdom and wide-eyed discovery. She cherished holding Meggie against her heart, rocking her and crooning to her and keeping her safe. *And she would lose Meggie forever if Drew sent her away.*

Cassie blinked back the flood of sudden tears and tried to plan. She had to find a way to stay with Drew. Surely she could agree with him instead of arguing, allow Drew to guide her as other husbands guided their wives. She must try to be that other Cassie, the woman she might have been if their dreams hadn't turned to dust nine years ago.

She dashed the tears from the corners of her eyes and fought for calm. She'd resolved what she must do; now she had to find the strength to do it. But tonight she felt so fragile, so small and alone. How could she go back and close herself up in that cabin? How could she go back and contrive to betray everything she'd come to be?

A voice came to her out of the dark. "Cassandra?"

She heard a rustle in the grass and spun around. A man was coming toward her down the bank. He was a big man, broad through the shoulders and chest, looking tall as a giant as he half-stepped down the slope.

"Cassandra?"

Her heart lodged hard against her throat. "Drew?" she whispered, terrified that he had come to drag her back.

"No, it's Hunter, Hunter Jalbert."

The breath went out of her so suddenly she almost laughed. "Hunter?"

"What are you doing here in the middle of the night?"

He loomed over her, barely more than a silhouette. Hunter was the one person in the world who might understand what she was feeling.

"I needed to hear the wind and see the sky," she told him.

She sensed more than saw the smile that grazed one corner of his mouth.

"When I lived with the Cheyenne," she went on, "I would lie in my blankets and listen to the night. I could hear the rattle of the grass and feel the pulse of the earth beneath me."

Hunter nodded and curled one hand around her elbow. He steered her toward a log midway up the bank, then lowered himself to the grass beside her. They sat as friends, united by the silence.

As they did, coolness crept up from the river. Moonlight caught and shimmered in the current. The scent of earth and night and growing things drifted to them on the freshening breeze. Cassie let the peace seep into her one cell at a time, felt the silence ooze into her flesh. She closed her eyes and let the strength collect inside her.

"Here in the quiet of the night it seems so clear to me," she whispered.

"What seems so clear?" His voice was a soft rumbling in his chest, as deep and dark as the night itself.

"Who I should be. What I should do."

She heard him shift on the grass to look at her. "And what is that?"

"A white woman who knows the rules and never breaks them."

He was silent for a long, long time. "And what is the alternative?" he finally asked her.

Tears sprang to her eyes again and diluted her voice when she spoke. "To be alone."

He reached across and sought her hand. His was warm, rough and sure against hers. "Don't be afraid. What is it you want?"

"I want to mother Meggie, to be with Drew, but it's so hard sometimes."

She felt his fingers tighten on her own. "And what will make that better?"

He was like a guardian spirit, a strong, steady presence protecting her while she sought a vision for herself.

"Getting away like this," she said. "Being able to breathe." She squeezed his hand by way of thanks. "And having you to talk to."

He didn't say anything more. He didn't have to; just his being there made the difference.

They sat together for a little while longer, watching the moon play hide-and-seek behind a cloud, listening to the river whisper past. When she was ready, he walked her back.

With Hunter beside her it wasn't so bad when the fort closed around her again: the rows of buildings, the smells of people, the stillness of the night that wasn't quite silence. The oppressive weight had lifted, and Cassandra felt able to live this life again.

She parted from Hunter without saying good-bye. She stood for a moment after he'd melted away, drew one last breath, and went inside.

She moved like a wraith through the silent house, slipped into the bedroom and removed her clothes. Drew murmured something in his sleep that made her turn and look at him. He was going away tomorrow, and all at once, she didn't want them to part in anger.

"Drew," she whispered, sliding into the bed. "Drew?"

She reached to stroke his cheek. He came awake with a jerk, catching her wrist in a crushing grip.

It took a moment for him to realize who she was, a moment more for his hands and lips to find her. He drew her close against his side, and they were lost to the sweet, indefinable alchemy that had claimed and enchanted them long ago.

Hunter saw the three of them coming toward him down officers' row. Drew had Cassie's fingers folded possessively in one gauntleted hand and was balancing Meggie on his opposite hip. The little girl's arms were wrapped tightly around her papa's neck and even in the hazy half-light of dawn, Hunter could see that when she looked at her husband, Cass all but glowed.

He stood as if he'd been turned to stone, his heart drumming in his ears and his chest on fire. He had been with Cass the night before. He knew what she'd been feeling. Only one thing could have changed all that—making love to her husband.

Fierce, irrational jealousy ripped through Hunter like a flood tide. He had no right to feel the way he did. He should be pleased that Cass had made peace with Drew; he'd encouraged her to do that. But nothing in the world could make him glad he'd sent Cass into another man's bed.

"I wasn't sure about those two when they married up," Lieutenant Anderson volunteered, coming up to where Hunter was tying his war club to the back of his saddle, "but things seem to have worked out well enough."

Hunter fumbled for words. No one must guess how he felt about the captain's wife.

"Looks like," he finally managed to mumble, and turned back to where preparations for leaving were well under way.

Two parties were forming up this morning. The one headed for Fort Laramie consisted of Man-Afraid-of-His-Horse and his two companions, Captain Reynolds, Sergeant O'Hearn, and a dozen troopers. The second party was the surprise the major had devised for the fort's distinguished visitor.

McGarrity made his way down the steps of the headquarters building toward where Man-Afraid-of-His-Horse stood waiting to mount his pony. Hunter joined them to translate.

"As a token of our friendship," McGarrity began, gesturing to the wagon of supplies, "we have decided to send a gift to the people in the Powder River camps, a few of the things we thought you'd need if the hunting has been less than satisfactory."

The Sioux chief eyed the wagon. "That is generous, very generous."

"Lieutenant Anderson and Mr. Jalbert will accompany the wagon," McGarrity went on. "I'm also sending a few extra soldiers to see that—"

Man-Afraid-of-His-Horse shook his head so vigorously his feathers danced. "You must send no troopers with the wagon. Only the young lieutenant, Lone Hunter, and two drivers may go into the camps."

"That doesn't seem to be nearly enough men to ensure—"

"More soldiers will be more trouble," the chief insisted.

McGarrity seemed unconvinced.

Man-Afraid-of-His-Horse turned and untied a tall crook-shaped staff from his saddle. "This will keep these four men safe."

Hunter eyed the standard with appreciation. It was wondrously ornate. The shaft was wrapped with narrow strips of fur and banded with copper and brass. The crooked head fluttered with eagle feathers. Tiny silver bells jangled in the breeze.

Man-Afraid-of-His-Horse offered the staff directly to Hunter. "This will grant you safe passage among my people," the old chief said. "Everyone in the northern camps will recognize that it is mine. They will see it, and it will be as if I ride with you. Tie a white handkerchief to the top to show you come in peace, and my people will offer you the same hospitality I would offer you if I were there."

Hunter was astonished that Man-Afraid-of-His-Horse was entrusting him with what was one of a brave's most prized possessions. He inclined his head and accepted the standard with the humility such an honor deserved.

"I thank you for giving something of such value and power to me," he said. "I will take care of this and see that it is returned to you when my visit to your people is over."

The Sioux chief smiled. "I offer this for both our sakes. Do as I tell you, and all will go well."

McGarrity waited for Hunter to explain, and when he was done, added his thanks for ensuring his men safe passage.

Once the extra troopers were dismissed, the mounting up began in earnest. The Indians sprang onto their horses. Anderson walked up beside the wagon to give a few last-minute instructions to the drivers.

Drew Reynolds mounted up, lingering at the head of his party while Cass and Meggie said good-bye.

Hunter tried very hard not to watch them, but couldn't seem to help himself.

Cass lifted Meggie up to her father for a final hug.

"You be good for Cassie," he admonished her.

"I will, Papa," the little girl promised.

"You be careful, Drew," Cass murmured, handing him a lumpy bundle of food to eat along the way.

Hunter would have sold his soul to have her bring him a rumpled bandanna of corn cake and biscuits.

"I'll be as safe on the way to Fort Laramie as I'd be in a featherbed," Drew assured her, and reached down to stroke the thick, glossy strands of her honey brown hair.

Even from this distance Hunter could see that Reynolds's eyes were warm and his touch gentle. That simple gesture made Hunter's throat rasp and his chest burn as if he'd been breathing trail dust for a week. Cursing his own stupidity, he turned away.

Up ahead, Lieutenant Anderson was swinging into the saddle. Hunter followed suit, taking special care with the standard Man-Afraid-of-His-Horse had given him. His roan danced a little with an impatience Hunter understood all too well. He couldn't wait to leave the fort.

In a cacophony of thumping hooves, creaking leather, and squeaky wheels, both parties pulled away. Reynolds's headed east toward Fort Laramie. Anderson's turned north toward the Powder River country. Hunter followed the wagon toward the bridge, but instead of just riding away, he made the mistake of looking back.

At the base of the headquarters steps Cass and Meggie stood waving and waving as if the captain might actually take a moment from his duties and wave back.

Chapter Thirteen

❋

"There, Lieutenant Anderson," Hunter said, pulling his horse to a halt at the top of the rise, "is the Powder River basin. Depending on who you believe, there are between five hundred and a thousand Sioux, Cheyenne, and Arapaho warriors waiting out there for a chance at us."

Beside him, the young lieutenant stared openmouthed.

Spread out across a shallow gold-and-green valley was the first of three Indian encampments. This one, Man-Afraid-of-His-Horse's compound, was neat, well kept, and comprised of nearly a hundred lodges laid out along the banks of a rippling creek. Smoke streamed upward from dozens of campfires. Vast herds of Indian ponies grazed on the thick, deep grass that carpeted the rising land beyond the camp.

It was an impressive sight, yet instead of reading the signs and evaluating the village, Hunter found himself seeking out shapes and colors and configurations he remembered from when he was young. He found himself recalling the smell of sage sprinkled into a campfire, the tepees glowing in the dusk, and the pulse of distant drums.

His heartbeat quickened as if he were coming home, but Lone Hunter was well aware that no Arikara was welcome among the Sioux, nor any army scout.

Mastering a surge of feeling he refused to name, Hunter

reached for his handkerchief and tied it to the top of the feathered standard Man-Afraid-of-His-Horse had given him. He raised the staff until the crisp, white cloth fluttered in the breeze.

The heat of the sun lay heavy across his shoulders, the sky shone flax-flower blue, and the wind tasted sweet. *It is a very good day to die,* he thought, and motioned the others to follow him.

As they rode nearer, Hunter spotted older boys clustered here and there across the plain guarding the compound's horses. He noticed women washing their clothes and bathing their children in the stream. He saw steam boiling out of the sweat lodge—which meant that the men were here and not off raiding. The camp dogs announced their arrival, and by the time they reached the central campfire, one of the subchiefs was there to greet them.

Hunter swung down from his horse and addressed him. "I am Lone Hunter, Arikara scout for the army, and this is Lieutenant John Anderson. We have been sent by Man-Afraid-of-His-Horse and Major Benjamin McGarrity with supplies from Fort Carr."

"I am Beaded Blanket," the subchief answered. "I see by the standard you carry that it is Man-Afraid-of-His-Horse who grants you passage."

"Man-Afraid-of-His-Horse spoke of your need for food," Hunter told him, "and we have come to help."

"And just where is Man-Afraid-of-His-Horse while you are here?" Beaded Blanket asked suspiciously.

"Man-Afraid-of-His-Horse has gone to Fort Laramie," Hunter answered, "to secure powder and shot for the buffalo hunt."

A murmur ran through the crowd, and one of the men stepped forward. Judging by his clothes and the feathers in his hair, he was another of the lesser chiefs. "Do you mean there is no ammunition in the wagon?" he demanded.

"By order of the army chief in Omaha, neither the traders nor the military can give ammunition to the Indians," Hunter explained. "No whites may go against his word."

Beaded Blanket curled his lip in derision. "Then why has

Man-Afraid-of-His-Horse gone to Fort Laramie?''

''He believes he can convince Colonel Palmer to change the big chief's mind.''

If these men did not believe him, if they thought that Man-Afraid-of-His-Horse had been killed or was being held against his will, he and these soldiers were as good as dead. They would be overpowered, stripped, and beaten, and would die by torture.

Beaded Blanket drew several of the other men aside to measure the truth of his words.

Sweat crawled down Hunter's ribs as they waited. His palm itched for the feel of his revolver, yet he did not move. The chiefs talked for what seemed a very long time.

''We will accept these supplies,'' Beaded Blanket finally agreed. ''We will give you and your men a place to sleep tonight, and you must leave when the sun comes into the sky.''

That didn't leave much time to reconnoiter, Hunter thought. ''Man-Afraid-of-His-Horse asked me to oversee the distribution of these supplies between this camp, Red Cloud's camp, and the Cheyenne camp of Buffalo Tongue,'' Hunter said.

Beaded Blanket seemed both startled and aggrieved by the request. ''But we have always seen to the equal distribution of goods.''

Hunter shook his head as if in confusion. ''Man-Afraid-of-His-Horse asked me to see to it myself—and I gave my word.''

Beaded Blanket clearly did not want to go against the peace chief's wishes and sought the counsel of the other warriors in a single glance.

''Then you alone may ride to the other camps,'' he decided.

It was more than Hunter had dared to hope for.

They spent the next hour dividing up the goods. When they were done, a tall solemn squaw showed them to a tepee. It was impersonally furnished, without woven rugs and animal skins on the floor, without an embroidered tent liner or colorful parfleches piled between the cots. Still, only Hunter missed the niceties. The others were astonished at how solid and snug the tepee seemed.

While the lieutenant and his troopers settled in, Hunter set off across the compound. By the shields displayed outside the tepees and the paintings of valorous deeds painted on their sides, he saw that many of the men were seasoned warriors. Still, there were no signs of martial activity. No stockpiles of food and arrows, no evidence of military training, no groups telling tales of glory or discussing tactics.

After he had walked the camp from end to end, Hunter sought admission to the sweat lodge, knowing that as an emissary of Man-Afraid-of-His-Horse, he would not be refused. Once inside, he made himself as inconspicuous as possible and listened to the men discussing village business. Though warriors from this encampment had probably been involved in the attacks on the Bozeman Trail and in the Fetterman massacre the winter before, their views were much like the ones Man-Afraid-of-His-Horse had expressed at Fort Carr. They wanted to find a way to maintain their way of life and live in peace. Since Red Cloud was the war chief, Hunter expected that the views expressed in his camp would be quite different.

Clean from his visit to the sweat lodge and a swim in the stream, Hunter returned to the tepee and found that the four of them had been invited to Beaded Blanket's lodge for the evening meal. They arrived at the appointed hour with their bowls and spoons. Following Hunter's lead, Lieutenant Anderson and his men entered the tepee, greeted their host, and seated themselves to the right of the door.

Beaded Blanket's wife served each of them strips of roasted antelope, a spicy stew, corn bread, boiled greens, and pemmican. The soldiers comported themselves like gentlemen, finishing every bite of their dinner and waiting politely for their host to light his pipe.

They smoked with him and spoke of inconsequential things. One of the troopers had a fine tenor voice, and Hunter suggested he sing since most Indians enjoyed the complex melodies of the white man's music.

When he and the others had offered their thanks and rose

to go, Beaded Blanket spoke to Hunter softly. "You will be ready when the sun comes up. The camps are near at hand, but it will take most of the day to distribute the goods."

Hunter was the only one of the four who slept soundly that night, and he was waiting at the wagon when Beaded Blanket and the others gathered just after dawn.

At Buffalo Tongue's Cheyenne village the chief accepted the goods with equanimity, but in Red Cloud's camp the warriors greeted the army's generosity with skepticism. Though he had very little chance to look around, Hunter saw that older men were painting their war shields and making arrows. The younger ones were practicing their fighting skills. Goods and weapons, which as far as Hunter could see included powder and shot, were stockpiled in tents on the north side of the camp. Hunter would have bet half of next year's pay that most of those supplies had come through licensed traders. But which ones? Hunter wondered. Who was making his fortune selling contraband?

Hunter had barely returned to Beaded Blanket's camp when Lieutenant Anderson came to him with something that verified his suspicions: a small tin can that had held condensed milk.

"They wouldn't have gotten that through the usual sources, would they, Mr. Jalbert?" the young lieutenant asked him, an edge of excitement to his voice. "It would have had to come from illegal trade."

"I suppose it would," Hunter answered, working at the label with his knife. "There seems to be some kind of stamp down in the corner. Maybe that will tell us where this milk came from."

And who's been trading illegally with the Sioux and Cheyenne.

Though the can had been used to mix the thick, viscous glue that the Indians boiled from buffalo hooves, Hunter managed to get the label off intact.

"I'll take this to Major McGarrity, and maybe with the information we get from it he can cut off the flow of contraband."

"Now, have whoever took this put it back. We don't want the Sioux to think we stole it."

Fort Laramie was very much as Drew remembered. Built on a rise at the junction of the Laramie and the North Platte Rivers, the installation was comprised of a dozen clapboard buildings organized around a rectangular parade ground. A dozen more buildings—mostly stables, storage sheds, and craftsmen's shops—lay off to the north. The post hospital where Laura died was off that way, too, as was the cemetery where she was buried. As they rode past, Drew glanced toward her grave and promised himself he'd come back to pay his respects. As much as it rankled him, Man-Afraid-of-His-Horse took priority. He had to be taken directly to Colonel Palmer.

They pulled their horses to a stop outside the graceful two-storied building known affectionately as Old Bedlam, where the commander kept an office on the first floor. As they dismounted, one of the colonel's staff officers sauntered out to greet them.

"Good afternoon, Lieutenant," Drew said, smartly answering the man's salute in spite of being stiff and saddle weary. "I'm Captain Drew Reynolds, and I'm acting as escort to Man-Afraid-of-His-Horse on orders from Major McGarrity at Fort Carr. Man-Afraid-of-His-Horse wishes to confer with Colonel Palmer at his earliest convenience."

"Indeed?" the lieutenant asked with a lift of his brows. "And just what business does this redskin wish to discuss?"

"I believe that is between the colonel and Man-Afraid-of-His-Horse," Drew answered.

The lieutenant gave a self-important sniff. "Colonel Palmer has very little time to chat with hostiles."

Drew had dealt with more than his share of supercilious staff officers during the war and skewered the man with a single glance. "You don't have any idea who this man is, do you, Lieutenant?"

"No, sir, I don't," the lieutenant answered. "And I'm not sure I care to learn."

Drew's anger flared like a bonfire in high wind. He was

tired and hungry and hot. He'd been passed over for a plum assignment and given duty he abhorred. It bothered him even more to have to take the Indians' part against some junior officer whom Drew both outclassed and outranked.

"Well, you damn well better learn, Lieutenant," he said, his voice ominously low. "Man-Afraid-of-His-Horse is the peace chief to the Oglala Sioux. He's a man the army needs to cultivate. He could make the difference between a peaceful summer and one that's drenched in blood. So I suggest you take your tail in there, Lieutenant, and inform Colonel Palmer that he has an important visitor.

"Or," he continued, holding the man immobile with the threat in his eyes, "you can direct us to quarters, and we'll wait to have our discussions with those peace commissioners I keep hearing about."

"Oh, Mr. Beauvais and Mr. Sanborne have already arrived," the lieutenant volunteered.

"Have they now?" Drew asked silkily. "Then dispatch someone to let them know that Man-Afraid-of-His-Horse has come to talk. That is what they're here to do, isn't it?"

"As you say, sir," the staff officer relented, and spun away.

Drew escorted Man-Afraid-of-His-Horse and his two companions to benches on Old Bedlam's wide, inviting porch. It wasn't long before Colonel Innis Palmer came out to greet them. The peace commissioners arrived soon after, panting for breath and trailing a translator, a secretary, and several junior officers.

With the situation well in hand, Drew slipped away to billet his men for the night. Drew supposed that either peace talks or negotiations for ammunition would begin in earnest the next day, and since he had no part in those, he meant to leave for Fort Carr in the morning.

As good as his word, Drew climbed the rise behind the hospital just after daybreak and sought out the spot where his first wife lay. He stood over the grave with hat in hand, suddenly regretting that he hadn't thought to bring flowers.

Laura had always liked flowers. She'd liked the novels of Sir Walter Scott, rustling silk dresses, playing chess, and sitting on the veranda in the shade. What else had she liked? Drew couldn't quite remember.

He stared at the neat wooden marker and wondered what he was supposed to feel. The single time he'd gone to where the troopers had buried his parents, the memories and the hatred had torn holes in him. He'd stood there sobbing like a child, shaking and cursing and vowing revenge. He'd left that canyon changed, devoted and impregnable.

Now he looked to where Laura lay and felt not loss, not grief, but betrayal. He had come to the fort as a married man and left a widower, come with a child and left with a responsibility. If Laura had lived, if she'd had relatives he could have sent Meggie to back in the States, he wouldn't be caught like this: saddled with a daughter he cared for but didn't understand, shackled to a woman he both loved and hated, or bound in a marriage that compromised everything he believed. If Laura had lived, he wouldn't be trapped between his responsibilities to the world of the living and the vows he'd made to the dead.

The wind picked up, ruffling Drew's hair, whipping his uniform tunic against his legs. He shivered a little in spite of the growing warmth of the morning sun.

It was lonely here. Quiet and peaceful, but lonely. As lonely as he felt sometimes when he watched Cassandra and Meggie playing together. As lonely as when he awoke from dreams of the massacre and found Cassie sleeping beside him. As lonely as he was when he painted the life and the people he'd lost. As lonely as . . .

Drew tried not to complete the thought, but his innate honesty wouldn't let him deny it. *As lonely as a man who wanted to love and couldn't let himself.*

Drew took a long, last look at his first wife's grave and knew she couldn't help him. Even when she was alive, she hadn't been able to help him.

He hadn't been able to help himself.

"Good-bye, Laura," Drew said quietly, and walked away.

Drew spotted the man as they topped the rise, a lone rider driving a herd of horses and mules. Even from this distance he could see that the man was an Indian. He wore leggings and a breechclout and rode as all the Indians did, as if he were part of his animal.

For a moment, Drew simply watched him driving the herd with nothing more than the wave of a rope and the cantering of his own horse, flowing with the same rhythm and gait as his thick-chested mount. There was poetry in the motion of the horseflesh, in the thick tan swirls of rising dust, and the play of light and shadow.

I'd like to paint this, Drew thought.

In the meantime, the Indian had driven his horses nearer.

Drew pulled out his pocket telescope and scanned the surrounding landscape. Though there was no sign of other hostiles, it paid to be wary. Once he had satisfied himself that the man was alone, he trained the telescope on the herd. He was looking for brands, proof that this redskin had stolen at least some of his stock. What Drew began to realize was that each of the animals was marked—marked with the "US" brand. This Indian had been stealing exclusively from the army!

For a moment Drew was stunned by the man's audacity, and then he laughed.

"Horse thief!" he shouted to the men drawn up behind him, and gestured to the Indian in the basin below.

That single word served as both order and condemnation. The troopers surged past him in a cloud of dust. Drew watched them charge down the rise. Half a dozen broke to the right of the Indian and his herd, while the rest rode around to the left. Drew galloped after them, howling with exhilaration.

The redskin spotted the soldiers and maneuvered his herd to the south, trying to snake beyond them. But no single man could offset the control of a dozen riders. The soldiers turned the horses, driving them in tighter and tighter circles.

Realizing the herd was lost, the Indian broke for the north like one possessed. Sergeant O'Hearn and Corporal Stockman lit out after him. The three of them thundered past to Drew's right, and after sparing one quick glance at where the rest of the troopers were balling the herd, he spurred his own mount after them.

The Indian was sprawled facedown in the dust with Stockman's boot between his shoulder blades when Drew caught up.

He dismounted on the fly. "Let him go," he ordered.

He pulled out his revolver and jerked the Indian to his feet. "Where did you get those horses?"

The Indian stared back, all tensed muscles and black-eyed fury.

"I want to know where those horses came from," Drew shouted as if the man were only being obstinate.

The brave made no reply.

"You want me to try some hand talk, sir?" O'Hearn offered.

Drew nodded grimly and watched as the sergeant made a series of gestures. The buck answered back.

"He says he rounded up some strays."

Drew gave a snort of laughter. "I'd be a damn sight more convinced if he told me those horses came in the overland mail."

The brave strung together a series of angry gestures.

"He says he heard that the army was paying a bounty for the return of their stock," O'Hearn translated. "He says he was headed for Fort Laramie to trade the horses back and collect his money."

"And a very nice business that could be for such an enterprising fellow," Drew observed.

"He says," Sergeant O'Hearn paused to watch the Indian's hands, "that he got most of the horses from a village of Arapaho up north. He says he'll show us where it is if we let him go."

"He can make that offer to Major McGarrity when we get back to Fort Carr this afternoon," Drew said with a nod. "In the meantime, tie his hands and put him on the back of one of the troopers' horses. I hear the hostiles teach their ponies tricks, and I don't want this one getting away from us."

Stockman did as he'd been bid, while Sergeant O'Hearn wound the Indian pony's bridle around his hand. "Do you believe what that young buck says about them paying a bounty for army animals?'' O'Hearn asked.

''I'll believe what a redskin tells me, Sergeant, only when I see pigs fly.''

Chapter Fourteen

"The government's mark is on the back of the label," Hunter insisted, bending over Ben McGarrity's desk and pointing to a stamped impression in the shape of an eagle. "It means that can of milk came from one of the licensed traders."

McGarrity moved the paper closer to the lit lamp and nodded. "And you think one of those men is trading with the Sioux illegally?"

"Condensed milk is too expensive to be on the list of approved trade goods," Hunter said, "yet this can got to the encampment somehow. Whoever traded it is probably trading for other things—like arms and ammunition."

"Like the cache you discovered in Red Cloud's village." The major sat silent for a moment. "And you think this second mark, this horseshoe, will tell us who the trader is?"

"Yes, I do."

"But why would any trader put his mark on contraband?"

"It might have been put there by mistake," Hunter suggested. "Or he might figure the odds of someone tracking down a single can of milk were pretty long ones."

McGarrity nodded and rubbed at his beard. "I'll have someone go fetch Jessup. He's probably more familiar with the traders' marks than anyone."

Tyler Jessup took his own sweet time answering Major

McGarrity's summons. When he finally made his way into the office, he was all bristle and blather.

"I don't see why you have to take a man away from his work to answer some damn question," he complained. "Now that the weather's better, the wagons are coming through thick and fast, and with the money freed up at payday, I'm down-right busy. I can't afford to have the store locked up for long, so you better tell me what's so all-fired important."

Hunter had seen McGarrity chew up far fiercer men than Jessup and sat back to enjoy the fireworks.

"Well now, Mr. Jessup," McGarrity drawled. "You're here in this fort at the behest of the U.S. Army in general and me in particular. You set your hours by my clock and the poker game in your back room goes on because I choose to look the other way. Don't you forget for a moment how all this works." McGarrity cleared his throat. "Now since we have that clarified, Mr. Jalbert and I have need of your expertise."

Jessup scowled in consternation, knowing he was caught.

"I have the label from a can of milk," McGarrity began to explain, "that was stamped and sold by one of the licensed traders. But on closer inspection, we discovered there's a second stamp."

"It's how we know whose goods are whose when they're shipped west," the sutler volunteered. "Each of us has a different mark."

"Then I would like you to identify the trader who handled this particular can." McGarrity handed the label across his desk and turned up the wick on the lamp.

"You get this up in Indian country?" the sutler asked. It wasn't a particularly inspired guess; everyone at the fort knew where Hunter had been.

"Well, damn!" Jessup exclaimed when McGarrity inclined his head. "I knew she was up to something when I sold her that milk."

"This is your mark?" the major asked. "This horseshoe?"

"It sure enough is," Jessup confirmed. "My mam used to call me 'Lucky' 'cause she won a big bet on a horse race the day I was born. I been using that horseshoe to mark things all my life."

"And how could you possibly remember who bought this particular can of milk?" the major wanted to know.

"I remember 'cause she bought 'em all. Eighteen cans."

"And who was that?" Hunter asked, his patience wearing thin.

Jessup grinned, knowing he was about to offer up someone's future. "That squaw woman."

"Squaw woman?"

"The one Captain Reynolds married."

Hunter's stomach pitched. "Cass Reynolds?"

"What would Mrs. Reynolds want with eighteen cans of milk?" McGarrity asked, glancing across first at Jessup and then at him.

Considering where he'd found this, the answer seemed obvious.

"Your West Point perfect captain knew about it, too." Jessup was taking a shine to the role of informant. "Reynolds came in on payday and chewed my head off over that bill. I told him then exactly what I'm telling you."

Hunter narrowed his eyes. He didn't doubt Jessup's word; the man was having too much fun causing trouble to have made this up.

Still, it didn't make sense. Hunter knew just how hard Cass was trying to be a good wife to the captain. Why would she deliberately jeopardize his position and her own by selling unauthorized goods to the Indians?

"You going to arrest that gal?" Jessup prodded McGarrity. "She's not to be trusted, not with that heathen mark of hers. Light-fingered, she is, too. She tried to steal from me when she first come. Could be spying for them redskins."

Anger flared in McGarrity's eyes. "We don't condemn people out of hand here, Mr. Jessup. If Mrs. Reynolds sold that milk to the Indians, there must be an explanation for it."

"Explanation, shit! She's a bad one. I knew it the first time I clapped eyes on her." When neither he nor McGarrity jumped on the bait, Jessup shoved to his feet. "So am I done? Can I get on back to my store?"

The major nodded, and Jessup left.

Hunter folded up in Jessup's chair, grappling with the sutler's revelations. McGarrity looked nearly as confused as he felt.

"It isn't possible Cassandra is more than she claims, is it? The Cheyenne didn't send her back to inform on us, did they?"

Hunter shook his head. "You know as well as I do that Cass is no spy, but it looks as if she's the one who gave the Indians milk. We're going to have to question her—"

"Major?" One of the orderlies knocked on the door to McGarrity's office and poked his head inside. "Captain Reynolds just rode into the fort, and it appears he's got a prisoner."

From the moment he turned his ambition to soldiering, Drew Reynolds had imagined a time when he and his men would ride back to their fort battered, victorious, and covered in glory. Returning with a single prisoner and a herd of rustled horses wasn't everything he'd dreamed about, but they'd recovered more than two dozen head of army stock and caught the redskin who stole them dead to rights. If he hadn't been all trussed up in military regulations, Drew would have hanged the thieving bastard on the spot.

He rode right up to headquarters with his prisoner in tow. He needed a sip of satisfaction after all the months of waiting to fight, and he intended to help himself to it.

Drew dismounted, tightened his fists in the Indian's clothes, and dragged him off his horse. The man's hands were bound behind him, and he fell facedown in the dirt. Drew grabbed the redskin's shoulders and hauled him to his feet just as Major McGarrity strode out the door and onto the porch.

"What's all this?" he demanded.

"My men and I caught a horse thief, sir, on our way back from Fort Laramie," Drew reported. "He had about two dozen head of army horses and mules and hadn't even bothered to doctor the brands. There's no telling where he stole them or how many soldiers he killed to do it."

McGarrity nodded in approval. "Good work, Captain

Reynolds,'' he said, ''but if I'm not mistaken, most of the stock the army loses is run off while it's grazing. Let's not make this worse than it is.''

Drew felt the color come up in his face. ''This man's still a rustler, sir.''

McGarrity acknowledged his point and turned to the Indian. ''And what do you have to say for yourself?''

When the thief didn't answer, Jalbert stepped up to take his part. ''I think he's Arikara, sir, and may not speak any English.''

''Arikara?'' the major echoed, his brows rising in surprise. ''What's one of your people doing this far south?''

''The tribe has been pretty much displaced by stronger neighbors,'' Jalbert answered.

''By the Sioux, you mean.''

Jalbert nodded. ''The tribes are old enemies. With settlers moving west along the Missouri River, they're rubbing against each other more than usual. When there's a confrontation, it's the Arikara who usually get the brunt of it. Let me see what I can find out.''

While the half-breed and the prisoner spouted gibberish, Drew swatted the dust from his hat and uniform and mopped the sweat off his face with the back of his arm. He was surprised how good it felt to get back to the rough-hewn cabins and more demanding duty. Being at Fort Laramie had unsettled him in a way he couldn't quite explain. It made him feel ineffective and isolated, as if army life weren't quite as satisfying as it had always been.

Jalbert concluded his conversation with the Indian prisoner. ''Many Buffalo is an Arikara who came south to see about signing on as a scout,'' Jalbert told them. ''Somewhere along the way he heard that the army was paying a bounty to anyone who returned their stolen animals.''

''That isn't true, is it?'' Drew demanded, already beginning to see the trend of the Indian's lies.

''Not that I've heard,'' McGarrity answered. ''But there's no telling what some post commander low on horses may have offered.''

''Whether it's true or not,'' Jalbert went on, ''Many Buffalo saw it as an opportunity to earn some money and endear himself to his prospective employer. He says he stole the horses and mules from a small band of Arapaho camped up near Lodgepole Creek. He was driving the herd to Fort Laramie in hope of collecting the bounty and signing on with Major North's scouts."

"If all that's true," Drew challenged, "why did he run when he saw us coming?"

"Wouldn't you have run if you were him?"

Goddamn Jalbert for taking the Indian's part. Drew could feel his face get hot again. "Certainly I would run if I were a horse thief caught red-handed."

"There will have to be a hearing in either case," McGarrity broke in. "We'll call it for eleven o'clock tomorrow. In the meantime, corporal"—McGarrity motioned one of the orderlies forward—"lock this man in the guardhouse."

As Jalbert translated, panic flared in his prisoner's eyes. Drew had heard redskins hated being locked up, but it took a corporal and two privates dragging him to get Many Buffalo the length of the parade ground into the guardhouse.

Drew had just gathered up the reins of his horse to leave when a towheaded fireball came charging across the parade ground toward him.

"Papa!" Meggie shrieked, throwing herself against him and wrapping her arms around his waist. "Papa! You've been gone so long!"

Drew grinned and caught his daughter up in his arms. Laughing, he bussed her on the cheek and suffered through a neck-snapping hug.

"We made rabbit-fur slippers while you were gone," she declared. "And frosted fried cakes. And built a bed for my dolly out of sticks."

Drew looked up and saw Cassie watching them. His belly suddenly buzzed with uneasiness and his palms were damp inside his leather gauntlets.

"I'm glad you both managed to keep busy. I thought about you and wondered what you were doing."

He extended his hand to Cassie, and she came toward him

across the dusty grass. She smiled, tentative and almost hopeful.

"Reynolds?" Major McGarrity's voice shattered the faint connection he and Cassie had made. "I know you must be eager to spend time with your family after being away, but there's something we need to discuss." He hesitated ominously. "Would you and Cassandra step into my office?"

Drew felt Cassie stiffen beside him. There was something in her eyes—dread or uncertainty or maybe even guilt—that turned the pleasure of his return to towering apprehension. Still, he acknowledged the order with a nod and guided Cassie up the steps.

Cassie handed Meggie off to one of the orderlies in the anteroom and followed Drew into McGarrity's office, uneasiness swarming over her like ants. When Hunter followed them inside and closed the door, the air in her lungs went cold and thin.

McGarrity motioned her and Drew to the chairs before his desk and settled himself behind it. "Jalbert has just returned from the Sioux and Cheyenne camps up along the Powder River," the major began. "While he was there he discovered something that seemed quite odd."

"Odd?" Drew asked.

He didn't seem to know what McGarrity was referring to, but Cassie had begun to suspect.

"Jalbert found a can of condensed milk that appears to be from one of the licensed traders," McGarrity enlightened them.

Cassie's face flushed with guilt.

"Condensed milk?" Drew asked as if he were genuinely confused. "What's so odd about that? Aren't goods traded to the Indians all the time?"

Drew was being noble. He was trying to protect her. Cassandra warmed all the way down to her toes just knowing that.

"Goods that are sent as annuities go through the Indian agents," McGarrity explained. "Things we send directly are from the commissary department. Both are distinctly marked.

Things that come from the licensed traders are marked, too, so they can be regulated.''

''It isn't as if we're talking about someone providing the Indians with guns or whiskey or ammunition,'' Drew argued reasonably. ''We're talking about milk . . .''

''Where there are cans of contraband milk,'' Hunter put in, ''there might well be other things.''

''It's something we have to investigate,'' McGarrity added.

Cassie knew what they were driving at and couldn't let Drew jeopardize his position here at the fort. She had to own up to what she'd done.

''I bought eighteen cans of condensed milk at the sutler's store'' she admitted, ''and gave them to one of the Indian women.''

Neither Hunter nor Major McGarrity seemed surprised by her admission.

''But why did you give an Indian woman milk?'' Hunter asked her. ''Didn't you know what you were doing was wrong?''

Cassie turned to look at him, surprised that what Hunter thought of her mattered so much.

''I knew I wasn't supposed to buy the milk,'' she admitted. ''I knew I was wrong to give it to Runs Like a Doe, but she came to me and told me her sister's baby would die without it. She asked if I could help her, and after all she'd done for me when I was a captive, I couldn't refuse.''

It had been a woman's transaction, based on things far too simple for men to understand.

''Did you give her anything but the milk?'' McGarrity asked.

Cassie shook her head.

''Did she ask for anything else?''

''Nothing at all.''

''Canned milk is expensive,'' he went on. ''How did you pay for eighteen cans of it?''

''I charged them to Drew's account.''

McGarrity shifted his gaze to Drew. ''And why didn't you report this, Captain Reynolds?''

Cassie spoke up before Drew could answer. ''He didn't

know about the milk until the bill came due. I'd bought and given it to Runs Like a Doe weeks before."

"But how did a can of contraband milk get from a Cheyenne woman to the Sioux encampment?" Hunter asked her.

Cassie looked from one man to the other. "I don't know. Sometimes the villages get together for a hunt or a feast." She realized that wasn't the explanation Hunter was looking for, but it was the best she could do.

McGarrity rubbed his beard and glanced at Hunter. "What do you think?"

Hunter shrugged and hunkered down next to Cassie's chair. "It's important that the army and the Bureau of Indian Affairs control what goods make their way to the tribes. You understand that, don't you?"

Cassie didn't see the sense in such control, but nodded anyway.

"Then give the major your word you won't pass supplies to the Cheyenne again."

It was the promise Drew had demanded of her a week or more before. She did what she'd done then; she lied to them.

"I won't," she said.

The major shifted uneasily before he went on. "You haven't seen anyone else you recognize here at the fort, have you, Cassandra? You haven't spoken to them or passed on information?"

Drew shoved to his feet beside her. "For God's sake, Ben, she doesn't pass on information! Nor will she. Nor will I. Nor will Meggie, for that matter. Are you satisfied?"

Cassie stared at him, surprised by the intensity of his defense.

McGarrity made a conciliatory gesture. "They are questions that need to be asked. You know that as well as I do."

"I won't tell anyone anything," Cassie promised, and meant it.

McGarrity drew a breath and nodded, still obviously troubled but satisfied.

"May we go now?" Drew asked his commanding officer. "I've been riding since well before sunup. I caught and delivered a horse thief and nearly thirty head of stock. And frankly, I'm tired."

He pulled Cassie to her feet.

"I'm sorry about this, Reynolds," McGarrity said.

Drew didn't reply, just eased Cassie toward the door.

"Don't forget I'll need you for the hearing tomorrow," the major reminded him. "That's another matter entirely."

Cassie saw Drew turn and give McGarrity a long, withering glance. "Oh, I'll be there to testify, sir. I'll be there to hear the verdict, too. And then, when all's said and done, I'll be there to watch that redskin hang."

Chapter Fifteen

News traveled fast. Gossip traveled faster. By noon the next day word that Cassie had been providing the hostiles with contraband had circulated through the fort. She could tell by the way the soldiers watched her, the way Alma Parker and Sylvie Noonan glared when they passed by. Two children had thrown stones at Meggie and her, and even Sally McGarrity's "good morning" had been decidedly chilly.

Cassie couldn't figure out how everyone knew. There had been four of them in that office. Drew was too ashamed of what she'd done to speak of it. Hunter would never say a word. And while the major might have told his wife about the milk, Sally didn't gossip.

Who else could have known?

Jessup. The man who refused to understand when she'd stolen those embroidery scissors. The man who persisted in calling her "that squaw woman."

Jessup must have been questioned about the milk. He must have identified the marks on the can and told Hunter and Major McGarrity who bought it. Now Jessup was spreading the story—and what better place for him to do that than in his own store.

She would have thought that everyone was too caught up in the hearing for the horse thief Drew had brought in to bother much with her. That didn't seem to be the way of it.

She and Meggie were hauling buckets from the water wagon when they all but collided with Lila Wilcox and her son. Since Lila knew everything that went on at the fort, she'd know about this. Cassie held her breath, waiting for Lila's reaction.

Lila grinned and propped a rough-skinned hand on one wide hip. "You sure do keep things stirred up, don't you, girl!"

"I had my reasons for doing what I did!" Cass spoke up, instinctively defending herself.

Lila laughed. "I'll bet money you did. But before you explain, meet my boy Josh."

Lila turned to where a gangly man in his early twenties stood hefting a loaded wash basket in either arm. "Corporal Josh Wilcox, this here is Captain Reynolds's wife Cassandra."

"Ma'am." Josh nodded, in no position to doff his cap.

"I'm pleased to meet you, Corporal," Cassie said.

"Hello, Josh." Meggie tugged on the cuff of Josh's jacket, determined not to be ignored. "Do you have time to play that walnut shell game with me?"

Josh gave Meggie a smile that lit his face and made him look remarkably like his mother. "Right now I've got these baskets of laundry to take to Ma's cabin, but when I'm done—"

"You're not neglecting your duties, are you, boy?"

"No, ma'am," Josh answered his mother. "I told you I just finished up with my fatigue duty and don't need to be anyplace special till evening mess."

"Good enough, then." Lila nodded. "Why don't you take Meggie with you and stop by Captain Reynolds's when you're done."

The two women watched them go, the tiny, fair-haired child running to keep up with Josh's long strides.

"He still seems like such a boy to me," Lila said with a sigh. "Too young to be serving his country the way he does."

"You have every right to be proud of him."

Lila smiled to acknowledge that mother's pride and took one of the buckets Cassie was carrying.

"I've been hearing Jessup's story this whole damned day. Since you're not denying it, I figured I'd better get your side of things."

"Has Jessup said what I gave the Cheyenne?" Cassie asked.

"Contraband," Lila told her. "Most folks figure that means whiskey or guns or ammunition."

"I gave them milk."

"Milk?"

"Eighteen cans of condensed milk."

"Well—well, damn Jessup's eyes!" Lila sputtered. "I suppose canned milk *is* contraband."

Cass climbed the steps to the cabin. "I want to tell you what happened, so you can judge for yourself."

Once they were settled at the table over cups of fresh-brewed tea, Cass began to talk. "When I first came to the Cheyenne village with my new husband," she began, "I didn't know either the Cheyenne language or Cheyenne customs. Since I had lived as a slave to the Kiowa, I didn't know what was expected of a wife or how to keep a warrior's home.

"Two sisters in the village took it upon themselves to befriend me and teach me everything I needed to know. Blue Flower was newly married, too, so we often did our chores together. We dug roots, picked berries and herbs, or gathered wood almost every day. Runs Like a Doe, the older sister, showed me her secrets for tanning the softest skins. She taught me how to make things from the skins and took me to the quilling and beading society."

"Sounds like they gave you a world of help when you needed it most," Lila said around a sip of tea.

"That's why I couldn't refuse when Runs Like a Doe came to see me two months ago. She said that Blue Flower had given birth to a son, but she had no milk."

"That happens sometimes."

"Though they had done everything they could to save the baby, he was growing weaker every day. Finally Runs Like a Doe decided to come to see if I was able to get them milk in cans. It was a debt of kindness I was glad to pay, so I bought the milk. I gave it to her so a child would live. It wasn't wrong to do that, was it, Lila?"

The older woman reached across and patted Cassie's arm. "Of course you weren't wrong. Saving any child, white or Indian, is never wrong."

Cassie's chest filled with gratitude.

"Still," Lila went on, a frown knitting her brows, "you need to make sure folks know the contraband you gave the Indians is only milk."

"But how can I do that? Not a soul at this fort speaks to me but you and Drew and Sally."

"I'll do what I can to spread the word," Lila promised.

"And I suppose I'll have to face up to Tyler Jessup." But Cassie was hardly prepared to confront the man. For the last nine years she'd submitted; she'd stayed alive by submitting. How could she find the courage to stand up to Jessup and a fort full of people ready to condemn her?

"You want me to go with you to Jessup's store?" Lila asked.

Cass was tempted but refused. "I have to do this by myself. But thank you for offering, Lila. And thank you for your friendship."

The laundress's ruddy face turned a few shades darker. "Posh, girl! You didn't think I'd throw Miss Meggie's mother to the wolves, now, did you?"

Miss Meggie's mother. That wasn't who she was, but Cassie was glad Lila thought of her that way.

Just then, Josh came stumbling through the kitchen door. Meggie was riding him piggyback and howling with delight. Josh backed up, settled her on the end of the table, then stood to tug his uniform back in place.

"That's a damn undignified thing for a United States Army corporal to be doing," Lila scolded.

"Aw, Ma," he answered, blushing in a way that made him look barely old enough to sign enlistment papers. "We were just funning."

"And guess what!" Meggie burst out. "I won three whole pennies playing that walnut game with Josh and his friends."

"Three whole cents," Cassie echoed, shooting Josh a quelling glance.

"I've never seen the like, Ma!" Josh exclaimed. "She picked the right shell every damned—beg pardon, ma'am—every time."

"That's all well and good, son," his mother said, "but I don't think Captain Reynolds would approve of you teaching his daughter *to gamble.*"

Josh's eyes widened. "Oh, I take your point, Ma!"

"And can we go up to the store?" Meggie asked. "I have three whole cents of my own, and I want to buy something."

Cassie's throat went tight. That store was the last place in the world she wanted to go.

"What is it you want that can't wait until later?"

"I want some peppermint drops. The kind Amy Noonan gave me when we were playing."

Cassie sighed, knowing Meggie's stubbornness and recognizing eventual defeat. "You won't need more than a penny for those. Go put the rest of the money away."

"In the rabbit-skin bag?"

"That would be fine."

While Meggie was gone, Lila climbed to her feet. "I'll do what I can to set things straight, but you need to talk to Jessup. And the more people who hear about that milk, the better things will go for you."

Though she knew Lila was right, Cass's hands were shaking as she tidied her hair and tied her bonnet.

The sutler's trading post was busy in midafternoon. More than half a dozen troopers were picking up the essentials the army didn't provide: like soap and bootblack and tobacco. A number of civilians were browsing, people on the Overland Trail who'd stopped for supplies. Several muleteers, a few men dressed in buckskin and fur, and a handful of Indians were buying this and that. It was as good an audience as she was likely to get.

She and Meggie waited their turn. When they reached the counter, Jessup sneered and asked her what she wanted. Cass let Meggie go first, and after fumbling in a jar behind the counter, Jessup handed over a paper cone of peppermint drops.

"And what about you?"

Cassie waited until Meggie was outside before she placed her order. "I'd like a pound of sugar, a can of peaches and one *large can of condensed milk.*" She spoke so loudly that even the poker players in the back could hear her.

Jessup rocked on his heels. "Condensed milk, huh?"

"Yes, Mr. Jessup," Cassie said, tightening both trembling hands around the handle of her shopping basket. "I'd like a can of *condensed milk*—just like the cans of *condensed milk* I bought from you some weeks ago. The very thing—*the only thing*—I ever gave the Indians. *Condensed milk!*"

Before Jessup could speak, Cassandra went on. "You haven't told anyone what contraband I gave the Indians, have you? You've let everyone think it was powder and shot. You haven't told them it was *milk to save a baby's life.*"

"There's some that wouldn't hold with doing that," the sutler warned her. "There's some who think that nits make lice."

"But others believe a child's life is sacred," Cassie countered, keeping her voice steady by dint of will. "A white child *or* an Indian. Those are the people who will understand what I did. Those are the people you've deliberately misled. Now if you'll be so kind as to give me my things, I've some baking to do before supper."

Scowling from under his brows, Jessup weighed out the sugar, took a can of condensed milk from his replenished supply, and added the peaches to her basket.

"Is that all, Mrs. Reynolds?" Jessup asked.

She could see the malice in his eyes and knew that he had just become an even more dangerous adversary.

"Enough for now."

"And how do you mean to pay for this?"

"Just charge these things to my husband's account," she answered, and spun toward the door.

Though her ears were ringing and her knees wobbled, Cass made her way outside. She braced one hand against the post of the sutler's porch and stood there gasping. Yet she was proud she'd stood up to Jessup and set the story straight. She felt stronger for having done that.

And then she saw the peppermint drops.

They were scattered at the bottom of the steps, small pinwheels of white and red ground into the dust, a white paper cone lying crumpled beside them. From around the corner of the store she heard someone wailing.

Meggie! Oh God, Meggie!

Cassie flew down the steps toward the child's sharp cry. *If someone had deliberately hurt that little girl . . .*

In the narrow, muddy passage between the sutler's store and the blacksmith's shop, Meggie had taken things in hand. She was sitting astraddle some boy who sprawled facedown in the mud, one of her small fists caught deep in his red hair.

"Take it back, damn you!" Meggie was shouting. "Take it back! My mother's not some Indian whore!"

Cassie stopped dead in her tracks.

"Is, too. She's got that mark on her face. And she's been givin' the In'juns—"

Meggie pulled harder.

"Ow! Ow!" the boy shouted, squirming to get away.

"Take—it—back!" Meggie repeated, tugging once for each of the words.

Cassie figured she'd better intervene.

"Meggie Reynolds, unhand that young man!" she ordered.

Meggie looked up, the set of her jaw mutinous. "He called you names."

"I heard what he called me," Cassie said. *And I heard you called me your mother.*

"And you're not mad?" Meggie asked incredulously.

"Of course I'm mad. But what he says isn't true, and anyone with brains in their head will know it!"

Cassie thought that sounded inane. But maybe the truth was that simple.

"Now, Meggie," Cassandra prompted her, "you're going to let that young man up, and then he's going to apologize. You are going to apologize, aren't you—"

"Homer, Homer Parker," the boy gasped. "Yes, I am."

It was Alma Parker's youngest son.

"Meggie!" Cassandra admonished her in her sternest tone, balanced somewhere between laughter and tears.

Meggie let go of Homer's hair and climbed to her feet. Homer took a good deal longer getting up.

He was bruised and battered, iced with mud all down one side. There was a smear of manure on his cheek. Meggie had defended her quite effectively.

"Now then," she said, "I believe I heard something about an apology."

"Y-y-yes, ma'am," Homer stammered. "I'm sorry, ma'am, for calling you an Indian—um—" His face got redder and redder.

"Lady," Cassie finished for him, letting him off the hook.

"And I'm sorry about spilling Meggie's peppermint drops."

"He knocked them out of my hand," Meggie accused. "A whole penny's worth of peppermint drops!"

Cassie chose to ignore the question of the peppermint drops.

"Go home, Homer," she advised. "Take a bath. And remember that Meggie doesn't take kindly to name-calling."

She and Meggie stood together as Homer limped down the passageway and turned toward officers' row.

Once he was gone, Cassie couldn't think what to say to Meggie. Should she thank her for defending her so valiantly? Should she admonish her for fighting? Should she tell her just how much it had meant to hear her claim her as her mother?

"So," she began awkwardly, swallowing down the knot that was near to choking her. "Do I need to buy you more peppermint drops?"

"I don't think I like peppermint drops anymore," Meggie said, her eyes clouding over with tears. "I don't think I will ever eat peppermint drops again."

Cassie came to her knees and gathered the child up in her arms. "Oh, Meggie girl, I love you," she whispered. "And I promise I won't ever make you eat peppermint drops."

"Oh, Cassie," Meggie sniffed. "I love you, too."

* * *

"They're going to hang him at dawn." Drew made the announcement from the kitchen doorway. Cassie looked up from where she was sewing at the table, letting down the hem of one of Meggie's dresses.

"Who?" she asked.

She could sense the energy dancing around her husband like rays of light. "They're going to hang the Indian. The horse thief we brought in yesterday."

"Is he guilty?" Cassie wanted to know.

Drew shrugged, moving nearer. "He claims he was bringing the horses in for a bounty, but that doesn't seem likely. The army wouldn't pay to get back something it already owned."

A bitter roux of misgivings swirled in Cassie's belly. "Did anyone make inquiries?" she asked, knowing she shouldn't question him. "Did anyone send telegrams to see if any of the forts' commanders—"

Drew scowled down at her. "He's just an Indian. Is this Many Buffalo someone you know?"

"Of course not," she answered. "He's Arikara. The Arikara have long been enemies of the Sioux and Cheyenne. I just thought someone should—"

"Jalbert spoke in his defense," he told her. "Not that it made much difference. This is a redskin we're talking about. Everyone knows they'd steal the pennies off a dead man's eyes."

"Drew—" Cassie cautioned him, aware of Meggie playing on the floor at their feet.

"For God's sake, Cassie. A man's entitled to his opinions."

But Drew's opinions were so narrow, so intolerant. Her husband was like a twig that had been bent by the wind and had grown into a tree that was twisted and misshapen. She had known what Drew was when she married him. He hadn't kept his hatred for the Indians a secret. She thought being with her could change him, that she could make him understand there were good and bad in any people, that she could help him return to the more reasonable views he'd held when they were young. She had been a fool to think that, but she had.

Drew reached to finger the faded fabric that puddled on the tabletop. "Meggie needs new dresses, doesn't she?"

Cass inclined her head.

"Then get what you need and make her some."

He shifted as if he were eager to leave. "What I stopped by to tell you is that I won't be home for supper. I have a report to write on how we captured Many Buffalo. Ben says we need to document everything that happened because the Peace Commissioners at Fort Laramie are bound to second-guess us."

"Then why not wait to hang Many Buffalo?" she dared to suggest.

"And what good would that do?"

"Well, once Many Buffalo is hanged, it's too late for anyone to intervene."

"Exactly."

Cassie shivered. The Arikara was going to die alone, away from anyone who could release his spirit to the afterlife. She'd faced her own death more than once while she was with the Kiowa and remembered how the cold, dark weight of her isolation pressed down on her. She'd wondered if anyone would dig a grave and mumble a few prayers over her.

Nor was hanging a noble way for an Indian to die. How could a warrior's spirit fly free if it were shackled by a rope to the earth?

Cassie looked up from her stitches, the words working their way up her throat. "Drew, do you think . . ."

"Think what?"

One look at her husband's face made Cassie's courage desert her. "Do—do you think—you should give Meggie a kiss before you leave? She'll probably be in bed when you get home."

Drew retraced his steps and squatted down in front of his daughter. Meggie grinned and offered him one of the clay cups, inviting him to join her and her dolly for tea.

Drew refused it with a shake of his head. He didn't seem

to understand that these days with Meggie would never come again, that every moment was precious.

"Give Papa a kiss," he instructed. "I won't be back until late."

"It's all right, Papa," Meggie assured him, coming up on her knees to buss his cheek. "I have Cassie."

After Drew left, Cassie couldn't get Many Buffalo out of her mind. He'd been shut up in that guardhouse for two days, away from the wind and the sky. She shuddered just thinking what that would be like for a man so used to running free, for a man who was going to die at sunrise. What could it hurt if she took him a few small things that would make his last night on earth more comfortable?

But Cassie knew what it would hurt. She knew what Drew would say and how the people at the fort would look at her if she went to visit the prisoner. She knew what she had promised herself and promised Drew. This was different from the milk. But no less important.

She quickly gathered up what she needed—a spoon, a container of fresh water and one of stew, a blanket, some sweet grass from one of her packets of herbs, a few wooden matches, and a handful of feathers. Still, Cass was wise enough to leave Meggie with Lila when she headed toward the guardhouse and the gallows out front.

She went inside and asked for the officer of the day. "I would like to see the prisoner," she told him.

Lieutenant Arnold gaped in slack-jawed shock. "Are you sure, Mrs. Reynolds?" he asked her. "What business could you possibly have with him?"

"I have brought him a meal, a bottle of fresh water, a blanket, and a few other things to make him comfortable," Cassie answered.

"This is highly irregular, ma'am," the lieutenant warned her. "Does your husband know you're here?"

"Is it necessary for me to have my husband's permission to visit him?"

"Well, no, ma'am. Not strictly speaking, ma'am. I just thought . . ."

"I'll take full responsibility for my actions," she assured

him. If she was capable of making this decision, she should be able to accept the consequences.

When the lieutenant hesitated, she went on. "If you were to die alone in an Indian camp, Lieutenant, wouldn't you want whatever small comfort some stranger might give you?"

Arnold shrugged and looked away.

After two corporals pawed through her things, they led her into a locked room at the back of the building. Many Buffalo was confined in a still-smaller cell. It was stifling inside. It smelled of pain and fear and unwashed bodies. A wave of panic rolled over Cassie when the guard locked the door behind her.

The prisoner was not a big man, not a particularly fierce-looking man. He wore his hair as most of the Arikara did, in two long braids wrapped in fur. Blue clamshells dangled from his ears, and his loincloth and leggings were made of buffalo hide.

Cassie swallowed hard and stepped farther into the cell to set the pail of stew, the blanket, and the other things she'd brought on the floor in front of him.

"I brought those to make these next hours more comfortable," she told Many Buffalo, first in Sioux and then in Cheyenne. She finally settled on hand talk to make herself understood.

When Many Buffalo made no move to take the things, she continued. "I know they must have told you that you are to be hanged tomorrow."

Many Buffalo nodded.

"I want you to tell me how a man of the Arikara should be buried. I cannot promise that these soldiers will do what I ask, but I will try to see that your customs are honored."

Many Buffalo gestured with his hands. "There is a man here who is half Arikara. He will see that I am painted and dressed and buried facing east. He will release my spirit to a better world before he closes the grave."

She should have known that Hunter would see to this. He was a good man and doubtless in a better position to see to Many Buffalo's burial than she was. Yet sometimes she thought Hunter's position at the fort was frighteningly tenuous. Major McGarrity respected him for his skills as a tracker, interpreter, and hunter. Yet he was a mixed-blood, and that would always make him suspect.

Cass blinked the flash of insight away and focused again on Many Buffalo. "Is there anything you need?" she asked him.

"Nothing more. I thank you for these things and your courage in coming here."

Cassie inclined her head and called for the guard.

She held herself together while the soldier unlocked the two stout doors. She thanked Lieutenant Arnold for allowing her to see the prisoner. She made it as far as the infantry barracks before the horror of that cramped little cell overtook her. She stepped into the shadows and stood there shivering.

The loud, deep-throated clanging of a bell woke them. Drew bolted out of bed, instantly alert.

"That's the firebell," he said, snatching up his pants.

Cassie ran to the window and peeked outside. "I can't see anything, but there's smoke in the air."

"Let's hope it's not one of the barracks."

"Or the stable!" Cass cried in alarm, but he was throwing on his clothes and didn't answer.

"Are the horses burning up?" Meggie asked, pushing back the curtain that separated her alcove from the rest of the bedroom.

"No, Meggie, no," Cassie assured her as Drew ran out. "I'm sure the horses are fine."

That didn't satisfy the little girl. Before Cassie could stop her, Meggie was across the parlor and out the door. Cass caught her on the porch, and the two of them stood staring.

On the far side of the parade ground the sky glowed vivid orange. A towering column of smoke spiraled upward. On the far side of the cavalry stable, something was fiercely ablaze.

"Is it the horses?" Meggie demanded, her voice quivering.

"It's not the horses," Cassie soothed, grabbing Meggie up in her arms.

Still, a score of men were leading the skittish animals out of the barn. Frightened by the smoke and confusion, the horses whickered and danced, making it difficult for the men to control them. Several soldiers had climbed to the top and were wetting down the stable roof. More men ran across the parade ground toward the fire.

Cassie spun back into the cabin to dress. She gave Meggie her clothes, jammed her own feet into shoes, and buttoned a skirt over her nightdress. She gathered her store of unguents and herbs to use in case someone got hurt. A minute or two later they were back outside.

Sylvie Noonan and her children were clustered on the porch next door. "Keep Meggie for me," Cass shouted, knowing Sylvie wouldn't dare refuse. Meggie protested being left behind, but Cass was already racing toward the fire.

On the far side of the barn a hayrick was spectacularly ablaze. Flames shot nearly fifty feet in the air. Smoke billowed into the black night sky. The air shimmered with sparks. She looked for Drew and found him at the head of a line of men with buckets. Hunter was throwing water on the fire from the opposite side. Cass wilted a little with relief at finding both of them safe.

The second hayrick ignited with a flash and whoosh. Fire clawed its way up the mound of straw. Bits of burning hay rained everywhere. Someone shouted and men with buckets ran in to throw more water on the fire. Their silhouettes shimmered against the red like wraiths as they were beaten back by the waves of heat.

Cassie had just joined the nearest bucket line, when a man ran toward her, his sleeve ablaze. She grabbed his opposite arm and flung him to the ground. Another soldier doused the man with water. The flames on his arm sizzled and went out.

Cassie dropped to her knees beside where he was writhing and howling in pain.

"It's all right!" she shouted at him. "It's going to be all right! I have medicines!"

As his screams of pain turned to moans, Cass turned to the man with the bucket who was hovering over them. "I'll take care of this. Get back to the fire."

The soldier went, leaving his bucket and the last of his water behind.

Bending over her patient, Cassie ripped away the charred remains of his sleeve and grimaced at what she saw.

The soldier moaned and pulled away from her.

"No, no," she soothed him. "You're going to be fine. It looks awful and I know it hurts, but I have herbs right here in my bag to make that stop."

She pawed through her pack and took out the last of the hyssop she'd collected and dried months ago.

"I can make the pain go away. Just trust me," she told him. She stuffed some of the leaves into her mouth and began to chew.

The man thrashed beside her and she held him down. He did his best to flinch away as she spit the moistened leaves onto his arm.

"Oh, no! I don't want that on me!" he wailed at her.

"It will take away the sting," she cajoled, patting the crumbly green paste onto the burn. "Don't you want that?"

"What *is* it?" he demanded.

"Hyssop," she mumbled, chewing and patting.

The man looked down at his arm, patently unconvinced.

She patted more of the paste onto the burn.

Slowly his eyes began to widen. "Why it—it feels better," the soldier said, sounding amazed.

When she had coated the burn to her satisfaction, Cassie moistened a strip of cloth in the bucket, and bound the poultice in place.

"Keep that bandage moist," she advised him, "and it should hold you until one of the medical orderlies gets a chance to look at it. And don't worry. You're going to be fine."

Cass helped the trooper to his feet. When they turned to look, the two hay wagons were roaring, turning the dark as bright as day.

Thank God the soldiers had left those hayricks so far from the stables, Cassie found herself thinking. Thank God there was no wind to carry the flames. That's all that had saved the fort and everyone in it from destruction.

There was nothing else to do but watch the wagons burn. The fire was magnificent, a pulsing white-hot core, flares of molten gold, licking forks of red-orange light raging skyward. It was like watching the sun being born.

The women and children who had been waiting back at the cabins crept up to join the sweaty, soot-stained soldiers. They all stood silent, awed by the fire's savagery and splendor. Among the families, Cassie found Meggie and took her up in her arms. Drew made his way to the two of them soon after.

"We were lucky," he whispered, slipping his arm around her waist. "So lucky. This could have spread and taken everything."

Cass looked up at Drew, at the streaks of soot on his face and the fear in his eyes. He'd been afraid for Meggie and her, and she could see he didn't like feeling that. It intruded on him somehow; it made him think of himself as a weaker, not a stronger, man.

"How—how did the fire start?" she asked him.

"No one seems to know. One of the sentries saw the flames and rang the bell."

She supposed it could have started from anything, a spark from someone's fire, a match carelessly tossed away, a bolt of summer lightning. It hardly mattered. What mattered was that they were safe.

She and Drew leaned together, listening to the hiss and roar of the fire. They watched the hay wagons shudder and flare. As they were consumed, their towering forms contracted and crumbled. They shrank and moaned until there was nothing left but a shimmering bed of coals.

The men were moving in to extinguish the embers when the officer of the day came pelting toward them.

"The prisoner has escaped!" Lieutenant Arnold shouted. "Many Buffalo has gotten away!"

"What do you mean, you let him escape?" McGarrity demanded, towering over the smaller man.

The people crowded closer to hear the details.

Arnold cringed before the major's wrath. "He must have gotten out during the fire, sir. We didn't discover he was missing until just now."

"Noonan, detail a search!" McGarrity ordered, and Noonan ran.

"I've sent my men out looking," the lieutenant reported. "He must have slipped past the pickets, or we'd have him by now."

"Or he's hiding somewhere here in the fort."

A shudder of apprehension rippled through the crowd. Men drew their families closer.

McGarrity looked around. "Jalbert!" the major bellowed.

"Sir?" Hunter appeared from somewhere off to Cassie's left.

"I know you can only do so much in the dark, but go see if you can figure out what direction that redskin took."

"Do we know how he got out of the guardhouse?"

Cassie could see the apprehension in Lieutenant Arnold's face. If something he'd done had enabled the prisoner to escape, McGarrity would break him back to private.

"When the firebell rang," Arnold began, "I myself checked on the prisoner. He was shut up in his cell and locked in the back of the guardhouse. I detailed Corporal Minter and Private Wallace to stay with him while the rest of us came to fight the fire."

"Goddamnit, Arnold!" McGarrity loomed up as if he meant to tear Arnold into little pieces. "How did Many Buffalo get past two armed men?"

"They came out onto the guardhouse steps to watch the fire, sir. Since the guardhouse is up on a rise, the view is—"

"I don't give a damn about the view, Lieutenant," McGarrity thundered.

"Yes—yes, sir. As near as I can f-figure, while they were out on the steps Many Buffalo got out."

"How, goddamnit?"

"I don't know how he got through two locked doors, sir. Once he reached the office, he climbed out one of the side windows and went around back."

"I'll see if I can track him," Hunter told McGarrity and trotted off.

"And you're sure those doors were locked?"

Lieutenant Arnold stiffened. "Yes, sir! I locked the cell door myself when we emptied the slops. I checked the lock on the one from the cells to the office before we left the guardhouse to fight the fire.''

''Has it occurred to anyone that the fire might have been set?'' Captain Parker put in.

A cold tingle ran the length of Cassie's back. The people around her muttered and glanced to where the wagons were still smoldering.

''Set as a diversion, you mean?'' Drew asked.

''The fire was certainly spectacular,'' Parker observed. ''It got everyone's attention.''

''But who—who would have done that?'' Sally McGarrity asked, nestling against her husband's shoulder.

The major turned to Lieutenant Arnold again. ''Did Many Buffalo have any visitors, anyone who could have helped him escape?''

Cassie felt the impact of that question in the center of her chest and waited for Arnold's answer.

He found her with his gaze before he spoke. ''Well, Mrs. Reynolds came to see Many Buffalo late this afternoon.''

Though his face remained impassive, Drew's fingers tightened at her waist, biting deep. Cass shuddered, knowing she was caught, knowing she'd betrayed both the promises she'd made to Drew and to herself. She would rather have faced a loaded gun than the accusation in his eyes.

Everyone within earshot turned and stared at her: Ben and Sally, several of the companies' laundresses, Lila's son Josh, scores of enlisted men. From a dozen feet away Jessup leered.

''What did Mrs. Reynolds do while she was with the prisoner?'' McGarrity asked the lieutenant instead of addressing Cassie directly.

''They made hand signs—first her, then him.''

''And did she bring him anything?''

''A blanket, some sundries, and a bucket of stew.'' Arnold spared her another glance. ''But we checked everything she brought before she went into that cell.''

''Are you sure you checked *everything*, Lieutenant?'' McGarrity asked.

The people around her speculated at what Arnold might have missed.

The lieutenant colored up, his blush visible even in the dark. "I checked everything a gentleman could, sir."

"And was Mrs. Reynolds Many Buffalo's only visitor?"

"No one came to visit Many Buffalo," the young lieutenant clarified, "except Mrs. Reynolds."

Cass could feel the hostility gathering and breaking over her like a wave. She knew she had invited everyone's censure by visiting Many Buffalo, but she just hadn't been able to ignore his plight.

Before Cassie could speak in her own defense, her husband straightened beside her. His face was devoid of expression, his eyes like mirrors reflecting back the darkness. Or perhaps that darkness was in Drew himself.

He wouldn't look at her as he spoke. He refused to look at anyone. "My wife may have gone to see Many Buffalo this afternoon, but she had nothing to do with his escape. She had nothing to do with setting this fire. She was home in bed when that firebell rang, and she'd been there all night."

Cassie knew that honor made him speak in her behalf, honor as brittle as prairie grass in November, as fragile as the bond that was breaking between them even now.

He'd been somehow defeated by what she'd done. By her promises, by his own dreams, by his own failures. By having his horse thief escape. He seemed so fragile standing there, like the spent shell of a locust disintegrating in her hands.

Yet that defense was what people expected of him, an honorable man defending his not-so-honorable wife. By those words, as futile as they were, he'd won their sympathy.

When Drew turned her and Meggie toward home, the crowd parted before them like winnowed wheat. Cassie and Meggie and Drew crossed the parade ground together, as if they were still a family. But once the stout cabin door was closed behind them, Drew took his hands away as if he might be tainted by touching her.

"I didn't do it," she whispered, her voice urgent in the silence. "I didn't have anything to do with Many Buffalo's escape."

Drew looked down at her for one long moment, then turned away. "It doesn't matter," was all he said.

Chapter Sixteen

Many Buffalo escaped without leaving a trace. No one had seen him go. No one could explain how he'd gotten through the two locked doors in the guardhouse. No one had been able to track him. Not even Hunter Jalbert.

Especially not Hunter Jalbert.

Not normally a duplicitous man, Hunter had taken delight in his own guile. By clever misdirection he'd released an Arikara warrior from his cage and let him fly free. He'd been inordinately pleased by what he'd accomplished until he returned to the fort and discovered the consequences—Cassandra Reynolds's ruination.

By the time he got back from his fruitless search, Cass Reynolds was paying for his deception. Short of turning himself in, there was nothing he could do to help her. He never thought a white woman would understand what it meant for a man of the Arikara to be shut away from the sun. He never thought that Cass would risk so much by visiting Many Buffalo. And even if he had imagined that, what else could he have done but set the Arikara free?

During the next two weeks, Hunter watched most of the people in the fort shunned Cass. He saw how they looked through her, how they turned away when she approached. He heard her degraded in whispers and denounced as a spy. He spoke in her defense in a meeting with the officers, but it was too late.

She was providing a focus for men already frustrated by weeks of tension and inactivity, for women frazzled by unruly children and the onslaught of the summer heat. And Drew Reynolds was behaving as if she were invisible.

Even the little girl was suffering for Cassie's disgrace. Twice Hunter had pulled Meggie out of fights defending her.

"You should tell Cassie that the other children are bothering you," he counseled as he held Meggie between his knees and blotted her bloodied lip with his handkerchief.

Meggie shook her head, valiant in a way even he could admire. "That would only make it worse."

His anger was instinctive, yet he knew the code white children lived by had its own complex and brutal hierarchy.

Nothing had changed since he was a boy in St. Louis, and *he* had been the one fighting the other children's taunts. Hunter hadn't forgotten what names they'd called him or that his father had brought him into the family parlor to lecture him on behaving like a gentleman. While Hunter stood with scuffed knuckles and a black eye, his father's city wife and his father's city children had laughed at him behind their hands.

Hunter had realized then that he had to answer the jeers all by himself. Meggie understood that, too. Sighing, he'd folded away his handkerchief and watched her limp toward the Reynolds's cabin.

As far as Hunter could see, Cass rarely left the house. He passed it whenever he could and wandered down to the riverbank at night, hoping for a chance to talk to her. He wanted to tell her what he'd done and apologize for the trouble it had caused. But he never caught so much as a glimpse of her.

Instead, it was Drew Reynolds who approached him in the cavalry barn one steamy afternoon. "I want to speak to you about Cassie," Reynolds said, standing there crisp and immaculate in spite of the setting and the heat.

Hunter's heart thumped hard against his ribs, and he nearly dropped the bridle he'd been mending. "Cassie? What about Cassie?"

"She's been after me about letting her leave the fort to gather herbs. She needs yarrow and milkweed and"—Reynolds frowned—"and some other things I can't remember. She says her supplies are getting low, and after what she did for Private Foster the night of the fire, we've had enlisted men knocking on our back door for one remedy or another." Reynolds shifted a little on his feet. "I thought you might have some idea where this damned stuff grows. I thought you might be willing to take her."

"You want me to take Cassie out to gather herbs?"

Images spun through Hunter's head—of riding out of the fort with Cass at his side, of taking her to the wide-water marshes downstream or to the thick piney woods on the slopes of Caspar Mountain. They could have a whole day to themselves. She could gather her plants, and he would have his chance—away from prying eyes and listening ears—to explain about Many Buffalo.

"I would like you to take her, Jalbert, if it wouldn't be too much trouble," Reynolds continued, "and you think it's safe."

"I'd be happy to take Mrs. Reynolds out to gather herbs."

"And Meggie, too, of course."

Hunter hadn't imagined taking Meggie. The visions he'd had of Cass and him hadn't included a child. Still, considering how the other children were treating her, a day away from the fort would do her good. It would do both the Reynolds women good.

"Of course I'll take Meggie."

Reynolds smiled, one of his rare, genuine smiles. "Meggie will like that. She loves horses, loves to ride. In a year or so I suppose I'll have to be getting her a pony of her own."

"Then I'll ask Mrs. Reynolds what herbs she needs," Hunter offered, turning back to the bridle. "We'll plan an expedition."

"Thank you," the captain said, and turned to go. "And you will have Cassie back before nightfall."

Hunter's mouth hooked up at one corner. He shook his head. While people at the fort were busy vilifying his wife as a spy, Reynolds was worried about what time she got home.

"I'll make sure we're back by suppertime," Hunter promised. Reynolds stopped just short of the door. Hunter noticed his hesitation and looked up.

"Jalbert?" There was something in Reynolds's voice that made Hunter's stomach bunch. "You don't think Cassie had anything to do with Many Buffalo's escape, do you?"

The unexpected question caught Hunter hard. Jesus, had he made this man doubt his own wife?

"No," he answered instinctively. "Why—why are you asking me?"

The captain turned and came nearer. He seemed suddenly almost haggard in the half-light. "I'm asking because I thought you'd know if Cassie was involved. Because I think you're man enough to tell me the truth."

Hunter let out his breath, strangely shaken by the captain's confidence. "I can see why people think she might have been involved in the escape," he began slowly. "She spent so long with the Indians, and she gave that woman milk. But I think she went to see Many Buffalo because she knows what it is to be held against her will. She understood what it meant for Many Buffalo to be shut up in that cell. She's a compassionate woman—your Cassie. I think she was just trying to help."

Drew shifted a little, like a man in pain. "I know exactly what Cassie is. I believed she wanted to do better, but she keeps making these mistakes."

The air went thick and hot in Hunter's lungs, but he couldn't seem to manage to let out his breath. Whatever Cassie hoped, however hard she tried, whoever she thought she could be for him, her life with Drew was over. Reynolds wasn't living with a phantom anymore. He was living with Cass, the real Cass, and he didn't want the woman his Cassie had become.

Hunter took care to meet and hold Drew Reynolds's eyes. He refused to give Reynolds cause to hurt her. "Mrs. Reynolds didn't have anything to do with Many Buffalo's escape," he told him. "Don't you doubt her for a moment."

Drew let out his breath and straightened. "I won't," he

said, and Hunter wished he could believe him.

Reynolds shifted and tugged his uniform jacket into place. "Very well, then," he said brusquely, almost as if they'd been discussing the weather. "I'll let Cassie know you've agreed to take her out to gather herbs. Perhaps you can go at the beginning of next week."

Hunter watched the captain leave, a dark regret creeping through him.

Once they'd ridden beyond the sights and sounds and smells of Fort Carr, Cass tipped her head back and devoured the bright new world around her. She drank in the hot, fierce blue of the cloudless sky. She turned her face into the wind. She breathed deeply, letting the scent and taste and feel of freedom soak into her.

She'd been preparing for this moment since well before dawn. She'd hauled and heated water, made the beds and breakfast, dressed both Meggie and herself, and packed up what they would need for the day. She'd kissed Drew goodbye by way of thanks, smiled at Hunter, and climbed onto the horse he'd brought for her.

For just today, she needed to be where the breeze ruffled the luxuriant carpet of buffalo grass and orange whips of curly dock overran the gullies. She needed to be where flax flowers poked their heads through the coarse gray-green clumps of sage that studded the rolling prairie.

This is how it's supposed to be, Cass found herself thinking. And Hunter had made this world his gift to her.

He had given her the prairie and the sky, and a chance to savor the solitude by inviting Meggie to ride with him. Cass glanced across at the two of them, the tall man patiently guiding his horse while the child in his lap chattered and pointed and wiggled. The contrasts between him and her touched some sweet, soft spot inside Cass.

Her gaze strayed as a pronghorn antelope bounded off ahead of them. Meggie crowed with delight, sending a dozen more antelope scattering. The mule deer proved far less skittish. They stood belly-deep in scrub, watching and chewing thoughtfully.

As they moved toward the ridge of green-black mountains to the south, the land tipped subtly upward. Rounded, velvety green hills rose from the rolling scrub country. Boulders seemed to be scattered across the lush baize hummocks like tumbled dice. The rocks became larger and more rough-hewn as they climbed. The wind blew more strongly here. Wispy cedars huddled among the rocks as if seeking protection from the howling gusts.

The slope became steeper as they entered the woods. Pine and hardwoods towered over them as they picked their way up a gravel trail. They had been climbing for the best part of an hour when Hunter turned into a steep glade at the edge of a rushing stream. It was cool and green and peaceful, as beautiful and perfect as anything Cass could have imagined.

Hunter came around to hold her horse's bridle while Cassie dismounted. "Is this place all right?" he asked her.

"It couldn't be more beautiful."

Calling Meggie back from the edge of the creek to help, Cass spread a length of gauzy cloth across the grass. She tied a pair of heavy scissors to her belt and settled the familiar weight of her gathering basket against her hip.

Hunter ambled back as she was preparing.

"Things up here look so green," she told him. "There should be wonderful clumps of mint and sheaves of goldenrod." She paused to look up at him. "Is there anything you want me to collect?"

Hunter glanced at her in surprise and shook his head. "I'm no healer."

"You still practice Arikara ways and use Arikara herbs, don't you?"

"Sometimes."

"Would you like to come with me and gather them yourself?"

"I thought I'd keep Meggie here. I like to fish, and I thought I'd teach her."

Cass knew he was giving her time alone, to wander and gather and think. Time to lie with her back to the earth and dissolve her soul on the wind.

"Stay on this side of the creek," he went on. "Don't go

too far. And take this." He held out an army revolver. "You know how to use it, don't you?"

Cassie nodded.

"I'm not expecting trouble, but bears and rattlers can be downright unpredictable. Captain Reynolds will have my hide if I bring you back any way but healthy and whole."

Cassie reached for the gun and tucked it into the pocket of her skirt. "I want to thank you for bringing me here."

Hunter gave a slow, self-conscious shrug. "It was the captain's idea," he answered, and flushed just a little. "Besides, it's going to give me a chance to catch some trout. Maybe if we're lucky, Meggie and I will get enough for lunch."

"I packed a meal in any case," Cass teased him.

Hunter gave her a we'll-just-see-about-that smile and sauntered away.

She resettled the basket on her hip and headed off.

"Be careful!" he called after her.

Cass shivered a little as she climbed through the coolness of the woods. The sharp, sweet scent of pine and the warm earthy damp mingled in her nostrils. Though it was late in the season to be gathering plants, she found a luxuriant growth of lacy sarsaparilla, a bank of wood sorrel, and another of bergamot. She stopped to scrape the bark from both aspen and chokecherry trees. Though they were best harvested in the fall, Cass dug for roots, dusting the cool crumbly earth from her hands when she was done.

Sunlight shafted through the branches of the trees like ribbons of gold, as she wandered from the woods into a mountain meadow. It lay broad and flat, a medley of colors and textures, hemmed on the far edge by a tumble of rocks. Cass waded in among the swaying plants, cutting yellow yarrow and mugwort, hyssop and goldenrod. She found the curly-leafed mint as much by its smell as by the shape of its stem, then searched out milkvetch and a few bright sunflowers.

She heard laughter as she came down the trail toward the clearing: Meggie's high-pitched giggle, underlain by a deep rumbling chuckle that seemed to find an answering vibration somewhere inside her. She couldn't think when she'd heard either Meggie or Hunter laugh.

She stopped on a boulder above the clearing to watch the tiny girl and the broad-shouldered man as they knelt together on the bank of the stream. The child's silver-floss hair gleamed bright beside a thatch of hair so black that even the sun got lost in it. She watched with a smile on her lips as Hunter bent above the child to help her bait her hook. His hands enfolded Meggie's tiny ones like broad dark petals around the delicate heart of a flower.

She supposed she should wish this was Drew spending time with Meggie, laughing with her and teaching her things, but somehow Cass couldn't manage that.

She spread the plants she'd collected on the gauze and went out for more without disturbing the pair fishing in the stream. When she returned well over an hour later, Meggie charged toward her across the clearing.

"We caught *six fish!* " Meggie declared. "We cut them open and took out *all their guts*. Now we're cooking them over the fire!"

Hunter looked up and motioned for her to come. "These are almost ready," he called out.

Taking a blanket and provisions from their packs, Cassie ambled over to where Hunter was tending their meal.

"I guess you had some luck fishing, after all."

"I guess we did."

"It's been a long time since I had trout cooked like this."

"Is that how the Cheyenne cook them?" Meggie asked.

Cassie nodded. "With a bit of salt and certain herbs." From the smell of things, Hunter knew the recipe.

While Hunter cooked, Cassie spread the blanket in the soft, cool grass. She took out tin plates and cups, bread and cheese, the cookies she'd baked the night before, and a canteen of lemonade. Now that they were finally beginning to harvest vegetables from the company gardens, the army thought to send lemons to ward off scurvy.

When the fish were done, Hunter brought them to their makeshift table. Cass burned her mouth on the first flaky bite, but the delicate flavor of trout and herbs made up for the discomfort. They shared the meal: Cass slicing bread and cheese, Hunter helping Meggie with the fish bones, Meggie offering around cookies when they were done.

Cass washed and then packed away the dishes and the rest of the food. Once she returned to the blanket, she unlaced her high-top shoes, took them off, and wiggled her black-stockinged toes. She smiled and stretched, wishing she could gather the whole of this day up in her arms and carry it back to the fort. Perhaps then the closeness of the cabin wouldn't chafe so much, and the slights of old friends wouldn't hurt. With a shake of her head, she put thoughts of the fort from her mind.

"I love it here," she said, half to herself.

"I love it, too," Meggie piped up from where she'd plopped down beside Cassie. Though she knew Meggie would never admit it, she was curling up for her nap. She pillowed her head on Cassie's thigh. "Let's stay right here and build a house."

Cass stroked the little girl's hair. "Now wouldn't that be nice—living someplace on the top of a mountain where you can see for miles and miles."

"Someplace with a stream where I can fish, and with a field where Cassie can gather herbs," Meggie wished generously. "And with a—" Meggie looked up at Hunter. "What do you want, Hunter?"

"I already have the place I want. It's in Montana."

Cass turned to look at him, and found he was concentrating on a spot beyond the trees where an eagle was riding the currents rising off the face of the hill. He was hiding from the admission—or trying to.

She allowed herself the sliver of a smile. "Where in Montana?"

He hesitated for a dozen heartbeats before answering. "Up between the Gallatin and Yellowstone Rivers. I staked my claim right after I got mustered out of the army."

"You served out here?"

"At what's become Fort Caspar. I decided I liked this part of the country well enough to want a piece of it."

She wanted to ask him more, but just then Meggie whimpered a little on her way to sleep. Cass bent to soothe her.

"It's been a busy day for her," Cassie said.

"And what about you? Has it been a good day for you?" Hunter wanted to know.

Cass smiled up into his eyes. Eyes that were warm and intent and dark, so dark she was surprised that they were such an extraordinary shade of blue.

"It's been a wonderful day," she told him.

"I'm glad," he said and reached across to pat her hand. His fingertips rasped against her skin, warm and rough and so compelling. A tingle of awareness danced up her arm.

"Cass," he said in a tone that made her stomach dip. "Cass, there's something I need to tell you. Something important."

Her heart lurched. Her throat went dry. There was something in the narrowed line of that generous mouth that she didn't want to acknowledge, didn't want to think about. She looked away, but it didn't help. She was aware of Hunter's height and breadth beside her, of the scent of woodsmoke that clung to his clothes, of his closeness and his warmth. Anticipation collected behind her breastbone like a log jam.

He cleared his throat twice before he spoke. "I—I wanted you to know . . ." he said and hesitated.

"Wanted me to know what?" she demanded, suddenly afraid to look at him, afraid of what she might see in those deep blue eyes.

"I wanted you to know I'm the one who helped Many Buffalo escape."

Cass let out her breath in a rush. "*You what?*"

It was the very last thing in the world she'd expected him to say. She stared at him, grappling with his confession and what it meant. She was glad he'd set Many Buffalo free, glad the Arikara had escaped from the fort with his life.

"You?" she demanded, stiffening one vertebra at a time. "You let him out?"

"I gave him the means to escape."

And had gotten clean away with it!

"Did you start that fire?"

"I did."

Outrage roared through her. She jerked her hand away. "Don't you know that people could have been killed in that fire? Don't you know we could have lost our families and our homes?''

''I had it under control.''

She was suddenly shaking inside, remembering the intensity of the blaze, the smoke spiraling into the sky. No one had that fire under control.

''What if those wagons had been closer to the barns? What if wind came up? What if no one had rung that bell?''

Hunter's jaw hardened. ''I made sure those wagons were well out in the field. I waited not a hundred feet from that firebell to make sure one of the sentries sounded the alarm.''

''So much could have gone wrong!''

He glared at her, color high in his face. ''What did you want me to do, Cass, let him stay locked up?''

She heard the low, stark shudder in his voice. He knew what it was like to be locked in that cage. He understood captivity, the way it strangled you, the terrible black futility.

''They would have hanged him!'' His voice frayed a little more as he went on. ''They would have marched him to the gallows and hanged him because of who he was, not what he'd done.''

She had stood in that cell and seen the panic in the Arikara's eyes. She'd understood it, wanted to set him free, and known she could not. Hunter had been able to save the man. Yet salvation had its price, and this time she had paid it.

''I didn't know you'd get blamed for what I'd done,'' he murmured as if he'd read her mind.

She heard the remorse in his tone, his guilt at having made her life more difficult.

She leaned a little closer, wanting him to know she understood. ''Of course you were right to help him. I know what being a captive means. I'm glad you set him free.''

He covered her hand with his, and again for a moment Cass allowed herself to absorb Hunter's warmth, his strength, the vitality that nourished her in ways she refused to even consider.

Then she pulled away. ''It doesn't matter about the blame. I've been an outcast half my life. It's Meggie who needs protecting, and as long as I can keep her from being hurt . . .''

''I've tried to look after her, too,'' he said.

''I know, Hunter, and I thank you for doing that.''

After a moment she tipped her head a little to the side and eyed him speculatively. ''So how *did* you break Many Buffalo out of the guardhouse?''

Hunter's mouth curled at one corner. She could see that in spite of her lecturing, he was pleased with himself.

''I made an impression of the extra guardhouse key in Ben McGarrity's office. Once I had an impression, it was easy enough to file a blank to fit the lock. I slipped the key to Many Buffalo during the hearing and told him to wait for his chance to use it.''

His smile faded away. ''I swear if I had any idea that you had gone to visit him, if I had any way of knowing they'd think it was you—''

''I told you it doesn't matter.''

''Of course it matters.''

''What matters to me, Hunter, is today. What matters is being out of the fort, being able to lie back in the grass and hear the wind humming in the trees. What matters is that you gave this world me—and I will always be grateful.''

Hunter nodded slowly. He understood in a way that no one else ever would. He loved the sun and the trees and the sky, just as she had learned to loved them. He saw the world as she did, through the filter of two lives, with the joy and pain of two disparate souls.

They were connected that way, and all at once she needed some more tangible connection. She leaned across and curled her fingers around the back of his hand. She smelled the wind and the sunshine in his hair. He raised his gaze to hers and she fell headfirst into those dark, dark eyes.

He turned his hand and caught her fingers in his own and pulled her closer. He stroked her hair, touching the wind-blown strands as if they'd been spun from gold. His breath slid over her like a veil of silk. She watched his mouth, mesmerized by the way the corners deepened and the way his lower lip softened as he smiled at her.

''Cass,'' he said, as if that single word could communicate a hundred things that needed to be said.

Her heart thumped in answer as loud as drumbeats on a windless night. A flush of longing rose in her so fragile and yet so compelling. Cass shivered and forced herself to pull away.

Hunter let her go and released his breath in a thready sigh.

In that moment Meggie stirred. She raised her head and looked from Cassie to Hunter. "Is it time for us to go already?"

Past time, Cassie thought and reached to lace on her shoes. Hunter levered himself to his feet and squinted out at the sky. "Well, Meggie," he said, "I promised your father we'd be back to the fort by suppertime."

"Then I suppose we should go," the girl said, her head drooping with resignation.

When Hunter went to see to packing up the horses, Meggie chased after him. Cassie wandered to the boulder above the stream.

From there she could look out over the glade, over the whole wide world that lay beyond it. She filled her eyes with the yellows and greens and golds of the towering hills and the plains that spread toward the horizon. She drank in the blazing hue of the sky, savored the caress of the wind against her cheeks and the scent of the pines. She listened to the murmur of the trees and the bright ripple of the creek as it danced down the mountain. She held on to this world as long as she could.

"Cass," Hunter finally called out to her. The word was as much an apology as a summons.

"Yes," she called back. "I'm coming."

"Oh, Soooo-ban-na,
Oh, don't shoe cry for meee
'Cuz I come from Aba-ba-lama
With my ban-jo on my kneeee."

Hunter laughed as Meggie warbled the last somewhat mangled verse of her favorite song. They had wound their way out of the boulder-studded hills at the foot of Caspar Mountain and were well out onto the rolling grassland. In an hour and a half, they'd be back at the fort.

As before, Hunter had taken Meggie up into the saddle with him and was letting her use the reins to guide his gelding. Cass straggled behind, keeping to herself. Hunter glanced back now and then, uncomfortable with the way the afternoon had ended, at a loss as to how he could have made things different.

He slowed his mount and waited for Cass to catch up. "Did you get what you needed today?" he asked her.

"Far more than I expected."

He shifted his gaze to the basket of cuttings tied to the back of her saddle. "Are there other things you need?"

She hesitated, looked across at him, then shook her head. "No," she said. "No, I can't think of anything else."

The light that had been burning so bright in Cassie's eyes was dimming, and Hunter didn't know how to stop it. Words of apology and concern pushed up his throat. "Oh, Cass—" he began.

Meggie cut off whatever wild and inappropriate thing he'd been about to say. "Hunter," she queried, "did you like my song?"

Hunter smiled with a flutter of relief. "It was a wonderful song, Meggie, and you sang it so well."

"Now you sing one."

"Oh, Meggie, I don't sing."

"Don't you know any songs?"

"No."

"Not even from when you were little?"

"Any songs I might remember would be in French."

Meggie cocked her head and looked at him. "What's French?"

"It's another language, like Cheyenne or Sioux."

"Sing one for me anyway."

"Now, Meggie," Cass warned. "I don't think Hunter wants to sing."

"I sang for him."

"Meggie." Cassie's voice held a note that suggested the child turn her attention to something else. Meggie puffed out her lip and slapped the reins against the gelding's neck. The horse ignored her.

"Where did you grow up speaking French?" Cassandra asked him.

"In St. Louis."

"St. Louis?"

He could hear curiosity in her voice, and it surprised him. No one at Fort Carr had ever asked him where he came from or what had brought him west. That Cass wondered about it, about him, brought her in too close, made him squirm a little inside his skin. Still, he knew so much about her that it didn't seem fair not to answer.

"My father came up the Missouri from St. Louis to trade at one of the Arikara camps. My mother was the daughter of an Arikara subchief. When she accepted my father's suit, it was considered a very advantageous match for both of them.

"My parents lived together for the next two summers. In the third year I was born, and when my father came, he told everyone how pleased he was to have a son.

"But that year the traders brought smallpox up the river to the Arikara. The sickness had visited the Assiniboine a year or two before, and many died. It had all but wiped out the Mandan nation. When it reached the Arikara, nearly everyone fell ill. Before my mother died she made my father promise that if I lived, he would take me with him to St. Louis."

Hunter drew a long, slow breath, picking through the memories as if they were shards of glass.

"Your father had a city wife, didn't he?" she asked softly, and Hunter was grateful for her perceptiveness.

"Madame Jalbert didn't want to know about my father's Indian wife or his half-breed child. All the years I lived in my father's house, she never once spoke to me directly. Her children thought it was their place to remind me whenever they could that I was less than welcome there. My father did see that I was fed and clothed and taught my letters. But only when I found my way to the Indians that lived on the edge of St. Louis did I feel as if I belonged somewhere."

Oblivious to what the two adults were discussing, Meggie clapped her heels against the gelding's sides, hoping to spur him to greater speed. Hunter eased the horse into a trot before he continued.

"One of the Osage men befriended me. When I was not at my father's house, I was with Man Who Stands Alone. He taught me how to ride as the Indians do; how to make and hunt with a bow; how to track and live on the prairie. One night he had a vision that I must go to the village where I was born and to the people who would recognize and honor me."

Hunter could feel the intensity of Cassandra's eyes on him. She understood the importance of such a vision. "Did your father let you go?"

"He took me himself. We found what was left of the Arikara—a few families living on what they could grow, a few small bands too weak to defend themselves from the Sioux. My grandfather was the only one of my family who had survived the smallpox. When my father asked White Water to take me and teach me the Arikara way, he said I was too old to begin training as a warrior."

"But you learned," Cassie said with admiration. "Anyone can see how well you learned."

Hunter smiled both at her compliment and at his memories of that tough old man and his gentle heart. "For seven years I devoted myself to warriors' ways, but the Arikara were weak. They could barely defend their herds from the Sioux and Pawnee. It wasn't much of a life for a man who wanted to fight.

"When one of the traders brought word that my father was dying, I took a steamboat to St. Louis to see him. While I was there, I got my chance to go to war. There were recruiters on every corner. They were signing men up to fight for the North and South. The Confederates seemed to have the finer leaders, so I signed up to fight with them."

Cass glanced out across the rolling waves of prairie grass. "My family and Drew's left Kentucky because they were afraid war was coming. I know both Drew and Ben McGarrity fought for the Union, though I don't know much about what happened."

"It's just as well you didn't hear about the war," Hunter

told her. "There wasn't any glory in it, at least not an Arikara's kind of glory. There wasn't much to make a man feel like a warrior—just marching and taking orders and being shot at."

"Is that all you did?"

"Sometimes we shot back," Hunter said with the hint of a smile. "Pretty early on, someone found out I could follow a trail, and General Forrest took me on as a scout."

"But how did you end up at Fort Caspar?"

"I got captured."

In spite of the sun beating down on his shoulders, Hunter felt the chill. He didn't remember much about the months he'd been locked away. There had been a pounding in his head, a panic that crawled over him like ants, a fury inside him that made him a menace to both the other prisoners and himself. Then a Union officer had come to Rock Island Prison and offered salvation.

The United States Army needed soldiers in the west. Any Confederate willing to take an oath of allegiance to the United States and fight the Comanche and the Sioux could leave the prison. Hunter had been ready to swear away his soul for a glimpse of the sun. He'd made his pledge, been given a new blue uniform, and marched into Fort Laramie eight weeks later.

"Hunter?" The concern in Cassie's voice shattered the spell of those dark days. "What happened after you were captured?"

"I got away" was all he said, and urged his horse into a canter.

Hunter maintained his silence for a good long while as a dozen mule deer ambled across their path headed toward the creek that lay just off to the east, as a hawk looped lazily across the sky hoping to spot his evening meal. They had ridden nearly three miles when a party of a half dozen braves suddenly crested the rise off to the west. With the sun casting them in silhouette, Hunter couldn't make out anything except that they were Sioux.

"Do they mean to harm us?" Cassie asked under her breath.

"I don't know," he told her, but prickles of danger kept dancing up his back. "Just keep riding."

The Indians followed them for more than a mile. Hunter fancied he could almost hear them speculating. Why were these whites so far from the fort? Did they have anything worth stealing besides the horses? Was the child strong and the woman pretty?

"You still got that pistol I gave you, Cass?" he asked, keeping his tone quiet and cool for Meggie's sake.

"Right here," she answered, her voice every bit as calm. He sliced a glance in her direction. Cassie rode tall, her back straight and her chin high. She had that cavalry pistol nestled in her lap and her hand around the grip as if she were ready to use it. There was color in her cheeks and resolution around her mouth. She was as worthy of being a warrior's woman as anyone he'd ever known. White-hot pride flashed through him.

Then all at once, one of the braves detached himself from the group at the top of the rise and galloped toward them.

Hunter pulled his horse up short. Whipcord taut, they watched the Sioux brave come at them.

He was bowed low over his horse, his body lithe and graceful, his hair and breechclout flying.

Hunter tucked Meggie into the crook of his left arm, and pulled the rifle from the saddle holster with his opposite hand. "Don't fire unless you have to," he told Cass. Without so much as a glance at her, he knew she'd stand her ground.

As the Indian bore down on them, they could see that he was broad-shouldered and strong, all done up in paint and feathers. A young buck out to prove himself—which meant he was unseasoned, inexperienced. And probably crazy.

As the youth thundered past, Hunter saw his face light with recognition. Lone Hunter the half-breed scout was known among the Sioux as a fierce fighter, a worthy adversary. In that instant, Hunter bore the weight of that hard-won reputation.

The brave circled around behind them and galloped back.

Hunter followed the man with his eyes. Two hundred yards beyond them, the brave hauled his horse to a prancing stop.

He pulled his war club from his belt, and howled with a challenge to single combat.

Hunter shivered with a thrill of response. He'd have to fight; to ignore the summons would insure their deaths. Yet a fierce, bright hostility ran deep in his bones and sinews, a hard-driving need to defend this woman and child. His horse danced beneath him, as eager as Hunter to fight. For an instant it was all he could do to keep from howling his answer and riding out to do battle.

"What—what's he doing?" Meggie asked, her quaking voice reminding Hunter of his obligations.

"It's going to be all right, Meggie. I'm going to take care of it."

He urged his mount a few steps forward in acknowledgment of the challenge, then glanced toward the Indians on the rise. Would they wait while he played this out or ride down on Cass and Meggie while he was fighting this single brave?

Cass was at his elbow when he turned. She didn't say a word, just grabbed Meggie and swung her into her own saddle. She took his rifle, and, once he'd stripped it off, his shirt.

She understood what a challenge to single combat meant. She knew exactly what he must do, and how she should comport herself while he was fighting.

"Both of you stay on that horse," he told her in an undertone. "Don't ride, don't move, don't give any hint of what you're planning unless the rest of those braves start down here." He gave the Indians on the hill another measuring glance. "If they head this way, kick that bag of bones and ride for the fort."

"Can we make it that far?"

Hunter gave her his most terrible smile. "If any woman can make it to that fort, Cass, you can. And if I lose out there," he went on, "you won't have a choice about reaching it."

"Then we'll be fine."

He had never heard a voice so calm or seen eyes that glowed with such ferocity. His chest burned and his throat tightened.

Then he turned away. He reached around to untie his war

club from the skirt of his saddle. He wrapped one palm around the heavy green-flecked stone that was bound at the head of the club. He could feel its power, its pulse, and its heat. He slid his fingers down the length of the leather-wrapped shank and slipped the rawhide loop around his wrist. He balanced the weapon in his hand. Its weight was familiar, almost comforting. Calm settled in his chest.

It is a very good day to die.

Yet he was fighting for Cass and Meggie, not just himself. Today his life mattered. That was not a weight he could carry into battle.

His challenger was growing restless out on the field, circling and circling. Hunter's own mount blew and snorted, ready to run.

"It is a very good day to die," he insisted under his breath. He nudged his mount forward across a wavering sea of yellow and green, where a lone Sioux warrior was waiting to kill him.

As he closed the distance between them, Hunter looked to the breadth of the man's shoulders. He measured the length of his reach. He gauged the speed his horse was traveling. He planned his strike.

The two warriors came at each other with their war clubs raised. Hunter feinted to the left as they came abreast. He swung the blow at his opponent's head.

The younger man twisted to block it. The clubs came together with a thud. Hunter felt the jar of contact the length of his arm.

The clubs caught head to head. The men glared into each other's eyes, then pulled away. The two of them swerved and circled back, scribing opposite arcs of a circle on the endless plain.

"I, Cry of the Hawk, challenge you, Lone Hunter, to a fight to the death," the young brave taunted, the cluster of feathers in his hair bobbing with his horse's gait. "You are too old to win such a battle. You are too soft from living with the whites to hope to triumph."

"Then my death won't be much of a victory," Hunter shouted back, gauging the younger man's eagerness.

"Even so, I look forward to spilling your blood, to taking the hair of a long-knife scout."

Hunter saw his opponent rein in and tightened his grip on his war club.

Yipping like a coyote, the Sioux warrior jerked his horse to the left and galloped toward the center of the circle. Hunter did the same.

Their horses met shoulder to shoulder, dancing and pushing against each other. The younger man swung his club at Hunter's head. Though Hunter battered it back, the stone at the top glanced off his shoulder. Numbing pain ran down his arm.

He gritted his teeth and swung in spite of it, knocking the young brave forward on his horse. Cry of the Hawk clung there, gasping for breath, as the horses danced away again.

This time as they circled both men rode as if they felt the toll the fight was taking. Hunter's shoulder ached up into his teeth. The younger man's face was the color of chalk.

Still, Hunter's nerves were singing, and the age-old bloodlust set every muscle afire. He craved the taste of victory.

"What is wrong?" Hunter called out as his horse pranced beneath him, kicking up a cloud of dust. "Has this old fox proved too cunning for you, cub? Have you lost your stomach for fighting?"

"I have lost nothing, Lone Hunter," the younger man called out breathlessly. "You have seen your death in my eyes."

"Or you have seen your death in mine. I am sorry about how much of life you are going to miss."

"I am not afraid," the younger man shouted.

"It is a good day to die!"

Across the width of more than a hundred yards the two men reined in their mounts. They turned them in tighter and tighter circles.

Hunter flexed his arm. The muscles were stiff and aching. Was he strong enough to strike the blow that would end this young man's life? Could he defeat this challenger?

With a howl of his own, Hunter turned his horse and urged it to a gallop. The Sioux brave drove his own horse forward. They came together with a jolt. Hunter swung his war club with every ounce of his weight behind it. It caught the younger man in the chest, battered up beneath his ribs, crushed his sternum, stopped his heart.

Hunter surged past him and pulled in his horse. He didn't bother to look back to where the young warrior sprawled broken in the dust. Hunter knew he'd killed the man and experienced a quick, hot surge of remorse for the brave who lay dead. He swallowed the yell of victory that swelled his chest and lifted his gaze to the rise instead.

The Sioux were there, like vultures waiting for a meal, like old men who had known the outcome of the battle and were compelled to watch it anyway.

Hunter didn't wait to see what they did next.

He turned his horse back to Cass and Meggie and rode like the fiends of hell were after him. If the other braves came to get them, he wanted to be armed, he wanted to be where he could defend this woman and child. If he was going to be granted his freedom, he meant for those men on the hill to understand that Cass and Meggie came with it.

When he reached her, Cassie held out his rifle and then his shirt. He donned one and checked the load on the other. Meggie didn't say a word.

"You think they'll come?" Cassandra asked.

"I think we should get out of here."

Cass nodded once and kicked her horse in the direction of the fort. For as long as Hunter kept looking back, the band of Sioux sat watching them.

Chapter Seventeen

The rifles were beautiful—brand-new breech-loading Springfields, specially reconditioned for use with metal cartridges. While Drew's men carried the boxes of "scrub brushes" and "brooms" into the powder magazine in the dead of night, he tested the weight and balance of one of those new rifles in his hand. His fingertips skimmed along the smooth steel barrel. He stroked the bright brass fittings with the pad of his thumb. He fit the flare of the stock in his half-open palm. These guns were simple and strong and dependable—and he wanted one for himself so much he could taste it.

But the rifles weren't meant for the men of Fort Carr. Because of transportation difficulties around Fort Reno, the rifles were being routed west then north to Forts Phil Kearney and C. F. Smith. Those Bozeman Trail installations were closest to the Powder River encampments and in the gravest peril. Besides, taking the rifles north was bound to be glory duty, and what Drew wanted even more than one of the rifles was that assignment.

The morning after the guns arrived, Ben McGarrity called his officers together to brief them on the mission.

Drew hunched at the end of the long, crowded table, his fingers wringing the life from a mug of cooling coffee. He deserved this duty. He'd honed his men. He'd studied maps until he knew every dip and draw between here and the Powder River. He could already taste the wild, sweet exhilaration of riding out of the fort with those munitions wagons.

It was a struggle to rein in his thoughts and turn his attention to the route Jalbert was indicating on the map.

"Since there have been troubles around Fort Reno," the scout was saying, "we'll head due north and intercept the Bozeman Trail a few miles south of Phil Kearney. The Sioux keep a close watch on the trail, and by staying closer to the mountains, we may get into the vicinity of the fort without drawing their attention."

"Isn't heading cross-country with such heavily loaded wagons going to be difficult?" Captain Parker asked.

"There have been trails through this area for years," Jalbert answered, pointing again, "so we'll have wagon ruts to follow. Most of the alternative routes were abandoned when the Bozeman was laid out, but there's no reason we can't use one of them to get the rifles through.

"This land's also a bit more rolling than the land to the east," he continued, "so we won't be quite so visible. And with the size of the contingent Major McGarrity plans to field, the Sioux may not detect our presence at all."

"Is the party to be a small one, sir?" one of the second lieutenants asked.

McGarrity nodded. "In order to make certain these rifles get where they're needed, we plan to make the wagons look innocuous. To that end, I've decided to detail forty men. About half will ride escort, as they might for a civilian wagon train. The rest will remain hidden in the wagons to surprise the hostiles if they attack.

"In addition, a decoy wagon train is starting out from Fort Laramie under full guard. We hope that if the Indians have heard about the rifles, they'll assume that's the party carrying them. We leave Thursday at dawn."

Drew breathed deeply, pleased with the plan and prepared to accept the assignment with equanimity. A good officer never gloated.

McGarrity cleared his throat. "Before I make the assignments, I'd like to say how pleased I am with the training you've provided your men. You've turned what were in some cases raw recruits into crack troops—''

Get on with it! Drew thought, impatience eating holes in him.

''—a pleasure to serve with all of you,'' McGarrity finished a few minutes later. ''Now then, about the rifles.''

Drew held his breath. Anticipation crackled along his nerves like current along a telegraph wire.

''Captain Amos Parker will command—''

Parker! Drew's face caught fire. What the hell was McGarrity thinking? Blood roared in Drew's ears. He hung on to the mug of coffee like it was salvation. What had Parker done to deserve this?

Drew was the one who had graduated at the top of his class at West Point. He'd distinguished himself in battle back East. He'd worked like hell since he'd been at Fort Carr. He'd trained nine long years to fight Indians. How could McGarrity pick someone else?

Only discipline kept Drew in his chair while the others asked questions and discussed contingencies. It was the change in the timbre of McGarrity's voice that cut through the buzz of anger in Reynolds's head.

''The Springfields are so far superior to anything being used on the frontier today,'' the major was saying, ''that a company of men armed with these guns could subdue the tribes in a matter of weeks. But let me caution you, should these guns fall into the wrong hands, they'll start a bloodbath. And we'll be the ones to mop up afterward.

''Speak of this to no one. For this plan to succeed, we need to maintain complete security. Now good luck, keep your mouths shut, and get back to work. Dismissed.''

Amid the hum of voices and the thud of boots on the wooden floor, Drew climbed to his feet. He stood there rigid while the others filed out, not sure where he wanted to go. No soldier worth his salt questioned orders, yet the need to confront McGarrity was raging through him like a bonfire.

The major must have guessed what he was feeling because he stopped beside Drew on his way to the door. ''I'm sorry about giving Parker this duty instead of you,'' he said. ''But

Parker's been out here longer and has a good deal more field experience.''

It was rare for a senior officer to explain his actions to a more junior man; that McGarrity had chosen to do so was a measure of his respect for Drew's abilities. Drew knew that, and still he couldn't seem to choke down his anger.

''Goddamnit, Ben,'' he finally said. ''I came out here to avenge my family's death, and I can't get any closer to Indians than the friendlies' camp!''

McGarrity laid one broad, sun-browned hand on Drew's shoulder. ''I know why you're here, son, and when I need someone to lead the charge, I'll send you. This action calls for something else, and I know I can count on Parker to behave with restraint.''

Drew shook his head, his nerves still humming. There had to be more to it than a question of experience. ''This—this isn't because of Cassie, is it? Because she's—''

''No,'' McGarrity answered gruffly and took back his hand. ''Cassie doesn't have a thing to do with how you fight. There may be times in your career when Cassie and what happened to her will make a difference. This isn't one of them.''

Drew had wanted so much for this to be Cassie's fault, but he squared his shoulders and nodded. ''As you say, sir.''

McGarrity paused as if he meant to offer something more, then moved along.

Drew stood there after McGarrity left, alone with his frustration and his failure. His head ached with the need for sleep, but the nightmare was waiting every time he closed his eyes. He'd been painting every night until almost dawn, even though his hands shook so hard he could barely control the brushes. He could feel himself coming apart.

If they'd just given him this command, he might have been all right. If they'd just let him go fight Indians, he'd be able to hold himself together. But he was failing to keep the most important vow he'd ever made, and he couldn't live with either that or with himself.

Drew yearned to put his ghosts to rest. He had a woman who should have been able to give him love and comfort. He had a child who should have brought him joy, but he couldn't let either of them close enough to touch him or ease his pain. He couldn't let anyone in—not while he was accountable to his family, not when the army denied him the vengeance he needed so desperately.

Drew scrubbed at his face with his hands and turned toward the door. He had to do something to silence the clamor inside him. He never allowed himself whiskey in the middle of the day, but today he'd make an exception. Now that McGarrity had denied him the chance to redeem himself, he needed something else—and whiskey would have to suffice.

Cassie didn't know why she'd decided to clean. It was hot. The bucket of water she'd brought from the water wagon was so full of silt she had to put it aside until the mud settled out. She had swept and cleaned the kitchen the previous day. Still, she hummed with a disquieting energy that propelled her through the house with her dustcloth and mop.

She started in the parlor. Since their wedding, she and Drew had acquired a few more furnishings. There was a spoke-backed armchair with a padded seat, a footstool, and a three-legged table just big enough to hold a book and a lamp to read it by. She dusted each of them, wondering how Drew's meeting was going, wondering if Meggie was having fun wading on the far side of the bridge with Lila and the other laundresses.

Perhaps she could have gone, Cass thought, knowing she would have been less than welcome. Still, it might have done her good to get away from the house. But then she would have remembered that day on the mountain with Hunter. The day she discovered who she was, or at least who she could be when she was with him. She had discovered Hunter that day, too, a man complete within himself. A slow, delicious shiver trickled the length of her back when she thought of how quiet and patient Hunter had been with Meggie and her, how wild-eyed and fierce he'd been defending them. That's why it wasn't safe to remember.

She swiped at the hair tumbling over her brow and moved on to where Drew's campaign desk sat against the wall. He always kept it inspection neat. The company books lay to the left of the blotter; an oil lamp stood on the right. His paint box sat dead center on top.

Cassie rubbed her cloth across the wooden case and wondered what enchantment it held for him. How could Drew spend so much time with his brushes, and so little time with Meggie and her? When she opened the box she saw only crinkled tubes of pigment, sheets of paper, and an ivory palette for mixing colors. She could discern no magic there.

She closed the lid with a snap and went on dusting. She whisked her cloth down the desk's narrow criss-crossed legs and encountered Drew's green morocco portfolio braced against the wall. This was where he kept his paintings. His secrets.

Cass could see the ruffled edges of the papers inside, hints of colors and shapes, elusive bits of a man who was inexorably turning from her. She bent over the loosely tied ribbons at the top, her fingers twitching. Perhaps if she glanced at them just this once, if she understood more about what drove him, she could be a better helpmate, a more loving wife. But Drew had hidden the paintings away deliberately. He didn't want her looking.

But as she bent to wipe the back legs of the desk, the hem of her skirt snagged on the portfolio and knocked it sideways. The ribbons came undone and paintings spilled everywhere.

They lay like a bright, tumbled patchwork across the floor, and for a moment Cass simply stared at them. Then, with a jolt of guilt, she sank to her knees and began to gather them up.

The first that came under her hand was a landscape of the prairie rendered with a skill and sensitivity that stole her breath. With a few swipes of his brush and a wash of color, Drew had captured the scope and beauty of this wide, stark land. He'd painted the breadth and clarity of her wondrous sky, shown the challenge and the freedom of those long horizons. Drew understood how this land could change a man, and Cass wondered if and how it was changing him.

She reached for the next paintings in the pile and realized that each was signed and dated. How like Drew, Cass thought, gathering up the papers in sequence.

Next came a series of watercolors that sparkled with wondrous vitality. A column of soldiers wound its way around a bluff. A muleteer leaned from the seat of his wagon cracking a whip. A party of men mounted up for patrol. The paintings were such a perfect depiction of life at the fort that Cassie smiled.

She gathered up several more papers and found that Drew had narrowed his focus to Meggie and her: Meggie hunkered down on the floor serving tea to her dolls, Cass whipping up some concoction in a crockery bowl. He had shown the concentration in her face, the errant curls that straggled along her cheek, the swipes she took with her wooden spoon. Drew took that moment in time and made it live again.

She caught her breath when she saw the next painting in the sequence. She and Meggie were curled together in the rocking chair. Depicting them in soft, subtle shades of sepia and mauve, Drew had shown the trust in his little girl's face, the love and pride in Cassie's eyes. He had captured the delight and heartbreak, the infinite complexity of the bond between mother and child. He had seen how things were between Meggie and her and set down not just their likenesses, but their emotions.

Cass stared at the painting through a sheen of tears. No man could paint his child with such tenderness or his wife with such sensitivity without loving them both. This painting proved Drew's feelings. The man who painted this was lurking inside her husband somewhere, close enough to access with a brush, close enough to see what he was missing. If that were so, Cass could reach him, touch him, make things better.

She clung to that image and that promise until the next paintings that fell under her hand extinguished all her hope.

They were portraits of Drew's parents, Julia, his brothers and their wives. Beautifully and meticulously done, they showed the resolve in his father's stance, the mischief in Julia's eyes, the steadfastness in both Peter and Matthew's faces. And each of the portraits had been smeared with blood.

''Oh Drew,'' Cass moaned, crushing the papers against her chest.

Until now Drew's art had been small, eloquent spills of color and emotion, ways of showing his joy, his love, and his awe. In those paintings he had been able to both express and control what he was feeling. In these Cass felt the pure, raw magnitude of Drew's pain. It was as if by acknowledging the massacre Drew had forfeited his control; torn open old, festering wounds; revealed himself in a way that wasn't safe; that wasn't even rational.

Cass tried not to look at the last of the pictures, yet she was drawn to them. With trembling hands, she spread them on the floor around her.

Each was more terrible than the last—that canyon with its hazy light and high, steep walls; their five tiny wagons red with flame; their two shattered families sprawled broken and bleeding on the earth.

A hot wash of horror swept through her as she stared at them, remembering her family dying before her eyes. Her wrists seemed to burn as if still chafed by her bonds. Her throat felt raw from screaming. Her eyes stung with smoke and tears. She did not need Drew's paintings to remind her of what had happened.

Yet somehow Drew's memories were even more vivid than hers, as if he'd courted those moments of pain and death to fuel his hatred. As if he hadn't dared to forget. These paintings were why Drew had no room in his life for Meggie and her.

Cassie swept the papers up in her hands, frantic to get them out of her sight. She'd been wrong to trespass inside Drew's world, inside Drew's mind. It was best for both of them if he never knew she had.

She froze at the thump of footfalls coming up the steps, at the rumble of boots across the porch. Cass's heart stood still as Drew loomed up in the open doorway.

She crouched on the floor, guilty as Cain standing over his brother's body.

Drew saw what she had done and tightened joint by joint, getting taller and taller.

"Oh, Drew, I'm sorry—"

"Jesus, Cassie," he muttered through lips so stiff she was

surprised that he could speak at all. "Not this. Not today."

She shuffled the papers, cowering. "I was dusting and the portfolio . . ."

Drew surveyed the scene with eyes as bleak as a January sky. "And once the paintings were out, you decided to paw through them, didn't you?"

Cassie's voice shook as she apologized. "I didn't mean to look. I didn't want to see—"

"Then put the paintings away, Cassie," he told her, his voice so low she could barely hear it. "We'll forget you ever saw them. We'll forget I ever painted them."

He dismissed her with a glance and headed for the kitchen.

Cass sprang to her feet and scrambled after him. "How can I forget what's there?" she demanded, surprising herself with her willingness to confront him. *"How can you?"*

"I don't want to talk about the paintings!" he shouted, and cleared the kitchen table with the swipe of his hand.

Tin plates and pewterware clattered to the floor. Wooden candlesticks bounced and rolled. A small glass of wildflowers shattered, staining the wooden floorboards with wet.

He looked down at the wreckage, breathing hard.

Cass shrank back against the doorjamb.

Drew was quivering as if he might shatter.

She ventured toward him, with the same care she might take in approaching a snarling wolf.

"What is it? What's wrong? This is about a good deal more than those paintings."

"Goddamnit, Cassie! Leave me alone!"

Drew stalked to the shelves where he kept his whiskey, poured himself a drink, and brought the bottle to the table.

"This is about the rifles, isn't it?"

The whole fort knew what had arrived the night before, just as everyone knew where they were headed.

Drew sank onto the bench as if he were a hundred years old.

Cass crossed the room and knelt beside him. "They aren't going to let you take the rifles north, are they?"

Drew poured himself another drink. "Parker's taking them," he admitted after a moment. "He and forty men are heading out on Thursday by some damned route Jalbert has found."

He took a gulp of the whiskey. "Goddamnit, Cassie, I'm the one McGarrity should have picked. My troops are better trained than Parker's. I'm a better officer."

He finished the liquor and set the glass aside.

"I've been waiting all this time for my chance to fight the redskins—waiting to get through West Point, waiting for the war to be over, waiting for the posting to Fort Carr, waiting for the goddamned orders to come. And now that there's finally a chance to see some action, McGarrity gives the assignment to someone else! After what the savages took from me, I deserve—"

Cass remembered what she'd seen in those last paintings, and tried to reach him anyway. "I know, Drew," she crooned. "I know. I lost my family, the same as you. But killing Indians won't bring them back."

She took his hands.

"Drew, please," she whispered, looking into his face. "That day destroyed everyone we loved, every hope we had. But it was long ago. It's time for you to forgive yourself for living when everyone died."

"I don't deserve to be forgiven."

Cass swallowed hard, thinking of Julia. "I didn't think I deserved to be forgiven, either, but neither of us could help what happened. Neither of us could change it."

Drew let out his breath on a sigh and looked away.

"I know what you're feeling. I know how to face the past and get beyond it. If you let me, I can help." Cass was all but pleading, both for his life and hers. "Please, Drew, I can help you forget. Please, let me do that."

Drew shifted his gaze to hers. She saw the weariness and longing in his eyes. He raised one hand to cup her face. With infinite deliberation he traced the lines that radiated across her cheek.

"Oh, Cassie," he whispered, shaking his head. "You can't ever help me forget. You're part of the remembering."

Cassandra read the truth in Drew's eyes. Inside her the hope that she's been nurturing crumbled away. She breathed the lingering dust of those shattered hopes and felt them rasp and burn inside her.

"I think—" she said, coming slowly to her feet. "I think I need to be by myself for a while."

When Drew didn't say a word, she ran out the kitchen door and didn't look back.

Hunter leaned against the porch of the headquarters building, scuffing up dust and waiting—though he couldn't say for what. Only when Cass came bolting out the door of her cabin did he realize he'd been waiting for her.

He lit out after her, lengthened his strides to keep her in sight. She scurried on ahead, her shoulders bowed, her head bent, and her arms wrapped around her waist as if she hurt.

As if the captain had hurt her. Bile washed up the back of Hunter's throat. If Reynolds had so much as laid a hand on Cass . . .

God knows the captain was coiled tighter than a watch spring these days. He'd been driving his men and himself. Everyone knew Reynolds had wanted to take those rifles north. It must have all but killed him to sit there and listen to McGarrity give the assignment to someone else. He'd held all that inside during the meeting, but he must have let loose once he got home. No wonder Cass had come flying out of that cabin.

Hunter caught up to her on the riverbank. She stood facing the water, her head bowed and her shoulders heaving. He slowed his steps. He didn't mean to startle or intrude on her.

"Cass?" he called out softly.

She swung around to face him, and Hunter froze.

Out on the prairie defending her own, Cass had been magnificent. She'd been tall and proud and possessed of a courage any warrior would envy. She was a husk of that woman now, pale and shrunken and small, as if Reynolds had sucked the life from her.

He wanted to gather her up in his hands and give back everything the captain had taken away: her pride and her vitality and her belief in herself. *He wanted to punch Drew Reynolds so hard he'd be spitting teeth for a week.*

"Are—are you all right?" he asked instead.

Cass nodded that she was.

Hunter didn't believe her—not when he could hear the uneasy cadence of her breathing and see how her hands were shaking.

"Is something wrong?"

"No, of course not."

Damn her for denying it. For denying him.

Hunter jammed his fists into his pockets and stepped beyond her down the bank. He ground his teeth and cursed the captain and convention and the people in the fort. He cursed everything that prevented him from taking Cass in his arms, and giving her the help and comfort she needed.

They stood there for a very long while. In the end it was Cass who broke the silence.

"Do you know how a Cheyenne husband divorces his wife?" she asked him, her voice all shivery and small.

Hunter shook his head. He didn't dare turn and look at her.

"He throws her away," she told him. "That's what Gray Falcon did. When he wanted to take a new wife, one who could bear him children, Gray Falcon took a stick out onto the floor at the dance lodge and danced with it. When he was done, he threw the stick away and announced he no longer wanted me as his wife."

She faltered for a moment. "Then he went to our tepee and threw out all my things. He said any man could have me after that. All my new husband would have to do to claim me was to offer Gray Falcon a brace of rabbits and a twist of tobacco."

Hunter stiffened as she spoke, angry at the low price Gray Falcon had set for her, angry that she had been bid and bartered for a second time.

"And though I was skilled in quilling and beading and preparing skins, no man wanted a woman who could not bear him sons. That's why the Cheyenne returned me to the whites, because no man would claim me, because no man would make such a worthless woman his responsibility."

Hunter choked back the words—words that might have softened those old hurts and whatever Reynolds had done to torment her today. They were words that praised her courage and her smiles, words that revealed a tenderness Hunter had never felt for anyone.

"I was so determined to make a place for myself when I came here." Cass sounded as if she were dying inside. "I thought that because Drew and I had loved each other once, we could make a life together."

Hunter turned and looked at her. "What is it? What's happened?"

Cassie's face was flushed and mottled from crying. "Drew says he'll never be able to forget the massacre—what happened to us, what happened to our families—because every time he sees my face the memories come back."

She scrubbed at the star burst on her cheek as if she could wash it away with the salt of her tears.

Hunter pulled her hands away.

"My husband hates this mark so much—" she said so softly he could barely hear "—that he only ever comes to me when it is dark."

Fool. Hunter's brain smoked with an image of creamy skin and tumbled hair, of rounded shoulders and slender thighs. *Goddamned fool!*

"Oh, Cass!" He breathed, holding her hands in both of his. "Do you know what I see when I look at you?"

She shook her head.

Hunter fumbled for words that could soothe her hurt. "I see a woman who is as beautiful as she is brave," he said slowly. "I see one who shines with compassion, who is always helpful and kind. Of course I see the mark, but it's only part of who you are. No more or less than the color of your hair or the gentleness of your hands or the goodness of your heart."

Cass blinked back her tears and smiled at him. It was a rare, soft smile that seemed to make the sun shine brighter. Hunter's chest filled with the pleasure at seeing a flicker of light at the backs of those pale eyes.

Then a wistful turn of her lips dimmed the sun. "If only Drew could see me the way you do," she whispered. "If only he could stop remembering . . ."

Hunter released her hands and glared past her to where the roofs of the buildings were visible at the top of the bank, thinking of what the people there had done to her.

He *could* have done better for Cass than Reynolds had. He could have protected her, cared for her, given her a place to belong. But he had been as big a fool as Reynolds. He hadn't even tried to claim her. He hadn't known his own mind. He hadn't trusted what he felt. He hadn't believed that anyone could matter as much to him as Cassandra did. He hadn't believed that he could be better for Cass than Drew could be. But he'd been wrong.

"What will you do?" he finally asked.

The question was inevitable; the answer was inevitable, too.

"I'll stay on. Meggie needs me, and I need her. Sometimes when I'm holding her," she admitted softly, "I pretend she's mine."

Hunter recognized the heartbreak in her eyes. Cass wanted so much more than it seemed likely she could ever have.

"Is Meggie enough to keep you here?"

She lifted her gaze to his, touching him in some extraordinary way that left him tingling.

"I have you, too, don't I, Hunter?"

His heart kicked hard against his ribs. She could have him any way she wanted, heart and mind, body and soul.

"You understand, what it means to live between two worlds," she continued softly. "You know what that demands, and you've helped me pay the cost. You've been my friend, Hunter, and I need you to stand by me now."

He needed her, too, in a hundred ways that went beyond understanding and friendship. He needed her strength when the way was hard, her tenderness when he'd had his fill of brutality. He needed the solace of her mouth and hands and body when he craved peace and beauty and pleasure.

He wanted to reassure her with his touch, but he didn't dare reach out to her. "Of course I'll stand by you," he told her. "Whatever you need, you have only to ask."

She held his gaze again, turning him breathless, making

him ache with a need so deep it seemed as if it had always been part of him.

"Thank you, Hunter," she whispered. "Now I need to go back."

Hunter nodded reluctantly. "Shall I go with you?"

Whatever had happened between them today had changed things.

"I don't think that would be wise."

Hunter swallowed down his regret. "As you wish."

She turned and started up the bank, alone and vulnerable, brave and fine. He stood and watched her go, a woman so special she shone like the sun, the woman Hunter Jalbert had come to love.

Chapter Eighteen

The attack would come today. Hunter knew it the moment he opened his eyes. They were three days out from Fort Carr and would reach the junction with the Bozeman Trail sometime before noon. If they got their cargo of rifles through, they'd sleep in the stockade at Fort Phil Kearney tonight.

If they got the rifles through.

Hunter sat his horse on the crest of the hill above the previous night's camp. He watched the cavalry finish saddling their horses and the infantry troops take their places in the three covered wagons. While he waited, Jalbert reviewed the plans they'd made to defend themselves. Parker and his men would engage the attackers while the muleteers circled the wagons and the infantry rolled back the wagons' canvas tops to give them fighting room. It was a more than adequate plan and could drive off a good-sized force of Indians. Still, Hunter felt the itch between his shoulder blades that always meant trouble.

"Keep an eye out, boys," he heard Captain Parker shout as he motioned the wagons forward. Hunter intended to do the same.

He galloped on ahead and spent the morning ranging to the right and left of where the wagon ruts cut through the rolling prairie land. He investigated every hollow where the enemy could hide. He rode to the crest of every ridge. It was inching on toward midday when he spotted a narrow passage where the trace wound down along the bank of a rippling stream. Low dun gray bluffs of broken stone hemmed the stream on the far side and a grassy plateau rose off to the right. The place felt oddly confining for all that it was in the midst of open ground.

Hunter rode both west and east, looking for a way to circumvent the creek, but any other course would take them miles out of their way. He rode back to where the wagons were approaching the little draw.

"I'm concerned about the narrows up ahead, sir," he told Parker, as he reigned in his horse. "I don't see any sign of hostiles, but it wouldn't hurt for us to be ready."

Parker took his advice and gave the order. "Stay in close, Jalbert, at least until we're through that draw."

It seemed ten degrees cooler along the rippling stream than it had in the flat. Birds chattered in the bushes that lined the opposite bank. Yellow and pink wildflowers poked their heads above the green-gold grass. It was a pleasant place, yet Hunter breathed a little easier when he saw the land opening up beyond it.

The first wagon was just pulling toward the mouth of the draw when Hunter heard the rumble of horses' hooves off to the west. He wheeled his mount and saw the Indians riding down on them. They galloped in an inexorable stream, yipping and waving their weapons. Hunter saw more attackers skidding down the slope at the rear of the little wagon train.

The front and rear guards rode out to engage the enemy. Though the draw was too narrow to circle the wagons, the muleteers managed to pull them far enough off the trail that the infantrymen would be fighting with the slope of the plateau against their backs.

Hunter grabbed for his pistol and nudged his horse toward where Parker and his vanguard were already battling hand to hand.

It is a very good day—

An image of Cassandra flickered in his head, accompanied by a sharp, hot pain of regret. He blinked the apparition away, angry that thoughts of her could intrude on him now, appalled that a warrior should be so weak.

He turned to the brave riding down on him, whooped his war cry, and fired on his attacker at point-blank range.

The man went down in a swirl of dust. A second challenger loomed up from where the first warrior had fallen. Painted and feathered, his face contorted in a leer of hatred, the second Sioux lowered his lance and rode at Hunter.

Hunter jerked his horse to the left to get out of the way, but he was hemmed in by the wagons on one side and a cavalryman on the other. He raised his gun, but he was far too late to save himself. The muscles of his abdomen contracted, anticipating the thrust of the lance, the searing pain, and certain death.

Then from almost directly behind him came the crack of a cavalry rifle. The lance went wide. The Indian pitched from his horse not a yard away.

Hunter swung around to see if he could tell whose shot had saved his life. Josh Wilcox paused in his reloading just long enough to lift his head above the wagon seat and grin. Hunter nodded in acknowledgment. He owed Corporal Wilcox a drink when they got out of this.

Hunter looked around and saw that the fight was far from over. More Indians were pouring down on them. He heard Parker shout for the cavalry to fall back. The troopers still in the saddle kicked their horses toward the shelter of the wagons. The captain did the same, but before he could reach safety, he clutched at his chest and slumped forward in his saddle.

Hunter pulled his mount's head around and spurred up the draw. He couldn't tell how badly Parker was hurt, but no man deserved what the Sioux would do to him if he was captured. Hunter fired as he rode and clawed the reins from the major's bloodstained hand.

The narrow seam between the hillside and the wagons provided a modicum of safety. Once he'd threaded their way inside, Hunter jumped from his horse and eased Parker out of the saddle. He laid the major on the grass and probed his wound.

"No use," the major gasped, and Hunter could see that he was right. "Go and try to hold the resistance together."

Hunter turned back to the fight, and what he saw made his blood run cold. Cavalry troopers' bodies were strewn across the grass along the course of the stream. Infantrymen lay crumpled behind the wagons. The gunfire had dwindled to the point where Hunter wondered if there was anyone left to fight at all. He reloaded his pistol as he ran the length of the wagon train, shouting for a response from soldiers still at their posts. He got almost two dozen answers out of what had been a company of forty men.

Near the end of the line, he encountered Sam Gifford, one of Noonan's first lieutenants. "Parker's wounded," Hunter told him. "I think that means you're in charge."

"Me?" Gifford gasped, going a shade or two whiter than he'd been before. He was new to Fort Carr and without a lick of field experience.

"I don't know how much longer we can hold out," Hunter went on. He picked up a rifle, reloaded it, and handed it to Gifford. "But whatever happens, we sure as hell can't let the Sioux get hold of these guns. I think we need to prepare to blow the wagons."

"Blow the wagons?" Gifford gasped, his mouth sagging like bunting the day after a parade. "Blow them up with dynamite?"

Hunter nodded. "There's some in that first wagon. Do you want me to rig it?"

"Rig it?"

"Rig the wagons to blow up in case we're overrun."

Gifford looked ready to wet himself. "Are we going to die, Mr. Jalbert?"

"I'm not making any plans for tomorrow," Hunter answered. He cast an eye to where the Indians were massing at the head of the draw.

Gifford saw them, too. It jolted him into action. "Very—very w-w-well, Mr. Jalbert. You rig the wagons. The rest of us will do our best to hold the hostiles off."

Hunter grinned at Gifford's sudden surge of gumption and headed back the way he'd come. He stepped over bodies as he ran. The sickly-sweet smell of blood soured in his throat. The shrill whoops of a hundred warriors drowned out the moans of men in pain. The rifle fire that answered the charge wasn't nearly enough to hold off the Indians.

They *were* going to die after all.

Hunter swallowed something that tasted suspiciously like fear and reached over the side of the first wagon. He rummaged for dynamite, clamped his hands around six fat sticks and a coil of fuse. Now where were the goddamned blasting caps?

Then above his own muttered curse, the yelling and the shooting, Hunter heard what sounded like a bugle call. With explosives in hand, he dropped down behind the wagon and listened hard. From up to the north where this trace connected with the Bozeman Trail came the clear, sweet notes of the call to arms.

The Sioux seemed to hear it, too, and decided, just as Hunter had, that the sound meant reinforcements. They broke off their assault on the wagons and headed south.

Moments after the last of the Sioux swept past, a detachment of cavalry came galloping into the draw. Most of the troopers lit out after the Indians. A few reined in and drew up before the wagons. Judging from their insignia, they must have been sent from Fort Phil Kearney to meet and escort them north.

Hunter leaned back against the wagon and let out his breath.

As the troopers from Fort Phil Kearney began to assess the wounded and the dead, Hunter went back to where he'd left Amos Parker lying in the grass.

Parker was still breathing, still barely alive when Hunter bent over him.

"We got reinforcements, Captain," he murmured, not sure Parker could hear him.

The captain's eyelids fluttered. He seemed to smile. "Good," he said. "We beat them back then, did we?"

"Yes, sir. The troops put up a good fight."

That seemed to satisfy Parker for a moment. Then he opened his eyes and looked into Hunter's face.

"A favor, Jalbert?" Parker rasped, his breathing thready.

"Of course, sir."

"Promise you'll give—my gold watch—to my oldest son Billy," he instructed.

Hunter nodded.

"Tell Alma"—the major grimaced—"I'm glad she chose me—for that quadrille. Tell her I—love her. That—I'm sorry I didn't—say it nearly enough . . ."

Hunter watched the light go out of Amos Parker's eyes. He hadn't known the man very well. He hadn't liked him or his wife and children because of how they treated Cass, but he was sorry Parker was dead. No man should die with words of regret on his lips.

But you can't tell Cass how you feel. You can't tell her you love her. Not while she was married to another man. Not even now that he knew that marriage was a sham. He couldn't burden Cass with knowing. He couldn't confuse her or compromise her. He might die without the words ever passing his lips, but Hunter would love Cassandra Morgan until the day he breathed his last.

Hunter closed Parker's staring eyes and pushed to his feet. He would see that Parker got a proper burial. He would deliver the watch and the messages to Parker's wife and family.

It had been a good day to die—just not for him.

"They're back!" Meggie crowed, bursting into the kitchen. "The wagon men are back!"

Cassie dropped the scissors she'd been using to cut out the pattern for Meggie's new dress and rushed out onto the porch. Three tall wagons were just pulling up in front of headquarters. She grabbed Meggie's hand and ran down along officers' row to where a crowd was gathering. Cavalry and infantry, laundresses and scouts, muleteers, pioneers and even a few of the friendly Indians had quickly assembled to welcome their boys home. Drew had to be here somewhere, and even Tyler Jessup had oozed out from under his rock to hear what had happened.

Word of the attack had reached Fort Carr by telegraph five days before. The message hadn't said much, just that the rifles were safe, that there had been some fighting, and that Captain Amos Parker had been killed in the line of duty. In typical army fashion, the telegram hadn't mentioned the fate of the forty men who'd ridden with him.

Drew had referred to this expedition as "glory duty." But as Cass shouldered her way through the crowd, she couldn't see anything glorious about the battered wagons and even more battered men who had returned to the fort.

"There are so few left," Cass whispered, half to herself.

The knot in her chest cinched tighter as she sought out one familiar face, one particular man. She found him standing at the rear of the third wagon, holding his horse. He looked tattered, dust-stained, and exhausted, but whole and safe.

Cass sucked in a long, deep breath, light-headed with relief. Then Hunter raised his head and caught her staring. Their gazes held, his eyes tormented and hot. She recoiled at the anguish she saw in him. She felt stunned by the intensity of his regret. Whatever had befallen this detachment of men, Hunter blamed himself .

At the head of the line of wagons, Lieutenant Gifford stepped forward and saluted Major McGarrity. "Detail from Fort Phil Kearney reporting, sir."

Though under normal circumstances the young lieutenant would have given his account of the mission in the major's office, McGarrity knew emotions at the fort were running high.

"You may speak, Lieutenant Gifford," he said. "We all want to know what went on out there."

As the lieutenant spoke, Cass watched Hunter's face. In spite of what had passed between them a few moments before, he was not a man who revealed much of himself. Still, she recognized the signs of his distress. His jaw broadened. His shoulders bunched. She saw the way his fingers clenched around his horse's reins. Though Lieutenant Gifford made it clear there was nothing anyone could have done to prevent the attack, Cass knew Hunter considered himself responsible.

When Gifford was done, McGarrity asked about the losses. "Have you a list of casualties from this action, Lieutenant?"

A wave of dread ran through the crowd. Cass picked Meggie up in her arms, as much to feel the weight and warmth of the child against her as to stop the girl's fidgeting.

Gifford withdrew the paper from his pocket.

Cassie saw Hunter dip his head and felt dread settle deeper. The news was bad.

"We lost one officer and six enlisted men, sir. Nine others are recovering from wounds at Fort Phil Kearney."

Sixteen men out of forty, Cassie thought.

"And will you read us the names of the dead, Lieutenant." McGarrity knew this was what everyone was waiting to hear.

Gifford cleared his throat. "Cavalry Captain Amos Parker."

Alma Parker, all done up in her widow's weeds, turned to sob against Sally McGarrity's shoulder. Her children, tear-splotched and uncertain, clung to their mother's skirts. Cassie ached for them, understanding what they were feeling. No one should be deprived of a parent so early in life.

"Also deceased are Cavalry Sergeant Shamus Mulligan," Gifford continued over groans of dismay, "and Corporal Johnny Wegman. Cavalry Privates Billy Boyle, Michael Longacre, and Alfred Spencer. And Infantry Corporal Joshua Wilcox."

"Josh?" Cass gasped on a breath that burned all the way down.

"Josh?" Meggie repeated.

Patting Meggie's back, Cass scoured the crowd for Lila and Will. She spotted them standing to the left of the headquarters' steps. They slumped together like two wax dolls. Will's eyes were fixed and flat. Lila clenched and unclenched her reddened hands, as if she were grabbing at something that was already gone.

Cassie buried her face against Meggie's throat. Cass didn't know how a mother lived with the death of her child, how Lila could accept the loss of all of her sons. What could Cassie say or do to comfort her?

How would she survive if she lost Meggie?

She nuzzled closer, unwilling to believe that such a thing could happen when she loved this child so desperately. Yet she knew she'd lose this baby forever if Drew sent her away.

Cass couldn't think about that now. Not when Lila needed comforting and Hunter looked so brittle and shaken.

Cass raised her head, suddenly aware of the strident, outraged voices rising around her.

"How did the hostiles know what route our men were taking to Fort Phil Kearney?" someone demanded of Ben McGarrity.

"And how did the redskins know what those wagons were carrying?"

Cass nodded, as eager for explanations as anyone here.

McGarrity held up his hands in a plea for quiet. "Those wagons were carrying army stores," he told the crowd.

His declaration stirred up hoots and catcalls.

"Hell, Major," one of the muleteers shouted around his wad of chaw, "even my lead Blue knew them wagons was carrying rifles."

McGarrity's jaw bulged dangerously. "No one knew that," he insisted. "No one knew the route those wagons were taking. No one knew when they were leaving."

But the major was wrong. Cass had known about the shipment of guns; Drew had told her. Other wives would have known, too. So would the bunkmates of the soldiers who'd been assigned to the detachment. So would the quartermaster and the baker and the cooks. There were no secrets on a post this size.

"Then, Major, if you're so certain you kept the shipment a secret," someone suggested, "there must be an informer here at the fort."

A speculative murmur rippled through the crowd like wind through wheat.

"It would have to be someone with connections to the Sioux," one man said.

"Someone who knew how to get word to the Indians."

"It needs to be someone with something to gain."

Cass had heard this kind of speculation the night of the fire and dread seeped into her belly.

Tyler Jessup was the one who shouted the accusation. "I think our spy is Captain Reynolds's squaw."

A hundred gazes turned on her.

"She only come from the Indians a few months past," someone added.

"She had truck with that redskin's escape."

It was like rolling a barrel down hill. Once the allegations got started, there was no stopping them.

"She admitted to giving that Indian woman milk."

Cass looked to Hunter, seeking calm and sustenance in his eyes. They were stormy instead, dark and glittering with anger.

She shook her head, hoping he had sense enough to hold his peace. He would only undermine his position by defending her.

"Ask her!" someone shouted. "Ask Reynolds's squaw what she knows about the rifles."

Half the crowd mumbled in agreement.

"Here, now!" Major McGarrity protested. "We aren't about to accuse Cassandra Reynolds of anything. This isn't some damned witch-hunt!"

Drew materialized at her side, all honor and obligation. Cass wasn't certain why he'd come. He hadn't believed in her since the night of the fire.

Cass recognized Jessup's voice again. "You're going to make inquiries, aren't you, Major?"

"What we're going to do," McGarrity answered, "is get back to our duties. Lieutenant Gifford?"

"Sir?"

"Since our men were buried at Phil Kearney, did you bring home their effects?"

"I did, sir."

"See that they are distributed to either the men's commanding officers or their families. I also want a written report on the incident on my desk by noon tomorrow. As for the rest of you"—McGarrity let his gaze sweep across the crowd—"you're dismissed. Get back to work!"

With a few mumbles of dissent, the crowd broke up. Rather than turn back to the cabin, Cassandra pushed toward where Lila and Will Wilcox huddled together.

"I didn't think the Lord would take my Josh," Lila was

whispering to her husband. "I didn't think He would see fit to take away all my boys."

Will didn't say anything. He rarely did. He just stood there rubbing Lila's hands between his own.

Cass suddenly saw how old their linked hands looked. They were reddened and scuffed and rivered with veins. These boys, Josh and his brothers, had been Will and Lila's life's work, their precious gift to a wondrous and dangerous world. And now they were gone.

Cass shifted Meggie in her arms and reached toward Josh's parents. "Lila, Will, I'm so sorry for your—"

Lila looked up. Her gaze sharpened as she realized who Cass was. "You!" she spit. "How dare you come to me now! How dare you tell me you're sorry! You knew those wagons were carrying guns. You sent the redskins word. You cost my Josh his life!"

"No!" Cassie gasped, wounded by her friend's accusation. "I had nothing to do with the attack on the wagons!"

"I was your friend," Lila seethed, as if she had not heard. "When no one else would speak to you, I came by. When the others called you an Indian whore, I defended you. And this is how you repay me—by killing my son."

"No, Lila, please believe me," Cassie begged. "I swear I didn't send word to the Indians. I would never do anything to hurt—"

"Liar!" Lila accused before turning her head into her husband's shoulder.

"I think you'd best leave us alone now, Mrs. Reynolds," Will Wilcox said softly, and turned toward soapsuds row.

Cass stood too shaken to move, too stunned to breathe. How could Lila believe she'd had a hand in this? What had she done to make these people think—

"Cassie?" Meggie's voice cut into her thoughts. "Did the Indians kill Josh?"

"Yes," Cass answered. "Josh is dead, and Lila's feeling very sad."

Meggie hesitated, then looked square into Cassandra's face. "She said you did it, that you killed him."

Cass felt her heart catch fire. Tears sprang to her eyes.

"You know better than that, Meggie," she answered, her voice broken and low. "You know how much I liked Josh. You know I would never do anything to hurt him."

"But Lila said."

Cass took a steadying breath and turned toward their cabin. "Lila heard what the other people were saying and got confused. Once she's thinking more clearly, she'll realize she's wrong about what happened."

At least Cass hoped she would.

Drew was waiting on the cabin porch like a sentry guarding the gates of a beleaguered citadel. He let her pass and followed her into the kitchen. She set Meggie on her feet and began to gather up the pattern and the scissors she'd been using. She wiped the table with a cloth, laying out the plates and cutlery for supper. She stuck doggedly to her tasks, pretending that today was just like yesterday.

Drew stood watching her. "You knew about the shipment of the guns," he finally accused. "I told you myself. You could have sent the Indians word—"

His distrust crushed down on her, adding its weight to the crowd's wild accusations and Lila's reproach. Still, she wasn't surprised by his defection. "Oh, Drew," she asked wearily. "Do you really think I'm capable of betraying everyone at Fort Carr?"

Drew shook his head. "Oh, Jesus, Cassie! I don't know what you're capable of anymore."

Cass hadn't expected his resignation to hurt so much. She burned inside, raw and aching for a child and a man and a life she now knew were unattainable. She didn't belong here any more than she had belonged anywhere else.

She fled out into the early twilight. She didn't know where she was going. She couldn't see for the blur of tears. She heard Meggie chase after her and call her name, but Cass couldn't go back.

She wasn't sure she could ever go back.

Hunter rose from sleep like a swimmer from a long deep dive, breathless, disoriented, with blood rushing in his ears. It took him a moment to realize he was awakening in his own lodge, in his own bed, and that someone was tapping at the door to his tepee.

"Who's there?" he called out.

"It's me. Cassandra."

"Cass?" Hunter mumbled and scrambled to his feet. He flung back the buffalo hide door and pulled her into his tent. Didn't she know the chance she was taking by coming here?

Dressed in nothing but his breechclout, Hunter stepped outside to look around. His end of Fort Carr's Indian encampment was all but deserted; no one could have seen Cass come to his tepee. In the dusk, he could see a bonfire and some sort of gathering down toward soapsuds row. He heard a fiddle's sweet lament and realized it was a wake for the men who'd been killed on the wagon train. The melancholy sound stirred Hunter's own regret. He'd done his best and failed those troopers, anyway.

Sighing, he ducked back inside his lodge.

Cass stood where he'd left her, her shoulders hunched and her head bent low. He thought she had been crying.

"Cass?" he said as gently as he could. "What is it? Why are you here?"

"I didn't know where else to go."

He heard the desolation in her voice, saw how frail and depleted she seemed. He eased her down into one of the canvas campstools drawn up to the edge of the fire pit and dipped water from the bucket by the door. He crouched before her and made her drink. Her hands were trembling when she gave the dipper back.

Hunter hunkered down again and waited for Cass to tell him why she'd come.

"Josh Wilcox," she began on a thready sigh, "was Lila's youngest son. Lila has been my closest friend—my only friend—here at the fort. She helped me with Meggie and stuck by me when all the other women turned away. But after what happened this afternoon, after what people said about me, Lila—" Cass lifted her gaze to his. "Lila believes I'm the one who told the Cheyenne and the Sioux about the rifles. She thinks I'm the reason Josh got killed."

Hunter recognized shadows of bewilderment and hurt in

Cassie's eyes. If Lila had been able to look beyond her own bitterness and grief, she would have seen them, too, and known that Cass couldn't betray anyone.

"Lila has just learned her son is dead," Hunter began, trying to explain away the hurt, to make excuses. "She isn't thinking clearly. Once she has a chance to reconsider—"

"Everyone thinks I betrayed Captain Parker and his men!" Cass burst out, her voice rising. "Lila and Sally and maybe even Ben McGarrity—"

"I don't believe you had anything to do with it," he assured her softly.

Cassie hesitated, reached out and brushed his arm by way of thanks. "You might not believe I betrayed them, but everyone else does—even my husband! Even Drew!"

Especially Drew, Hunter thought.

"He told me about the plan to transport the rifles, and now he's convinced—" Cass looked down at her hands.

Hunter's blood hummed through his veins like a swarm of bees. *Goddamn Drew Reynolds!* Damn his obsession with revenge and damn his blind expedience.

"After Lila accused me," Cass went on, "after Drew questioned my loyalty, I had to be by myself. I went down to the river so I could hear the water and see the sky. That always helped before." She raised her head and looked at him. "But this time you weren't there with me."

Her words surprised him, delighted him, and made him wary. But if Cass needed him, needed him enough to risk coming here, he couldn't deny her the comfort she was seeking. He closed the scant distance between them, gathered her up in his arms, and was suddenly awash in her scent, fresh as the wind off the prairie; in the lushness of her hips and breasts; in the silken texture of her skin and hair.

He'd wanted to hold her like this for what seemed like forever. He'd wanted to shelter her, offer her his strength and his protection. He'd wanted to let her know that she would always be safe with him.

Hunter just hadn't understood how much he'd needed that closeness himself.

She curled against him, her face nestling into the curve of his throat, her shoulders bowed beneath the contour of his palms, her long graceful limbs flowing against him. She fit him in a way no woman ever had, the curves of her body finding a perfect complement in the unyielding angles of his own. She seemed so fragile in his arms, yet her warmth and her compassion and her humanity seeped into him like rain to dry, parched earth.

Cass knew. She had wandered the wasteland between two worlds. She had experienced the isolation of never belonging anywhere. She understood how lonely that could be. And even in the depths of her own distress, Cass seemed able to soothe him with the warmth of her body and the stroke of her hands. He closed his eyes and let the doubt, the tension, and the terrible regret of these last days drain away. He allowed himself to absorb her unexpected tenderness.

"Is there anything I can do to make Drew and Lila believe I didn't betray our soldiers?" she whispered.

Hunter could barely believe that after all she'd faced in these last five months, in these last nine years, this would be what broke her. But as she raised her head he could see that those pale eyes, the eyes he had once thought devoid of emotion, were sad and wet. Tears tracked down her face, shimmering like crystal in the half-light.

His chest filled. He went breathless and weightless and dizzy. He lifted his hands to cup her face. And then he kissed her.

The brush of his mouth on hers was delicate and tender, something he meant as comfort and consolation. Her lips were soft beneath his, full and pliant, spiced salt-sweet with tears. He tasted deeper, sipping at the corners of her mouth, laving the bow with the tip of his tongue. She opened to him, exposing the inner contours of her mouth to his slow, deliberate exploration. She brushed his tongue with hers and shyly curled away.

Hunter's heart tripped high in his throat. He deepened the kiss, savoring a suddenly fierce and compelling communion. He trailed his fingers down the ivory-smooth column of her neck, across her shoulders, down her back. He pulled her against him, length to length, her body conforming to his, chest and belly, hips and thighs. He caught her up in the breadth of his hands. Her flesh was warm against his palms, so vital, so feminine and ripe.

"Oh Hunter," she breathed into his mouth, and he felt as if he were coming home.

Never had Hunter known such fierce possessiveness, such a need to hold and defend and sustain and cherish. He wanted to kiss Cass awake in the morning and make love to her while the soft scent of sleep still lingered in the curve of her throat and the hollow between her breasts. He wanted to lie with her and whisper secrets in the dark—about how beautiful she was, how wondrous and special, how much he loved her. He wanted to hold her and tease her and pleasure her until she cried out with breathless joy.

Together he and Cass could make a place for themselves where the rest of the world didn't matter. Together they could start again. Together they could find—

Together? The word echoed in Hunter's head. He and Cass had no right to be together.

Cass was a married woman. Not happily married, not content with her life, but committed just the same. And he didn't have any more to offer her now than he had when she first came to the fort. Nothing but himself, nothing but his devotion and his understanding. He wished with all his heart that was enough—and knew it was not.

Hunter dug deep inside himself for the strength to break the kiss. When he raised his head he felt deprived of hope, of sustenance. Staring down into Cassandra's face, he thought she seemed as lost and bereft as he was. Still, he lurched to his feet and put the width of the fire pit between them.

He was breathing hard. His hands were shaking. By both white and Arikara standards, what he and Cass had done was wrong. Yet he refused to feel dishonored by loving Cass, by kissing her—just this once.

"I didn't mean to make things more difficult," he told her.

Cass resettled herself on the stool, curling up, withdrawing inside herself. "I wish we could just run away."

Hunter stared at her. He had not expected a woman like

Cass to consider that course. That she would gave testament to how hopeless she felt, how tired of trying. But even if they really considered running away, he had nowhere to go.

Except Montana.

The idea of taking her up into the mountains where no one could find them, of living suspended between earth and sky, teased the edges of his imagination. But he couldn't lure her with promises of that life when she was bound by love and honor to people here.

If he loved her, he must hold his peace. If he loved her, he must help her keep her vows—even if they were promises she'd made to someone else. If he loved her, he must offer her hope.

"Perhaps by tomorrow everyone will realize how foolish their accusations are," Hunter said almost desperately. "Perhaps McGarrity will discover who really sent word to the Sioux and Cheyenne about the shipment of rifles."

"Perhaps," Cass said on a sigh, and rose from the camp stool. He hated to let her go like this. "What are you going to do?" he asked.

Cassandra shrugged. "Go back to the cabin. Make peace with Drew as best I can. Mother Meggie. Hold my head high and wait."

"Wait for what?"

Cassie didn't answer him. She smoothed her hair and wiped away the last traces of tears with her fingertips.

Hunter had never felt more helpless. "Do you want me to walk you back to the cabin?"

She shook her head. "I don't think we dare take that chance anymore." And then she was gone.

Alone in the tent, Hunter sparked up the fire and stared into that red-orange glow. Now that he was taking time to think, he realized that someone here at Fort Carr must have sent word to the Sioux not only about when the new rifles were being shipped, but by what route. How else would the Indians have known where to ambush the wagon train?

Hunter straightened. There *was* a traitor among them. Someone had forfeited those men's lives. Someone was offering Cass as scapegoat to hide his own treachery. But who would have been privy to the details of the trip north, the timing and the route? Who could have sent word to the Indians without arousing suspicion?

Who had turned the blame on Cass?

He thought back to the confrontation on the parade ground this afternoon. He remembered the heat of the setting sun on his back, the bone-deep weariness, and the bitter taste of failure. He heard angry voices in his head, filled with pain and rage and grief.

Then one voice rang out above the rest. Though the man really hadn't said much—just a word here and there to goad the crowd—Hunter realized who the informer was. But he needed proof before he could approach Ben McGarrity with his suspicions. He'd need a confession from the man to clear Cassandra's name. He'd need to settle his own score with the traitor for offering up the lives of Captain Parker and those young troopers, lives that had been entrusted to him.

Hunter was sure now who had betrayed them. Seeing what other people missed had always been his gift.

Cass fled from Hunter's lodge into the deepening dark. She fled with her skin on fire and her heart fluttering inside her like a moth trapped in a lantern. She fled with the taste of Hunter on her mouth and the heat of his flesh still warming her palms. She left when she desperately wanted to stay. She had committed herself to Meggie and Drew months before, and she would remain with them until everything was settled.

Hunter knew that as well as she. It was why he hadn't asked her to stay with him. And while she might ache with denying herself, she knew where she belonged.

The music drifting up from soapsuds row matched her mood. The high, clear promise of a tin whistle's tune was offset by the soft, sweet weeping of some trooper's violin. In a better world, she might have been invited to join the women who were crying for their friends and sons and lovers, and the men who were mourning their fallen comrades. But not tonight, not when she was who she was, not when everyone thought she had betrayed them.

Still, the music soothed her, made returning to the cabin

she shared with Meggie and Drew less difficult. She paused just shy of the front steps and glanced back to where Hunter's tepee stood, to where the man who knew her heart was all alone. To where—for one agonizing moment—Cass longed to be.

She turned her gaze to the wide dark sky, to the round ripe moon and the spattering of stars. To its height and breadth and freedom. To its promise of a better day tomorrow.

She turned slowly back to the house, where Meggie should be washing up for bed and where Drew might, for this one evening, have relented and read his daughter a story. To where she needed to be.

Once she crossed that threshold she'd be caught again in things she could not change, but Cass had made the only choice she could. She climbed the steps and went inside.

Hunter prowled along the river in the direction of the bridge, past tepees glowing in the dark, past clusters of braves sitting around their campfires smoking pipes, past the telegraph office, where an endless stream of messages clattered down the talking wire. He found a place in the shadows directly across from the sutler's store and watched for his chance to slip inside.

He knew now that Tyler Jessup was the one who'd sent word to the Sioux about the wagon train. But Hunter needed proof before he could go to Ben McGarrity or clear Cassandra's name. If that evidence existed, it was in the sutler's store: in the trading post itself, in the storeroom behind it where Jessup slept, or in the "gaming room" where Fort Carr's perpetual poker game was just getting started. Judging from the men he'd seen headed inside, two muleteers, an infantry corporal, and a drifter were about to be fleeced by Grenville and Lloyd, Fort Carr's resident cardsharps.

Once Hunter was sure the game had begun, he eased inside. The darkened front room was ripe with the smell of Virginia hams, briny pickles, horse liniment, and new cloth. He crouched low, moving along beneath the level of the counters and tables where Jessup displayed his goods.

Hunter decided to look first for Jessup's business records

and found a big, clothbound ledger lying open at the counter at the back. He took it and hunkered down on the floor behind the counter, studying its pages by the light spilling out of the gaming room.

The entries marched down the page in perfect formation, profits and losses and expenditures. Goods ordered, received, and distributed. Credit extended and repaid. To Hunter's untutored eye, everything appeared just as it should be.

Hunter put the ledger back. Jessup might be a scoundrel and a spy, but he kept good records. He'd just bet there was a second ledger around somewhere, here or in back.

A burst of masculine laughter and the jingle of money changing hands, reminded Hunter how close discovery was.

To start his search, he felt his way along the shelves beneath the counter. He discovered boxes of nails and cans of paint, bolts of cloth and packets of seeds, three dozen toothbrushes and several ladies' hat-forms. He nearly set off a mousetrap baited with a sticky cheese, and jabbed himself on a paper of pins.

He had almost reached the wall when he encountered what felt like a metal-banded strongbox. Hunter pulled it toward him and inched his way to the head of the aisle, where the light was better. It was heavy, made of wood, with stud-work on every side. It was very sturdy, very imposing—and with a lock a child could pick. He flicked it open with the blade of his knife.

Several wads of greenbacks were tucked inside. He had to move a sack of coins to reach the ledger at the bottom. Hunter had a feeling that the records in this book were going to cast an entirely different light on Jessup's enterprises.

But before Hunter had a chance to open the ledger, Tyler Jessup strode into the trading post and turned down the aisle behind the counter.

Balancing a stack of cigar boxes in one hand and a felling ax in the other, Jessup saw Hunter and slammed to a stop.

"What are you doing there, *In'jun?*" he demanded. "You stealing from me?"

"Just looking for something to read."

"And you thought you'd find my ledgers interesting?"

"Fascinating," Hunter answered. "And I think this second volume is going to be even better than the first. I think it's going to show you've been carrying on unauthorized trade with the hostiles. I think it will show you've been selling them powder and shot—and maybe even rifles."

"Is that what you think?"

Hunter came slowly to his feet with the ledger in hand. "I think somewhere in here, I'm going to find proof that you're the one who told the Sioux about the rifles. And I'd bet a year's wages that's not the only information you've sold them."

Jessup shifted the cigar boxes onto the counter beside him. "Everyone seems to think it's Reynolds's squaw who did that," the sutler hedged. "Like as not she was sent to the fort to spy on us. Who knows what else she's passed along?"

I know, Hunter thought.

"Besides, *half-breed,*" Jessup went on, wrapping both hands around the handle of the ax, "without proof, who'd believe you? And you're not taking that ledger anywhere."

Hunter jumped back as Jessup swung the ax. The blade whistled past his chest and slammed into the counter to Hunter's right. Fragments of wood flew in all directions.

Jessup worked the ax head free and stalked Hunter farther down the aisle. Hunter came up short, with the wall against his back.

Jessup smiled as if he figured he had Hunter cornered. He raised his ax.

Hunter vaulted the counter and struck out for the door.

Jessup bolted for it, too, and reached it a step ahead of Hunter. He stood poised to attack, the ax cocked over his shoulder.

Hunter grabbed for something to defend himself. A garden shovel came under his hand. He threw the ledger aside and wrapped his fingers around the shovel's handle.

Hunter and Jessup jockeyed for position.

Sounds from the poker table quieted. "Jessup?" one of the men called out. "What the hell is going on out there?"

Jessup ignored the question and feinted left. Hunter raised

the shovel to block the blow. The ax and iron shovel blade clanged together, spraying sparks.

The sutler shuffled back, sidestepped a pyramid of cans, and swung the ax as if he were felling a tree.

Hunter dodged out of the way and brought his shovel around, slamming Jessup across the shoulders and back. The sutler dropped like a rock and lay still.

"Jessup?" one of the gamblers called out. "You all right out there, Jessup?"

Hunter rolled the sutler over, trying to assess his injuries. The man had to be all right. Jessup had to be alive to clear Cass's name.

As Hunter felt for a pulse in the man's throat, Jessup twisted beneath him. He grabbed the knife at Hunter's waist and jerked it from its sheath, driving the blade up toward Hunter's chest.

Hunter dodged to the left, but the blade scraped a fiery path along his ribs. In spite of the pain, he tangled his hands in Jessup's clothes and jerked him sideways. They rolled across the wooden floor, kicking and twisting, grappling for the knife. A table went down. Cans bounced and spun in all directions.

Jessup thrust to his knees and forced Hunter onto his back. He plunged the knife downward. Hunter jerked away, though the point snagged in the muscle below his collarbone. Pain seared along his arm and up his neck. He hissed and twisted sideways.

He shoved at Jessup and rolled over him, twisting the blade between their bodies. Jessup's hand slipped on the knife handle as the blade swooped in a downward arc with every bit of Hunter's strength behind it. The blade plunged through flesh and muscle and bone. Blood welled warm over Hunter's hands. The big man shuddered and lay still.

Hunter hung above him, panting, cursing, dizzy with effort and regret. He crouched there, angry at Jessup. Angry with himself. He hadn't meant to kill the bastard. He needed Jessup alive.

And then he realized what he'd done. Lone Hunter Jalbert—an Arikara Indian—had killed a white man. It wouldn't matter that he'd killed Jessup in self-defense, or that he'd been a trusted scout. It wouldn't matter that Jessup had betrayed the troopers on the munitions train. What mattered was that Jessup was white and Hunter was an Indian.

He jerked the knife from the sutler's chest and pushed to his feet. Not three yards away one of the cardsharps from the poker game stood waving a pepperbox pistol at his head.

"Now just you hold on there, Indian!" Lloyd shouted. Grenville and one of the muleteers hovered at Lloyd's back, reluctant reinforcements.

Hunter looked at Jessup, the gamblers, and the door. He was as good as dead if he kept standing here.

"I—I swear I'll shoot!" Lloyd threatened when he saw the trend of Hunter's thoughts.

Hunter knew a bluff when he saw one. And even if Lloyd wasn't bluffing, it didn't matter much. Hunter ran for the door and out into the street.

Someone had left a horse tied outside the telegraph office. He gathered up the reins, sprang into the saddle, bent low over the horse's neck, and kicked the animal toward the bridge.

The gamblers stumbled out of the trading post a dozen steps behind him. "Shoot him!" they shouted to the soldiers guarding the bridge. "Shoot him!"

Hunter swept past the sentries before they could collect themselves. The horse's hooves drummed across the layers of wooden decking. Rifle fire blossomed behind them. The guards at the north end of the bridge ran to cut him off, but Hunter rode them down. They fired after him, but as bad as their marksmanship was and as fast as he was traveling, it was a waste of lead.

Hunter galloped as far as the first rise and pulled up to look back at the fort. He'd destroyed his life tonight. Destroyed any chance he might have had to clear Cass's name. Destroyed any hope for the future. He could never go back.

If he wanted to live, he had to head for Montana. Head so deep into the mountains that only the coyotes could find him. Yet as long as Cass was at Fort Carr, he couldn't go. He couldn't leave because he loved her, because he was afraid for her. Because he couldn't imagine building a life in those distant mountains with anyone else. He had to stay. And when Cass needed him, he would find a way to help her.

Chapter Nineteen

A polished silver sun beat out of a lowering sky, casting a harsh, stark light across the landscape and turning the Platte River to a ribbon of quicksilver. It soaked up the shadows, drained the dimension from the buildings, and leached the life from people's faces. Clouds like dirty batting rolled up in the west, promising rain that never came.

Cass stepped out onto the porch of the cabin hoping to catch a breath of breeze. She couldn't seem to get enough air in the August heat. She couldn't swallow for the knot always lodged in her throat, or lie down to rest without the walls closing in on her. Whenever she could she fled onto the porch.

Today, while Meggie was taking her nap, Cass had brought her sewing outside to stitch on the dress she was making for the little girl. She settled on the bench and stared up at the tattered bit of sky that hung above the fort. Just being able to see it calmed her, made it easier to breathe. But it also left her hungering for changing colors, bellowing wind, and racing clouds. Only Hunter had ever been willing to give her the sky, and Hunter was gone.

She balled the fabric of Meggie's new dress in her fists, remembering how Drew had burst into the kitchen that night two weeks before.

"I knew we were wrong to trust that Indian," he announced, bristling with news.

Cass looked up from where she had been wiping the wide pine table. She could see the malice in Drew's smile, smell his almost feral satisfaction. Her stomach turned inside out.

"It's your friend, Jalbert," he said, as if he were testing her. "He killed the sutler."

"Hunter killed Jessup?" Cass breathed. Her fingers tightened around the cloth, deepening the pool of water on the tabletop. She had been with Hunter not much more than an hour before.

"What—what happened?" she stammered.

Drew sauntered toward her. "They say Jalbert was stealing from the trading post, and Jessup caught him. He knifed Jessup to get away," Drew went on, "and he killed him in front of witnesses."

Cass had seen the warrior in Hunter Jalbert. If he had killed someone, he had done it honorably and effectively—and only if he'd had no other choice.

"Hunter wouldn't steal," she answered almost reflexively.

Drew moved in closer. "All Indians steal."

Cass staggered under the scope of that condemnation. *All Indians*—as if the nations and the tribes and the clans were a single entity. As if instead of seeing the human face, what Drew saw was a paper silhouette.

What did Drew see when he looked at her?

But Cass knew. He didn't see his Cassie anymore. She had become someone else. Someone Drew didn't know how to bring into focus, someone he would never in this life recognize or understand.

She straightened slowly, thinking back to her first encounter with Jessup and the incident with the embroidery scissors. That first mistake had marked her, in Drew's eyes, in the eyes of everyone here. In some odd way it had declared what she was even more clearly, even more decisively than the mark on her face. It showed them how she thought, what she felt—what she was beneath her skin. Now it was time to confirm what both she and Drew had been trying so hard to deny.

"While *I* may have stolen," she told him softly, "you'd

be wrong to judge *all* Indians by me.'' Cass brushed past him, knowing now that she'd declared herself, there was no going back.

The days since Hunter left had passed for Drew and her in stewing heat and icy silences. He stayed away from the cabin as much as he could. She toiled from dawn until dark and stared at the fort's small swatch of sky, as if it was all she had.

But for now at least, she had Meggie.

As August crawled by, Cass treasured every question Meggie asked, every snuggle they shared, every scrap of foolery and laughter. She tried not to cling to the little girl and very nearly succeeded. On nights when she couldn't sleep, Cass paced to the foot of Meggie's bed and drank in the sight of that soft, sweet face and those delicate hands. Cass remembered how they'd felt against her skin as they'd traced the lines of her tattoo. She remembered how they'd looked tucked into Hunter's larger ones the day he'd showed Meggie how to fish.

Sometimes she allowed herself to wonder where Hunter was. Far away from here, she hoped. Off to his land in Montana. His tepee had disappeared from the fort's encampment, and she hoped that meant he was beginning a new life somewhere safe.

When Cass came back out onto the porch after checking on Meggie, she noticed that a light wind had begun to ruffle the parade ground's yellowed grass. Halfway down its length she saw Lila Wilcox lumbering toward soapsuds row. She was loaded down with wash baskets and walking as if her bowed back hurt. A few weeks before Cass would have hurried out to help her, but not today. Not ever again.

Cass thought back to the last visit she and Meggie had paid to Will and Lila's cabin.

Lila had been elbow deep in soapsuds when Meggie ran toward her, waving a bouquet of wildflowers. Lila had wiped her hands and hugged the little girl.

''Cassie says Josh went away like Mama did,'' Meggie began. ''She says you're feeling sad, so I brought you flowers.''

Lila took the wilting bouquet. ''I thank you for your kindness, Meggie girl.''

''Cassie says mothers come back from heaven to watch over their children, so maybe Josh will come back to watch over you and Sergeant Wilcox.''

''Maybe he will,'' Lila said, and blinked back tears.

Cass instinctively reached out to comfort her. ''Lila, I want you to know how sorry—''

The older woman jerked away and glared at her. ''I told you what I thought the day the wagons came, and I haven't changed my mind.''

''Lila, please just let me explain.''

''I can't think how explaining would matter much.''

Then, ignoring Cass, the older woman squatted down and spoke to Meggie. ''I like the flowers, Meggie-girl. And I appreciate you saying you're sorry about Josh. But I'm busy here, and I really need to get back to work.'' She gave the child a shove in Cassie's direction.

''Lila, please,'' Cass tried again.

''No,'' Lila said, and went back to her washtubs.

Cass bent to her sewing again, swallowing down the memory. She'd valued Lila's friendship and Sally McGarrity's kindnesses, and she'd lost it all.

At the sound of footsteps thumping along the path, Cass raised her head. Drew was striding toward her, his shoulders stiff and a scowl twisting his handsome face. Her stomach flip-flopped at the sight of him. He never came back to the cabin in the middle of the day unless something was wrong.

He stomped up the steps. ''I have a report to write,'' he offered by way of explanation.

She stuffed her sewing into her basket and pushed to her feet. ''Would you like some lemonade?'' she asked, following him into the house.

Drew didn't answer, just jerked to a stop two steps inside the door.

''Meggie!'' he yelled at her. ''What the devil are you doing with my things?''

Cass stepped around him to see what Meggie had gotten into now. She was perched on the seat of Drew's desk chair, with a paintbrush in one hand and Drew's shaving mirror in the other.

"I painted my face," she announced, and turned her head so they could see.

The child had copied the design of Cassie's tattoo with surprising accuracy—that circle with a star burst radiating from the center. Cass raised one hand to her own cheek, flushed with overwhelming tenderness.

Beside Cass, Drew was quivering like an aspen in a gale.

Reading their expressions, Meggie tried to explain. "I—I just wanted to look pretty—like Cassie."

Drew burst across the room and jerked Meggie out of his chair. "Goddamnit, girl!" he bellowed, shaking her. "Why would you want a filthy tattoo. You're not an Indian. You're *white!*"

Meggie shrieked and stiffened in her father's grasp.

Cass flew at him. "Don't you hurt her!" she spit. "Don't you dare hurt her. Meggie doesn't understand what she's done. She doesn't understand how much you hate the Indians. How much you hate me!"

Drew released his hold on Meggie and turned on Cass.

The child scrambled back and slumped against the wall. She was tousled from her nap, barefoot, half-dressed, and terrified. Cass wanted to go to her, but knew she had to face Drew first.

"Oh, Meggie understood perfectly well about redskins until you came here," he told her. "She understood everything until you told her your wild stories and your heathen superstitions. She was my sweet, obedient girl until you turned her into a savage."

"You don't deserve a child like her!" Cass shouted back. "You don't know how to care for her or give her the love she needs! You're so bent on avenging your parents' deaths that you can't spare a thought for—"

Drew grabbed Cass's arm and hustled her out onto the porch. "I don't want you here anymore," he shouted, his eyes black with rage. "I don't love you. I don't need you. I don't even know who you are! *You're not my Cassie!*"

"I'm *not* your Cassie," she answered, her throat suddenly

aching with regret. "Your Cassie died in the Indian camp."

Drew seemed to comprehend—at last. "Like Julia," he said.

"Just like Julia."

Cassie's last and most terrible secret bubbled up inside her. It pushed at her sternum, clawed up the back of her throat. She'd held her peace for all these months, hoping Drew would never have to know how Julia died. But if this was the end of everything between them, she owed him the truth.

"Your Cassie was too weak to survive, so she died just like Julia. She had to be abandoned, left behind."

It took a moment for Drew to realize what she'd admitted, and when he did, his eyes flared bright with rage again.

"Is that how it happened?" he breathed. "Is that how my sister died?"

"That's how all of them died, all the old and the frail and the sick. The Kiowa left them and went on."

She remembered how she'd kept looking back to where they'd left Julia in a grove at the edge of a stream, how Cass had wanted to sink to her knees and weep for her lost friend. How she'd managed to keep on walking.

"And you did nothing?" he accused.

She'd been captive, powerless. Drew had never understood how powerless she'd been. He kept blaming her for things she couldn't help.

"Goddamn you, Cassandra!" he shouted, and shoved her away.

She stumbled down the steps and sprawled in the dust at the bottom, shaken by Drew's ferocity.

"I don't want you here!" he declared. "I don't want you as my wife! I should never have married you—no matter what we were to each other once. Now get out!"

When Drew spun back into the cabin, Cass climbed slowly to her feet. She could see Meggie staring out at her, hear her crying in loud, gulping sobs. Cass yearned to go to her, to snatch her up and take her away. But for all that Meggie was her child, she had no claim on Drew Reynolds's daughter.

Drew himself came back a moment later carrying the wooden trunk Sally McGarrity had given Cass months before.

"Here's what you came with, *Sweet Grass Woman.* Take it and leave."

He heaved the wooden box off the porch.

It landed with a bang at Cassie's feet. She looked up at Drew, and their gazes held for one charged moment. She'd loved him once so long ago, and he'd loved her.

How could their dreams have gone so horribly wrong?

Then Drew spun back into the cabin and banged the door shut behind him.

Drew stumbled back against the rough wooden panel and stood there shaking. Goddamn Cassandra Morgan! Goddamn her for what she was, for living when Julia had died, for leaving his sister behind. How could Cass have abandoned her?

How had he abandoned both of them?

He should have shot Cassie that day in the canyon. He should have shot them both. He would have had a modicum of peace if they had died there beside the wagon. Instead Julia had perished somewhere out on the prairie all alone. Instead Cassie had lived as an Indian whore, a traitor to her own people. A traitor to him.

Drew heard the whoops of their attackers again, tasted dust on his tongue, and felt the imprint of that pistol in his hand. A shiver racked him as he remembered.

He'd never needed a drink more than he did now.

He pushed away from the door and stumbled toward the kitchen. He took down the pitcher with the bottle inside and reached for a glass. He sat at the end of the bench, filled the tumbler with whiskey, and downed the drink in a single draft.

The liquor bit the back of his tongue, seared his gullet, and vaporized halfway down his chest. He'd learned to like the harsh, unrepentant burn of it. He'd learned to crave the ease it brought, the way it blurred both memory and reality when he couldn't own up to the world anymore.

As the burning subsided, Drew let out his breath. He wondered where his daughter was.

"Meggie," he called out.

The house was silent.

"Meggie?"

Damn the child. She was sulking because he'd yelled at her. Hiding somewhere. Under the bed or around the corner of the house. How far could a four-year-old go, anyway?

She'd come back when she was hungry. She'd come back with that goddamned paint on her face—Cassie's mark, Cassie's shame. If he had to scrub off every bit of her skin, he'd wash that mark off Meggie's face. Just thinking of her painted up like that made his stomach curl.

He picked up the bottle and poured again.

Now that Cassie was gone, he could admit how angry he was that she'd come back. He hated that she hadn't been the girl he remembered. He hated that she'd stirred up memories he thought he'd tamed. He hated her for making him question everything he'd done since that day in the canyon and everything he hoped to do. But most of all he hated her for making him face how he had failed both Julia and her.

Drew wrapped his trembling hand around his drink and brought the glass to his lips. He took a long, deep swallow and hissed with satisfaction at the liquor's spreading heat.

It helped him admit that he had failed them twice. He hadn't aimed that pistol and killed them when he'd had the chance. He hadn't searched for them once he was well.

How did a man endure knowing that he'd chosen to believe that his sister and the woman he loved were dead rather than accept what their time with the Kiowa would make them? How did he admit that he hadn't wanted to bring them back to scorn and degradation? Instead, he had chosen to dedicate his life to avenging the dead.

Drew's eyes blurred with tears. For nine long years revenge had been the whole of him. It had taken the place of loyalty and friendship and love. It had meant more than Meggie's smiles, Laura's embraces, than either Julia's or Cassie's lives. Had it been worth it?

He drank down what was left of the whiskey in his glass, but its heat never seemed to melt that icy place inside him. Nothing did.

Nothing but vengeance drenched in blood would ever

quench it. That was how he was. How the past had made him. There was no going back.

Drew looked out the kitchen door, north toward the river, toward where the Sioux and Cheyenne encampments were located. North where glory and satisfaction awaited him.

He rubbed his hand across his mouth and poured himself more whiskey.

"To vengeance," he said, raising the glass to his mouth. "May it finally be worth the cost."

Cass stood with the trunk at her feet staring up at Drew's cabin, at the empty windows and the tightly closed door. As hard as she'd fought it, she had known this moment was inevitable. Still, she hadn't expected it to end like this, with Drew accusing her of things she hadn't done and her declaring her last and most closely guarded secret.

The heat of those emotions slowly died, leaving the taste of ashes in her mouth. As much as she loved Meggie, as much as she had come to understand the dark motives that were driving Drew, she hadn't been able to change things.

She'd failed again.

As Cass turned from the cabin, she realized that a number of people had witnessed the shameful display of Captain Reynolds divorcing his wife. A full half dozen troopers heading back from fatigue duty had stopped to watch. A trio of laundresses stood balancing baskets of clothes on their hips. Sylvie Noonan was sweeping her porch and gawking, probably thrilled to have a prime bit of gossip to tell over afternoon tea.

Cass ignored the lot of them and flung open the lid of the trunk. She pulled out her beaded blanket and her medicine bundle; her tools, her jewelry, and her herbs. She took out her leggings and her moccasins, slammed the lid, and sat on the top.

She tugged the laces from her heavy, shin-high shoes. She'd worn these horrible shoes every day since she'd married Drew. She'd worn them even though they pinched her feet. She'd worn them without complaint and told herself she'd get used to them, that she'd break them in—but she never had.

Now it was time to take them off for good, time to give up the pretense of being something she could never be. She removed one of the stiff, high-polished boots and then the other. She set them aside with both distinct relief and unexpected regret. She wiggled her toes into her elkskin moccasins. It felt good to be herself again.

Except for losing Meggie.

Losing Meggie ripped Cass raw and left her bleeding. She refused to leave Fort Carr without saying good-bye, without holding Meggie one last time. She needed to wrap the girl close against her heart; stroke that soft, fair hair; and breathe in the scent of her childish innocence. Cass could not go without telling Meggie she loved her. This small, precious girl was the child she could never have. She had made Cass a mother in every way but one, and Cassie would carry the regret of leaving Meggie for the rest of her days.

Drew would never let her talk to Meggie after what had happened between them, but Cass would watch and wait. She would find her chance to say good-bye.

She sweated out the thickening afternoon heat in the shade of the cavalry barracks, but while she watched, neither Drew nor Meggie came out of the cabin. They didn't draw water from the water barrel, take down the short line of wash she'd hung out that morning, or use the privy. The longer Cass waited, the more restless she became. But it was only when she saw the cavalry troopers heading back from afternoon stable call that she dared approach the house.

The kitchen door was propped open with a flat iron, just the way she'd left it. She paused outside, leaning closer, listening for the sounds of movement, the ring of Drew and Meggie's voices. Everything was deathly still. The fist in her belly clenched tighter as she peeked inside.

After the hazy gray brightness of the overcast afternoon Cass couldn't see much, but as her eyes adjusted to the dimness, she saw Drew slumped over the kitchen table. His head was on his arms and beside him sat the pewter pitcher, a glass, and a whiskey bottle drunk down to the dregs.

"Oh, Drew," she breathed around the disappointment that clogged her throat. "Oh, Drew!"

She slipped past him on silent feet, prowled through the parlor and into the bedchamber. She drew back the curtain and looked in Meggie's bed. The child was not there.

Cassie's heart went cold.

"Meggie?" she call out softly, her voice wavering a little. She waited, but there was no answer.

Cass crept back through the silent house, looking everywhere she could think of, trying to keep her fear in check.

Where had Meggie gone? To Lila's or Sally's? To the stables or the bake house? She wondered if she should awaken Drew and ask him where his daughter was.

She stared down at where he sprawled flushed and slack-jawed. Drew wouldn't know what had become of his daughter.

Cass stepped outside, trying to decide where to look for Meggie next. As she gathered up the bundle she had made of her belongings, she noticed the print of one small, bare foot pressed into the mud that was left from dumping her wash water. The footprint appeared again a few yards away. Judging from the stride, Cass would say Meggie had been running.

Running away.

Cass knew it suddenly and certainly. The realization chilled her all the way to her toes.

She followed the signs, trotting along to the east, following the course of the Overland Trail. A mile or more out, Meggie crossed the dusty wagon ruts toward the river. The ground was softer here, the blowing grass taller, the trail easier to follow. Cass wondered just how far a four-year-old would dare to wander by herself.

She'd covered nearly four more miles of Meggie's trail when she suddenly saw the ring of trampled grass. She ran toward it, feeling the surge of foreboding prickle through her blood. She recognized the sign of horses, the cut of unshod hooves in the sandy earth.

Indians, she thought, though it wasn't immediately clear whether they had been here before or after Meggie. Then Cass found the doll she had made lying tranpled in the grass.

Cass stumbled to her knees, crushing the bits of cloth and buttons and horsehair to her chest. "Meggie!" she screamed in the rising wind. "Meggie!"

But Meggie didn't answer. She had been taken by the Indians, stolen away.

Cass wrapped her arms around herself and doubled over. Sobs ripped up her throat. Cass knew how Meggie would be treated. She would lose herself just as surely as Cassie had, and Cass refused to let that happen.

She pushed to her feet and studied the ground. She didn't read sign as well as warriors did, but she could see that the riders had been on stallions, which meant it was a war party. They had passed through half an hour before. Too long ago for Cass to overtake them on foot.

Cass had almost decided to go back to the fort and tell Drew and Ben McGarrity about Meggie when she found the clear, unmistakable print of a Cheyenne moccasin. If Meggie had been taken by the Cheyenne, Cass had a far better chance of getting her back if she went alone. Once the army was involved, there would be bloodshed.

She forged ahead, running along beside the war party's trail. The Cheyenne had crossed the Platte at a gravel-bottomed shallows well hidden by the overhanging bank. They had ridden across with what appeared to be very little difficulty. Cass had to ford the river on foot.

The storm that had been brewing all day came to a boil directly overhead. Thunder mumbled menacingly. The trees along the river churned. The sky hazed darker and darker. If she didn't cross the river now, she'd get cut off.

Cass stripped down to her chemise and drawers and waded in. She had to fight the current to keep from being swept downstream. She had to fight to keep to the narrow ridge of stones that marked the ford.

Above her, lightning cut jagged streaks across the sky. The clouds roared in answer. Rain gushed down in torrents, dimpling the river like waves of gooseflesh.

Cass fumbled on. The river swept up to her chin. Rain washed down her face and blurred her vision. She gasped for breath, and then, when she could barely see or breathe, the footing evened out. She waded on, stumbling up the northern bank into the raging storm.

She donned her skirt and moccasins and headed off, tramping through the rain, peering at a trail that was quickly being obliterated. Long, wet grass dragged at her as she stumbled forward. Her breath rasped in her throat and her muscles burned. If she could follow this track until the Cheyenne turned north, she would have a fair idea of where they were taking Meggie. But the hoofprints were swiftly being washed away and the trampled grass was springing back.

Then all at once a man on horseback loomed out of the storm. Cass screamed and swung at him instinctively, slamming her bundle of belongings into the horse's side.

His gelding danced and reared, his hooves flying.

One grazed Cassie's shoulder and knocked her back onto the grass. She scrambled to her feet, her heart jerking wildly. She raised her pack again, ready to fight. Then she heard her name.

"Cass! Goddamnit, Cass!"

She peered up at the man.

The rider was wearing a white man's hat and a white man's duster. Yet in the shadows she could just make out the breadth of his jaw and the faint, soft bow of his lower lip. "Hunter?" She gasped. "How did you find me?"

He reached out a hand to help her mount. "I've been waiting and watching the fort. I guess I knew you'd need me."

Cass went breathless and wobbly now that she knew who he was. Still, she ignored the gesture, standing stiff and straight in the pouring rain.

"The Cheyenne have taken Meggie! I have to keep following their trail so I can get her back!"

"Take my hand," Hunter instructed.

"I have to get her back!" Cass's voice grew shrill. "I can't let them keep her."

The brim of his hat dipped, spilling rain. "Take my hand."

"Are you going to help me find her?"

She thought she saw him smile. "Of course."

Cass slid her foot in the stirrup on top of his and swung up onto his horse. His arms closed around her, and he pulled her back against his chest. Even through the duster she could feel his heat. Even through the frenzy of her own desperation, she felt her muscles trembling and sensed she'd reached the limits of her strength.

She felt Hunter's warm breath brush her temple. "Which way do you think the trail was heading?"

Cass gestured off to the right.

He nudged his horse in that direction. "We'll find her, Cass," he whispered against her ear. "We'll find her, and we'll get her back."

Chapter Twenty

What the hell had they done to her? Hunter shrugged out of his dripping duster and crossed from the door of his lodge to where Cass lay crumpled, half-dressed, and dead asleep on his bed of skins. Even in the dim light of the smoldering campfire he could see her eyes were ringed dark with fatigue. Her hip and collarbones stuck out and the turning of her jaw seemed unbearably delicate. What in God's name had these last weeks been like?

He'd gathered the rudiments of her story as they rode back through the storm: that she and Drew had argued and Meggie had run away, that the child had been taken by the Cheyenne and Cass intended to get her back.

He knelt beside the bed and smoothed his fingers through Cassie's rain-wet hair. Her skin was cold to the touch, and he pulled a blanket up around her. He had given Cass one of his shirts and the privacy to put it on when they first got back to his campsite. Now the soft, dark fabric lay open down the front, baring a long, inviting vee of creamy skin. At the sight of it Hunter's breath snagged in his throat. His heart tripped a little unsteadily.

He wanted to take Cass in his arms and hold her, please her, and offer her comfort. He wanted to comfort himself with the feel of that long, sweet body against his own. He wanted to kiss her until neither one of them could breathe. He wanted—

But it didn't matter what Hunter wanted. Not when Cass was so exhausted and needed his help.

He shoved to his feet and went about building up the fire, exchanging his own wet clothes for a dry shirt and buckskin breechclout, and preparing a meal. He didn't wake Cass until everything was ready.

She sat up sloe-eyed and disoriented. "Oh, Hunter," she murmured, glancing around. "I didn't mean to just—"

"And how long has it been since you slept?" he asked, handing her a plate of venison stew. "Or ate enough to keep a bird alive?"

"I haven't felt much like eating."

"Eat tonight, get a good night's rest, and we'll look for Meggie in the morning," he advised her, trying to make it sound as simple as that.

Above them thunder rumbled across the sky, and the walls of the tent billowed in the wind.

"Will we be able to keep to the trail after such a storm?" Cass asked him.

"Ben McGarrity claims I'm the best tracker west of Omaha."

"Oh, are you, now?" she asked, venturing a smile.

Cassie's smiles were so rare that Hunter paused a moment to watch her. "I am," he assured her. "Now tell me what happened at the fort."

"Only once you've told me how you ended up killing Jessup."

Hunter scowled but explained his suspicions about the sutler. He told her about finding the extra set of books, how Jessup had come after him, and what he'd done to defend himself.

"I shouldn't have blundered into the trading post the way I did," he chided himself. "I should have been more careful."

"Still, I think you had it right," Cass said, setting aside her plate. "Jessup had to be the one who sent word about the rifles."

"But I didn't get the proof we need to clear your name." What was worse, he'd killed a white man. Nothing he'd done or been before mattered now that Jessup's blood was on his hands.

"Major McGarrity might listen if he knew what you'd found," Cass offered. "Ben's a fair man, and it might make a difference once he knows you killed Jessup in self-defense."

Hunter wished what Cass said was true. "But I didn't get the ledgers. And if Grenville and Lloyd are swearing I killed Jessup in cold blood, what chance is there that anyone will believe me? "

He shoved to his feet and stood over her. "I am what I am, Cass—half-Arikara. Half-savage and not to be trusted. No one will believe a word I say when it comes to this, not even Ben."

He paced to the far side of the fire. "Now, tell me what happened this afternoon."

Cass wound her fingers together in her lap. "What happened with Meggie, you mean?"

"What happened with *you.*"

High, mottled color flared in Cassie's cheeks. She lifted her head. "This afternoon my husband divorced me."

Hunter's gut tightened. There was so much he didn't understand about Cass and Drew. He didn't know whether Cass loved the captain in spite of everything. He couldn't seem to comprehend what other loyalties bound them together or what had forced them apart. What he *did* know was that Reynolds had the power to hurt her, and Hunter resented that beyond all else.

"I know how much you wanted to make your marriage work," he told her evenly.

She acknowledged his words with a delicate dip of her chin, a subtle compression of those pale, pale lips. "Drew said he'd been wrong to entrust his daughter to me." She repeated the words like some vile litany. "He said he'd been wrong to marry me, no matter what we'd been to each other once."

Anger flared in Hunter like burning pitch. The bastard

didn't have a right to blame Cass because their marriage failed, to make her feel as if the destruction of the life they'd tried to make together lay with her.

Months before, Hunter had convinced himself that Drew Reynolds would be better for Cass than he could be. He'd told himself that the captain could offer her more, protect her better, love her in a way Hunter could never aspire to. He knew now how much of a fool he'd been not to take his courage in his hands and court her, give Cass a choice.

Cass swallowed hard before she went on. "Drew threw me out of the cabin. He brought out the trunk where I kept my things and heaved it off the porch. He said he didn't want me as his wife anymore."

Goddamn Drew Reynolds for making Cass feel small and worthless again.

Hunter came to his knees beside Cass and took her hands. They were cold in his, and he willed her his warmth. She was shaking, and he willed her his strength.

"I stayed near the house," Cass went on, "to say good-bye to Meggie. I knew she wouldn't understand what had happened between her father and me. I didn't want her to think I was leaving her because I didn't love her or that this was her fault."

"Why would Meggie think that?"

"Because she's the one who set him off. She got into Drew's paints. She put a tattoo on her cheek that was just like mine."

Hunter held his peace by dint of will.

"I waited hours before I realized she was gone, hours before I went after her . . ."

Cass began to cry.

Hunter gathered her up in his arms. Cass curled her fingers into his clothes and dragged him closer. She shivered and twisted against him, her tears hot against his throat.

"Oh, Hunter, you've got to help me get Meggie back. I don't want her to be afraid all the time," Cass whispered, as if even now she must keep the truth about her captivity a secret. "I don't want her to have to fight so hard to survive.

I don't want her to be different, always separate, always alone.''

''We'll find her, Cass. I promise.''

She shivered again. He felt that tremor pass from her flesh into his at the places where their bodies touched. He felt the fear for Meggie pass from her heart to his.

''Just hold me,'' she whispered, sounding raw and desperate and so very much afraid. ''Don't let me go.''

Hunter couldn't have refused her if he had wanted to.

The wooden bed frame creaked and sighed as he eased them both down into the nest of blankets and skins. Cass settled into the crook of his shoulder, seeming calmer, satisfied.

''We're safe here,'' he whispered, and they were. With the tepee tucked out of sight in the grassy vee between two outcroppings of crumbled stones, no one could find them. Nothing could touch them, not even the storm still raging around them.

Yet even while he assured Cass she was safe, Hunter's blood had begun to burn. He was too aware of her pressed close against his side, of her hand lying lax at the base of his throat. Sensation rippled through him, faint shimmers of heat dancing along his skin. He was possessed of a feverish restlessness that made him want to claim her mouth and move against her.

Hunter summoned honor to keep the wanting at bay, but he no longer believed that Cassandra was Drew Reynolds's wife. The way the captain had treated her, the way he'd disavowed her today at the fort nullified the bond between them—at least in Hunter's eyes. In the eyes of the Arikara and the Cheyenne.

He turned his face into her tumbled hair and tried to will the wanting from his blood. But she smelled of clean, cool rain; of wide, bright fields of wildflowers. She felt wondrously right in his arms, all delicate and womanly, all willing and warm.

He raised one hand to touch her cheek, and she turned her face to his. He pressed a petal-soft kiss onto her mouth and heard the rasp of her indrawn breath. He deepened the kiss, the slow, soft friction devastatingly tender and blissfully sweet. He brushed the contours of her lips with the tip of his tongue and stroked the smooth inner surface. He tasted of her honeyed warmth and lingered over her.

It was an innocent enough exchange, yet when he raised his head, Cass seemed as dazzled by the kisses as Hunter felt.

He wanted to tell her right then that he loved her, to promise to cherish and keep her all the rest of her days, to give her a place to belong. But it was far too soon to offer so much.

They had to get Meggie back. Cass needed time to lament what she'd lost with Drew. Only when that was over could he tell her what he felt for her.

Still, he couldn't seem to stop touching her, stroking her, tangling his fingers in her hair. He nuzzled from her temple to the turn of her jaw, nibbled down her neck and along the ridge of her collarbone. He paused in the hollow at the base of her throat.

The creamy expanse of her upper chest lay bared to him. He pressed tiny, down-soft kisses along her breastbone and into the dusky valley below. He breathed the warmth of her, the elusive essence of her femininity. He swirled his tongue against her skin, branding her with his heat.

Cass gasped and rose against him.

Tempting as she was, Hunter refused to take her while she was confused and exhausted and vulnerable. He refused to make her his when what she needed was a guardian who was sane and strong, someone who was man enough to hold and soothe her, and do nothing else.

Meaning to ease her away, he braced one hand against her hip. But instead of the blanket or the fabric of his shirt, smooth, bare flesh came under his palm.

Hunter sucked in his breath, as if he'd been burned. Instead of pulling back, he closed his fingers over the jut of her hipbone, the firm, cool silk of her skin.

Desire moved through him like a deep red stain. It invaded every cell, sharpened his senses, and set his pulses thundering. His head went light at the thought of all the wild and wondrous things they could do together. He tried to hold back, tried to think, tried to be sensible. But with his hands on her, with her body gathered close, all he could think about was making love to her.

In the seconds before his skein of reason ran out, Hunter turned to her. "Please, Cass, don't let me make this mistake."

Cass smiled at him, a slow, heartbreaking smile that stole his breath. "Would it still be a mistake," she asked him, "if we made it together?"

And Hunter was lost.

Cass looked up and saw the blue flame flare in those dark, dark eyes. A frisson of anticipation danced through her. She wanted this. She wanted it, and the strength of her wanting astonished her.

In the years since she had been taken by the Kiowa, she had learned to trade in the only coin a woman had. She had given herself because she would have died if she didn't submit. Because it was her duty as a wife. In an attempt to recapture the past and secure her place.

She wanted Hunter for herself. She needed him to help her forget all she'd hoped for and all she'd lost. She yearned for him to make her feel whole and desired and beautiful. She had tasted the promise of fulfillment in his kiss, in the brush of his hands, in the press of his body against her. And she needed the pleasure he could give her.

As if he understood, Hunter whispered her name, caressing it, giving it depths and inflections she'd never known it could have. He moved over her, taking her mouth in a kiss that was desperate and desiring, a kiss that made her feel like a woman from the surface of her skin to the depths of her soul.

As he began to tease the buttons along the front of her shirt from their holes, Cass allowed awareness to seep into her on levels and in ways that she had never been able to acknowledge before. She had looked into his face and read concern and tenderness and anger in those harsh, familiar features; but she had never let herself see the stark beauty in the sharply delineated brow and cheekbones, in the breadth of his jaw and the curve of his mouth.

She had taken shelter in his arms, relied on his strength, but she had never questioned why he made her feel so safe.

She had watched those broad, brown hands guide a child and wield a war club, but she had never let herself feel the tantalizing friction of his callused palms against her skin. Cass shivered with new awareness, new sensations, new possibilities.

With the slow, ticklish glide of his forefinger he eased the panels of her shirt out of the way. The air was cool against her chest. His gaze was hot as it moved over her.

A flush prickled upward from her diaphragm. Following the wash of color, Hunter skimmed one hand up the rise of her ribs. He cupped the weight of her breast in the curve of his palm.

His skin was dark against the paleness of her flesh, rough against her smoothness. She took unexpected joy in the wondrous differences between them.

He circled her nipple with the pad of his thumb. Her body arched as those long, capable fingers rasped against her. She liked the brush of his hands, the way her breasts tingled at his touch, the heaviness that seeped deep down into her loins.

Cass squirmed and pressed her legs together.

Hunter smiled as if he knew very well what she was feeling and slid his big hand down the midline of her body. He cupped her mound in the sweet, penetrating warmth of his palm.

Cass breathed his name. He lowered his mouth to hers and lapped up the sound of her pleasure. He took her with the sinuous thrust of his tongue as his fingers sought the nether core of her. Each stroke sent delight spiraling through her, the heady glide and press of his hand, the nibbling pleasure of his mouth.

She went restless, feverish, and dizzy. Sharp, unexpected voluptuousness swept up her spine. She arched her back and reached for him.

Dressed only in a breechclout and opened shirt, he was wondrously accessible. She spread her palms over the breadth and bulk of his shoulders. He was so much bigger than she, so much stronger, yet she sensed her power over him. She felt his muscles grow taut beneath her touch, saw how his nipples pearled beneath the graze of her fingertips. She felt the thrust of his manhood against her with only his breechclout between them.

She pushed the shirtsleeves down his arms. She skimmed her palms along the smooth, straight arch of his spine. She sought the ties at the sides of his breechclout. The buckskin fell away and she touched him, stroking him and pleasing him until he began to tremble.

He rolled above her, whispering her name, calling to her, pleading with her, needing her as much as she needed him. She lifted her hips against him, as open and ready as a furrowed field.

He pressed her down into the bed of skins and blankets. She felt the weight of his arousal against her mound. She felt the thrust of his body inside her. She shuddered with the joy of it, with the depth of the connection, with the sense of being home at last.

She saw the same sweet wonder in his eyes.

They lay together savoring the brush of flesh on flesh, the miracle of being bound together, the sense of endless unity.

Slowly he reached to touch her cheek, tracing the radiating lines of her tattoo. She mewed in protest and tried to turn away. But Hunter held her fast, his fingertips caressing the mark, his eyes holding hers, his lips a mere breath from her own.

"This makes you special," he whispered. "It makes you beautiful. It makes you mine." He lowered his head and claimed the tattoo with his lips.

His words spread through her like a balm, easing the shame, the stigma of being scarred.

Tears of hope and gratitude burned in Cassie's eyes. She had finally found someone who saw her for herself.

With a sob, she drew him to her. She wanted this man with all his tenderness and strength. She needed him, just as she was coming to need the soul-deep communion of his body moving in concert with hers. She raised her hips, and he sank into her. They sought the age-old rhythm that would both bring exquisite joy and bind them irrevocably.

He was there with her in a way no man had ever been before, looking inside her as no man had ever looked, courting her pleasure as if it were more important to him than his own. He stroked into her until she could not breathe, until the blood roared in her ears, until she was shivering with a delight that bordered on frenzy.

Then the world went hazy around her, and there was only Hunter. She lost herself in him, in the intensity of his eyes, in the hard, hot waves of sensation that swamped them both. They flowed together, melting and molten, fierce and fragile, him and her. Each sought pleasure beyond themselves and found sensation so fine and sweet that it bound them and held them and granted them a deep, resounding peace that joined their souls.

Cass curled against him in the aftermath. If there were words for what had just passed between them, she did not know them.

Hunter seemed to feel the fulfillment as deeply as she did. He drew her to him as if he never meant to let her go. And safe in the circle of his arms, Cassie slept.

Chapter Twenty-one

❁

"Do you think she's there?" Cass asked, peeking over the edge of the low, grassy bluff toward the tepees clustered on the far side of the creek.

Hunter sprawled on his belly beside her, scanning the scene with field glasses. "It's where the trail leads. She's got to be down there somewhere."

Cass let out her breath. With it went a little of the tension, a little of the thick, hot fear. She'd seen for herself how fine a tracker Hunter was. He could learn more from a broken leaf and a clot of dirt than most men could from a signpost. If Hunter said Meggie was in that camp, Cass believed him.

He handed the glasses across to her. "You lived with the Cheyenne. See what you make of it."

Cass put the glasses to her eyes and squinted against the glare of the afternoon sun. The village sprang into focus before her. It was familiar, almost welcoming: the neat formation of buff-colored tepees, the cookfires trailing smoke, people at work and play. Though it was too far away for Cass to identify individuals, she recognized paintings on the sides of several tepees. They represented families she knew, and she could not help but wonder if Gray Falcon, her Indian husband, and his new wife were down in the village somewhere.

"I think this must be Standing Pine's band of Cheyenne," she told Hunter. "He sets a high store by his horses and may have broken off from the main encampment during the dry spell to look for better grazing."

She felt Hunter turn and look at her. "Isn't Standing Pine the chief who traded you back to us last winter?"

"And organized the ambush." The knot in Cass's belly pulled taut again. She hadn't known what Standing Pine meant to do, but she'd been caught up in it anyway.

"Do you have any suggestions about how we should go about getting Meggie back?"

"I haven't thought about much but holding her," Cass admitted. "I wish we had more to offer in exchange."

In addition to the horses they were riding, Hunter had brought a skittish sorrel gelding and a dappled mare. If it came to bartering for Meggie, that was all they had.

That didn't seem to worry Hunter as much as it did her. "Those braves don't know what a hornets' nest they stirred up when they took Meggie. We'll let them know and see if we can't convince them to send her back before the whole United States Army descends on them."

Cass lowered the field glasses, uneasiness lapping through her again. "How long do you think we have before they get here?"

"Two days, maybe three. We don't know when the captain realized Meggie was gone, and some of the trail is bound to have been washed out by the storm." A smile hitched up one corner of his mouth. "Besides, the army's best tracker is here with you."

Hunter was doing his best to tease her. Cass did her best to smile back. "I know he is."

He grinned and nudged her away from the edge of the bluff.

Cass and Hunter entered the Cheyenne camp a few minutes later. Yapping dogs heralded their arrival, but no one challenged them. Instead people pointed and put their heads together as they passed, speculating, Cass supposed, about why she was here. She rode with her head held high. Returning to the Cheyenne in the company of Lone Hunter, the army's famed Arikara scout, gave her a credibility she wouldn't have had if she had come alone.

Still, what Cass wanted most was to see some sign of Meggie. But her little girl was neither among the children who ran along beside them, nor in the care of any of the women who trailed them toward the central campfire.

Standing Pine was waiting when they dismounted. Though he gave no outward sign, Cass knew he must recognize both of them.

Hunter stepped forward. "Standing Pine, revered chieftain of the Cheyenne, allow me to introduce myself. I am Lone Hunter of the Arikara, come to offer you and your people my greeting and my friendship."

The Indian's eyebrows rose. "We have met before, I think."

"Some months ago," Hunter answered, "in a situation not quite so cordial as this."

Standing Pine's mouth curled as if he were remembering that day when he and his men had ridden down on the party of cavalrymen. "It had to do with returning your companion to the whites."

Hunter nodded. "I am pleased that you remember Cassandra Morgan."

"The woman I remember was known to us as Sweet Grass Woman," the Cheyenne corrected him. "Has this woman forsworn her Cheyenne name now that she lives among the whites?"

A Cheyenne woman would have allowed Hunter to answer for her, but Cass wasn't a squaw anymore. She was no longer the wife of a United States Army captain, either. Not belonging to anyone seemed to give her the right to speak for herself.

"I have forsworn nothing," she told the man who had once decided her fate. "Sweet Grass Woman will always live within my heart, as will the friends I made among the Cheyenne. But it was necessary for me to become someone else in order to make my way in the white man's world."

"She is Cassandra Reynolds now," Hunter put in. "She married the long-knife captain who claimed her months ago."

"So the high-nosed Reynolds took you for his own. Why then is he not here with you? Why have you come to us at all?"

"We have come with an important message for those who would live in peace," Hunter answered.

Standing Pine's eyebrows rose. "How do you know peace is what we seek?" he demanded. "Our ally Red Cloud rides out against the white soldiers in their forts."

"But you are here," Hunter pointed out, "not in Red Cloud's encampment."

Standing Pine's mouth narrowed and his nostrils flared. "I can be in Red Cloud's camp before moonrise tomorrow. Red Cloud would welcome me and my warriors."

Hunter seemed to shrug off the Indian's boast. "We have come to speak of peace, not of Red Cloud."

Cass held her breath, wondering how Standing Pine would respond when Hunter told him why they'd come.

As it was, Standing Pine gave Hunter no chance to explain. "Before we speak of important matters, surely you wish to refresh yourself," he suggested, suddenly all smiles and generosity. He gestured for a small, moon-faced woman to come forward. "Blue Flower, will you show these visitors the way to their lodge."

Cass instantly recognized her old friend and bit back a smile when she saw that Blue Flower was carrying a fat, gurgling baby on her hip.

They followed Blue Flower through the camp to a small tepee nestled against a rise above the creek. It was freshly aired and stocked and swept. Wood stood stacked on one side of the door and buffalo bladders of fresh water hung on the other. Beds were made up with blankets and furs, and there were woven mats spread out across the floor.

It was only when the proprieties of welcoming had been observed that Cass could reach out for Blue Flower's child.

"Oh, he is beautiful!" she cooed, taking the baby in her arms. "What is his name?"

The child looked up at her, his soft mouth bowed and his black eyes wide with wonder.

Cass smiled, enchanted by the perfection of his pudgy

hands and the rosy roundness of his cheeks. She had wanted a baby of her own for as long as she could remember, and holding this child in her arms made her ache with delight and envy.

"We called him Little Sparrow," Blue Flower told her, "because he was so small when he was born. But see how he has grown since then."

"He's a wonderful big boy."

"That it is so, I owe to you. He would have died if you had not sent the cans of milk."

Cass glanced up at her friend, pleasure warming her cheeks. "I am glad there was something I could do to help."

Cass wanted to ask Blue Flower if Meggie was here. She wanted to find the little girl, to go to her, and hold her as close as she was holding the other woman's child. Even if they succeeded in getting Meggie back, her time with the child could be counted in hours. Cass couldn't bear to miss so much as a single heartbeat.

Hunter paused for a moment to admire Blue Flower's child, then he excused himself to see to the horses.

The Indian woman watched him go. "Lone Hunter is a good man," she observed.

"Yes, he is," Cass answered.

"An able warrior."

Cass nodded.

"A man the women will watch with hungry eyes."

Cass looked up, startled by Blue Flower's words.

"Will you sleep with him tonight," the woman asked, "or do you wish to stay with Sharp Knife and me?"

Though Cass supposed it would be wiser to pretend to be Captain Reynolds's devoted wife, she couldn't abide the thought of being separated from Hunter when there was so much at stake.

"I will stay here," Cass told her friend.

"And what of your white husband?"

Cass sighed, remembering. "I am no longer welcome in his home, but I love his child."

"The white-haired girl."

Cassie's pulse leaped. "Is Meggie here?"

"Since yesterday," Blue Flower confirmed. "Runs Like a Doe said she must be yours. The paint was faded, but the child wore your mark upon her cheek."

"Is Meggie safe?" Cass demanded. "May I see her?"

"Is that why you have come—to get this bright-haired child?" When Cassie nodded, the younger woman went on, "It is Runs Like a Doe's nephew who brought her in. He means to give her as part of the bride price to the family of the woman he wants to marry."

"Is there any way we can dissuade him?"

Blue Flower nodded thoughtfully. "Perhaps if you made him a better offer, you could change his mind."

Cass thought about the horses they had brought and dread clamped like talons around her heart. What would they do if the horses weren't enough to buy Meggie back?

"Where is she?" Cass demanded. "I need to see her for a little while."

The Cheyenne woman compressed her lips. "I think it is better that you wait. Man on the Right might take exception if you were to see the child. That could make negotiations more difficult."

Cass glanced down at the baby in her arms. He had pursed his lips and was blowing bubbles.

"Could you wait if it was Little Sparrow they were keeping from you?"

Blue Flower hesitated, then inclined her head. "I would wait. You have forgotten how a Cheyenne woman behaves."

"Sometimes I think I never really learned."

"Then you must pretend," the other woman offered sagely. "It is what they will expect of you."

Cass bit down hard on her impatience. Blue Flower was right. As much as she wanted to turn the camp upside down looking for Meggie, she must not antagonize the people with whom they would barter for Meggie's life.

As if she could read the acquiescence in Cassie's face, Blue Flower took the baby back.

"You should know," she said, tucking a blanket around her son, "that your Cheyenne husband is dead."

Cass was startled by the news. Though she harbored no

affection for Gray Falcon, her enmity had faded. "What happened?" she asked.

"He has been with Red Cloud since the spring. He was killed only a few weeks ago in a battle near the fort they call Phil Kearney. They say the troopers had some magic guns . . ."

The rifles, Cassie thought. Those rifles had cost Fort Carr so dearly; they had cost Lila Wilcox her son and Alma Parker her husband. Now Cass learned that though the rifles had saved the lives of other soldiers, they had cost the lives of Cheyenne and Sioux warriors. What was she to think of that? Was she to grieve for those men's families? Or was she to grieve for two great peoples who refused to find a way to live in peace?

Cass drew a ragged breath. "Thank you for telling me this. I had wondered if he was here in camp."

Her duty done, Blue Flower moved on to other matters. "I would invite you and Lone Hunter to come to my husband's lodge for your meal tonight."

Cass smiled. "That would be nice."

"It pleases me to do it after all you have done for me. Do you need anything else before I go?"

Cass looked down at her grimy skirt and rumpled bodice. "I wish to be clean," she said.

"Then I will have fresh clothing brought to you," Blue Flower said as she turned to go. "Come to our lodge tonight and after the evening meal we will see who else comes by to join us."

Hunter prowled around Standing Pine's camp for the rest of the afternoon. Under the guise of seeing to the horses, he talked to one of the older boys who was tending the herd. He learned that when five warriors had returned to the camp the day before, they'd brought in a dozen head of horses and a fair-haired child. As Hunter wandered back along the neat perimeter of tepees, he saw the drying racks behind each lodge hung thick with jerky, which meant the summer hunt had been successful. It also meant there would be food enough for winter, that the men could go to war. He noticed men preparing, repainting their war shields and fletching arrows.

Still, this band was here and not with Red Cloud. Hunter puzzled over what that meant until he chanced to offer a twist of fresh tobacco to two old men who were sitting in the sun. While he smoked with them, they explained that the camp was deeply divided between those who wanted to escalate the war and those, like Standing Pine, who favored a negotiated peace. Feeling as if he finally understood what was happening in the Cheyenne camp, Hunter headed down to the stream to bathe.

He had just donned his clean shirt, breechclout, and moccasins when a Cheyenne woman stepped out of the trees at the edge of the creek. Even though the years had streaked her hair with gray, she stood as lithe and straight as the shaft of a spear.

"Have you come for the white-haired girl?" she asked him.

Everyone in the village must have guessed why they were here. Hunter inclined his head in answer. "Do you know if Meggie is safe?"

The woman smiled a little. "She has been with me."

Hunter found comfort in that, though this woman was a stranger. "Then I thank you for seeing to her care. Is she all right?"

"She was frightened by being carried away. And she wants her mother."

"Then may I bring Sweet Grass Woman to see her?" he asked.

The woman pursed her lips, then shook her head. "That is not wise. Sweet Grass Woman has long been a friend to me and my family. Tell her Runs Like a Doe will see no harm befalls her little girl."

"And if she still wishes to hold her child?"

"Sweet Grass Woman learned the lesson of patience with great difficulty, but she will wait."

The woman's insight pleased him. "And will the brave who captured Meggie be willing to trade?" he wanted to know.

Runs Like a Doe compressed her lips again. "My nephew is a fool if he refuses."

Hunter fought down a swell of concern. Surely once Standing Pine understood the risk of keeping Meggie here, he could persuade the young warrior to accept what they were offering. Still, he needed to provide an alternative course for Cassie's sake.

"But if he does refuse," he said softly, "I will need to know where you are keeping Meggie."

Runs Like a Doe hesitated. She knew what he was asking—that by answering she would betray her nephew and perhaps even her tribe.

"I will bargain honestly with the man who took Meggie," Hunter promised. "I will address the council on Sweet Grass Woman's behalf. You are wise enough to see that this is no time to antagonize the whites by stealing their children. We must take Meggie back, or a great misfortune will befall your people."

The woman watched him narrowly, weighing his arguments and his sincerity. "We are in the lodge farthest to the north in the circle," she finally said. "It is the one painted with three buffalo."

Hunter inclined his head. "I thank you for trusting me. I will not misuse the gift you have given me."

"And now I must trust you with something else." Runs Like a Doe eyed him for a moment, then dipped her hand into the beaded medicine bag that hung on a thong around her neck. She extracted a small cream-colored square of paper folded over and over upon itself. She came forward and placed it in Hunter's hand.

"Do not look at this now," she instructed him. "Do not look at it while you are in this camp. Blue Flower says you care for Sweet Grass Woman, and I trust you to use this to help her if there is need."

Hunter battled down a swell of curiosity. "If you believe this is important, I will guard it well." He tucked the tightly folded paper away in his own medicine bag and turned to Runs Like a Doe with a new round of questions. But she was gone.

Cass was bathed and dressed when Hunter returned to their lodge. Her hair was neatly plaited down her back and bound with beads and leather. Her dress was made of doeskin, with a wide fringed yoke and narrow skirt. The buttery fabric warmed the tone of Cassie's skin and delineated every curve.

He let his gaze drift over her and smiled. "You are very beautiful."

Cass ducked her head, though she was smiling, too. "It seems odd to be wearing just this after the months of corsets and stockings and petticoats."

He was struck again by the difference between who she was and who she seemed to be. She bore a white woman's delicate features and pale, bright eyes, an Indian woman's tattoo and simple grace. Yet her strength, determination, and courage were uniquely her own, as much a part of her as breathing.

Still, Hunter couldn't help wonder what she would do when they got Meggie back—where she would go and how she would live when this was over. He couldn't help wondering if she would be willing to share her life with him.

"Would you come back here if you could?" he asked her.

Cass looked past him as if she were seeing things he could not see. "I was never able to make a place here. I was not able to make a place among the whites. I want to find where I belong."

The question was out of his mouth before he could bite it back. "And where do you think you'll find that?"

Anywhere with you, Hunter willed her to say. Anywhere we can live and be free to love each other.

Cass averted her eyes and turned away. "I don't know."

Hunter tasted the dust of desperation on his tongue. He wanted to grab her and kiss her until she couldn't breathe. He wanted to touch her and hold her and lie with her, to bring her fulfillment again and again. He wanted to find what it took to make her want him as much as he wanted her.

He squatted down and poked at the fire instead. "I think I'll bring in a bit more wood. It's going to be cool come morning."

Cass let out her breath as if she had been waiting for the

dangerous moment to pass. "Perhaps you can do that later," she suggested. "We have been invited to supper at Blue Flower and Sharp Knife's lodge."

Carrying their bowls and spoons, Hunter and Cass walked the short distance to her friends' tepee. Lone Hunter of the Arikara was immediately accepted as a welcome guest. They ate and talked and laughed together through a pleasant meal. Just as they were finishing, Standing Pine called out and asked to enter.

Cass flashed Hunter a long, acknowledging glance as the chief spoke to each of them and settled himself by the fire. Standing Pine obviously wanted to negotiate Meggie's release in private rather than taking the matter to the council. It was another sign that all was not as it should be in this camp.

A young brave arrived and swaggered into the tepee a few minutes later. From the arrogance in his face, Hunter surmised this wasn't going to be an easy negotiation.

Man on the Right dressed like the brash young warrior he was. His clothes were thickly adorned with beads and fringe. A red-tipped roach bristled from the crown of his slicked-down hair. He wore six beaded necklaces and bracelets high on each arm.

Once the introductions had been made, the newcomer took his place at Standing Pine's side and accepted the offer of Sharp Knife's pipe. Hunter took it in his turn and observed the age-old tradition of offering it to the earth and sky and to the cardinal directions before he smoked.

Once they had put the pipe away, Standing Pine turned to him. "Lone Hunter, what has brought you and Sweet Grass Woman to this camp?"

Hunter spared a glance to where Cass and Blue Flower were seated on one of the beds sewing, almost as if the discussion the men were having was of no consequence to either of them.

"We have been following the trail of a child," Hunter answered, "a little girl whose hair is as pale as winter sunshine."

Standing Pine nodded. "And what would you say if I told you we have not seen a child like that?"

"I would say I am too good a tracker to be mistaken about where she was taken."

"And why do you seek this little girl?"

"We seek her for her mother's sake."

Standing Pine looked down at his hands. "And if the mother wanted this little girl back, how much might she be willing to pay for her?"

Man to the Right stiffened. Hunter could see that the younger brave resented Standing Pine opening negotiations when he clearly preferred to keep the child.

Hunter ignored Man on the Right and played the only card he had. "Perhaps," he said, leveling a long, speculative glance at Standing Pine, "you might better ask what price the girl's father might extract from those who took his daughter."

"His daughter?" Standing Pine repeated in stunned surprise. "Whose girl is she?"

Hunter smiled. "She belongs to Sweet Grass Woman's husband, Captain Drew Reynolds."

Man on the Right sucked in his breath.

Standing Pine swallowed hard before he spoke. "Reynolds hates all Indians."

"Indeed he does," Hunter confirmed. "Imagine what will happen if he follows his daughter to this camp. Reynolds will not come to trade for her. He will come with fire in his eyes and a full company of cavalry at his back. He will want revenge on the men who stole his daughter."

Hunter glanced across at Cass. Her face was pale as the winter moon, flat and impassive. But her eyes—oh God, her eyes—seethed with fear and impatience and hope. And with the faith that he could get Meggie back for her.

Hunter tried his best not to disappoint her. "Reynolds will come riding down on this encampment like Chivington's volunteers did at Sand Creek. His men will find his daughter, and once they have, he won't care who they kill. If you do not want that to happen, give the child to us. No one need know who took her. We will make Reynolds believe that she wandered away from the fort and got lost. You and your village will be safe."

Standing Pine turned to the young warrior beside him. The choice was his to make.

Man on the Right sat silent.

"Surely you have brought something to trade," Standing Pine said, attempting to open negotiations a second time.

"There was no opportunity for me to gather trade goods," Hunter told him. "I have brought both of my extra horses, a sorrel gelding and a sweet gray mare. I trained them both. They are good ponies, deep-chested and strong."

Standing Pine looked to the younger man. "He offers two horses for the child."

"It is not enough," Man to the Right answered.

"I will give you my pistol," Hunter offered.

"It is not enough," the young brave insisted.

"My rifle and all my ammunition."

"And my beaded blanket," Cass added softly.

"And her beaded blanket," Hunter repeated. That was all they had between them.

"Reynolds will trade for his daughter," Man on the Right insisted. "He traded a wagonload of goods for *her.*"

Without so much as looking in her direction, Hunter knew how the brave's words had wounded Cass.

"Reynolds will not trade," Hunter maintained. "The men in the forts have been waiting all summer for a reason to attack the Sioux and Cheyenne villages. Because there are treaty negotiations going on at Fort Laramie, the soldiers have not been allowed to campaign against the tribes. Stealing this child may be the spark that sets that tinder aflame."

"People may die if you do not do this," Standing Pine entreated Man on the Right.

The younger man shoved to his feet. "Then this is for the council to decide. It is a matter of war and peace. We must call a council, now, tonight. Only if *they say* I must trade for the army captain's child will I accept what this man has offered me."

Hunter read the trepidation in Standing Pine's face. He had come here hoping to avoid taking this question to the council where he might lose not just this question but his position of leadership.

The older man sighed and heaved to his feet. "Very well then," he said. "Call the council together."

Man on the Right nodded his thanks to Sharp Knife and Blue Flower for their hospitality and burst out of the tent to start gathering the men together.

When Man on the Right was gone, Hunter turned to Standing Pine. "May I attend the council and explain how dangerous it is to keep the child?" he asked.

Standing Pine shook his head. "It will be better if I tell them. I will do everything I can to convince them how important it is to make this trade."

"I will speak on the child's behalf, as well," Sharp Knife offered.

It wasn't all that Hunter had hoped for, but it was all they had.

"How long will it take the council to make its decision?" Hunter asked.

Standing Pine frowned. "Most of the night, I fear. I will send word to you when we are done."

The two men left.

Hunter thanked Blue Flower for the meal and steered Cass back toward their lodge. She was coiled tight, ready to act, though certainly she realized that for this night there was nothing she could do.

Hunter wasn't sure how she would keep from coming apart while they waited for word. He wasn't sure how he could help her ease the strain. But once they had gone into the tent, once he was alone with her, Hunter realized the only thing he could offer her.

Without saying a word, he bent and caught the hem of the buckskin dress and skimmed the sleek soft fabric up her body. He dropped his own shirt and breechclout to the floor and pulled her against him.

Cass hissed like water meeting flame as their bodies brushed. Color flared up her chest and into her cheeks. Sparks leaped between them as if they were flint and steel instead of flesh and bone.

He kissed her hard, demanding a response with the heat of his mouth, the thrust of his tongue. Cass surged against him and kissed him back. Desire swept through them like a firestorm.

They fumbled toward the bed. Her skin was like pearl in the nest of furs. He rolled above her and fit his hips to hers. He brushed his manhood against her mound. Cass shivered and arched and opened her legs. In a single thrust he was inside her.

They stared into each other's eyes. Hers were wide and reckless and hot, but no wilder than Hunter's eyes must be. They panted for a space, one encompassed, one fulfilled. But neither of them satisfied.

They waited without moving, balanced, teetering, ready to fall. Tension danced through them. Excitement throbbed at the place where their bodies joined. The headlong flight to oblivion beckoned. Yet they held still, lost in each other's gaze, tempting and tempted, holding the world at bay.

He lowered his head to kiss her. His mouth moved down against her cheek, grazed her temple, lingered at the corner of her eye. She was holding her breath, waiting. And he made her wait. Made himself wait.

He did his best to make the waiting worthwhile. He teased away the frown between her brows with the brush of his lips. He kissed along the narrow bridge to the tip of her nose. He tasted the point of her chin with the swirl of his tongue.

Cass braced up on her elbows and captured his mouth with hers. Slow, taunting kisses flowed between them, their mouths drifting together and retreating, the rhythm suggestive, promising. He slid his tongue into her mouth, a sinuous second invasion nearly as intense and inflaming as the first.

She moved beneath the kiss, circling his tongue with hers, arching her back to brush her breasts against him, lifting her hips. Hunter answered her movement, pleasuring her and pleasuring himself.

Cass moaned softly, the sound a prelude, an invitation.

He moved again. She fell back against the bed, her mouth drawn in a gasp of wonder, of wanting.

He buried his face in the curve of her throat, breathing in her sweetness and her spice. He nuzzled the lobe of her ear and felt her squirm beneath him. The sensation was delicious, enticing, arousing to a man already deep in his pleasures.

He wanted her. But more important than that, he wanted her wanting him.

And it seemed she did.

"Please, Hunter," she whispered. "Will you take me now?"

As she spoke, her hands moved over him, teasing the hair that lay long against his neck, clinging to the breadth of his shoulders, trailing along his ribs. Gooseflesh blossomed wherever she touched, shivers of awareness and delight.

"Oh, Cass," he whispered, his senses filled with her. "Oh, Cass . . ."

Her fingers danced down his back. Her palms stroked slowly and rhythmically over his hips. He smiled to himself, pressed one more kiss against her skin, and gave her what they both wanted.

The deeper merging of their bodies brought a rush of joy scalding through them. The pleasure spread, mounting waves of delight from the point where their bodies joined. Shimmers of heat radiated down their arms and legs as they clung closer.

She arched against him, offering all of herself. He took her, moved within her, and gave back. In the splendor of endless kisses, the friction of skin on skin, white-hot need devoured them. They rose together, finding satisfaction and succor, fervor and forgetfulness in each other's arms.

When it was over they lay spent and lax and silent for a very long time. As he held her, Cassie slept. But in the darkest hour of the night, when the moon was down, Hunter felt her stir beside him. He felt the worry and the tension creep into her. He was waiting for the question when it came.

"What will we do," she whispered, "if the council decides we can't have Meggie back?"

Hunter smiled into the dark. "Then I know where they are keeping her, and we'll take our chances."

She's down there somewhere. Drew Reynolds smiled as the knowledge whispered through him. The treacherous bitch who'd stolen Meggie was in that Indian village. And so was his daughter.

Drew hunched his shoulders against the predawn chill and trained his field glasses on the encampment laid out in the bend of the stream. Thick, woolly fog all but hid it from his view, yet he could make out the sprawl of flimsy tents, the smoke of a few dying fires, and a horse picketed here and there. He could almost smell the stench of grease, dirty blankets and buckskins, and even dirtier bodies. This was where Cassie had chosen to bring his daughter, his precious Meggie. To this hellhole in the middle of the prairie. To this nest of vermin.

The banked fire in Drew's chest flared hotter when he thought how his poor little girl had been taken against her will. When he thought about how she might be cowering in one of those tepees even now, hungry, lonely, and afraid—waiting for her papa to come for her.

Perhaps he'd failed with Julia and Cassie, but he had every intention of rescuing his daughter from the savages. He was a man this time, not a frightened boy. He was an army officer with a company of men at his back, not a youth who would have been heading off into the wilderness alone. This time he wasn't trying to find two girls who were probably dead. This time he wasn't trying to do the impossible.

Drew lowered the field glasses from his eyes as one of his young lieutenants pulled up beside him on his horse.

"The men are in place, sir," Lieutenant Sparks informed him in an undertone, "set out all along the stream."

Drew nodded in acknowledgment. They were poised to sweep through the sleeping village just at dawn. It was best to take the redskins by surprise, charge in when they weren't prepared to defend themselves. John Chivington had proved that at Sand Creek. Only Chivington's volunteers had been such raw, undisciplined bastards that something that might otherwise have been heralded as a success had become an unmitigated disaster.

Drew's men, however, were meticulously trained. They all knew Meggie was in the Cheyenne camp. They all understood his objective was to get his daughter back. His men were instructed to shoot only the Indians who resisted.

"On my signal, Lieutenant Sparks," Drew confirmed

softly, and listened as Sparks rode down the line passing the word.

Drew turned his eyes to the village one last time, his nerves on edge, his heart thudding. Cassie was asleep in one of those huts, too, and Drew couldn't wait to get his hands on her.

The conniving bitch had come to Fort Carr as a spy, and every single one of them had been taken in. She'd played them all so well, pretending not to understand, eliciting their sympathies, worming her way into their confidences. Everyone from Ben McGarrity on down to Lila Wilcox had been deluded.

But Cassie had made Drew the biggest fool of all, both as a military officer and as a man. He had taken her into his heart and home. He had let himself believe he could still love her, that they could somehow recapture what they'd felt for each other when they were young. He'd even married her and entrusted her with the care of his daughter. And Cassandra had betrayed him on every count.

Now she'd had the audacity to steal his daughter.

Well, Drew would bring her to justice. Every one of his men knew he wanted Cassie alive. Soon he would have her back, and when he did, he'd make Cassie pay dearly for wronging him, for wronging all of them.

Drew looked to his right and left down the long line of troopers poised to fight. They were sharp and finely trained, eager and brave. He could see it in their faces.

He nodded to the bugler and raised his hand.

The men drew their pistols in perfect unison.

Drew Reynolds smiled. "Charge!" he ordered, and the bugler began to bray the call to arms.

Now that it was too late for her to escape, he wanted Cassie Morgan to know he was coming for her.

Hunter couldn't say why they needed to be dressed and packed and saddled up well before sunrise. It was that itch, that portent he'd learned to trust. And Cassandra hadn't questioned him.

Once they were ready, he prowled around their campsite, his belly balled tight and his chest on fire. He tried to blame the uneasiness on waiting to hear Meggie's fate. He tried to tell himself that if they had a chance of getting Meggie back without a fight, he could wait this out.

But everything about this dawn unsettled him, the sudden chill of cooler weather that sent the dense drift of fog rising up from the creek, indistinct sounds that somehow didn't fit this place or situation. They were noises he couldn't quite place, that teased the edges of his memories. The rustle of grass, the muffled jingle of harnesses.

And then he knew.

"Jesus, Cass," he whispered, gathering up their horses's reins. "The army's out there. They're getting ready to attack."

He read the acknowledgment in her face; she felt it, too.

"It's like Sand Creek," she whispered, and grabbed his arm. "We have to get to Meggie. We have to take her out of here."

"She's with Runs Like a Doe," Hunter told her. "In her lodge."

He saw Cass nod, and with the horses in tow, they set off across the compound. She raced after him as they dodged between tepees and barely smoldering cookfires.

They were just crossing the center of the camp when the bugle sounded. Chills shot up Hunter's back at the disembodied trill.

"Hurry!" Cass shouted. "Hurry!"

Behind them, the earth rumbled with the sound of hoofbeats. The first fusillade of gunfire rattled down near the stream. It tore through the foggy silence, shattered the peace.

People burst from their lodges, half-asleep and partly dressed, disoriented by the milky dawn.

Hunter pulled his revolver and forged ahead, north toward the tepee where Meggie was being kept, the tepee painted with three buffalo.

The sound of hooves beat nearer and Hunter turned to look just as the first cavalrymen loomed out of the mist.

The Cheyenne men grabbed up their guns and bows to defend their families. The women wailed and clutched their children. Some crouched in fear. Others scuttled away, hoping to escape.

The mounted soldiers rode them down.

Cass ran ahead of him, shouting Meggie's name.

A trooper thundered down on her, his weapon drawn.

Hunter blew him out of the saddle.

Cass kept on moving, fighting her way through crosscurrents of women and children, barking dogs and stray horses. Hunter followed, dragging their own horses after him.

By the time Cass and Hunter reached the tepee painted with three buffalo, troopers had engulfed the village. Hunter handed the horses' reins to Cass and ducked inside. A fire burned in the fire pit and the beds were still warm to the touch. There was no sign of either Runs Like a Doe or the child she was guarding.

"Meggie!" he bellowed as he spun back outside. "Meggie!"

Cass clamped his arm, dragging furrows with her finger nails. "You mean she's gone?" she yelled at him. "You mean Meggie isn't there?"

Hunter shook his head.

"How are we going to find her now?"

Chaos had erupted around them. Not five yards away a trooper trampled a woman beneath his horse's hooves. A tepee went up in flames off to their right. A brave and a cavalryman fought hand to hand, rolling through the remains of last night's fire.

"Meggie!" Cassie screamed, her face contorted with fear. "Oh, please! Meggie!"

A tiny girl came flying toward them from around the back side of the tepee. She was sobbing and covered with blood.

Cassie stumbled to her knees. "Are you hurt?" She dragged her palms over the little girl, searching for injuries. "Oh God, Meggie, are you hurt?"

"Cassie," Meggie gasped. "Oh, Cassie, they shot the Indian lady."

"Where?" Cass demanded.

Hunter grabbed her arm. "We don't have time—"

But Meggie had disappeared around the back of the tent. Cass jerked away and followed her.

Runs Like a Doe lay sprawled and broken in the grass.

"Oh, my friend!" Cass cried, and dropped to her knees beside her.

"I kept her safe—for you," Runs Like a Doe whispered. "I covered your child with my body so the bluecoats would not see . . ."

"And I thank you," Cass whispered back. "Now, let me help—"

"Too late—" she breathed, "—for me. You go." She nodded toward where Hunter stood. "He is a good man. Let him take you where it is safe."

Hunter grabbed Cassie's arm. "Come on."

Cass hesitated for one long moment to squeeze Runs Like a Doe's hand in a final farewell.

In that moment a cavalry officer loomed out of the dust not ten yards away. Hunter instinctively raised his gun. But though the man stared hard at them, he made no move to come nearer. Cass thrust to her feet and pushed Meggie behind her, standing straight, staring back at the man as if the rest of the world had fallen away.

All at once, Hunter realized it was Drew. Drew who had come for Meggie. Drew who had unleashed this carnage. Hunter reached for Cassie to pull her away.

Then Drew swung his arm in a wide, encompassing stroke and shouted something Hunter couldn't hear.

But Cass had heard. She pulled Meggie up onto her hip and darted toward the edge of the compound. Hunter caught up and took the lead. Now more than half of the tepees were ablaze. The air was thick with smoke, alive with cries of challenge and fury and pain. Bursts of gunfire rattled around them.

Cass stayed at his heels, holding Meggie against her with one hand and carrying a cavalry pistol she'd picked up somewhere.

The horses danced and fought the reins, growing ever more restive with the constant firing and the smell of smoke and blood. If they could get beyond the outer ring of tents, Hunter thought, if they could get into that little dry gully to the west of the camp, they could mount up and get out of here.

Just then a pair of cavalrymen rode in from their right. Their bullets kicked up dirt just ahead of Cass and Meggie. Hunter wheeled on the troopers and fired.

One of the men slumped over and fell from his saddle. The other turned and aimed. Hunter dodged to the left, but he wasn't quick enough.

The bullet slammed into his thigh. Hunter went down hard, pain tearing the length of his leg and up into his groin. Cass suddenly stood over him, still holding Meggie. She raised her pistol and fired. When he looked, the second cavalryman's saddle was empty.

"You shot him!" he said.

"Yes," she answered, and bent beside him to probe the wound.

The pain flared up like grease on a fire. Hunter went clammy and sick.

"It hit muscle, not bone," she told him.

"That's good," he panted. "Now help me up."

"I need to clean this, tie it up, stop the bleeding."

"There isn't time."

He could see she knew that, too. With Cassie's help Hunter fought his way to his feet. She wrapped the horse's reins in one hand and slid her other arm around Hunter's waist.

"Meggie, stay close," she ordered.

Together they stumbled forward. Hunter went sweaty and cold. His stomach lurched. He could hear that Cass's breathing was nearly as ragged as his. He wondered just how much farther that gully was. He couldn't seem to judge distances in the swirl of dust and fog and smoke. But all at once they were at the edge of it.

The three of them plunged over the rim and stumbled down the shallow slope. Pain swept over Hunter as his legs worked. Blood soaked down his pants. The sick, clammy feeling swept over him again.

He grabbed for the skirt of one of the saddles and held on hard. His heartbeat reverberated inside his ribs. There was a roaring in his ears. The world went white around him.

"Hunter?" Cass's voice reached him from far away.

"This always happens when I get shot," he told her, and then wasn't sure he'd said the words aloud.

"How many times have you been shot?" It was Meggie's voice, Meggie's insatiable curiosity. He tried to answer, but his thoughts seemed so disjointed and slow.

All he knew was that Cass was kneeling beside him, touching him, wrapping something around his leg. He was shaking, tingling all over, cold down to his bones. He longed to lie down somewhere, but was afraid he'd never get back on his feet.

"This makes four," he said when his head began to clear.

"Can you ride?" Cass was standing beside him, half-holding him up.

Hunter could hear the battle going on, could see that there were others who had taken refuge in the gully. It wouldn't be long before the army found them. He just couldn't think where to go from here.

"Can you ride?" Cass asked again, more than a little impatient.

He smiled at her, or tried to. "I can ride."

"Good," Cass said. "And I know where we'll be safe."

It took three tries for Hunter to get onto his horse, and once he was in the saddle, the whiteness came again. He heard Cass cut the extra horses loose, toss Meggie into the saddle, and climb up behind her. He felt the jerk as they started off and hung on to the saddle horn with all the strength he had.

Cass was taking them someplace safe. He closed his eyes and trusted her.

Chapter Twenty-two

The cave was exactly where Cass remembered it, tucked half-way up a ragged hillside amidst a cluster of cedars and scrub pine. She dismounted at the foot of the trail that led to the cave and swung Meggie down. Hunter had clambered out of the saddle before she got back to help him. He seemed steady on his feet and more clearheaded than he'd been since morning.

"The cave's up there?" he asked, eyeing the climb.

"I discovered it a year or two ago when some of us came here to dig roots. There's grazing and a creek just off to the north. We can hole up here while I tend that wound."

She'd been wanting to get at it for hours. The longer the bullet stayed in his leg, the greater the danger of fever and putrefaction. The high color in Hunter's face worried her. She stifled an urge to lay her palm across his forehead, sure he wouldn't let her near him until they got settled.

Doing that took the best part of an hour. By the time Hunter was stretched out on the bed of blankets Cass had made, she could smell the flat, hot scent of fever on him. As desperate as she was to tend his wound, she had to see to Meggie first.

"I need you to do a very important job for me, Meggie," Cass began, easing the child toward the mouth of the cave. "While I'm busy bandaging Hunter's leg, I want you to keep watch outside. Do you think you can do that?''

Meggie nodded, solemn and resolute.

''Then sit right here at the top of the path and let me know if anyone comes,'' Cass instructed carefully. ''You can do that, can't you?''

''You're going to be able to fix Hunter, aren't you?''

''Of course I can fix him,'' Cass assured her, and hoped it was true.

''Hunter's nice. I like him. I don't want him going away like Mama did.''

Cass's fears fluttered at the base of her throat. ''I don't want him going away, either. Once I fix him, Hunter will be fine.''

Meggie hesitated and then whispered, ''I wish Hunter was with us all the time.''

All the time. Cass couldn't think about ''all the time.'' About what that meant. About what it might be like. She couldn't think about anything but how she must see to Hunter's hurts before her gumption deserted her.

''Are you going to be all right here, Meggie-girl?''

Meggie nodded and Cass left her at the head of the trail.

Hunter was propped up on his elbows when she entered the cave.

''I've posted Meggie as a lookout while we do this,'' Cass told him as calmly as she could. Though her hands were slick and the blood was drumming in her ears, she took out her knife and sliced away both the blood-soaked bandages and the leg of Hunter's trousers. Beneath them the wound looked ragged and dark, the blood still oozing. She tried not to notice how Hunter sucked in his breath as she probed around the edges.

''That ball's deep and barely missed the bone,'' she told him.

''Then once you get the bullet out, you're going to have to cauterize the hole.''

Cass squirmed at the prospect, but when she looked up into his face, she took care to meet his gaze head-on. ''I know that,'' she said. ''I can boil up some herbs that will help the pain.''

She'd never seen such resolution in any man's face. "I want to keep my wits about me as long as I can."

Cass fanned the little fire she'd made and nestled the blade of Hunter's bowie knife into the bed of glowing coals. She put her own more delicate knife in a basin of water steaming over the fire. Crumbling white pine bark into a cup, she mixed up a gray, lumpy paste to use as a poultice, and boiled up catnip tea to fight his fever.

Cass had treated gunshot wounds before and loathed what she must do to him. She gritted her teeth and gently wiped away the steady seep of blood on Hunter's thigh.

"Just get on with it," he whispered.

Though her hands were steady, Cass's heart beat thick inside her as she took up her blade and began to explore the wound.

Hunter sucked in his breath and stiffened.

Trying to block out the signs of his pain, she followed the furrow downward with the point of the knife. She felt his muscles quiver as he tried to hold himself still, saw how the sweat beaded up on his face and rolled in rivulets down his throat. She hated that she was hurting him.

The ball was buried deep in the long, hard muscle of his thigh. As she worked it toward the surface, she fought to ignore the way Hunter's jaw hardened, how the air hissed in and out between his teeth. She tried to ignore the burn of sickness rising at the back of her throat.

At last she plucked the misshapen bit of lead from the open wound. She sat back on her heels, breathless and dizzy with relief. She sucked in huge, shaky lungfuls of air as if she'd been running for her life.

Hunter's hair hung wet and lank along his jaw. A rim of white outlined his mouth.

Only when she bent to wipe his face with a damp cloth did Cass realize how badly her hands were trembling. "Are you all right?" she asked him.

His eyes met hers, hot as hell and twice as dark. "I want to get this over with."

With a shudder, Cass nodded.

Her already-tattered resolve frayed a little more as she

plucked Hunter's knife from the fluttering flames. The blade glowed as if it were alive, pulsing and shimmering in the half-light. Before either of them could lose their courage, Cass pressed the tip of the red-hot blade into the heart of Hunter's open wound.

His body jerked taut beneath her hands. The acrid stench of charring flesh spiraled up to singe her nostrils. He ground out a curse between his teeth, collapsed back against the blankets, and lay still.

While Hunter was lost in oblivion, Cass finished her work. She spread the wound with the poultice she'd made and covered the paste with moistened strips of willow bark. She tied everything in place with the bandages, then washed and stowed away her herbs and tools.

When she was done, she sought the dark at the back of the cave, curled in upon herself, and wept silently into her hands.

"You said he was going to be all right," Meggie chided Cassie in a small, fretful voice. "You promised."

Cass turned from placing a dampened cloth on Hunter's brow. "Of course he'll be all right," she insisted. "He's only got a little fever."

In spite of the words of reassurance, Cass was worried. Hunter had been drifting in and out of a restless sleep for the best part of two days. She'd been changing the poultice of powdered pine bark every two hours. She'd been dosing him with fever tea, and his skin was still like fire beneath her hands.

Bending above him, she stroked his hair.

He tossed, muttered something under his breath, then opened his eyes. They were hazy and dark with confusion. "Cass?" he murmured. "Is this the cave?"

She dampened the cloth again and wiped his face. "Yes, Hunter, we're safe in the cave. Are you feeling any better?"

He pushed up on his elbows and blinked, as if he were trying to bring the world into focus around him. "I'm so thirsty—"

Gesturing for Meggie to fill the dipper with the fresh water they'd brought from the stream, Cass put the cup to Hunter's mouth. He drank deeply and dropped back onto the bed as if that simple effort had exhausted him.

"I've made some soup. You'll feel stronger if you eat a little."

She turned toward the pot she'd kept simmering all afternoon, but Hunter reached out and caught her wrist.

"Promise you won't leave here until I can go with you," he insisted, his big hand clamped tight around her arm. "Promise you won't go back to Fort Carr without me."

It was a conversation they'd been having by fits and starts for the last two days, and Cass had run out of ways to reassure him.

"Of course I'll wait," she answered him. "Of course, I won't head out alone."

She made the promise knowing that if she went back, she couldn't let Hunter accompany her. If the army found him anywhere near Fort Carr, he would be arrested, tried, and hanged for Jessup's death. Cass simply couldn't risk that. But then, neither could she leave him here until she was sure he was out of danger.

She spooned thick buffalo broth into a tin cup for him to drink and dosed him with more fever tea when he was done. She sat beside him until he slept.

"Hunter is going to be all right, isn't he?" Meggie asked a few minutes later as Cass tucked her into the nook she'd chosen for her bed.

"Why don't you mention him in your prayers tonight," Cass suggested.

"Do you think God will listen if I pray for Hunter?"

"God hears everyone's prayers, Meggie," Cass assured her. Which God heard what prayers was something Cass had never been able to reconcile. Whether God chose to answer was something else entirely; He had never seen fit to answer hers. But if God answered anyone's prayers, Cass supposed it would be someone like Meggie, someone who deserved to have them answered.

Cass listened through Meggie's usual recitation. "And please make Hunter all better again," she added at the end.

Cassie smiled and kissed the child good night when she

was done. "I love you, Meggie," she said. *I love you every bit as much as if you were my own little girl.*

Meggie snuggled with the battered doll Cass had given back to her. "I love you, too, Cassie," she whispered, and drifted off to sleep.

Cass sat staring down at Meggie, thinking how bleak life would be without her. She took such delight in her giggles, in the wide-eyed joy of her discoveries, in her sticky hands and spontaneous kisses. In parts of his daughter Drew could never see or appreciate or understand. He could never love Meggie the way Cassie loved her.

Yet how could she take Meggie from her father? As long as he lived, Drew would search for her.

Where would she go if she took Meggie and ran away? She'd have to find someplace where the war between the Indians and the whites couldn't reach, where Meggie could grow up untouched by the prejudices that had eaten away at her father. Where could the two of them live together, anonymous and safe?

Cass couldn't turn to Hunter, couldn't ask him to take the risks the two of them would face. Her vision blurred at the thought of leaving him behind—Hunter who had known who she was the moment they looked into each other's eyes, Hunter who had come to feel like the other half of herself.

She looked across the fire to where he lay, tossing and mumbling in his sleep. The question of Meggie's future would wait. Hunter was the one who needed her now. She blinked back hot, useless tears and went to him.

Cass worked over him most of the night, bathing his burning body with water from the stream, wiping his face and corded throat, drizzling cool water across his collarbones and down his chest. She slid a wet cloth down his arms and moistened the pulse that beat in the hollow of his wrists. She bathed his belly and his legs. He was a strong man, brown and sculptured and beautiful, so beautiful that just touching him made her feel hollow and weak inside.

He was a man who defined himself in a way she had never experienced before. He was a warrior with a generous heart, a soldier with vast reserves of compassion and humanity. He was a friend who gave his friendship and his tenderness and his compassion with selfless ease. What they'd shared in these past months, in these past days, made her think of him as hers, even when such fancies were impossible. It made her wish for so much more than she could ever ask of him.

Hunter mumbled and tossed as she worked over him. Sometimes he slept. Sometimes he stared up at her with fever-bright eyes, seeing someone or something else. Sometimes he talked in French and Sioux and Arikara. Often he relived the moments they'd shared together, asking about the herbs she'd gathered, repeating advice about living among the whites, telling her she was beautiful.

Cass clutched those words against her heart. No man had spoken to her with such tenderness. No man had told her that she was beautiful, for all that she had longed to hear the words. No man had whispered how much he needed her . . .

Sometimes he mumbled, "Don't leave me." But the request came hard, as if the syllables had been torn from his throat, as if he hated needing to ask her to stay.

As if he knew she could not.

And though she soothed him with her assurances, quieted him with the brush of her hands, she feared leaving him was becoming inevitable.

His fever spiraled higher in the dark hours before dawn. Cass worked over him, cursing and praying and cajoling. She whispered his name, as if she could keep him with her by the sound of her voice. She battled for his life, as if she could hold him with the skill in her touch and the force of her will.

And then all at once he was better, cooler. Hunter's skin went damp, and his breathing came easier. He slept peacefully, dreamlessly, exhausted from having passed through the fire.

Wearily Cass pushed to her feet and gathered up the buffalo bladder they had been using to carry water. She paused as she stepped beyond the mouth of the cave. The moon was down, but a handful of stars were sprinkled across the wide expanse of graying sky. The breeze blew cool against her throat, ruffling the skirt of her buckskin dress and lifting the strands of her tumbled hair.

Cass raised her head and spoke to the world beyond her own. "Thank you," she whispered, and from around her in the rolling hills the wind hummed in answer.

Cass toiled up the path toward the cave, the buckskin sling across her shoulder heavy with firewood. Meggie ran on ahead, leaping from stone to stone, shouting with the pure exhilaration of the bright, crisp day. Cass laughed a little breathlessly, wanting to set aside her burden and follow Meggie, wanting to lie back in the grass and fill her eyes with the color of the sky. She needed the scope of it to nourish her, to help her dream her secret dreams, to fill her mind with possibilities.

Especially now when the threat to everything she loved was so tangible and real.

Meggie reached the head of the trail a dozen steps ahead of Cass. "Hunter," she crowed. "You're all well!"

He was settled on a rock at the mouth of the cave, pale and shaking and breathing heavily.

Cass brushed past him without saying a word. She clattered her load of branches onto the pile beside the fire, and stood there fighting down the urge to weep. How could she be anything but pleased that Hunter was better?

Yet his recovery meant that if she intended to take Meggie back to the fort, they had to leave—tomorrow or the next day, before Hunter was strong enough to follow them. Her time with the two most precious people in her world was running out.

"Cass?" Her name echoed hollowly around her, and she could hear the concern in Hunter's voice. "Cass?"

Damn him for sensing her mood, for seeing more than she wanted him to see. She dashed the moisture from her eyes and went outside. Only then did she notice the soap and fresh shirt piled up at his feet.

"Is there someplace I can bathe?" he asked. "I smell like fever."

She glanced at the trail to the creek and back at him. "It's a bit of a walk."

Hunter managed to limp as far as the little stream, and

though Cass was tempted to stay and watch him bathe, she and Meggie went back to gather up blankets and food. Cass had relived that day at Caspar Mountain scores of times, and she yearned to store away a few more memories.

Once they'd eaten the sparse meal of pemmican and jerky, Cass lured Meggie into her lap where the child fell asleep almost instantly. Hunter stretched out on his back beside her, good leg bent and arms crooked behind his head. She could tell by the high, fresh color in his face that the outing had done him good. Still, she reached across to brush back a strand of that black, black hair and surreptitiously check for fever.

He smiled at her, a slow, contented smile that sank straight into her heart. She hastily looked away, afraid he would see the longing in her eyes.

"Have you ever thought," he began, almost as if he'd read her mind, "about keeping Meggie?"

Cass's head came up; she stared at him. "Of course I've thought about keeping her. But I have nowhere to go, no way to provide for her."

"What if I could take you somewhere safe?"

"Somewhere safe," she repeated. "And just where is that?"

"To Montana, to my land up in the mountains."

"Montana," Cass whispered, the word soft, melodious and seductive. Hunter had told her about Montana, about the cabin he meant to build, about the life he planned to make for himself.

"We could be happy there," he told her. "We could grow the things we need, cut a little timber, raise a few horses. We could take care of Meggie as if she were our own little girl."

The temptation that had been whispering in Cassie's ears became a shout. If she let Hunter do this, she could keep the little girl.

"You'd do all of that for another man's child?"

His deep blue gaze bore into her. "I would do it for you."

The words kindled a hot, sweet tenderness for this man who understood what she needed and was willing to sacrifice himself to make her happy. Cass had never dreamed she would find anyone willing to risk so much to make her whole.

"You could marry me," Hunter went on, his voice so low and persuasive that gooseflesh shimmied down her arms. "Meggie can be the child we can never have together, and I'd do my best to be her father."

Cass lost herself in the heat and conviction in his eyes. This man had fought for her and cared for her and watched over her. He had made love to her with a passion and a sweetness that thrilled her and left her mindless with pleasure. He was worthy of her trust, worthy of her love.

"There's a spot in a stand of pine at the top of the ridge," he told her, his face alight, "where we can build the cabin. You can see for miles from there, ridges of mountains running off to the west, forests bristling on every hand, the river shimmering in the valley miles below. And the sunsets you can see from there fairly set the sky ablaze. If we leave here by the middle of next week I can get our house built before the first of the blizzards come."

Hunter was sharing his dreams with her, trusting her with his hopes and his ambitions. Plans he might never have shared with anyone. It sounded so wonderful.

"But what about Drew?" she had to ask.

Hunter's eyes shone a little less brightly. "Not even Drew knows what became of Meggie back at the Indian village. She could still be a captive. She could be dead. She could have run off on her own."

"He'll keep on looking."

His wide mouth narrowed. She saw the condemnation in his face. "He never looked for you and Julia."

Which was why Drew would search for Meggie until the day he died.

"Cass," Hunter said, and she could hear the urgency in his tone, "you love that girl. You want to be her mother more than anything. I want to give you that. I want the three of us to be a family."

A family. Ever since she'd lost her parents and her sisters, she had been searching for a family, a place to belong.

"But Drew is Meggie's father," Cassie whispered. She could still see Drew's face, the way he'd looked back in the

Indian camp. She could still hear the words he'd shouted to her over the din of battle.

"You're her mother," Hunter insisted softly. "The woman who birthed her could not love her more than you. Please, Cass, let me make a life for you and Meggie in Montana. Let me give you something that will make all of us happy."

When she didn't immediately answer, Hunter fell silent. He was giving her the chance to decide their future: hers and Meggie's—and his own. She held the power for joy or contentment or heartbreak in her hands, and she didn't know how to make the choice.

As she stared intently at the rushing stream, the exertions of the day caught up with Hunter. He drifted into an easy sleep. Cass watched over both him and Meggie. She stroked the child's pale hair; brushed the sweet, pink bow of her babyish mouth; felt the warmth and the trust of that small, warm body curled against her.

She stared down at Hunter, filling her eyes with his fierce beauty. She let her gaze trace over that wide, determined jaw, the blatantly sensual turn of his lips, the fringe of thick, black lashes. She had never known a man like this, a man of such gallantry and strength, of such tenderness and honesty. She wanted to marry him and live with him in peace far up on his mountaintop.

But how could she betray the man she'd seen in Drew during the battle at the Cheyenne village? She had looked up from where she knelt by Runs Like a Doe's body and seen an officer loom out of the smoke and dust. She'd seen the blur of his dark blue uniform, his horse wheeling and prancing beneath him, his saber glinting in the half-light. And then she realized it was Meggie's father.

Panic had sent her jolting to her feet. She'd swept Meggie behind her and gripped her gun, ready to protect herself and her child. But Drew hadn't tried to shoot her or ride her down. He hadn't made any move to take Meggie.

Instead, across the yards of smoky clearing, their eyes had held. She had steeled herself for the hatred in his, for the rage, for the zealot's fire. Instead those silver-gray eyes were filled with disillusionment. They were wide with horror at the carnage he'd unleashed on Standing Pine's village. They were dark with shame that in the midst of the fight he had lost control of his men.

In that moment Drew had known that the tenets that governed his life were wrong. Cass had sensed his confusion and his grief and instinctively reached out for him.

As if in answer he'd swung his sword arm in an arc above his head. His face contorted as he shouted and desperately gestured to the west. Over the rattle of rifle fire, the thud of hooves and moans of pain, Cass could just barely make out Drew's words.

"Run!" he'd shouted at her. "Run! Save Meggie! Save yourself!"

Then he had wheeled his mount and galloped back the way he'd come.

In that single act, Cass had seen there was hope for Drew. Meggie was that hope, Drew's last chance to redeem himself. How could Cassie deny salvation to the man she'd loved since childhood? How could she deny Drew his daughter?

Cass closed her eyes and let the hot, hopeless tears seep down her cheeks.

After she'd served their evening meal and put Meggie to bed, Cass made her way to where Hunter sat propped up on his bed of furs and blankets.

"How are you feeling?"

"Better. A little tired. How are you?"

"Fine," she lied. *I feel as if my heart is breaking.*

He frowned as if he'd caught a glimpse of the sadness in her eyes. "You aren't considering taking Meggie back to her father because you think you don't deserve her?" he asked softly. "You don't feel guilty about us being together because you're still Drew Reynolds's wife?"

Cass looked deep into his eyes, knowing it was so much simpler than that. "What Drew and I thought we had was over long ago," she told him. "I made him take me for his wife when he didn't really want me. In the end, he threw me away. What happened after that was only between the two of us."

Hunter drew her down onto the blankets and into his arms. She nuzzled into the solid strength of his shoulder. He stroked her hair. Cass breathed the scent of him, the warmth and woodsmoke. She would never smell woodsmoke again without thinking of him, without feeling the longing for him way down deep.

But she needed more than the scent of him tonight, more than mere companionship. She craved the brush of his hands against her skin, hungered for the dulcet seep of his passion. She wanted pleasure and joy and moments to cherish.

She raised her head and sought sweet solace in his mouth. He kissed her back, his lips brushing over the contours of hers, molding and clinging. That kiss swept into the next, warming, consoling, seeking, filling the aching need in her.

Cass slid her hand along the thick, corded column of his throat and felt the beat of his vitality beneath her palm. Curling his arm around her as the intensity of their kisses grew, Hunter eased both of them down onto the pallet of blankets. They lay there length to length, their lips fused in slow, elegant kisses. His tongue sought hers, the taste and the textures and the tenderness merging between them.

"Oh, Cass," he murmured into her mouth. "I need you so."

The tight, hot pain of a silent sob rose inside her. She fought it down and turned her head so he could not read the emotions in her eyes. "I need you, too," she whispered back.

He tugged at the hem of the doeskin gown, and as the buttery soft leather fell away, he skimmed his big, callused hand along her shoulder. The roughness rasped against her, pointing up the delicious divergence between a man and woman, the difference between him and her. He curved his palm around her breast and she gasped with the pleasure spilling through her. He brushed her nipple with the pad of his thumb and took her mouth again.

As they kissed she spread the panels of his shirt and slipped the ties that held his breechclout in place. She reveled in the expanse of his warm, taut flesh against her. He groaned as her hand swept down along his side and over the jut of his hip as she drew him against her.

They touched, his eyes holding hers as if he needed to watch the pleasure grow in her. He brushed his hand down her belly and pressed it between her legs. She stirred beneath him as he circled against her mound. The delight came thick and heavy and honey-sweet.

''You seem more womanly every time I make love to you,'' he whispered. ''More lush and lovely.''

He eased his fingers inside her with slow, languorous strokes that made her arch against him. She whispered his name. He swallowed the sound in a lingering kiss.

She stroked him, too, needing to see the same fierce wanting in those blue-black eyes, needing to merge their bodies and their souls. And when she saw that he was as consumed by desire as she, as lost to sweet sensation, Cass rolled above him and took him into herself.

Being one with him brought a kind of completion, a soul-deep satisfaction. It was the ultimate joining of two lost people who had found in each other the missing part of themselves.

''All I want, Cass,'' he whispered as his hands moved over her, sensual and worshipful, tender and enticing, ''is to make you happy. All I want is to make our life together wonderful.''

''Oh, Hunter,'' she murmured, the need to weep burning at the back of her throat. ''That's all I want, too.''

Cass watched his eyes as the two of them began to move together. She saw the heat of his desire and the strength of his joy, the love she had never in this life expected to find. She gave herself up to it, to him, to the splendor of this joining.

Knowing the decision she must make made the brush of their bodies and their mouths more poignant, edged with exquisite pain, filled with exquisite tenderness. As the chorus of delight swelled between them, she saw his pleasure flare like a hot blue flame. She consigned herself to the conflagration, rising with him like a shower of sparks from the heart of a white-hot blaze, drifting with him like wisps of smoke spiraling upward to be lost in the nebulous darkness of the sky.

Cass was clinging tight to Hunter when she came to herself again. She didn't want it to be over. Not the loving, not her time with Hunter and Meggie, not this small, brief swatch of happiness in a world of war and death and loneliness. But it was. And there was no help for what came next.

After a time, Cass dragged one of the blankets around her and went to the fire to boil up a special herbal tea.

"What's this?" Hunter asked when she brought him a cup of the brew.

"A tonic I prepared for you. Something to help you regain your strength more quickly."

"Do you think I need it?"

Cass nodded, unsmiling and adamant.

He took a sip and grimaced at the taste. "What's in it?"

"Vervain, some mountain mint, a bit of juniper . . ."

He swallowed it down, hissed between his teeth, and handed back the cup. "That's wretched stuff."

"I'm sorry," Cass said, and didn't dare look at him.

"Well, as long as it serves its purpose. Now come to bed."

Cass lay down beside him, nestled into the crook of his shoulder and waited. In didn't take long for Hunter's body to go lax or for his breathing to deepen. It was done now. She had prepared and made him drink the tea that would ensure he would sleep like the dead until well past midday.

"I'm sorry, Hunter," she whispered again. "I'm sorry I can't take what you've offered me. I'm sorry I've had to betray your trust. I'm sorry I haven't been able to tell you how much I love you. But I do."

Cass reached across to stroke his hair, to trace the rise of those chiseled cheekbones and the sensual curves of his mouth. "I love you. You are the only man who knows who and what I am and cares for me still. I love you, Hunter. I will love you forever."

With tears in her eyes, Cass curled into Hunter's warmth, into his strength, into the shelter only he had ever afforded her. And knew it was for the very last time.

Chapter Twenty-three

"Aren't we going to wake Hunter and say good-bye?" Meggie whispered as Cass gathered up their few belongings. They were both washed and dressed and ready to leave the cave.

Cass shook her head. "Hunter has been sick. He needs to sleep." With the herbal tea she'd given him after they'd made love, he wouldn't stir until at least midday. Far too late for him to catch up to them, even if he wanted to.

"But won't Hunter wonder where we went?" Meggie persisted.

"He'll know where we went," Cass assured her, and fought down the urge to look back at him one last time.

"Where *are* we going?" Meggie demanded as she trailed Cass out to where their horse was saddled and waiting.

"Back to the fort. Back to your father," Cassie answered, lifting Meggie into the saddle. She gathered up her tattered calico skirts and swung up behind her.

Meggie craned around to stare at her. "Will we have to tell Papa we're sorry we ran away?"

"I expect we will." Cassie's heart thumped a little harder at the thought of facing Drew.

"Won't Papa be angry?"

Cass straightened in the saddle and turned her mount down

the slope. "I think he'll be so happy to have you back, nothing else will matter."

Meggie was silent for a moment. "I don't want to go back to the fort. I don't like it there. I want to go to Montana with Hunter and you."

Cass still yearned to accept what Hunter had offered her—a place where the wind whispered through the pines and the sky was at your doorstep, a place where the three of them could make a life together and truly become a family. The strength of her regret squeezed her throat, all but choking off her answer.

"I'm not going to Montana."

"Are you going to stay with Papa and me?"

Cass could hear the excitement in Meggie's voice and didn't know what to say to her. She couldn't tell her the truth. They had a two-day ride ahead of them, and Cass needed Meggie's cooperation. She hated to lie; the child had been lied to far too often in her young life. Instead she tightened her arms and drew Meggie back against her chest.

"We'll talk to your father about it once we reach Fort Carr," Cass promised.

And with that, Meggie seemed satisfied.

They reached the base of the hill where the trail wound along the edge of the prairie, and Cass couldn't keep from turning and looking back. She'd stood over Hunter in the dawn, staring at the inky darkness of his tumbled hair; at the fierce, almost elegant features; at the length and breadth of his body beneath the blanket, trying to commit every feature, every facet of this man to memory.

Later he would awaken and find them gone. Cass knew it was better like this. She'd run fresh out of choices, out of hope, and out of strength. Once she'd given Meggie up to Drew, there wouldn't be much left of her to offer to anyone. This was the way it had to be.

With a sigh of resignation that came all the way from her toes, Cass turned their horse southward toward Fort Carr.

Hunter wished he could remember what he'd done to deserve feeling so battered and queasy this morning. He kept trying to wake up and kept on drifting. He wondered if he was sick again, but he didn't feel all hot and close and restless like before, and Cass would be here nursing him if he was.

Cass. His memories seemed to snag on Cass, of pulling her down beside him the night before, of making sweet, languorous love to her.

He stirred a little and opened his eyes. Light ricocheted around inside his head. He blinked the world into focus by dint of will. He was in the cave, in his bed.

"Cass," he called out softly, his voice thick and thready with disuse. "Cass, are you here?"

The cave was silent. Utterly silent, as if it had been empty for a very long time.

He bolted up in his bed, fear grabbing at the heart of him. His head reeled with the sudden movement. He braced himself and waited for the world to settle again. When it had, he hauled himself to his feet, shaking and cursing.

He stumbled toward the mouth of the cave. He looked at the empty pallet laid out on the floor, at the fire burned to ashes hours before. He saw Cass had taken all her things, her blanket and her herbs and her medicine bundle. Meggie's few belongings were gone, as well.

"Cass!" he shouted, though he knew it was futile. Only his own agonized shout came back to him.

Cursing steadily, he ran out into the tiny meadow beyond the cave. His horse was grazing at the fringe of the trees—his horse alone. He didn't have to think twice about where Cass and Meggie were headed. Cass was going to Fort Carr to give the girl back to her father.

He spun back into the cave, gathered up what he would need, and went to saddle his horse. It was well after midday. They must be hours and hours ahead of him by now, far enough to make catching them nearly impossible. But that didn't mean he wasn't going to try.

He rode as if the hounds of hell were at his heels. He rode with his head reeling from the effects of whatever Cass had given him the night before, rode sick with concern for a woman and a child traveling alone.

He worried that Cass had given up, that in taking Meggie

back, Cass had decided to stop caring, stop hoping, stop being able to risk her heart. He couldn't blame her for feeling that way. Losing his parents had destroyed Drew Reynolds. Cass had lost even more than he, and now she was giving up the child she loved with all her heart.

Hunter just couldn't let it be too late for Cass, not when he hadn't told her how much he loved her, hadn't convinced her they could make a life together. With or without Meggie, they could find happiness, here on the plains or living in the mountains. He had to find her before she stopped believing in the future and shuttered herself away as Drew had done.

The sun was down and Hunter was riding through the blue half-light that preceded full dark, when he saw a flicker of light and a twist of smoke spiraling skyward.

"Cass," he breathed in exasperation, both relieved to have found her and angry that she had taken the chance of lighting a fire out here in the flat where even the smallest spark blazed like a beacon.

He took care to tether his horse some distance away and came into the campsite on foot. But Cass and Meggie weren't huddled by the fire. Instead he found a battered cavalry trooper bent over a rabbit he was trying to cook on a stick. The man dropped his dinner into the flames as Hunter came at him out of the dark.

"Who're you?" the man demanded once he realized Hunter had the drop on him. "Wait, I know. You're that scout from Fort Carr, the one that killed that sutler fellow a few weeks back. Jobbert, or something like that. You going to shoot me, too?"

"Alain Jalbert," Hunter corrected him. "And I didn't shoot the sutler. I knifed him. Who are you?"

"I—I'm Corporal Mason Manus," the trooper told him.

"From Captain Reynolds's company?"

Manus nodded.

"What are you doing way out here? Is Captain Reynolds still looking for his daughter?"

"It's hard for me to say. I got separated from my troop in the battle at the Indian camp. Someone banged me on the head. When I woke up a tepee had fallen on top of me and everyone was gone.''

''How long ago was that?''

''It took three or four days before I was fit enough to travel. I lived off things I found in the village. I didn't see a soul there once I woke up. I been walking since yesterday noon, trying to get back to the fort without my horse.''

''Have you seen any sign of Mrs. Reynolds or Reynolds's little girl?''

''The child his Indian bitch run off with, you mean?'' The corporal spit. ''I ain't seen much of anyone, until tonight.''

''Ran off with?'' Hunter pressed him, determined to ignore the man's unflattering reference to Cass. ''Who said she took the child?''

''Why the captain, I guess,'' Manus told him. ''The captain had a warrant for her arrest for taking that child and spying for the Indians.''

''Ben McGarrity issued a warrant for Mrs. Reynolds's arrest?''

''I guess. The captain had one, all right.''

Hunter shivered with the chill that ran up his back. There had been a whole lot more to Reynolds's enmity than either he or Cass had guessed. ''Are you sure about this, Corporal Manus?''

''I ain't used to conferring with the captain directly, you know, but everyone at the fort was in an uproar about her taking that girl. We rode out the morning after Captain Reynolds found her gone, followed the trail right to that Indian camp.''

''You say the trail led right to the camp?''

''Well, no sir. Not now that you mention it. We tracked them to a tepee set off by itself. We burned the son of a bitch and followed the trail north from there.''

Concern for Cass roiled up inside him like thunderheads on a muggy afternoon. Whoever had been tracking for Drew had followed not the war party that had taken Meggie, but Cass and him. That's how they'd found the Cheyenne camp and why they were so sure that Cass had Meggie. It was also why it was so dangerous for Cass to ride into that fort all by herself.

Hunter had to get there before she did. He had to warn her that Drew—that everyone—thought she'd kidnapped Meggie. He had to try to persuade her that it wasn't too late go to the mountains with him.

"I'm heading for Fort Carr, Manus," Hunter said. "I'd take you with me if I could, but I've only got one horse, and I need to make time with him. I'll let them know you're out here so they can send a patrol to bring you in."

"You're not going to shoot me, then?"

Hunter couldn't help but grin. "Not unless you're crazy enough to try to shoot me first."

Manus shook his head. "I 'bout done all the crazy things I intend to for a while."

Hunter nodded and turned toward where he'd tethered his horse. "And Manus," he called over his shoulder.

"Sir?"

"Put out that fire. You can see it for miles, and the next folks it attracts might be a whole lot less friendly than I am."

Chapter Twenty-four

Fort Carr lay before them on the far side of the Platte. Cassie's breath caught in her throat as they paused on the rise to look down at it: at the long, wooden bridge; at the cluster of rough-hewn barracks and cabins set in the swishing expanse of prairie grass; at the tepees of the friendly camp nestled off to the west. Drew was in the fort somewhere, waiting to take his daughter back and break Cassie's heart.

Blood and honor demanded that she return Meggie to her father. Yet as hard as she'd tried to prepare herself, Cass wasn't ready to say good-bye. She curled her arms more tightly around the child who rode before her in the saddle and pressed her cheek to Meggie's hair. Her eyes stung with tears she dared not shed as she breathed the scent of Meggie's little-girl sweetness and her little-girl dreams. Yet Cass had no choice about taking her back.

She straightened in the saddle, blinked away the tears, and eased her horse down the bank toward the fort.

The sentries stopped her at the near end of the bridge. "Halt!" the corporal of the guard called out, his rifle at the ready. "Dismount and state your business."

Cass swung down from her horse, taking care to leave Meggie in the saddle. "I'm Cassandra Reynolds. I've come to Fort Carr to bring Captain Reynolds his daughter."

The man shifted his gaze to the riverbank, to where the cottonwoods grew thick along the sides of the bridge. "You alone, Mrs. Reynolds?"

Cass's nerves began to hum. The corporal suspected she and Meggie had been sent by the Indians as some kind of diversion.

"There are just the two of us, Corporal," she assured him, tightening her grip on the reins. "May we pass?"

"I'll escort you to the fort myself, ma'am. You're under arrest."

Cass spun and jabbed her toe into the stirrup, trying to mount her horse and spur away. The corporal was too fast for her. He caught her around the waist and flung her to the ground.

Meggie screamed. The horse began to dance.

Cass scrambled to her feet and felt the thump of the trooper's rifle barrel against her breastbone.

"Get the girl!" the corporal ordered, and the other sentries jumped to obey. One of the privates grabbed the horse's reins and a second dragged Meggie out of the saddle.

The little girl kicked and scratched, shrieking Cassie's name. The private cursed, and in spite of the gun pressed tight against her chest, Cassie turned.

"It's all right, Meggie," she shouted. "The man won't hurt you if you're good."

Meggie's struggles subsided. She hung clamped against the private's chest, dangling against his legs like a rag doll. Her face was splotched with tears. "They're going to make you go away," she sobbed, "just like Mama!"

"No, Meggie, no! I'll be fine. They're going to take you to your papa."

"I don't want to go to Papa. I want to stay with you!" Meggie wailed. "I want to take a rest with you!"

A rest. In spite of herself, Cassie laughed. This had to be the first time Meggie had ever volunteered to take a nap.

"You can take a rest back at the cabin. I'll come and lie down with you as soon as I can."

The burly private heaved Meggie onto his hip and started toward the fort.

"No!" Meggie yelled, twisting and kicking again. "No! I want to take a rest with Cassie!"

The trooper kept walking.

Once the private and Meggie had cleared the bridge, the corporal gathered up her horse's reins and prodded Cassie toward the fort.

"Will you tell me why I'm being arrested?" she asked him.

"Don't you know what you did, Mrs. Reynolds?"

"I rescued the captain's daughter from the Indians and came to bring her back to him."

The corporal snorted and spit. "Well, then, I guess the officer of the day will tell you what the charges are when we get to the guardhouse."

To the guardhouse. The air burned cold as hoarfrost in Cassie's lungs at the memory of visiting Many Buffalo in the close little cell. She'd be screaming by nightfall if they locked her up in there.

"And my husband?" she asked, her voice quivering just a little. "I'd like a word with Captain Reynolds."

The corporal snorted and spit again.

They started collecting a crowd the moment they stepped off the bridge. It was just like the day she'd been exchanged and ridden in with Drew. She remembered how she'd shuddered as the people and the buildings closed around her, how the sights and smells had made her head pound and stomach pitch.

It was worse today. She knew these people, their hatreds and their prejudices, their perfidy and their ruthlessness. She could hear their muttered threats and see the hostility in their faces.

Ben McGarrity stood on the steps of the headquarters building waiting for her. The corporal nudged her toward him with the barrel of his gun. She saw no sign of Drew, and Cass was suddenly grateful that Meggie wasn't with her now. Whatever was about to happen was far more daunting and dangerous than anything Cass had imagined she would face by coming here.

McGarrity looked down at her, his eyes weary and dark

with something that looked very much like disappointment. "So you came to give yourself up, did you, Cassandra?" he asked her.

Cassie stiffened. "I came to bring Meggie to her father."

She heard the hiss of whispers around her and knew better than to discount their malevolence. A creep of foreboding inched across her shoulders.

"I didn't want to believe you could do this, Cassandra," McGarrity went on with a shake of his head. "I didn't want to believe you were in league with the Indians all this time. But three different troopers saw you during the attack on the Cheyenne camp. They said you were armed and dressed like an Indian. They told me you had Meggie with you. Surely that proves Drew's allegations."

Cass swallowed hard, her throat as dry as tinder. "His allegations?"

"That you abducted Meggie, for one."

Cassie's heartbeat stumbled. Was that what Drew thought? Was that what they had charged her with?

Before she could answer, McGarrity continued. "That you carried on illicit trade with the Cheyenne."

"I gave an Indian woman a few cans of milk so her sister's child would live!" Cass declared. "I swear that's the only contact I've had with the Cheyenne since I came here."

The furrows in McGarrity's brow deepened. "That you aided in the escape of Many Buffalo."

"Major, please!" Cass's voice rasped with the strain of trying to make him believe her. "I had nothing to do with Many Buffalo's escape."

"And most serious of all—that you sent word to the Cheyenne and Sioux about the munitions wagons."

The crowd's angry murmurs rose in a groundswell of curses and accusations. Around her she saw the somber faces of Parker's cavalry troopers, men who had lost their leader and their comrades in that fight. She saw thick-bearded muleteers scowling; three of them had died driving those wagons. She saw Lila, her eyes alive with blame for Josh's death. These people wanted the men who'd died avenged, and they sounded ready to hang her up without so much as the courtesy of a hearing.

Ben McGarrity's face went grimmer still. ''We also had reports that Jalbert was in the Cheyenne camp, that you've been in league with a murderer.''

Cassie glared up at Ben McGarrity, her anger on Hunter's behalf overwhelming concern for herself. ''Haven't you looked into what happened that night?'' she challenged him. ''Don't you know Hunter killed Tyler Jessup in self-defense?''

''So you *have* seen him. Drew figured you'd go looking for Jalbert when you ran off.''

''Hunter helped me follow Meggie's trail.''

''Follow Meggie's trail?'' There was derision in the major's voice. ''Don't you know the way to the Cheyenne camp?''

Panic churned hot in her belly. ''Damnit, Ben!'' she shouted. ''Are you going to let me tell you what happened, or have you already condemned me?''

McGarrity looked down at her, his mouth narrowing with consternation and something that might very well have been regret. ''What am I to believe, Cassandra? You admit to giving an Indian contraband, and then you help a horse thief escape. You pass word to the Sioux about the rifles. You were seen in the Cheyenne camp when the troops rode in. And now you've come back to the fort with the child you've been accused of abducting.''

''I didn't take Meggie with me when I left. I never told anyone about the rifles. Please, Ben, just listen!'' Cass's voice dipped and cracked with desperation.

Ben McGarrity's face hardened, like water glazing with ice. ''You'll have ample chance to defend yourself at the hearing tomorrow.''

Cass went on as if she had not heard. ''If any of this were true, would I come back here? Would I have brought Meggie to her father?''

McGarrity just shook his head as if he were unspeakably weary and called her captor forward. ''Corporal Hoskins?''

''Yes, sir.''

"See that Mrs. Reynolds is removed to the guardhouse."

No-o-o! she wanted to moan. She wanted to plead with Ben not to lock her away, but how could she show her weakness in front of all the people who hated her?

As the corporal grabbed her arm, fierce, biting cold spread down her limbs. Spangles of white rose in her head like whorls of snow in the prairie wind.

But just as they turned, a rider appeared at the far end of the parade ground. He was a tall man astride a long-legged roan, a dark man with a clutch of eagle feathers tucked into the band of his broad-brimmed hat.

Hunter! Cass's hopes soared with a sudden elation, then swooped toward desperate fear. She jerked free of the corporal's grip and ran toward Hunter waving her arms.

"No!" she screamed at him. "Don't come here! Go back!"

Still, he galloped toward them. People scattered to make way, as Hunter pulled his lathered horse to a stop just short of the headquarters steps. The moment he swung out of the saddle, the guards swarmed over him, grabbing his arms, taking his weapons. He made no move to resist.

McGarrity looked stunned, like a man who thought he'd seen all life's surprises and was being proved wrong.

"Well, then, Mr. Jalbert," Ben greeted him. "Have you come to turn yourself in, too?"

The crowd edged closer, eager to hear Hunter's answer.

He glanced in her direction. "I came for Cass."

As if he thought Jalbert was about to snatch her away, Corporal Hoskins tightened his grip on Cassie's elbow.

"I know what you think she's done," Hunter went on, "and I came to tell you the truth."

"The truth," McGarrity huffed. "If you're so damned eager to tell the truth, you can do it at her hearing tomorrow. And while you're at it you can answer the charge of murder that's been lodged against you. Corporal Hoskins—"

"Goddamnit, Ben!" Hunter broke in, shaking off the guards. "Isn't Meggie here somewhere, confused and afraid? Even if she's with her pa, she's scared because she's losing

Cassie. Can't we get the charges against Cass settled now so she can go comfort that little girl?''

McGarrity cursed volubly under his breath.

Cassie watched him, her chest squeezed so tight she could barely breathe. Even if Ben gave them the chance to tell him the truth, could she and Hunter make him believe it?

McGarrity scrubbed agitatedly at his beard. ''All right, goddamnit. Bring the prisoners into my office. I'll hear what they have to say—for Meggie's sake.''

The crowd rumbled their disappointment as Corporal Hoskins and two guards prodded Cassandra and Hunter up the steps.

Once inside, Ben settled himself behind his desk. The office was a familiar room, close and overly warm, smelling faintly of cigars. Cass stood beside Hunter before the desk, knotting her hands to still their trembling.

''Now then.'' The major glared at both of them. ''Start at the beginning—and this had better be good.''

Cass explained about Meggie getting into Drew's paints and the argument she'd had with him. She told him how she'd waited to say good-bye, and how she'd discovered Meggie had run off.

''About five miles from the fort, I found signs that Meggie had been taken by a Cheyenne war party. I picked up their trail and started following it north.''

Ben McGarrity's thick brows snapped together. ''A war party that close to the fort? But if Meggie had been taken by Indians, for God's sake, Cassie, why didn't you come back to us for help?''

Cass remembered how she'd parted from Drew, about what would have happened if she'd told him Meggie had been captured.

''I almost did. Then, because they were Cheyenne, I decided to follow them, on the chance I could explain who Meggie was and get her back. If I'd come here, Drew would have ridden those men into the ground. There would have been a fight, and Meggie could have been hurt.''

McGarrity sat impassive, watching her.

''Hunter found me while I was tracking the Cheyenne,''

she went on. "He helped me follow the signs to Standing Pine's village. We were trying to negotiate Meggie's release when Drew's troops attacked."

"You're telling me there were two trails leading to the village?" he asked, incredulous. "Yours and Meggie's?"

"Two trails that ran together, but hours apart," Hunter offered quietly. "Any fool should have been able to see that. Who was tracking for Reynolds, anyway?"

"Bartell," McGarrity admitted with a scowl.

"Bartell!" Hunter gave a snort of derision. "He couldn't track a company of artillery through fresh snow!"

"Reynolds wanted him," McGarrity conceded.

Drew had picked a white man to follow the trail, Cass realized. He had thought he could trust a white man.

"Well, there's one sure way to find out what happened," Hunter said. "Ask Meggie."

McGarrity's scowl deepened. "Jesus, Jalbert, how can I ask that little girl?"

"How can you refuse to talk to her with lives at stake?"

The major rubbed at his beard again and turned to Hoskins. "Bring Meggie Reynolds to me."

Cass all but wilted with relief. Why hadn't she thought to have Ben ask Meggie about what had happened? But then, she hadn't wanted Meggie involved any more than McGarrity had. This would give her a chance to see Meggie again, to hold her, and explain why she was leaving her with her father. But it also meant facing Drew. The thought of that sparked up a fire in Cassie's chest.

"Abduction, however," McGarrity was saying, "is not the only charge that has been leveled against you, Cassandra. There's the question of what you passed on to the Indians about the munitions wagons. Drew admitted he told you when they were leaving and what trail they meant to follow. And we know you've had contact with the hostiles."

Cass hung her head, the tattoo like a brand against her cheek. "I have no way to prove that I am innocent, nothing to give you but my word."

"That's not enough."

Cass shook her head in defeat. She had nothing else to say.

Beside her, Hunter was tugging on the thong of the medicine bag that hung around his neck.

"Perhaps I have the proof you need."

He spilled the contents of the small leather pouch onto his palm. Cass stared at the objects, bits of wood and stone and shell, feathers and beads. Hunter's sacred objects. Among them was a folded square of paper not much bigger than his thumbnail. He pulled it out, held it for a moment in his hand, then passed the paper to McGarrity.

"Where did you get this?" the major asked as he began to open the crisp, cream-colored stock.

"A friend of Cass's gave it to me in the Cheyenne camp."

"And how will this help?"

Hunter's arched brows rose. "I don't know."

McGarrity's head came up.

Cass turned to him in disbelief.

"One of the Cheyenne women gave it to me the night before the attack," Hunter confessed, "and I haven't thought about it since. I believe that whatever Runs Like a Doe entrusted to me is all she claims."

Cass swallowed around a knot of grief. Runs Like a Doe had proved to be a good friend to her, even in death.

As McGarrity unfolded the paper, they could all see what it was: the wrapper from around a can of Cathcart's beef. It bore the army's eagle stamp in one corner and Jessup's horseshoe in the other. McGarrity stared down at it.

"I don't see how this will prove anything except that this tin of beef came from Jessup's trading post."

"Is there something on the back?" Hunter prodded him.

Ben turned the paper over, and all three of them caught their breath. "There *is* a message here. It says: 'The wagons of rifles leave Fort Carr by western route Thursday morning.' "

"Is it signed?"

McGarrity nodded. "With that horseshoe symbol."

"It's from Jessup, then!" Cassie declared.

"Of course it's from Jessup," Hunter agreed. "Everyone shopped at his store. That's how Jessup knew everything that went on at the fort. Who can say what other information he gleaned and passed along to Red Cloud?"

McGarrity wasn't so easily convinced. "Where did Cassie's friend get this?" he wanted to know. "Where is she so that I can question her?"

"I don't know where she got it," Hunter answered. "Probably from one of the warriors."

"And she died in the attack on the Cheyenne camp," Cass added as the memory of that morning swirled through her head, of how she'd held her old friend's hand as she lay dying. Cass's head rang with the sounds of shouting and gunfire. She smelled the smoke, tasted the bitter salt of tears, and knew she was responsible for that death and destruction. She had brought it down on all their heads by going after Meggie.

Cass shivered, going cold down to her bones. McGarrity's office swam before her eyes. Her knees gave way.

McGarrity rushed around the desk and helped Hunter ease Cass into one of the chairs. He gestured for the guard to bring them water.

When she had drunk it down, Cass turned to where McGarrity was kneeling beside her. "Oh, Ben," she whispered, her voice quivering, "do you know what happened in that camp? It was like Sand Creek. The troops rode in at dawn and shot down everyone they saw. They started firing the tepees and killing the horses.

"As much as Drew hated Indians, that couldn't have been what he meant to happen. I saw him for just a moment in the midst of the battle. He seemed shocked by the carnage, appalled that he'd lost control of his men. It seemed as if he meant to stop the killing. Did he stop it, Ben? Was Drew able to stop it?"

McGarrity looked at her, his eyes unreadable. "You don't know what happened?

Cass shook her head, a swell of foreboding pressing up beneath her ribs.

"Drew was killed."

"No," she whispered, going weak and cold again, the room wavering around her. "Oh, no."

"I'm sorry, Cassie."

She felt Hunter's hand come warm against her shoulder, offering her his compassion and his strength. She drew on it, trying to absorb what Ben McGarrity had told her.

Drew was dead, killed in battle perhaps only minutes after he'd loomed out of the smoke. Cass could scarcely take it in.

She covered her face with her hands and let the tears she had been holding inside for half her life spill free. She wept silently, as her years with the Indians had taught her to weep, crying for the boy she'd loved and lost so long ago, for the man so scarred by surviving that he could never free himself from the past. She cried for the years they'd lost and the dreams they'd failed to realize.

But even as grief for Drew tore through her, Cass recognized that she'd grieved for him before. She'd grieved and accepted his death and given Drew up. She would be able to do that again, with time and patience and regret. But before she could begin to accept his passing, she had to know how Drew had died.

She wiped away tears with her fingers and raised her head. Ben McGarrity was offering her his handkerchief, a crisp, pristine handkerchief that had to be something Sally insisted he carry. Cass smiled up at him through her tears.

He seemed relieved that he could do that much for her. Some of the concern and helplessness that etched his broad, rough features smoothed away.

Cass mopped her cheeks and blew her nose. "How did it happen?" she finally asked him.

McGarrity hesitated for a moment, as if he were deciding what to tell her. "Drew managed to stop the fighting," he finally said, "but by the time he did half the village was aflame and there were wounded and dead on both sides. Even then there was sporadic gunfire, and Drew took a ball full in the chest. It was over in an instant, Cass. He didn't suffer. And it was how he'd want to go, in the field, living up to his honor."

Cass sat limp, lost, her thoughts drifting to days when she and Drew had made daisy chains and picked blackberries and waded in the stream. To a kitten Drew had given her and the way he'd liked to watch the sunset from the hill behind her house. On days long gone, but not forgotten.

While she sat remembering, the men were returning to other matters, the question of the note.

"How can I tell if the paper that Indian woman gave you is genuine?" she heard McGarrity demand of Hunter.

"You could take my word," Hunter answered, "or compare the writing on that note with something else."

"To Jessup's ledgers, maybe," Ben said almost grudgingly, as if he were angry at not thinking to do that sooner. "I've been taking a very close look at Jessup's ledgers."

McGarrity took a book from one drawer of his desk and opened it. All three of them edged forward as Ben laid the wrapper in the center of the page.

The same scrolled copperplate script tracked across both the wrapper and in the page of the ledger. Runs Like a Doe had done well by her, Cass thought with relief.

McGarrity looked up from the book and pinned Hunter with his gaze. "You figured Jessup was the one who sent word about the munitions wagons to the Sioux."

"I suspected," Hunter admitted, "but I needed proof. That's why I was in the store that night. It's there in the ledgers, isn't it?"

McGarrity nodded. "There are notations in his second set of books to make me suspect that Jessup had connections to Red Cloud. He caught you reading them, didn't he?"

"And came after me with an ax."

"So you're claiming you killed Jessup in self-defense." When Hunter inclined his head, McGarrity went on. "We have two witnesses who swear they saw you stab him in cold blood."

"Then both of them are liars," Hunter said simply.

McGarrity settled back in his chair. "Well, then maybe I should ask Lloyd and Grenville exactly what they saw that night. Private, is Corporal Hoskins back?"

"No, sir."

"Then you head on over to the sutler's store. Mr. Grenville and Mr. Lloyd are probably in the back. You tell them I want a word with them."

Cass let out her breath. The charges against her and Hunter were dwindling. Perhaps once Ben talked to Meggie, all of this would be settled.

But then, if Drew were dead, what would happen to Meggie?

As if he sensed her concern, Hunter smiled at her. She took comfort in that strong, uncompromising face, in eyes that shone the deep, dark blue of midnight skies. In spite of how she'd tried to thwart him, Hunter had come for her, come to protect her, to offer himself in her place. He would stand by her no matter what.

The sound of footfalls and cursing came from the headquarters' main room. The infantry private shoved the gamblers Grenville and Lloyd through the door of McGarrity's office.

"Mr. Grenville and Mr. Lloyd." The major rose to greet them and offer them chairs.

The two gamblers exchanged wary glances when they realized who else was in the office.

McGarrity waited until they were settled, then stalked out from behind his desk. "I have a few questions I'd like to ask," he said.

"Questions?" Grenville queried.

"Questions regarding the night some weeks ago when Mr. Jessup was killed. You remember that night, don't you?"

"Clear as day," Lloyd answered.

"Indelibly," Grenville added.

"Good," the major replied, standing over them. "And you remember Alain Jalbert, our hired scout. Was he the one you saw in Jessup's store that night?"

"The very man," Lloyd confirmed. "I tried to hold him for the guards, but he ran out on us. But then, we told you all this before."

"Yes, you did."

"We saw him murder Mr. Jessup in cold blood," Grenville volunteered. "Stabbed him with his knife, he did!"

McGarrity braced his hand against the chair back and bent close over Lloyd's shoulder. "Was Mr. Jalbert in any way provoked that night?"

"Provoked?"

"To do violence to Mr. Jessup? Did Jessup have an ax, perhaps?"

"I—I'm sure there were a-a-axes in the store," Lloyd stammered. "Do you remember seeing a display of axes, Albert?"

"Certainly I do."

"Well, was Mr. Jessup using one?" the major went on.

"I didn't see any trees that needed felling," Grenville snapped, obviously pleased with the rejoinder.

Cass wondered how McGarrity was going to get these men to admit to what they'd seen. They were a slick and wily pair. She glanced across to where Hunter stood braced against the wall, his attention focused on the major.

But all Ben McGarrity did was settle back on the corner of his desk and stare at the two men. He stared and stared. His presence and his silence seemed to expand to fill the corners of the room. He raised the temperature ten degrees just sitting there as impassive as a stone.

The men fidgeted, shifted in their chairs, and moved their feet. Lloyd ran a finger around inside his collar. Grenville ruffled like a bird whose perch had been disturbed.

Even Cass began to perspire.

Still, McGarrity didn't say a word.

"Well, maybe the two of them were fighting," Lloyd finally conceded.

"Then Jalbert didn't knife the sutler in cold blood?" McGarrity clarified.

"Maybe not exactly cold blood," the little gambler answered.

McGarrity rose, looming over them. "Are you saying that Mr. Jalbert killed the sutler in self-defense?"

"Hell, Jalbert's just a half-breed," Grenville burst out. "What does it matter if he was trying to defend himself. He killed a white man!"

A bright red flush crept into McGarrity's face. "It matters to me," he said so softly Cass could barely hear him. "Now, was Jessup's killing self-defense?"

"You might call it that," Lloyd admitted.

"So Mr. Jalbert was in the trading post trying to find proof that Jessup had been selling information to the hostiles when the sutler attacked him. Is that right?"

Clearly neither Lloyd nor Grenville had suspected Jessup of spying for the Sioux. They exchanged startled glances.

"I suppose it is," Grenville admitted.

"And Mr. Jalbert killed the sutler in self-defense?"

"I suppose he did," Lloyd agreed.

"Very well, then," McGarrity said around a heavy sigh. "If that's what you saw—Mr. Jalbert defending himself when he knifed Tyler Jessup—I want the two of you to let folks know."

"You want us to clear that red bastard's name?" Grenville all but choked.

"There's some that won't believe that," Lloyd warned in a more conciliatory fashion, "Mr. Jalbert being a half-breed and all."

"Then I leave it to the two of you to convince them," McGarrity threatened. "And to pass the word that Jessup was our spy."

Lloyd and Grenville seemed scandalized by the major's pronouncement.

"Mr. Lloyd?" McGarrity asked. "I want your word on this, and God help you if I don't get it!"

"Yes, sir. I'll swear it was self-defense."

"Mr. Grenville?"

Grenville scowled. "I suppose we can let folks know about Jessup spying for the Sioux."

The weight on Cass's chest seemed to lighten.

The two gamblers rose to go, but McGarrity stopped them. "Oh, and gentlemen, I hope you manage to spread the word before you pack up and leave Fort Carr. I'm closing that poker game down. I'm sure you'll find some other sutler who'll welcome your talents and some other post commander willing to look the other way. But I won't; not anymore. Do I make myself clear?"

"Perfectly, Major McGarrity," Lloyd answered.

"Exceedingly clear," Grenville agreed.

The gamblers slunk out.

McGarrity frowned at Cass and Hunter. "Well, I suppose I owe both of you an apology for thinking the worst."

"Does that mean you believe that Meggie Reynolds wandered off on her own?" Hunter asked, seeming to need the confirmation for Cass's sake. "And that Jessup was the spy?"

McGarrity nodded. "I need to speak to the child, but it will only be a formality. From the way she was yelling to be with you, Cassandra, I can't believe you've done anything to hurt her. As for the other charges—I think we can dispense with those now that we've discovered Jessup was in cahoots with Red Cloud."

There was the sound of voices in the anteroom and Sally McGarrity and Meggie came into the office. The minute Meggie saw Cass, she ran into her arms.

"O-o-oh, Cassie," she wailed. "Sally said that Papa went away to be with Mama and with God, and I didn't think I had anyone left to be with me!"

Cass swept Meggie up into her lap, doing her best to absorb some of her fear and grief. "Oh, Meggie, I'm so sorry about your papa."

Meggie tightened her hold around Cassie's neck. "He was busy all the time," she whispered between sobs. "He didn't play with me much, but I love him. I don't want him to be gone away."

"I know, Meggie. I know." Cass held her and rocked her gently. "Sometimes in battles soldiers die. Ben says your father died very bravely. He died saving other people's lives."

The major came to kneel beside Cassie's chair. "Your papa was a good soldier and a valiant leader," he told Meggie softly.

Cass burrowed against Meggie's neck. "Thank you, Ben," she whispered. "That's how Drew would want his daughter to remember him."

Ben stayed where he was, waiting patiently until the child quieted. "Meggie," he finally said. "There are some things I need to ask you. Is that all right?"

Meggie nodded and looked up, her fingers in her mouth.

"We were all worried about you when you ran away, especially your papa."

Meggie sniffed. ''I know. I'm sorry.''

''Were you afraid when the Indians took you?''

''They looked so mean.''

''Were their faces painted?''

''Un-huh. Except the lady.''

''What lady?''

''The one in the Indian camp. She was nice until the soldiers hurt her. But then Cassie came and got me.''

Ben glanced up, distress in his face. He'd obviously pieced together what had happened. He shook his head, reaching across to stroke Meggie's sun-bright hair.

''What's going to happen now?'' Hunter wanted to know.

Ben sighed and leaned back against his desk. ''That's something we need to discuss. Sally—'' He glanced up at his wife. ''Would you mind taking Meggie back to our quarters?''

''No!'' Meggie objected. ''No, I want to stay with Cassie.''

Sally cooed and patted and promised Meggie cookies.

''We'll be over as soon as we're finished here,'' Cass told her, and reluctantly Meggie agreed.

On their way out Sally McGarrity paused in the doorway. ''You do the right thing by this child, Ben,'' she told him, her soft, pretty face gone suddenly fierce, ''or don't you bother coming home to me!''

When Meggie and his wife were gone, Ben eyed the two of them. ''We need to talk about Meggie's future.''

The grim tone of McGarrity's voice frightened Cass. She had been Drew's wife. She should be the one to take care of Meggie now, but Ben seemed to have other concerns.

''I don't think either Drew or his wife had any kin,'' Ben was saying when Cass looked up. ''If they did, Drew would have sent Meggie back to the States long before this.''

''Then what do you mean to do with her?'' Hunter asked quietly.

She could see the concern in McGarrity's eyes. ''Since you're not blood kin, Cassandra, regulations say I have to send Meggie back East, to Fort Leavenworth or to Jefferson Barracks at St. Louis, where they'll search for relatives and decide what's to become of her.''

"Oh Ben! How can you send her away? I'm her mother!" Cassie cried. "I've been taking care of her these last six months."

"I know," Ben answered solemnly. "There will be a hearing. You'll have a chance to petition for custody."

All three of them knew how little chance they had of convincing a military panel to let them take Meggie and raise her as their own. They'd take one look at Cass's tattoo and know what she'd been through. They'd see that she'd been accused of spying and abduction. They'd look at Hunter, a half-breed scout who had fought for both the North and South, and make their decision. It wouldn't matter that the two of them loved the little girl, or that Meggie wanted to be with them. And if there were blood kin somewhere, they wouldn't even have a chance to ask for the little girl.

"Ben," Hunter said, his voice gone low, "let Cass take Meggie and leave today. You know how much she loves her. She's been more of a mother to Meggie than Drew ever was a father."

Cass glanced up at Hunter, gratitude swelling around her heart. Everyone Meggie had ever loved had been taken from her, her mother and Drew and now even Cass herself.

This was worse than losing Meggie to Drew. He had loved Meggie in his way and would have taken care of her. There would have been Sally and Ben here at the fort to oversee things, and Lila to rock Meggie and pet her and hold her when she cried. But Cass couldn't let Meggie go back East, where she wouldn't have a soul who cared for her. She couldn't let that baby know that kind of loneliness, lovelessness.

"Ben, please." Cass's voice was raw with misery.

"I'm sorry, Cassie. This isn't what I want for Meggie, either, but my hands are tied. Even if I let you take her, how could you care for her? Drew didn't leave any money, only his clothes, a few household goods, and a portfolio of paintings."

"I'll take care of them," Hunter answered. "I have some land up in Montana, and I've saved nearly enough to buy some stock. I have plans to turn the place into a damn fine horse ranch. If Cass agrees to marry me, we can give Meggie everything she'll ever need, a home and a family."

"Damnit, Jalbert! I'm not authorized to make this kind of decision."

"Do it anyway." Hunter's eyes were dark, his voice rough-edged with emotion. "Do it because it's what's right. Do it because it will make Cass and Meggie happy."

McGarrity looked down at the floor. He looked at the two of them and heaved a sigh. "The army will have my head for this," he grumbled.

Cass shot to her feet, giddy and laughing. Hunter gathered her up in his arms and hugged her hard. Joy welled up between them.

"Ben," Cass gasped, reaching out to clasp his hand. "Thank you. Thank you. You've made us both so—"

McGarrity scowled. "I don't know how I'll ever explain this to General Crook in Omaha. Or to the War Department." Then abruptly his scowl became a smile, and he reached for his hat. "Oh, hell, I'll worry about them later. Let's go tell Meggie she's got a brand-new set of parents."

Meggie saw them coming the moment they stepped onto the parade ground. She bolted down the steps of the McGarritys' cabin and ran the length of officers' row, directly into Cassie's arms. Cass stood holding her, laughing and crying. Hunter pulled the two of them against him.

Cass smiled at where Sally McGarrity had come to stand beside her husband. "Thank you," Cass whispered. "Thank you both for giving me everything I've ever wanted."

Late that evening Ben McGarrity dipped his pen and signed his name at the bottom of his report to the War Department outlining the incident at the Cheyenne camp. He'd labored over it for hours. He always had trouble justifying a mission that had failed, one that had cost brave men their lives. One that, in this case, had robbed the army of as fine an officer as Drew Reynolds.

He sighed and rubbed his eyes, wondering if he could have changed the way it had all turned out. But Reynolds had come west with his prejudices intact. He'd seemed sincere in his desire to marry Cassie Morgan and accept responsibility for her when she'd been returned to the whites. He'd been determined to avenge the deaths of his family. Ben didn't know what he could have done differently. Still, every officer had his share of regrets. He just knew that giving Meggie Reynolds to Cass and Hunter wasn't going to be one of them.

Ben smiled to himself, remembering how the three of them had looked as they'd headed off for Montana this afternoon. Jalbert had ridden tall and protective, obviously proud of his newly acquired family. Meggie was subdued by news of her father's death, but was obviously pleased to be riding up in front of the man who had taken her on as his own child. And then there was Cassandra—a bright new wedding band gleaming on her finger, her tattooed face aglow, her eyes filled with a happiness Ben had never expected to see in them. And now he'd done his best to ensure that no one would disturb the contentment they'd managed to find together.

Ben could hear Sally puttering around behind him in the cabin's kitchen, grinding beans and boiling up a final pot of coffee. He heard her pull out the cookie crock she kept tucked away, and smelled the dark, rich sweetness of molasses. She set the crock on the table and came to stand behind him.

''Have you found a way to make sure Cassandra and Alain Jalbert can keep Meggie Reynolds?'' she asked him, wrapping her arms around his shoulders and pressing her cheek against his hair.

Ben tapped one finger on the page that lay on the table before him, indicating the paragraph at the end.

In spite of an intensive search of the village and the surrounding area, no sign of Meggie Reynolds was ever found. As with many of the whites who have been taken captive over the years, we may never know Meggie's fate. There seems to be no clue to her whereabouts, and I hold very little hope for her return.

Sally leaned around and kissed his cheek. ''You're a very clever man, Ben McGarrity.''

He turned and pulled his wife into his lap. "I've done my best—everything I can do to keep them safe."

"And they will be," Sally whispered, kissing him. "This is the way it was supposed to turn out."

Epilogue

Late October 1867
Southwestern Montana

Cass stood on the porch of her brand-new cabin surveying the world Hunter Jalbert had given her. She looked out across the thick, rusty brown of the broomsedge meadow; out through the filigree frame of leafless trees; out at the sky. Bright veils of color streaked the length and breadth of it: deep blue-lavender wrapped closest to the night, scarlet and peacock blue hanging in the middle ground, a tracery of pure rich gold outlining the crests of the peaks off to the west.

The sound of footsteps rustling through the grass made her turn from the sunset to where Hunter was coming toward her from the stream. His hair was damp and his fresh shirt clung damply to his chest and shoulders. He carried a bucket of water in either hand.

"Are we all moved in?" he asked her as he dumped the buckets into the barrel at the end of the porch.

"Meggie's putting the last of her things away," Cass said.

Hunter came to stand beside her at the top of the steps. "And does my wife approve of the view from her new front porch?"

Though she could feel his gaze on her, Cass continued to

stare at where the last orange sliver of sun was winking out.

"It's wonderful," she answered. No words she knew were adequate to express what the cabin and the life he was making for them meant to her.

He had worked from before dawn till well past dark to get this cabin built before the winter rolled in. He had laid up a proper stone foundation, hewn logs and set them in place, and shingled the roof.

"Is it everything you hoped for?" he asked her. "Do you have everything you need?"

Cass slowly turned to him. "Almost."

She saw the smile on his wide mouth lose its crispness and concern crimp a line between his brows. A stillness settled over him. "What is it?"

Cass gathered every scrap of her courage and looked into his face. "I'm going to have a child," she said. "I didn't—didn't think I could have children. That's—that's why it took me so long to notice the symptoms and—and realize . . ."

The spark of apprehension in his eyes danced away, replaced by a look of dawning wonder. A grin broke across his features.

"Oh, Cass, that's wonderful. I've always wanted children, but I didn't dare hope—" His voice deepened, turning just a little husky. "When do you think we—"

Cass sucked in her breath, knowing she had to tell him all of the truth. "We didn't," she answered with deep and genuine regret. "The child I'm carrying isn't ours. It's—it's Drew's."

She waited, anticipating his disappointment or his anger or his censure, but the light in his eyes didn't change. They still shone that clear, dark blue that was so like the color of the midnight sky. They shone with the same softness, the same warmth as when he thought the baby was his.

"I'm glad, Cass. I know how long you've wanted this, to carry a baby of your own."

"Does it—" She didn't know how to ask the question, and yet she knew she must. "Does it matter that it isn't yours?"

Hunter hesitated, his mouth bowing just a little. "I wish it were mine," he told her. "I wish we had made this baby together. But I think this is the way it was meant to happen. It's something you owe Drew for the old times when the two of you had dreams together.''

She felt tears thicken in her throat and burn beneath her eyelids. She had stood over Drew's grave in the little burying ground at Fort Carr more than six weeks before and promised never to forget him or how they'd loved each other once. Cass knew she would always have Meggie to remind her of Drew, and now there was a new life, a new child, a new reason to keep the good memories of their life together alive.

She just hadn't expected Hunter to understand what she owed Drew, why it was important that this baby carry on Drew's legacy. But Hunter had known her down to her bones from the very beginning and had accepted her as she was. He had given her a security she had never expected to have.

Hunter pulled her against him, and she nestled close as they stood together on the porch. He was broad and strong against her. He smelled of pine and woodsmoke, of earth and wind, of freedom and home. She curled her hand around his neck and clung to him, to the fortitude and goodness of the man who was her husband.

''I love you, Cass,'' he murmured against her hair. ''This child is part of you, just as Meggie is part of you. And you are part of me. Yours and mine are ours to share. And where one child finds purchase and grows strong, others will follow. Someday soon the child you carry will be yours and mine. I can wait. As long as I have you with me, I can wait.''

She raised her head and looked into that broad, handsome face, into those calm dark eyes. ''Thank you, Hunter, for accepting this child. Thank you for giving me all of this.''

He kissed her then, slowly and deeply, as a lover kisses his mistress, as a man kisses his wife. She sighed with contentment and delight.

This man was her heart; he was her home. Here beneath the wide, wide sky, Cass had found the place where she belonged.

Author's Note

The photograph of Olive Oatman sent chills up my spine. I found it in one of the *Old West Series of Time-Life Books* and I couldn't stop staring. It was a picture of a woman dressed in Victorian clothes, a woman with sweeping skirts and wide pagoda sleeves, a woman with her hair carefully parted and curled. A woman with fascinating and intricate Indian tattoos curling over her chin. I was struck by the contrast in the way Olive was dressed and the way she must have been perceived from the moment her brother arranged for her return to the whites.

The dichotomy in that photograph whispered to my writer's mind about the conflicts Olive Oatman must have faced, about the difficulties she must have had reconciling a part of her life she could never deny and the simple joys Victorian women were raised to appreciate.

With that photograph the story and character of Cassandra Morgan began to take shape in my mind. Though in the end, the life I created for Cassie was vastly different from the one Olive Oatman lived, I suspect the difficulties of being marked in such a way and living in what seems to us a very repressive society must have been similar.

In creating that society, I took Fort Caspar, Department of the Platte, as my model. Initially, and as late as when the excerpt of *So Wide the Sky* appeared in the back of my previous novel, *A Place Called Home*, I was using the fort itself. But as the story and characters took on a life of their own, I began to feel I might be intruding on the lives and personalities of people who may well have felt and thought very differently from the lives I was inventing for them. In other words, I decided to change the names to protect the innocent. Doing this also allowed me the freedom to move the story back a year. By August of 1867, Fort Caspar had been abandoned in favor of Fort Fetterman farther east. Still, the descriptions and the layout of Fort Carr are very much based on my research into the site and early garrisoning on Fort Caspar.

In writing this book, certain volumes were crucial in creating the ambience of life on a frontier fort. First among these was *Frontier Regulars* by Robert M. Utley, who initiated me to the organization of the U. S. Army in the period following the Civil War. I also drew heavily on *Forty Miles a Day on Beans and Hay* by Don Rickey, Jr., and for the parts of the book that deal with women living on the frontier outposts I used *Glittering Misery: Dependents of the Indian Fighting Army* by Patricia Y. Stallard. I also read a number of diaries and memoirs left by the wives of soldiers serving in the west. My visits to both the reconstructed forts at Fort Caspar and Fort Laramie were instrumental in helping me create what I hope is the flavor of life on the plains.

Reconstructing the past from a twentieth-century perspective is a business fraught with peril. Perhaps the best test of what I accomplished lies with you and the viability of the characters and the story I have created. My fondest wish is that you have enjoyed them both.

E. K. G.
P.O. Box 260052
St. Louis, Missouri 63126
June 1996